A MAN WITHOUT MERCY

BY
MIRANDA LEE

Miranda Lee is Australian and lives near Sydney. Born and raised in the bush, she was boarding-school-educated and briefly pursued a career in classical music before moving to Sydney and embracing the world of computers. Happily married with three daughters, she began writing when family commitments kept her at home. She likes to create stories that are believable, modern, fast-paced and sexy. Her interests include meaty sagas, doing word puzzles, gambling and going to the movies.

CHAPTER ONE

'WHAT DO YOU mean, I *can't* have Vivienne?' Jack said. 'I *always* have Vivienne.'

Nigel suppressed a sigh. He didn't like disappointing his best client but there was nothing he could do about it.

'Sorry, Jack, but as of yesterday Miss Swan doesn't work for Classic Design any longer.'

Jack's head jerked back with shock. 'You *fired* her?'

Now it was Nigel's turn to look startled. 'Hardly. Vivienne was one of my best designers. No,' he added, with true regret in his voice. 'She quit.'

Jack could not contain his surprise at this second piece of news. Admittedly, he didn't know Vivienne all that well, despite her having worked for him on his last three building projects. She was an extremely self-contained young woman who didn't engage in idle chit-chat. When on a job, her focus was always on her work, which was simply brilliant. He had asked her not long ago why she didn't open her own interior design firm, and she'd replied that she didn't want that kind of stress, especially now that she was engaged to be married. She'd said she didn't want to live just for work any longer, a sentiment which Jack had not appreciated—till yesterday.

He'd been driving around the Port Stephens area, looking for suitable land for another retirement village, when he'd come across a small acreage for sale which had totally blown him away. It wasn't what he was looking for, not even remotely. Not the right kind of land, for starters; not flat enough. There'd also been a huge house smack dab in the middle of the lot, perched on top of a hill. A house unlike anything Jack had ever seen, with a name that was as unique as the building.

Despite knowing he was wasting his time, Jack had still felt compelled to inspect Francesco's Folly. From the moment he'd walked inside and out onto the first of the many balconies which all faced the bay, he'd known he wanted the place. Not only wanted it but wanted to live in it. Crazy, really, since Port Stephens was a good three-hour drive north of Sydney. Jack's normal place of residence was a conveniently located and relatively modest three-bedroomed apartment in the same CBD building which housed his construction company's head office. Aside from its inconvenient location, Francesco's Folly was as far removed from modest as a residence could get, with eight bedrooms, six bathrooms and an indoor/outdoor swimming pool which would have put a Hollywood mansion to shame.

As a confirmed bachelor who never entertained at home, Jack had no need for a house this size, but it was no use. He simply had to have it, telling himself that maybe it was time for him to relax and live a little. After all, he'd been flogging himself for two decades, working six and sometimes seven days a week, making millions in the process. Why shouldn't he indulge himself for once? He didn't actually have to live in the place twenty-four-seven. He could use it as a weekender, or a holiday home. So could the rest of his family. Thinking of their pleasure at having such a dream place at their disposal had sealed the deal for Jack, so he'd bought Francesco's Folly that very afternoon, getting it for a bargain, partly because it was a deceased estate, but mostly because the interior was hideously dated—hence his need for an excellent interior designer, one whose taste and work ethics matched his. It annoyed Jack considerably that the one person whom he could trust to do the job, and do it well, was unavailable to him.

But then it suddenly occurred to Jack that maybe that wasn't the case.

'So who was the sneaky devil who head-hunted her?' he demanded to know, excited by the possibility that he could still hire the decorator he wanted for the job.

'Vivienne hasn't gone to work for anyone else,' Nigel informed him.

'How do you know?'

'She told me so. Look, Jack, if you must know, Vivienne's not feeling well at the moment. She's decided to have some time off work.'

Jack was taken back. 'What do you mean, not feeling well? What's the matter with her?'

'I guess it doesn't matter if I tell you. It's not as though it isn't public knowledge.'

Jack frowned. It certainly wasn't public knowledge to him.

Nigel frowned also. 'I'm guessing by the look on your face that you didn't read the gossip columns in Sunday's papers, or see the photos.'

'I never read gossip columns,' Jack replied. He did sometimes skim through the Sunday paper—mostly the property section—but he'd been busy yesterday. 'So what did I miss? Though, truly, I can't imagine a girl like Vivienne making it into any gossip column. She isn't the type.'

'It wasn't Vivienne. It was her ex-fiancé.'

'*Ex*-fiancé… Good Lord, when did that happen? She was solidly engaged last time I saw her a few weeks back.'

'Yes, well, Daryl broke off their engagement about a month ago. Told her he'd fallen in love with someone else. The poor girl was shattered, but she was very brave and soldiered on. Of course, the rat claimed he hadn't cheated on her whilst they were still engaged, but yesterday's paper proved that was just rubbish.'

'For pity's sake, Nigel, just tell me what was in the darned paper!'

'The thing is, the girl Daryl dumped Vivienne for wasn't just any old girl. He left her for Courtney Ellison. You know…? Frank Ellison's spoiled daughter. Vivienne did the decorating job on the harbourside mansion you built for Ellison, so I guess that's how the two lovebirds met. Anyway, the bit in the gossip column was announcing their engagement. In the photos—there were several—the Ellison girl is sporting a diamond engagement ring the size of an egg—as well as a much bigger baby-bump, meaning their affair's been going on for quite some time.

'Naturally, there was no mention of Courtney's handsome husband-to-be having been recently engaged to another woman. Darling Daddy would have quashed that. You don't get to be a billionaire mining magnate in this country without having lots of connections in the media. As you can imagine, Vivienne is very cut up about it. She was in tears on the phone yesterday, which is not like her at all.'

Jack could not have agreed more. Tears were not

Vivienne's style. He'd never met any female as cool and collected as Vivienne. But he supposed everyone had their breaking point. He shook his head, regretting now that he'd recommended her to Frank Ellison. Jack hated to think that he was in some way responsible for Vivienne's unhappiness. But how could he possibly have known that Ellison's man-eating maniac of a daughter would get her claws into Vivienne's fiancé?

Still…if ever there was a man willing and ready to be eaten by the likes of Courtney Ellison, it was Vivienne's now ex-fiancé.

Jack had only met Daryl once—when he'd briefly dropped in on Classic Design's Christmas party last year—but once had been enough to form an opinion. Okay, so darling Daryl was movie-star good-looking. And charming, he supposed, if you liked silver-tongued talkers who smiled a lot, touched a lot and called their fiancée 'babe'. Clearly, Vivienne did, since she'd been planning on marrying him.

It saddened Jack that Vivienne had been unlucky enough to lose her heart to one of that ilk, but he had no doubt that she would, in time, see that she'd had a narrow escape from long-term misery as a result of Daryl's defection. Meanwhile, the last thing that girl needed was to be allowed to wallow in her present misery. Jack understood that Vivienne was probably feeling wretched, but nothing would be achieved by cutting herself off from the one thing she was good at and would make her feel good about herself: her work.

'I see,' he said, quickly deciding on a course of action. 'You wouldn't have Vivienne's address, would you, Nigel? I'd like to send her some flowers,' he added before Nigel gave him some bulldust about privacy issues.

Nigel stared at Jack for a long moment before looking up the company files on his computer and writing down the address.

'I don't like your chances,' he said as he handed the address over.

'My chances of what?' Jack replied, poker-faced.

Nigel smiled a dry smile. 'Come now, Jack, you and I both know you don't want Vivienne's address just to send her flowers. You're going to hotfoot it over to her place and try to get her to do whatever it is you want her to do. Which is what, by the way? Another retirement-home project?'

'No,' Jack said, despite thinking that Francesco's Folly would make a perfect retirement home, when and if he ever actually retired. 'It's a personal project, a holiday house I've bought which badly needs redecorating. Look, it'll do Vivienne good to keep busy.'

'She's very fragile at the moment,' Nigel warned. 'Not everyone is as tough as you, Jack.'

'I've often found that the gentler sex are a lot tougher than we men think they are,' Jack said as he stood up and extended his hand in parting.

Nigel tried not to wince when Jack's large hand closed around his much smaller one. But truly, the man didn't know his own strength sometimes. Didn't know women as well as he thought he did, either. No way was Vivienne going to let herself be bulldozed into working for him. Aside from the fact that she was in a dreadful emotional state at the moment, she'd never overly liked the owner of Stone Constructions—something which Jack obviously didn't know.

But privately she'd expressed the opinion to Nigel that Jack was a pain in the neck to work for, a driven workaholic with impossibly high standards which, whilst admirable in one way, could be very trying. Of course, he did pay very well, but that wasn't going to help him where Vivienne was concerned. Money had never interested her all that much, possibly because she'd inherited plenty of her own when her mother had died a couple of years ago.

'If you want some advice,' Nigel called after Jack as he headed for the door, 'Actually taking Vivienne some flowers—not red roses, mind you—might improve your chances of success.'

Though Nigel seriously doubted it.

CHAPTER TWO

VIVIENNE'S ADDRESS WAS easy to find. It was located in
Neutral Bay, only a short drive from Classic Design's
office in North Sydney. Finding a florist first was not
quite so easy. Neither was deciding what flowers to buy.
By the time Jack parked outside the two-storey red-
brick building which housed Vivienne's apartment, an
hour had passed since he'd left Nigel.

Not a man who liked wasting time, it was a somewhat exasperated Jack who climbed out from behind
the wheel of his black Porsche, carrying the basket of
pink and white carnations the florist had finally convinced him to buy.

A sudden autumn shower had Jack bolting up the
narrow front path and into the small lobby of the apartment block. Thankfully, he didn't get too wet, just a few
drops on his shoulders and hair; nothing that couldn't
be easily remedied.

There wasn't any security panel anywhere, he noted
as he smoothed back his hair. The building was quite
old, possibly federation, though in reasonably good condition. He pressed the brass door-bell, hearing only a
faint ring coming from inside. No one came to answer
straight away, giving rise to the annoying possibility
that Vivienne wasn't at home. Jack now regretted not

ringing first. He had her mobile number in his phone. He'd just presumed she'd be at home after what Nigel had said.

'I'm a bloody idiot,' he muttered under his breath as he pulled his phone out of his pocket and brought Vivienne's number up on the menu. He was about to call when he heard the dead lock being turned. It wasn't Vivienne who opened the door, however, but a plump, middle-aged woman with short blonde hair and a kind face.

'Yes?' she said. 'Can I help you?'

'I hope so,' Jack replied, switching off his phone and slipping it back into his jeans pocket. 'Is Vivienne at home?'

'Well, yes, but…um…she's taking a bath at the moment. I presume those flowers are for her? If you give them to me, I'll make sure she gets them.'

'I'd prefer to give them to her personally, if you don't mind.'

The woman frowned at him. 'And who might you be?'

'The name's Jack. Jack Stone. Vivienne's worked for me on a number of occasions.'

'Ah yes. Mr Stone. Vivienne has mentioned you once or twice.'

Jack was taken aback by the dry tone in the woman's voice when she said that. He wondered momentarily what Vivienne had said about him, but then dismissed the thought as irrelevant.

'And you are?' he shot back.

'Marion Havers. I live in number two,' she said, nodding towards the adjoining door. 'Vivienne and I are good friends as well as neighbours. Look, I presume since you've brought her flowers that you know what's happened.'

'Actually, I didn't know a thing till I went to Classic Design's office this morning to hire Vivienne for a job. Nigel explained the situation, saying how upset Vivienne was, so I thought I'd come round and see how she was.'

'How very kind of you,' the woman said with a soft sigh. 'As you can imagine, the poor girl's devastated. Can't eat. Can't sleep. She did get some sleeping tablets from the doctor, but they don't seem to be working too well. Anyway, after this latest catastrophe, I think she'll be needing some serious anti-depressants.'

Jack had never agreed with the way people turned to medication to solve life's problems.

'What Vivienne needs, Marion,' he said sternly, 'is to keep busy. Which is the main reason I'm here: I was hoping to persuade her to come and work for me.'

Marion looked at him as though he were delusional, but then she shrugged. 'You can try, I suppose. But I don't like your chances.'

Frankly, he thought he stood a darned good chance. Okay, so Vivienne was very upset at the moment, but beneath her distress she was still the same sensible young woman he'd come to respect enormously. She'd soon see the logic in his proposal.

'Could I come inside,' Jack asked, 'and wait till Vivienne's finished in the bathroom? I really would appreciate a personal word with her today.'

Marion looked doubtful for a moment, until she glanced at her wristwatch. 'I suppose it will be all right. I don't have to leave for work for another half hour. Vivienne should be out of the bath by then.' She looked up at him and smiled. 'Meanwhile, I could do with a quick cuppa. Would you like to join me? Or would you prefer coffee?'

Jack smiled back at her. 'Tea will be fine.'

'Good. Here, give me those flowers and follow me. And close the door after you,' she threw over her shoulder.

Marion led him down a narrow hallway which had a very high ceiling, white walls and polished floorboards the colour of walnut. Jack passed three shut doors on his left before the hallway opened into a living room which surprised him by being so starkly furnished. It didn't look anything like the stylish but comfy living rooms Vivienne decorated for him in his show homes.

Jack glanced around with disbelieving eyes. Where were the warm feminine touches which were her trademark? There were no colourful cushions or elegant lamps; no display cabinets or shelves; no ornaments of any kind, not even a photo on display. Just one long black leather sofa with a neutral-shaded shag rug in front of it and a chunky wooden coffee-table varnished the same colour as the floors.

Only one picture graced the white walls, a black-framed painting showing a girl dressed in a red coat, walking alone along a rain-spattered city street. Obviously a quality painting, but not one Jack found pleasure in looking at. Despite wearing red, the girl looked sad and cold. Like this whole room.

It occurred to Jack that possibly dear old Daryl had stripped the room of some things when he had left, which could account for its ultra-bare look. He wasn't sure how he knew Daryl had been living here with Vivienne, but he *was* sure. She must have said something at some stage. Or maybe Daryl had, at that Christmas party. Yes, that was it: he'd mentioned he was moving in with her in the New Year. Whatever; maybe there had been more furniture in this room before he'd left and more pictures on the walls, plus the odd photo or two. The TV was still there, Jack noted, mounted on the wall opposite the sofa. But one would have expected a piece of furniture underneath it—a sideboard of some kind. There was room for it.

Marion stopped briefly to deposit the basket of carnations on the coffee table before leading him on into the kitchen which, though smallish, was brilliantly designed to incorporate every mod con and still leave enough space for a table and four chairs. Obviously, it had been remodelled recently, since the bench tops *and* the table top were made in the kind of stone which had only become popular during the last few years. White, of course; white was *the* colour for kitchens these days. That and stainless-steel appliances. Vivienne always insisted on that combination in kitchens she designed for him. But she usually introduced a bit of colour in the splashbacks as well as other decorative touches: a bowl of fruit here and there. A vase of flowers. And, yes, something colourful on the walls.

There was nothing like that here in Vivienne's place, however. If it *was* hers? Jack suddenly wondered. Possibly this was a rental. He hadn't thought of that. Only one way to find out, he supposed.

'Does Vivienne own this place?' he asked as he pulled out one of the white leather-backed chairs which surrounded the table.

Marion glanced over her shoulder from where she was making the tea. 'Sure does. Bought it when she inherited some money a while back. Had it refurbished from top to bottom last year. Not quite to my taste, but we all like different things, don't we? Vivienne's one of those women who can't bear clutter.'

'I can see that,' Jack remarked.

'Would you like a biscuit or two with your tea?' Marion asked.

'Please,' Jack replied. It was nearly one o'clock and he hadn't eaten since breakfast.

'How do you have your tea?'

'Black, with no sugar.'

Marion sighed a somewhat exasperated sigh as she carried Jack's mug of tea, plus a plate of cream biscuits, over to the table. 'Lord knows what Vivienne's doing in that bathroom. She's been in there for ages.'

Their eyes met, Jack's chest tightening when sudden alarm filled Marion's face.

'Perhaps you should knock on the door and let her know I'm here,' he suggested.

'Yes. Yes, I think I'll do that,' Marion said, and hurried off.

Jack listened to her footsteps on the polished floorboards, then to her knocking on a door, along with her anxious-sounding voice. 'Vivienne, are you nearly finished in there? I have to go to work soon and you have a visitor—Jack Stone. He wants to speak to you. Vivienne, can you hear me?'

When Jack heard even louder knocking and obviously still no answer from Vivienne, he jumped to his feet and raced down to where Marion was standing at the first door past the living room.

'She won't answer me, Jack,' the woman said frantically. 'And the door's locked. You don't think she's done anything silly, do you?'

Jack wasn't sure of anything, so he banged on the door himself.

'Vivienne,' he called out loudly at the same time. 'It's Jack. Jack Stone. Will you open the door, please?'

Not a word in reply.

'Bloody hell,' he muttered as he examined the bathroom door which was solid wood, as opposed to chipboard, but also ancient and hopefully the victim of termites over the years. Telling Marion to stand back, he shoulder-charged it with every ounce of strength he had, splintering the lock in the process and taking the door right off at the hinges.

Jack half-fell into the bathroom, taking a second or two to right himself and see what the situation was.

Vivienne wasn't lying comatose or drowned under the water, the victim of an overdose of sleeping tablets. She was alive and well, bolting upright in the bath as the commotion of the door being shattered finally penetrated the earplugs she'd been wearing. Her piercing scream testified to her shock, her mouth staying open as she gaped at Jack.

On his part, Jack just stood there in the mangled doorway, totally speechless. He hadn't stopped to think about Vivienne being naked. All he'd been concerned about a few seconds earlier was her safety. Now, suddenly, all he could think about *was* her nakedness. His eyes were transfixed on her bare breasts which were, without doubt, the most beautiful breasts he'd ever seen. They glistened at him, two lushly rounded globes, their smooth, pale flesh centred with dusky-pink aureoles and crowned with the most tantalisingly erect nipples.

Jack had never thought of Vivienne as busty before, perhaps because she always wore tailored suits and shirt-like blouses, which obviously covered up her curves. He recalled that, even at that Christmas party he'd attended, she'd worn a loose-fitting dress which had successfully hidden her knockout figure, one which would have any red-blooded heterosexual male salivating over her.

Unfortunately, Jack was a red-blooded heterosexual male who hadn't been with a woman since back in early March, over two months ago. Hell, had it been that long? It obviously had, by the uncomfortable stirring in his jeans.

Thank goodness Marion pushed past him at that stage and started rapidly explaining things to a still gaping Vivienne. Dragging his eyes off those stunning breasts, Jack spun round and marched back to the kitchen, telling himself ruefully as he sat down and munched into a biscuit that he really had to get himself a life. A sex life, that was. He was, after all, only thirty-seven years old, a fit, virile man still in his sexual prime. He couldn't keep restricting himself to holiday flings, or the occasional one-night stand. He needed sex on a more regular basis.

But that would mean getting himself a proper girlfriend, something Jack was reluctant to do. He'd had girlfriends before and they had always wanted more than just sex. They wanted to go on regular dates, attend family gatherings and, ultimately, they wanted a ring on their finger. Even if they were prepared to bypass marriage and just live with a guy, inevitably they still wanted children.

Jack didn't want children. For the past twenty years he'd been father as well as big brother to his two younger sisters, protecting and providing for them, along with his mother, who'd been totally useless when she'd unexpectedly become a widow at the young age of forty. Jack himself had only been seventeen when his father had been killed in a motor-cycle accident. After it was discovered that his dad had been hopeless with money, with no insurance premiums up to date and more debts than you could poke a stick at, his mother had promptly fallen to pieces, leaving it up to him to become the man of the house. Jack had been obliged to leave school immediately and get work so that they could survive.

It had nearly killed him to abandon his ambition to become an engineer, but he'd had no alternative. There was simply no one else he could turn to for financial help. Jack had worked as a builder's labourer seven days a week to cover the mortgage and put food on the table. Fortunately, he'd been a big lad who could handle the gruelling workload. Also, he'd been smart enough to learn most of the building trades in record time and eventually set up a building business of his own, one which had earned him more than enough over the years to provide for himself and his family.

Jack no longer regretted not becoming an engineer. He loved what he did. He loved his family, too; very much. But providing for and protecting them all these years had taken an emotional toll on him. There was simply no room left in his heart for another family. He didn't want a wife of his own. Or children. What he did want, however, was more sex.

But getting more sex wasn't as easy as some people seemed to think. Okay, so Jack didn't have much trouble picking up women when he put his mind to it. But at thirty-seven his appetite for one-night stands had faded somewhat. Nowadays, he preferred to have sex with a woman he actually liked, not just one he lusted after.

What he needed, he decided, was a mistress, someone attractive and intelligent he could visit on a regular basis but who wouldn't put any emotional or social demands on him.

Jack was mulling over this problem when Marion bustled into the room.

'Sorry, Jack, but I really must go get changed for work. Vivienne said for you to wait here. She won't be long. Nice to have met you,' she added before hurrying off through a back door.

Jack grimaced at the thought of being left alone with a no doubt even more upset Vivienne. Lord knew what she must have thought when he'd burst into the bathroom like that.

'I dare say she's not too happy about the bathroom door, either,' he was muttering when the woman herself swept into the kitchen wrapped in a fluffy white robe and matching slippers.

'You can say that again,' Vivienne snapped as she tightened the sash around her waist.

The thought that she was still naked underneath her dressing gown was decidedly unsettling. So was the fact that her hair was down, long auburn waves falling in disarray around her shoulders. Jack had never seen her with her hair down before. Had no idea it was that long. Or that pretty. It was usually pulled back off her face into some kind of roll thing which was both practical and professional-looking. He was sure she hadn't worn it down at the Christmas party he'd attended, either. He would have noticed.

Or would he?

Jack never paid too much personal attention to females he worked with, or who belonged to another man. He'd learned over the years not to complicate his life by inviting trouble with members of the opposite sex. Yes, he'd been aware that Vivienne was an attractive girl, but that was as far as his observations had gone.

Now, as his eyes lifted to study her face more closely,

he discovered that she was more than attractive. She was really quite beautiful, with delicate bone structure, a small, straight nose, full lips and the most gorgeous green eyes. How in hell he hadn't noticed those eyes, he had no idea. Perhaps because she wore sunglasses most of the time.

He sure as hell noticed them now, since they were glaring at him with the kind of fury that might have made a lesser man quiver in his boots.

'I expect you to have that door fixed as soon as possible,' Vivienne demanded.

'I'll get right on to it today,' he agreed.

'I can't imagine why you thought I was actually in there topping myself,' she went on heatedly. 'The very idea is ludicrous!'

Jack wished he'd trusted his instinct that Vivienne wasn't the suicidal type. But it was too late now.

'Marion said you'd been in there a very long time,' he explained, hoping his calm tone would soothe her temper. 'And then, of course, there was what Nigel told me earlier this morning.'

'Oh yes?' she said, crossing her arms and giving him a very droll look. 'And just what did Nigel say about me?'

Jack decided sarcasm was a definite improvement on white-hot rage. 'He said that I couldn't hire you for a job because you'd quit.'

'Hmph!' Vivienne snorted. 'I'll bet that's not all he said.'

'No. He told me what had happened with Daryl and the Ellison girl.'

'Indeed,' Vivienne said, her chin suddenly beginning to quiver as it did when a girl was about to cry.

Jack was very familiar with the symptom. He held

his breath, not sure what he would do if she started weeping. He didn't like the thought of having to comfort her physically. Hugging crying sisters and mothers was rather different from hugging a woman he was finding terribly sexy all of a sudden. And there was something provocative about Vivienne spitting fire at him just now. He had an awful feeling that if he took her in his arms at this moment he might do something really stupid. Like kiss her. Which would put a swift end to his plan to get her to redecorate Francesco's Folly. Vivienne would no doubt slap his face then tell him in no uncertain terms to get lost. As it was, Jack knew he would still have the devil of a time persuading her to take the job.

Luckily, she didn't dissolve into tears, her jaw firming and her eyes flashing with a defiant glitter.

'Well, that was yesterday!' she stated with the kind of spirit Jack could not help but admire. 'Today is another day. So, Jack,' she went on, sitting down in the chair opposite him, 'what is this job you wanted to hire me for?'

CHAPTER THREE

Vivienne found the surprised expression on Jack Stone's normally stone-like face somewhat satisfying. So, he was not a machine after all! Okay, so he *had* stared at her breasts in the bathroom just now. But not the way most men would have stared. There'd been no lust in his piercing blue eyes. There'd been nothing but shock. Possibly because she wasn't dead, as he'd imagined.

It had shaken Vivienne when Marion had explained that was what they'd both been thinking, making her see how her very uncharacteristic behaviour—especially her rather hysterical quitting of her job—would worry the people who truly cared about her. Not Jack, of course. Vivienne wasn't silly enough to think Jack Stone cared about her. She knew him better than that. His showing up here and bringing her flowers was just a ploy to get her to do what he wanted. He didn't give a damn if her heart was broken, as long as she agreed to what he had in mind work-wise.

And her heart *was* broken.

It was bad enough to be told that the man she loved no longer loved her. Worse was finally finding out who it was he'd left her for. Even worse was seeing the size of Courtney Ellison's baby bump.

The realisation that Daryl had been cheating on her for months had been devastating. Mostly because she'd believed him when he'd insisted he hadn't slept with his new love as yet.

God, she couldn't bear to think about how stupid and gullible she'd been where that man was concerned.

She would *not* think about it any more, she vowed staunchly. Instead, she steeled her spine and eyed Jack with what she hoped was a steadfast gaze. The last thing she wanted to do was break down in front of the likes of him.

'Well?' she said sharply. 'Out with it.'

His blue eyes darkened, his thick dark brows bunching together in a puzzled frown.

Another first, Vivienne thought with perverse triumph. First surprise and now confusion.

'Are you saying you'll actually consider my proposal?' he asked.

Vivienne laughed. 'Not if it's a proposal of marriage. But I'm prepared to consider a work proposal. It's occurred to me that I was foolish to quit my job, especially if it's going to make people think I'm about to top myself. So yes, Jack, tell me what you want me to do, and if I like the idea I'll do it.'

Once again, Jack gave her a look unlike any he'd ever given her. He also did something else: he smiled, a slow almost amused smile which was annoyingly unreadable.

Vivienne wondered what she'd said that had tickled his fancy. Possibly her crack about a marriage proposal. It was well known around the building world that Jack Stone was a confirmed bachelor. No surprise there. How could he be anything else? The man was a workaholic. He wouldn't have time for a wife and a family. She'd never seen him with a girlfriend in tow, either. Not on site at any of his building projects, or even at last year's Christmas party.

Vivienne suspected, however, that he didn't live the life of a monk. He was too male for that. 'Testosterone on legs' was the way one of her female colleagues at Classic Design had once described him.

Vivienne knew what she meant. Well over six feet tall, Jack possessed the same broad-shouldered, powerful body that you saw on wood-chopping champions. Just look what he'd done to her bathroom door! His face was all male as well, with a high forehead, strong nose, granite jaw and a wide, uncompromising mouth. Short dark hair and thick dark brows completed the macho picture.

There was no doubt a lot of women would find him quite attractive, despite his lack of warmth and charm. He did have nice blue eyes, Vivienne conceded, but they were usually hard and cold. They rarely twinkled with humour as they had a moment ago. Not that that made any difference to her. Jack was not her type and never would be.

For some reason, however, she couldn't help wondering just who *his* type of woman was. Who *did* he sleep with? When he could find the time, that was. It occurred to Vivienne that maybe he had a mistress stashed away somewhere who made herself available to him just for sex without expecting anything else. Except money, of course. Which Jack had plenty of.

Vivienne looked deep into his eyes, trying to see if he was that kind of man. His eyes didn't waver, boring back into hers, their expression no longer amused. A strangely erotic shiver ran down Vivienne's spine as she realised that, yes, he probably would have a mistress. How odd, she thought, that she would find such an arrangement rather titillating. She should have been disgusted. But she wasn't. Not even remotely.

'You've gone very quiet all of a sudden,' Jack said, breaking into her somewhat shocked silence.

'Sorry. Just thinking. I've been doing a lot of thinking today. That was what I was doing in the bath all that time—thinking.' After which she'd listened to music, some very loud, mind-numbing music. Hence her not hearing anyone knocking on the bathroom door.

'Not much to be gained by too much thinking,' Jack said. '*Doing* is the solution to most of life's problems. You need to keep busy, Vivienne. Whether it's working for me or someone else is immaterial. But you need to do something, not just sit around, not eating and not sleeping whilst your mind torments you with depressing thoughts. Next thing you know you'll be stuffing yourself with pills every day, weeks will go by and before you know it you'll be unemployable.'

'Oh dear… From the sounds of things, it wasn't just Nigel telling tales but Marion as well.'

'They only have your best interests at heart, Vivienne.'

'And you, Jack? Do you only have my best interests at heart by offering me this job?'

He shrugged. 'I have to confess your best interests weren't my first priority when I came here today. But that doesn't mean I'm totally heartless. Trust me when I say that one day you'll be glad that you didn't marry that bastard.'

Vivienne's teeth clenched hard in her jaw at Jack's possibly well-meaning but still wounding words. She'd loved Daryl and it would take her longer than one miserable month to get over his betrayal.

At the same time, she wasn't about to crawl into a

hole and let him destroy her entirely. Jack was right. She did still have her work.

'Perhaps,' she bit out. 'All right, run your proposal by me and I'll see what I think.'

Five minutes later, Vivienne had to admit that Jack had surprised her. And also intrigued her. The last thing she would have expected him to want her services for was to do a complete refurbishment of a holiday home he'd bought out in the bush. Well, not the bush exactly. Port Stephens was on the coast not that far north of Newcastle, which was the second biggest city in New South Wales and not too long a drive from Sydney— two and a half, maybe three hours.

Because of its location, Port Stephens had become a popular holiday and retirement area. Vivienne had never been there herself, but she'd seen a segment about the area on a travel programme not long ago. Whilst the beaches and bays did look spectacular, and the various townships dotted along the coast perfectly civilised, there was still a lot of rugged bush around. Not only that; from what Jack told her, the house he'd bought wasn't a typical beach shack sitting just off the sand. It did have water views but it was set back in the hills, and was simply huge, with a décor that was a mad mixture of Mediterranean villa and a fifties Hollywood mansion.

All in all, Francesco's Folly sounded fascinating, and would no doubt be a challenge to fix up. A distracting and consuming challenge which would take ages. Just what she needed right now.

'I have to admit you've surprised me,' she said.

Jack leant back in his chair. 'But are you interested in doing the job?'

'Absolutely,' she said in a firm voice.

'Now *you've* surprised *me*,' Jack admitted. 'I was sure you were going to say no.'

Vivienne shrugged. 'I only said I was interested, Jack. I haven't said a definite yes yet.'

'Fair enough.' Jack glanced at his watch then up into her face, his blue eyes no longer twinkling with humour. He was back to business. 'Look, I don't know about you, but I'm starving. Marion said you don't have much food in this place so I suggest you get yourself dressed and we'll go find a local restaurant. We can work out the details of the job over lunch. I can't actually sign you up till contracts have been exchanged on the property, but that shouldn't take long. I rang my solicitor last night and told him to hurry things through. Meanwhile, I'm sure the estate agent handling the sale will be only too happy to give us the keys so that you can look through the place. I'll drive you up there tomorrow.'

'Tomorrow!' Vivienne exclaimed.

'What's wrong with tomorrow? Don't tell me you have anything else you have to do, because we both know you haven't.'

Vivienne suppressed a sigh. She supposed it was too much to ask Jack to act any differently than he usually did when he was on site, charging through each minute of the day like he was perpetually on a deadline. If the man did have a mistress, she could just imagine how his visits to her would go. He'd ring her in advance and tell her to get her gear off so that she could be ready to service him the second he walked in the door.

Once again, Vivienne was shocked that she found such a scenario perversely exciting. Shocked that her body thought so too, her belly and nipples tightening underneath her robe. Thank the Lord it was a thick fluffy robe which hid everything. But her cheeks still

flushed slightly as a wave of heat raced involuntarily
through her veins. Her teeth immediately clenched
down hard in her jaw as she battled for control over
her mind, and her uncharacteristically wayward flesh.
Vivienne wasn't used to being sexually excited by her
thoughts. She'd always needed romance to turn her on.
And a man she was in love with.

Her immediate somewhat panicky response was to
tell Jack that she wasn't hungry and he should go get
himself something to eat then come back later. But then
Vivienne decided she was being silly. Jack didn't know
her secret thoughts, or feelings. On top of that, she *was*
hungry.

'Well, go on,' Jack ordered. 'Go and get dressed.'

Vivienne rolled her eyes but still stood up and headed
for her bedroom, hopeful that the irritation Jack's bossy
manner always evoked in her would douse the unexpected heat he'd been somehow generating. Not that it
was him exactly who'd been turning her on: it had been
her imaginings over his mistress, the one who probably
didn't even exist. Why she'd invented her, Vivienne had
no idea. But she vowed to put her and what Jack did
with her right out of her head.

But typically that was easier said than done. As she
put on her underwear—white cotton bikini briefs and
a white stretchy bra, which minimised rather than enhanced her double-D-cup breasts—Vivienne started
wondering what kind of underwear mistresses wore.
Something very sexy, no doubt. Nothing made of cotton, that was for sure. Or possibly nothing at all.

'Oh God!' Vivienne cried, and dropped her head
into her hands.

CHAPTER FOUR

JACK ANSWERED FIVE missed calls, arranged for a man to come and look at Vivienne's bathroom door tomorrow and booked them a table for a late lunch in the time it took Vivienne to make her reappearance, dressed in bone-coloured slacks, a white T-shirt and a black linen jacket. Her hair was still down and she was wearing only a minimum of make-up, especially around her eyes, which were bloodshot and red-rimmed.

'You've been crying,' he said stupidly before he could think better of it.

Vivienne shot him a droll look. 'No kidding. It's what women do when the man they love turns out to be a two-timing rat. I'm sorry, Jack, but if you want me to work for you in the coming weeks you'll have to risk being on the end of a few crying jags.'

'Fine,' he said. 'As long as you don't expect me to do anything about them.'

She looked taken aback. 'Like what?'

'I have two sisters and a mother,' he informed Vivienne. 'If I didn't hug them when they cried in front of me—which is depressingly often—I would be banned from their lives for ever.'

'You have two sisters and a mother?'

Jack laughed at the astonished expression on her

face. 'What did you think—that I was a foundling, abandoned on a building site when I was a few days old?'

She smiled. She actually smiled. Not a common trait of Vivienne's. She was one serious girl.

'Not quite,' she said. 'But you don't come across as a man in touch with his feminine side.'

'Then you'd be wrong. Living with three women for a good chunk of my life meant I had no choice. Though it was more *their* feminine side I had to be in touch with rather than my own. I have to confess I'm not the kind of guy who cooks and cleans and sends soppy cards, but I do hugs very well.'

'And you bring the right flowers, when required.'

Jack wasn't sure if she was being sarcastic or witty.

'Which I haven't thanked you for,' she went on with seeming sincerity. 'Sorry, Jack. It's not like me to be rude. Or ungrateful. I guess I'm not myself at the moment.'

'Apology accepted. Now, shall we get out of here? Time's marching on and I've booked us a table for lunch.'

She blinked. 'You have? Where?'

'Why don't I just surprise you again?'

He certainly did surprise Vivienne again, in more ways than one. Not only by taking her to a very trendy seafood restaurant which overlooked nearby Balmoral Beach, but by the way he was treated there by the staff—like he was an extremely valued client who deserved the very best table and the very best service. Which he definitely got, with drinks brought and their orders taken in no time flat.

Clearly, Jack had been there more than once, which gave rise to the speculation that he might not be as much of a workaholic as she'd imagined him to be. Maybe he did have an active social life. And a proper girlfriend as opposed to a mistress. Not that she would ever ask such a personal question. Not directly.

But a certain amount of curiosity got the better of Vivienne in the end.

'I gather you come here often?' she said casually as she lifted her glass of mineral water to her lips. She'd declined his offer of wine. If she started drinking, she might become maudlin again.

'Often enough,' he replied noncommittally. 'My mother lives on that hill over there. She loves seafood so I usually bring her here at least once a month. We also came here this year for Mother's Day. The rest of the family came too. Given both my sisters are now married with children, we had to book a seriously large table.'

'I see,' Vivienne said, then decided, what the heck? She wanted to know more. 'And you, Jack—why aren't you married with children?'

It was a reasonable enough question and he didn't seem to mind her asking, judging by his nondescript expression.

'If I said I never had the time, or the energy, you probably wouldn't believe me. But it's true. My dad died when I was seventeen, leaving the family in terrible debt. I had to leave school and get to work straight away. I wasn't happy, I can tell you; I'd made plans to go to uni to become an engineer. But that quickly went by the board. Still, I'm not complaining about that. I made good with what I did.'

'You certainly did,' Vivienne agreed. 'Your company is not only successful, it's one of the few construction companies in Sydney with a reputation for finishing projects on budget, on time *and* with good workmanship.'

Jack smiled at her. 'You forgot to mention that I hire only the best in the business as well, which includes interior designers.'

'And you forgot to mention why, after you made good, you still didn't have time for marriage and children. Let's face it, Jack, you've been at the top of the building ladder for some time now.'

'True. But getting there was a hard slog. Then there was the responsibility of looking after my two younger sisters and my mother. My mother in particular. Mum's not the strongest woman, emotionally. After my dad died, she totally fell apart. Even now, she has a tendency to fall into a depression at the drop of a hat. Some people are like that, you know. It's hard on them and hard on the people who love them and care about them.'

'Yes,' Vivienne said with more empathy than he could possibly realise. 'I'm sure it is.'

'It's a difficult situation to understand unless you live it,' he said, assuming—mistakenly—that she wasn't personally acquainted with such problems. 'Anyway, like I said, by the time I was making serious money I just didn't want to take on any further commitments or responsibilities. I still don't. I… Hell, Vivienne,' he broke off suddenly, his blue eyes startled. 'Why on earth am I telling you all this?'

Vivienne rolled her eyes. Truly, anyone would think he'd committed a crime by unburdening his soul a bit. At least he had one. Unlike some people!

'For pity's sake, Jack,' she said, a little more sharply than she intended. 'Don't go all "macho male" on me. There's no harm in expressing your feelings occasionally. Women do it all the time. You should hear Marion and me when we have a girls' night out. If you must know, I think it's sweet the way you've looked after your family, especially your mother. As for your not wanting marriage and children… Well, there's nothing wrong with that either. You have the right to live your life as you see fit. I was just curious. After all, you're quite a catch. I dare say you've had loads of women running after you over the years.'

'I've had my moments of being targeted.' He opened his mouth to say something more then shut it again. Vivienne was wondering what he'd been about to say when their meals arrived—his and hers lobsters, along with French fries and side salads.

'Oh my God,' she said with a groan as she salivated over the food. 'I didn't realise till this very moment just how hungry I was.'

'You and me both. Come on, let's stop with the chit-chat and tuck in.'

Tuck in they did, all conversation ceasing as they went about the all-consuming task of totally stuffing their faces. Vivienne gave the occasional satisfied sigh whilst Jack did nothing but crunch and munch. It wasn't until there wasn't a morsel of succulent flesh left on her lobster that Vivienne lifted her head, only to find that Jack had just finished his lobster as well and was licking his fingertips with relish.

No, not licking. *Sucking.*

'That was seriously good,' he said between somewhat noisy sucks.

Vivienne didn't say a word. Because she was staring at what Jack was doing and having the most inappropriate thoughts about his fingers. His amazingly long, thick fingers…

When a decidedly kinky fantasy involving herself

and Jack filled her head, Vivienne sat up straight, pressing her spine hard against the back of the chair. She was totally rattled, not just by the erotic nature of her thoughts, but by the way her muscles had tightened deep inside her, as though in anticipation of being invaded by Jack's fingers. She took several deep, calming breaths whilst she struggled to make sense of her behaviour. This was the second time that day that Jack had somehow turned her on. Not consciously, of course. Or deliberately. He would have no idea what mad thoughts he'd been evoking, first about his having a mistress stashed away somewhere, and now about his doing seriously intimate things to her with his fingers.

She wondered dazedly if her focus on things sexual had something to do with Daryl leaving her. Vivienne had been plagued over the past month by thoughts that she hadn't satisfied him in bed, despite his always having said that she did. She'd wondered, during her thinkfest in the bath, if Courtney Ellison did kinky things to Daryl that he'd always secretly craved, and which he now couldn't live without. Maybe her own weird behaviour today was a rebound or a revenge thing, a crazy desire to prove to herself that she could be as wildly sexual as any woman.

Whatever, Vivienne could not deny that she was turned on at this moment. If only Jack would stop sucking those damned fingers!

She turned her eyes away, then did what she always did when life threatened to overwhelm her: she concentrated on work.

'So, Jack,' she said, looking back at him with her business face on. 'Tell me exactly what the terms of my employment will be.'

Jack frowned as he picked up his white linen serviette and wiped his fingertips.

'I can't really give you specifics yet,' he said. 'Not till I see the place again. If you come with me tomorrow, you can inspect Francesco's Folly for yourself and tell me how long you think the job will take to complete. I always prefer to pay designers a lump sum rather than so much per hour. At the same time, given you would be doing me a special favour by taking this job, I am prepared to be generous.'

Vivienne's eyebrows lifted. Jack Stone was not known for his generosity. He was a fair businessman, but tough.

'*How* generous?' she asked.

'*Very* generous.'

'But why? I'm sure you could get any number of up-and-coming young designers to do the job for next to nothing. It would be a feather in their cap.'

'But I don't want any other up-and-coming designer, Vivienne. I want *you*.'

CHAPTER FIVE

·

WHEN JACK SAID he wanted Vivienne, he'd meant it as a strictly professional statement, the same one he'd made to Nigel earlier that day.

But as he looked deep into her gorgeous green eyes—eyes which had widened slightly at his words—the thought hit Jack that he didn't want Vivienne just professionally, but physically as well.

It was a stunning realisation, one which left Jack speechless. After all, not until today had he seriously fancied Vivienne. Okay, so he'd been aware of her good looks, and had occasionally given her a second glance as she'd walked by.

But she'd never given him a hard-on. Not once.

Yet she'd already done that twice today. Once, when he'd seen her naked in the bath, and right now, here, in this restaurant.

It was this second unexpected erection which totally threw him, because there was nothing happening which should have stirred lust in him: no nakedness; no flirtation. Hell, they were just discussing business.

But lust was very much in control of Jack's body at that moment. *And* his mind. Effortlessly, it stripped Vivienne of her clothes until she was naked before him, the mental image of her sitting there in the nude bringing his arousal to an almost painful level.

God in heaven, he thought frustratedly, *what on earth am I going to do now?*

Absolutely nothing, he decided ruefully. Because there was nothing he *could* do. To make a play for Vivienne in her present emotionally charged and highly vulnerable state was both unconscionable and extremely unlikely to be productive.

But what of later? he wondered. The job he'd asked her to do would take weeks. No, probably months. Could he wait that long before making his move? Probably not, if the bulge in his jeans was anything to go by. Hopefully, it wasn't Vivienne herself sparking all this urgent desire, but his long stint of celibacy.

'But *why* do you want me?' Vivienne persisted.

Jack hoped his face didn't betray the thoughts which immediately ran through his head. Because they had nothing to do with work.

'Why? Because you're seriously good,' he replied, all the while wishing that she wasn't. At this moment, he wished she were seriously bad. The Courtney Ellison type of bad. If that were the case, the possibilities were endless.

The waiter arrived fortuitously at that moment, sweeping away their plates and asking them if they wanted dessert. Vivienne declined. So did Jack, briskly ordering them coffee instead. By the time they were alone again, he'd managed to stop the X-rated images bombarding his brain, his conscience castigating him at the same time for reducing a nice girl like Vivienne to little more than a sex object.

Vivienne was seriously glad that the waiter arrived when he did, stopping her from making a fool of herself by asking more stupid questions as to why Jack wanted her specifically for the job. What had she been expecting him to say, for pity's sake? She already knew that he liked her work. He'd said so on many occasions. Had she been looking for more praise? More ego-stroking? Or something else—something which she hardly dared admit, even to herself...

When another embarrassing wave of sexual heat started flowing through Vivienne's body, she stood up so abruptly that her chair almost tipped over backwards. She grabbed it just in time, throwing Jack a weak smile as she excused herself and headed for the rest room.

It was a flushed and confused Vivienne who leant on the washstand and stared into the wall mirror above the twin basins. Lord, what was happening to her here? First, she'd entertained kinky fantasies involving Jack's fingers, then she'd started hoping he'd say he wanted her and her only for the job because he wanted *her*. Which was even crazier, considering any female with a brain in her head knew when a man fancied her. And Jack didn't. Never had. The same way she'd never fancied him. Until today, that was. Suddenly, she seemed to be finding him extremely attractive. No, not just attractive—sexy. Dead sexy.

The logical part of Vivienne's mind told her this definitely had something to do with Daryl leaving her. His desertion had unhinged her and she'd become desperate. Desperate for someone, if not to love her, than at least to want her. Women sometimes did stupid things after being dumped. A girlfriend of hers had once cut her hair very short and bleached it white. Another had gone out and had a boob job. A third had slept with a different man every night for a month. You didn't reach the age of twenty-seven without having witnessed a few of your female friends lose the plot over men.

Vivienne had no intention of cutting her hair. Or of going blonde. Or having a boob job. Neither was she about to cruise bars every night in search of one-night stands. But she was awfully tempted—awfully, *awfully* tempted—to try to make Jack Stone want her for more than redecorating Francesco's Folly. She wanted him to look at her with fire in those hard blue eyes of his. Wanted him to want her so badly that he'd stop at nothing to have her.

Vivienne shook her head, her shoulders slumping. Who was she kidding? None of that was ever going to happen. She wasn't the kind of girl who could turn a man's head against his will. She wasn't a flirt, let alone a *femme fatale.* Before Daryl, she'd had less than a handful of lovers. She was, if truth be told, on the shy side when it came to bedroom matters. Daryl had been the one to pursue her, to seduce her, to make her fall in love with him.

Vivienne frowned at this last thought. Was that true? Had Daryl somehow *made* her fall in love with him? How odd that sounded, as though she hadn't had any choice. If there was one thing Vivienne was proud of, it was her ability to make choices in life. To decide. That was what she'd been doing in the bath today—deciding what to do with the rest of her life. Not that she'd come to any solid conclusion in the matter. She'd still been too upset to think rationally. In the end, she'd just lain back in the warm water and listened to music, unaware of time passing and the water cooling.

Jack breaking down the door had shocked the life out of her, not to mention seriously embarrassed her. She hadn't enjoyed his getting an eyeful of her bare breasts.

An exhibitionist, she was not! Which made her subsequent sexual responses to him even harder to fathom. None of it made any sense at all!

When another woman came into the rest room Vivienne scurried into one of the cubicles where, with a bit of luck, she could sit and think in peace. She hated not being able to think clearly.

So what are you going to do about this job offer from Jack, Vivienne? came that stern voice that would pop up in her head on the rare occasions she began to waffle over something. *You don't have to do it. He can't force you. Come on, girl, make a decision!*

Vivienne gnawed at her bottom lip as she considered the pros and cons.

To knock him back would not be the best of moves work-wise, if she wanted to continue being a designer. Jack was a powerful man in the building industry. At the same time, it was going to be awkward, being alone with him in the car tomorrow and then working with him on such a personal project. No doubt they would have to spend more time together than when she usually worked for him. Not an enjoyable situation, if she kept being besieged by hot thoughts about him all the time.

But what was her alternative? Say no and stay home, wallowing in her misery? Vivienne shuddered at the thought. She supposed she could pack her bags and go on a holiday somewhere. But she would still be alone. Alone and unhappy, with nothing to distract her. She'd rather take back her resignation and return to work for Classic Design than do that. Running away never solved anything. You had to face things in life. Face reality!

Okay, so face it, Vivienne! For some weird and wonderful reason today, you're madly attracted to Jack.

Madly attracted and seriously turned on. That's the truth of the matter.

But there's absolutely no basis for this sudden attraction, she argued with herself. Jack wasn't even her type, physically. Vivienne had always found big men intimidating, not appealing at all.

Maybe it was just a temporary aberration. Maybe she'd wake up tomorrow and these mad feelings would be gone. Maybe when she saw him in the morning, she'd only feel what she used to feel for him. Which was a mixture of irritation and exasperation at his bossy ways and less than charming manner.

Soothed by such sensible reasoning, Vivienne decided not to make a hasty decision. She'd wait and see what happened tomorrow. If the drive up there with Jack was a nightmare of frustration and confusion, she'd decline his offer, saying she was sorry but she simply wasn't up to such a big job at this time.

Surely Jack would understand?

It was a relief to find, as she made her way back to their table, that when she looked over at him, sitting there drumming his index finger on the white linen tablecloth, her only feelings were wry ones. He really was a most impatient man. Impatient, demanding and not happy, unless things were going his way.

Remembering this, Vivienne conceded Jack probably wouldn't react well if she rejected his proposal. No doubt he would argue with her then offer her more money, neither of which would work. If he knew her better, he'd know she couldn't be bullied, or bribed into anything she didn't want to do.

But maybe it wouldn't come to that. Clearly, she was already over what had taken possession of her earlier.

Her brain was now crystal clear and firmly in control of her body.

'Coffee not here yet?' she said politely as she pulled out her chair and sat down.

'Nope. So, is it a yes or a no, Vivienne? Give it to me straight.'

Vivienne almost smiled. Oh yes, things were right back to normal. But she still wasn't about to be bullied into saying yes prematurely.

'I think, Jack, that it would be wise for me not to commit myself till I see Francesco's Folly in person.'

'Okay, I'll pick you up early tomorrow morning. Around seven. So don't go taking too many of those sleeping tablets the doctor gave you.'

Vivienne gave an exasperated sigh. 'Marion's a good friend but she talks too much. What else did she tell you about me?'

'Not much. She did say that you owned rather than rented your apartment. But that was only because I asked her. She didn't volunteer the information.'

'I see. And why did you want to know that?' she asked, thinking to herself that he'd probably been trying to gauge her financial situation. Knowledge was power, after all.

'No good reason. It surprised me, that's all, how starkly furnished the place was. It didn't have your signature warmth and style.'

'Oh,' she said, taken aback that he would notice. Her chest tightened as it did whenever she thought of the reasons why her apartment was the way it was. You couldn't explain something like that. When Marion had asked her the same thing, she'd just said she hated clutter. Of course, it went deeper than that. Much, much deeper.

'I haven't long had the apartment renovated,' she said. 'The decorating's not finished yet.'

'Ah. That explains it, then. I thought maybe the boyfriend had taken some things with him when he left.'

Vivienne rather liked the disdain with which Jack said 'the boyfriend' rather than Daryl's name.

'Daryl didn't own anything,' she bit out. 'Only his clothes.' And she'd bought most of them. His salary as a mobile phone salesman didn't extend to trendy designer wear. God, but she'd been a fool where that man was concerned. Quite unconsciously her right hand went to the fourth finger on her left hand, where her engagement ring had resided until a month ago.

She'd bought that, too, Daryl having promised faithfully that he would pay her back.

But he never had.

Currently, it was languishing in the top drawer of her bedside table, a visual testament to her stupidity.

Vivienne realised suddenly that Courtney Ellison must have paid for the rock she'd been proudly displaying in those photographs published in the gossip section of last Sunday's paper. No way could Daryl have afforded a diamond that size, not unless it was a fake one. Actually, it wouldn't surprise her if it *was* a fake diamond. A fake diamond to go with his fake persona.

The coffee arrived at that point, in a silver pot, along with a jug of cream and a plate full of after-dinner mints. The waiter poured the coffee then left them to do the rest. Vivienne added cream and two cubes of sugar to hers. Jack left his black.

'He didn't leave you because of *you*, Vivienne,' he said abruptly after taking a sip of his coffee. 'It was because of the fortune he stands to inherit as Courtney's husband.'

Vivienne gritted her teeth before looking up. 'Maybe.'

Marion had said the same thing, and of course the logical part of Vivienne agreed with her. But she still couldn't get it out of her head that somehow she was at fault as well. Perhaps Daryl had got sick of her obsession with tidiness, not to mention her sexual inhibitions. She wasn't keen on oral sex, or adventurous positions where she felt exposed and vulnerable. Even being on top bothered her. Daryl had always said that he didn't need her to do any of that stuff if she didn't want to; that making love to *her* was enough for him.

'No sane man would leave a nice girl like you for a woman like Courtney Ellison,' Jack said. 'Not unless the carrot was gold-plated.'

Vivienne might have been flattered, if the thought hadn't struck her that if Daryl was such a cold-blooded fortune hunter then he'd probably pursued *her* because of her money. She might not be in Courtney Ellison's financial league but she wasn't poor either. She owned her own apartment and car, and still had a substantial bank balance. On top of that, as one of Sydney's most successful young designers, she earned a six-figure salary.

The conclusion that Daryl had *never* loved her, that their relationship had been nothing but a con from the start, was even more shattering than his leaving her.

When Jack saw Vivienne's face go ashen, he decided a quick change of subject was called for.

'Before I forget,' he said as he plonked his coffee cup back onto its saucer. 'The chap I've organised to come look at your bathroom door will be at your place the same time as me—seven. Not that he can fix it on the spot. When I told him the door would need replacing, not repairing, he said he'd have to take measurements to make sure he got the right door.'

Vivienne made a scoffing sound. 'And you trust a tradesman to arrive on time? When I had my apartment renovated I soon discovered that tradies have a totally different time schedule to the rest of the world.'

'Then you should have called in my company to do the work,' Jack said. 'Trust me when I tell you the carpenter I've booked will be at your door bang on seven. He knows that if he's late I won't be hiring him again.'

'I'll have to see it to believe it.'

'Then you will. I'll be on time, too. Just make sure you're up and ready.'

'You don't have to worry about me,' came her rueful reply. 'I'm nothing if not punctual.'

Jack frowned at the underlying depression in her words, anger quickly joining his concern. That bastard had done a real number on Vivienne's self-esteem. If he ever came across him again, he'd flatten him, and to hell with the consequences!

'You sound tired,' he said. 'Come on; drink up your coffee and I'll take you home. I can see you're in need of some serious sleep.'

Vivienne opened her mouth to tell him that he wasn't her boss—yet—so he could stop with the orders. But then she realised that he was only trying to be kind. He just didn't know any other way but bossy and controlling. So she drank her coffee and let him drive her home. Once there, she declined his offer to walk her to the door, but he just ignored her and did it anyway. Vivienne decided not to argue. She was beyond arguing.

'Are you sure you'll be all right?' Jack asked as she went about slowly inserting her key into the lock.

She sighed as she turned and glanced up at him. 'I'll be fine,' she said somewhat wearily. 'Thanks for the very nice lunch, Jack. I did thank you for the flowers before, didn't I?'

'Yes.'

'Good. I'm not quite all there at the moment.'

'I can see that. But you'll be better tomorrow. And even better the day after that.'

'I certainly hope so.'

'I *know* so. All you have to do is do what Dr Jack tells you. Till tomorrow morning, then,' he said, giving Vivienne no warning before his head bent to deliver a goodbye peck.

It was just a platonic kiss but, when his lips made contact with hers, Vivienne's heart stopped beating altogether. Thank God he spun away immediately and strode off without a backward glance. Because if he'd looked down into her face after lifting his head he would have seen something not so platonic in her eyes.

'Crazy,' she said with another sigh. 'I'm definitely going crazy.'

CHAPTER SIX

'I'm a bloody idiot,' Jack muttered to himself as he jumped into his car, slammed it into gear and accelerated away.

He knew he should go back to the office. There was always work to be done. Instead, he drove back down to Balmoral Beach where he turned off his mobile phone then sat in his car for a ridiculously long time, thinking. Then, when he couldn't stand trying to work things out in his head a moment longer, he did something even more futile: he drove to his mother's house.

She was home, of course. His mother was always home nowadays, recently having added agoraphobia to her long list of anxiety disorders. The only time she'd been out of the house during the past year was on Mother's Day, and for her birthday back in February. Jack had tried to get her to go to Vanuatu with him in March but to no avail.

'Jack!' she exclaimed when she opened the front door, looking surprisingly well, he noted. *And* very nicely dressed. Sometimes, when he came to visit, he found her still in her dressing gown in the middle of the day. 'It's not like you to visit on a weekday,' she added. 'There's nothing wrong, is there?'

'Nope,' he lied. No point in telling his mother about

his personal problems. It would only upset her. 'I was in the area for work and decided to pop in and see you.'

'How nice. Come in, then. Would you like some coffee?' she asked him as he followed her down to the kitchen.

'I won't say no,' he replied.

The kitchen was super-tidy today, he noted. His mother had always been a fastidious housekeeper when they'd been growing up, but after his father had died you could always tell how depressed she was by the state of her kitchen. Clearly, if the shining sink and benchtops were anything to go by, his mother was far from depressed at the moment.

'You going out somewhere?' he asked as he sat down at the large wooden kitchen table.

His mother sent him a sheepish look from where she was standing by the kettle. 'Actually, yes, I am. But not till five. Jim next door—you know Jim, don't you?—has asked me out to dinner. We're going to a restaurant way up at Palm Beach. There aren't too many restaurants open on a Monday night, it seems.'

Jack could not hide his surprise that his mother would go out at all, let alone accept a date from a man.

'Yes, yes, I know,' she said. 'It's been a long time coming. But I finally got so sick of myself last week that I started talking to Jim over the fence when we were both outside gardening. We have spoken before, but only to say hello. Anyway, he was just so easy to talk to, and when he asked me over for a cup of tea I went. It was then that he asked me out to dinner and I said yes. I know he's a good few years older than me, but he's just so nice, and I thought, what have I got to lose by going out with him?'

'Absolutely nothing, Mum. I think it's great.'

'Do you?' she said as she brought his mug of black coffee over to the table. 'Do you really?' she repeated as she sat down opposite him.

'Of course. Jim's a decent man.' Jack had got to know Jim over the years his mother had lived in this house. He was always out in the garden and happy to have a word or two.

'I'm glad you approve. Because this isn't the first date I've had with him. We've been going out to dinner every night for almost a week.'

'Wow. No flies on Jim.'

When his mother blushed, the penny dropped.

'Wow again, Mum,' Jack said. 'And good for you. Good for you both, actually.'

'We don't want to get married,' his mother confided, her voice dropping to a conspiratorial whisper. 'We just want company.'

'I haven't seen you this happy in years,' he said.

Her blue eyes sparkled.

His mother astonished him further by lifting her chin and looking him straight in the eye. 'Now, I have to go put my make-up on, Jack. Stay and finish your coffee by all means but I would prefer it if you're gone by the time Jim comes to pick me up. I don't trust you not to say something embarrassing.'

'Who, me!' Jack exclaimed, doing his best to stop himself from smiling.

'Yes, you. You can be extremely tactless at times.'

'Who, *me*?' Now he was grinning widely.

'Oh for pity's sake,' she said, rolling her eyes at the same time. But she bent and kissed the top of his head. 'You're a good son and I love you dearly, but may I suggest you ring before you just pop in next time? I might have a visitor and I wouldn't want to shock you.'

It wasn't until Jack left the house ten minutes later that he stopped smiling and started thinking again. Not about his mother and Jim but about himself and Vivienne.

As he drove at a snail's pace back towards the city and home—rush-hour traffic had more than arrived—his thoughts ran over the events of the day, right up until that last moment when he'd kissed Vivienne goodbye. That had been the moment when it had hit home to him—with considerable force—that if he took Vivienne up to Francesco's Folly tomorrow there was a very real danger of his doing something which would spoil their working relationship for ever.

Jack didn't want that to happen. He valued Vivienne as a business colleague and respected her as a woman. But there was no denying that she'd stirred a lust in him today that was almost beyond reason. He'd imagined he'd got it under control back in the restaurant, but then he'd kissed her and all hell had broken loose.

'Worse than hell,' he muttered aloud, recalling how the second his lips had brushed over hers he'd been instantly besieged by the most violent urge to sweep her into his arms and kiss her properly. His struggle not to succumb to the temptation had almost exhausted his will power, so much so that he doubted he would be able to resist a second time.

Of course, he would not be stupid enough to kiss her a second time. That was a given. But it was still likely that he'd be plagued by ongoing thoughts about doing a lot more than just kissing her. Which would result in his getting turned on again.

Jack didn't want to spend tomorrow with a hard-on. So he guessed it was off to a club tonight, and sex with a virtual stranger.

Such a scenario would have excited him once upon a time. But no longer, it seemed. What Jack really wanted was to have great sex with a woman he knew and liked. A woman with gorgeous green eyes, long auburn hair and breasts to die for.

Jack banged his hands on the steering wheel, swearing in frustration.

His frustration grew all the way across the Harbour Bridge, reaching a furious peak by the time he let himself into his apartment. There, he stripped off all his clothes and jumped into a steaming hot shower. After a few minutes, he turned the tap abruptly to cold and stood there under the icy shards of water till his body was numb. Not so his brain, however. Nothing was going to rid his mind of the annoying reality that he wanted Vivienne as he had not wanted a woman in his entire life.

For a man who was used to achieving his goals, it exasperated Jack that he could not have what he wanted. If only he wasn't a modern man, he thought irritably, constrained by the rules of civilisation and society. Cave men had had it so much easier. If a cave man had seen a female he fancied, he'd just banged her on the head with a club then dragged her back to his cave, where he'd ravaged her silly, after which she'd become his woman.

Jack had to laugh at what would happen to him if he did that to Vivienne. He certainly wouldn't have to wait for the power of the law to punish him. She'd up and kill him the first chance she got. God, what he would not give to have her in his bed, not just once—once was not going to be *nearly* enough!—but on a regular basis.

By the time he'd exited the shower and wrapped a towel around himself, Jack had come to two decisions. One, he wasn't going to go pick up some stranger tonight. To hell with that idea! Two, he didn't care how long it took, or what he'd have to do to make it happen—one day, Vivienne Swan was going to be become his lover!

CHAPTER SEVEN

'THAT DIDN'T TAKE long, did it?' Jack said as he popped on his sunglasses then started up the powerful engine of his Porsche. 'I told you the door man would be on time.'

Vivienne gave him a cool smile in return before putting on her own sunglasses. After sleeping for fourteen hours straight, she'd woken at six this morning with a clear head and a determination to take control of her life once more—which included not falling apart over Daryl's lies, and not entertaining any further wanton thoughts about Jack Stone.

It was a still a relief, however, when he arrived and she was able to open the door to him without instantly wondering if he'd spent last night with his mistress, or whether other parts of his body were as big as his fingers. Yes, she did still find him more attractive than she had in the past. He looked *extremely* good in those tight blue jeans, white T-shirt and a navy zip-up jacket. But her thoughts didn't turn lustful, even when he bent over to show the door man the broken hinges.

Vivienne was also able to fold herself down into the low passenger seat of his sexy black sports car without worrying that being alone with him would prove too much for her. She felt rested and relaxed and almost back to her normal self. Thank heavens!

'I'll remember to call you the next time something goes wrong in my place and I need a tradie,' she said. 'You seem to have all the right contacts.'

'Call me any time you like,' he replied.

Vivienne frowned at the uncharacteristic warmth in his voice. She supposed he was just being nice so that she'd do the job he wanted her to do, the same way he'd been nice to her yesterday. But she seriously wished he'd go back to being as brusque and matter-of-fact as he usually was. That way, there'd be no chance of a repeat of what had happened to her yesterday.

'Do you mind if I ask you something personal?' he said.

Vivienne's frown deepened. '*How* personal?'

'It's about Daryl.'

'What about Daryl?'

'I only met him the once. Last year at your Christmas party. I've been puzzling over what was it about the man to make you fall in love with him?'

It startled Vivienne, that phrase Jack used about Daryl *making* her fall in love with him. For that was what she had thought herself: that somehow Daryl had *made* her fall in love with him.

'It sounds like you didn't like him much,' she said.

'You could say that.'

'But why? You only spoke to us that night for a few minutes.'

Jack shrugged. 'It doesn't take me long to form opinions of people.'

'In that case, what was your opinion?'

'He was a slick-talking, superficial charmer whom I wouldn't trust an inch.'

'Goodness! You really didn't like him, did you?'

'No, but obviously you did.'

'Well, yes…yes of course I did. I *loved* him.'

Jack liked the way she said that in the past tense. He liked also that his questions were making her think about the rotter she'd been planning to marry. He needed Vivienne to get over him fast. To move on with her life. Because that was his only chance of success with her in the near future.

Jack was not a patient man at the best of times. Seeing Vivienne again this morning had done little to dampen his desire for her, despite her wearing a rather androgynous black pants suit and having put her hair back up. He knew now what she looked like with her hair down, and what her breasts were like underneath that crisp, white schoolgirl blouse.

'But why, Vivienne?' he persisted. 'What was there to love about him? Surely it wasn't just because he was handsome?'

'No,' Vivienne denied, though Daryl *was* handsome. Very handsome. 'It was more the way he treated me.'

'You mean he said all the things you wanted to hear. Conmen are very good at lying, Vivienne. And giving compliments.'

'True,' Vivienne agreed. Daryl had paid her never-ending compliments. Looking back, she could see that they had been over the top. She wasn't drop-dead gorgeous. Or *that* good a cook. And facing the evidence of her ex-fiancé's character was beginning to make her angry again. Though the anger this time was more directed at herself than him. How *could* she have been so stupid as to be taken in by that creep? What kind of idiot was she? It was some comfort that she hadn't finalised any arrangements for their wedding— as though deep down she'd known the wedding would never take place.

'Would you mind if we stopped talking about Daryl?' she said a bit sharply.

'Sorry,' Jack said. 'Do you want me to shut up altogether? It's just that it's a rather long drive. It could get a bit boring if we just sit here in silence. I could turn on the radio if you prefer, or put on some music. I have a flash stick with heaps of songs on it.'

'What kind of songs?' Vivienne asked, vowing to forget all about Daryl. He wasn't worth thinking about, anyway.

For a minute there, Jack had thought he'd made a big mistake, bringing up the subject of Vivienne's ex. She'd become very uptight with his questions. Clearly, she was still in love with the bastard. Or thought she was. It irked Jack that dear old Daryl had probably been great in bed. Men like that usually were. But what the heck? He wasn't too bad in the sack himself.

Jack felt confident that, if and when he managed to seduce Vivienne, she'd be happy enough in the morning. Not that he wanted actually to *seduce* Vivienne. Seduction suggested sneaky methods, such as excessive flattery, which had obviously been one of Daryl's tactics for getting a girl into bed. Jack had never learnt the art of flattery. He called a spade a spade. If he told a girl she was beautiful, it was because she *was* beautiful. Jack hated liars and manipulators, hated empty chit-chat as well. He was a doer, not a talker.

Or he usually was. It had come as a genuine surprise to him that he'd talked to Vivienne more yesterday than he'd ever talked to any woman. He'd even told her about his family background, and the problems he'd had with his mother. Which was a thought…

Jack decided not to bother with music for now and to stick to chit-chat.

'You'll never guess what my mother's gone and done,' he said.

Vivienne seemed momentarily taken aback by his sudden change of subject, her head whipping round to look at him.

'Er…no, I couldn't possibly guess. What?'

'She's having an affair with her next-door neighbour.'

'Heavens! I hope she's not best friends with his wife. That's not very nice.'

'No no, Jim's not married. Recently widowed.'

'Then it's not really an affair, is it? I mean, an affair suggests something illicit. Or secret.'

'True. Call it a fling, then. She's having a fling. They're not in love, or anything like that.'

'How do you know?'

'She said so. They're just good friends. And you know what? I've never seen her happier. Or more confident. I was somewhat shocked at first but, once I thought about it, I realised it was the best thing to happen to her in years.'

'So when did you find all this out?' Vivienne asked.

'Yesterday afternoon. I dropped in to see her after I left you.'

Jack was pleased when she smiled at him.

'You love her a lot, don't you? And worry about her a lot.'

'Mothers who live on their own can be a worry, especially ones who are on the emotionally fragile side.'

'Yes. Yes, that's so true.'

Jack detected a touch of irony in Vivienne's remark. Maybe her mother was a widow as well. Or divorced. But then he recalled Marion saying something about Vivienne inheriting some money recently. That usually meant a death in the family. But who? He would have to tread carefully. He didn't want her getting upset.

'You sound like you've had some personal experience with emotionally fragile mothers,' he said.

'Yes. Yes, I have, actually. Dad divorced Mum when she was still quite young and she never got over it. She died a couple of years ago. Heart attack,' Vivienne added, hoping it would stop Jack asking further questions about her mother's death. If she told him the truth it would be like opening Pandora's box, which she preferred to keep solidly closed.

'That's sad, Vivienne. And your father?'

'Oh, I haven't seen him since he walked out on Mum when I was about six. He went overseas and never came back.'

Jack's sidewards glance showed true shock. 'What kind of man would do something like that?'

Vivienne knew that there were excuses for her father's behaviour but to explain them would be delving into that Pandora's box again.

She shrugged. 'To give him credit, he did leave us well provided for. He gave Mum everything they'd accumulated during their ten-year marriage: the house. The furniture. Two cars. And he paid child support for me till I was eighteen.'

'And so he should have!' Jack said, clearly outraged. 'He should also have kept in touch. Been a proper father to you. I presume it was just you, Vivienne? Sounds like you don't have any other brothers or sisters.'

'No. There was just me,' she said, her chest tightening with the effort of staying calm in the face of memories which were better kept buried.

Jack shook his head. 'It never ceases to amaze me how some men can just walk away and turn their backs on their families, especially their children. Why have children if you're not going to love and care for them? Bloody hell, did you see that?' he growled, thumping the steering wheel at the same time. 'That stupid idiot in that four-wheel drive almost took my front off.'

Vivienne was extremely grateful that that stupid idiot in the four-wheel drive had interrupted what was becoming an increasingly awkward conversation, giving her the opportunity to deflect Jack's attention onto other less painful subjects.

'So how long do you think it will take us to get to Port Stephens?' she asked.

'Mmm. Let's see… It's going on eight and we're about to turn onto the motorway. It took me two and half hours last Sunday from here, but I didn't stop anywhere.'

'You don't have to stop anywhere for me,' Vivienne said. 'I'll be fine. I had a big bowl of porridge for breakfast which usually keeps me going till lunchtime.'

Jack's eyebrows lifted. 'Fancy that. I had porridge too. And you're right. It does stick to your ribs. But I think we might still have a coffee break at Raymond Terrace.'

'I'm not sure where that is. I haven't been up this way before.'

'Really?'

'To tell the truth, I haven't done much travelling of any kind. Never even been out of Australia.' Or Sydney, for that matter, she didn't add. No point in courting more awkward questions.

'I haven't travelled all that much, either,' Jack replied. 'If and when I do take a break, it's to places that it doesn't take long to fly to, like Bali or Vanuatu and Fiji. You know me—busy, busy, busy.'

'Maybe it's time you slowed down a bit.'

'I couldn't agree with you more. That's one of the reasons I bought Francesco's Folly.'

'Francesco's Folly,' Vivienne repeated thoughtfully. 'Do you know why it was called that?'

'The estate agent said Francesco was the name of the Italian who built the place back in the late seventies. The folly part will be self-explanatory once you see the place. I gather our Italian had a large family, most of whom he outlived. He finally passed away a couple of months ago at the age of ninety-five. His two great-grandsons inherited the place but they both live in Queensland and wanted it sold, pronto. Which is where I came in.'

'I can't wait to see it,' Vivienne said.

'And I can't wait to show it to you,' Jack replied.

CHAPTER EIGHT

IT TOOK THEM longer than anticipated to reach Port Stephens, stopping for over half an hour on the Pacific Highway just north of Newcastle. Jack answered several missed business calls and Vivienne had a nice long chat with Marion, who was pleased to hear that her friend was feeling better and planning to get back to work, though not necessarily with Classic Design.

After leaving Raymond Terrace, it took them a good forty minutes to drive to Nelson's Bay—the main seaside town in Port Stephens—where they picked up the keys from the agency handling the property, then made their way to Francesco's Folly, which was near an area called Soldier's Point. Despite having enjoyed the drive and the scenery, by the time Jack turned his Porsche into the driveway of their destination, Vivienne was keen to see the house.

And what a house it was! Only two storeyed, but it looked like a mansion perched up on top of a hill. Mediterranean in style, it was cement-rendered in a salmon-pink colour and had more archways and columns than Vivienne had seen outside of a convent or a museum.

'Heavens to Betsy!' Vivienne exclaimed as Jack drove up the long, extremely steep driveway.

Jack grinned over at her. 'It's pretty spectacular, isn't it?'

'Not quite a traditional Aussie holiday house, I have to admit. A mad mixture of Tuscan villa and Greek palace. What's it like inside?'

'Extremely dated. Trust me when I say you'll have your work cut out for you to transform it into something I could live with on a permanent basis. But the views, Vivienne. The views are to die for.'

'But Jack, it's enormous!' she said as they drew closer and she began to appreciate the true proportions of the place. 'Are you sure you want to buy a place this size? I mean…it would be different if you were married with a big family, like Francesco was.'

Jack shrugged. 'I have two married sisters with a total of five children between them. And a mother with a lover. They'll use the place, too. Though, to be brutally honest, I'm not buying it for them. I'm buying it for myself.

'I knew the moment I walked out onto one of those balconies up there that I wanted to live here,' he said, pointing to the balconies, which spanned the full length of both floors. 'Maybe not twenty-four-seven just yet, but at least at weekends and for holidays. Call me crazy if you like but that's the way it is. Now, stop trying to talk me out of this, Vivienne,' he said as they drove round to the back of the house. 'It's a done deal.'

The back of the house was where the garages were located, along with the main entrance to the house, guarded by two huge brass doors with equally huge brass locks. The tarred driveway also gave way to a gravel courtyard, the wheels of the Porsche making crunching noises as Jack brought his car to a halt in front of the multiple garages.

'Leave that behind,' Jack ordered when she picked

up her bag. 'I don't want us being interrupted by phone calls. I'll leave my phone behind as well.'

'What about my camera?' she asked. 'I'd like to take photos.'

'No photos first up. Just your eyes. Come on.'

She did as ordered, despite thinking to herself that if she agreed to do this job she would have to learn to bite her tongue a lot. Jack really was a control freak, in her humble opinion. She smiled a wry smile when he made her stand back while he unlocked the brass doors and pushed them wide open, after which he turned and stood, still barring her way.

'Now, before you call me a liar,' he said. 'This first part of the house is not too bad.'

Vivienne almost laughed when she walked inside. 'Not too bad' was a serious understatement! The foyer alone was quite magnificent with a vaulted ceiling and an Italian-marble floor, an elegantly curved staircase on each side leading up to the first floor. Straight ahead was a wide columned archway, beyond which lay a huge indoor swimming pool, which seemingly stretched for ever, before running under another columned archway and ending out in the sunshine.

'Wow,' was all she could think of to say.

'Yes. The pool is Hollywood wow,' Jack agreed. 'Not solar heated, however, something which I would want to have done. But that wouldn't be your problem. Yours is the décor of the rooms, which are many and varied.

'On each side of the pool there's a self-contained three-bedroomed apartment,' he explained as he took Vivienne's hand and led her along the left side of the pool. 'In recent years, Francesco used to let them out in the summer. But that was before he became ill. After that, he just lived upstairs, the downstairs apartments were left empty and the whole place became run down.'

'It doesn't look that run down,' Vivienne said, trying to keep her focus on her surrounds and not on her hand in Jack's. Lord, but she wished she could extract her hand without such a move being rude, but before she could do so his fingers tightened around hers. Her breath caught as a violently electric current raced up her arm and down through her entire body, tightening her nipples and belly on the way.

So much for her having this insane sexual attraction under control!

'I gather the estate agent got in a team of cleaners before the place was opened for inspection,' Jack said as he walked on, a totally rattled Vivienne in tow. 'The great-grandsons took away what furniture they wanted, so all the rooms are half-empty, which perhaps didn't serve the sellers well. It highlighted how neglected everything was and I was able to negotiate a bargain. But enough of that for now. Come and see the view.'

Thankfully, he let go of her hand once they reached the sun-drenched balcony, and Vivienne was quick to put some distance between herself and Jack, walking swiftly over to stand at the iron railing, which she gripped with both hands as though her life depended on it. And it did, actually, there being a considerable drop from the balcony onto the rocky hillside below.

Not that she gazed down for more than a split second, her eyes soon returning to admire the view, which was as spectacular as Jack had promised.

In truth, Vivienne had never seen a view like it, not just for its natural beauty but for the sheer size and expanse of the panorama. It felt like she was standing on a mountaintop looking out over treetops at the bay beyond. She had no idea how large Port Stephens was but it looked enormous! And so beautiful and blue. Of course, it was a cloudless spring day, so the colour of the water reflected the blue of the sky. Perhaps on a rainy day it might not look so spectacular. But today, Mother Nature was on show and it took Vivienne's breath away.

Though not quite to the degree that Jack's holding her hand a minute ago had taken it away.

Vivienne still could not get over the intensity of her physical response to something as simple as hand-holding. Her mind boggled at what she might do if Jack ever kissed her, or touched her in a more intimate fashion.

Not that he was likely to, so she was safe on that score. But just thinking about it sent an erotically charged shiver trickling down her spine. Her hands tightened on the railing when Jack moved to stand beside her.

'Well?' he said somewhat smugly. 'It is an incredible view, isn't it?'

Vivienne gritted her teeth as she turned to face him. '"Incredible" hardly describes it, Jack,' she said, proud that she could sound so calm when she felt anything but. It was as well, however, that she was wearing sunglasses. They gave her a degree of safety. 'I guess, if I had the money, I'd be tempted to buy this place too. That is one seductive view.'

'It's even better from the top floor,' he said. 'Shall we go take a look?'

What could she say? *No, I don't think so, Jack. And no, I'm sorry, but I won't be taking this job after all.* He'd want to know why and she couldn't tell him the truth, could she? Couldn't confess suddenly to lusting after him with a lust to rival what Paris had felt for

Helen of Troy. He'd think she'd gone barmy! Which, of course, she had. Totally, tragically barmy!

'Shouldn't you show me the downstairs apartments first?' she said.

'That can wait. Come on.'

'You lead the way,' she said quickly before he could reach for her hand again. 'I'll be right behind you.'

Being behind Jack wasn't totally without trouble; Vivienne was having difficulty keeping her eyes off his very nice butt, especially once he started up the stairs. In desperation she dropped her gaze to her feet until she reached the upper level which opened out into a spacious semi-circular landing, over which hung a very elaborate crystal chandelier.

'I gather this was once Francesco's private art gallery,' Jack said. 'But, as you can see,' he went on, waving a hand towards where several paintings obviously had once hung against the heavily embossed wallpaper, 'All the pictures are now gone.'

'Would you like it to be an art gallery again?' Vivienne asked, doing her best to refocus on business.

Jack shrugged. 'I'll leave that decision up to you. I know I'll like whatever you do with it.'

Oh dear, Vivienne thought with some dismay, only too aware that she was slowly being sucked into a situation from which there was no escape. Because in truth she really wanted to do this job, wanted to transform Francesco's Folly into the type of home Jack would love. His faith in her abilities was extremely flattering. And the house itself was a fantastic challenge. It was impossible to say no. And yet she knew she should. Nothing good was going to come out of working side by side with Jack. She could feel it in her bones—and several other parts of her body as well!

'This way,' he said, and walked over to the double doors in the centre of the semi-circular wall, throwing them both open and waving her inside with a flourish of his right arm.

Vivienne walked past him into a massive rectangular-shaped living room, which she knew instantly would look fabulous if and when it was properly refurbished. Her designer's eyes were picturing the room with its hideous wallpaper stripped off, the walls painted white and the dated furniture replaced by more modern pieces. The marble fireplace at the far end of the room could stay, but the rest would have to go, especially the heavy brocade curtains which framed the glass doors leading out onto the balcony, and which were simply horrible.

'I can see that decorating head of yours is already ticking away, Vivienne,' Jack said, smiling as he headed over to the glass doors. 'But first things first, madam. The view!'

Even from where she was standing Vivienne could see that the view from up here was even more spectacular than from the lower balcony. But to get there she had to brush past Jack, who was still standing in the half-opened doorway, waiting for her. She somehow managed to move past him without actually making bodily contact, hurrying over to the railing like the hounds of hell were after her. But as she closed her fingers over the top rung, leaning her weight against it at the same time, the whole thing suddenly shifted.

CHAPTER NINE

JACK SAW THE railing give way a split second before Vivienne screamed. With a burst of fear-fuelled adrenaline, he covered the distance between them with a speed which would later amaze him, grabbing at Vivienne as she began to lose her balance, her arms flailing wildly, her sunglasses flying off her face into the valley below. All he got hold of at first was the back of her suit jacket but it was enough to stop the momentum of her fall. Finally he managed to wind one firm arm around her waist and pull her back from where she was still teetering on the edge of disaster. She fell back against him, her scream silenced as she gasped for air. By the time he dragged her body back further from the edge of the balcony, her shock had turned to an almost hysterical sobbing.

This time, Jack didn't hesitate to comfort her, turning her trembling body in his arms and holding her close.

'There there,' he murmured, one of his arms wrapped tightly around her lower back whilst the other gently stroked the nape of her neck. 'Stop crying. You're safe.'

But she didn't stop crying. She wept on and on, Jack suspecting that her close brush with death might have released more emotions than just relief. Possibly she was crying over what had been happening in her life recently.

Whatever, having her pressed hard against him was not conducive to his peace of mind. Or the peace of his body. Despite willing his sex-starved flesh to stay calm, it did not. Common sense demanded he push her away from him. But to do so whilst she was still sobbing so disconsolately seemed heartless. All he could hope for was that she wouldn't notice he was getting an erection.

Things went from bad to worse, however, when she moved her arms from where they'd been jammed between their chests and wound them tightly around his back, her head nestling into the crook of his neck. Now he could feel the soft fullness of her breasts, not to mention the warmth of her breath against his skin. When her crying finally stopped, he tried moving his lower half away from hers but it was almost impossible with the way she was clinging to him.

'Vivienne,' he said a bit brusquely.

Her head lifted, her tear-stained face no less beautiful, her lovely green eyes searching his with a strange intensity. And then she did something which shocked him. She planted her hands on his shoulders, reached up on tiptoe and kissed him full on the mouth. When he jerked his head backwards, her hands fell away and she sank back down on her heels, her face crumpling.

'I'm sorry,' she choked out. 'I thought…I thought… Oh, it doesn't matter what I thought. Obviously I was wrong.' And she staggered back from him, her shoulders slumping, her eyes wretchedly unhappy.

'No. You thought right, Vivienne. I've been struggling with my desire for you since I saw you naked in that bath yesterday. It's come as a surprise to me, I admit, but I want you, and I'd like to take you to bed more than anything. But not like this, Vivienne.'

She lifted startled eyes to his. 'What do you mean, not like this?'

Jack sighed as he pushed his sunglasses up on top of his head. 'Your kiss just now. It wasn't for me, not really. It was just a reaction to your close call with death. An instinctive wish to feel still alive.'

'No,' she denied quite fiercely. 'That isn't true. It *was* for you.'

Jack stared at her, shock rendering him speechless.

'I'm not sure I understand this sudden sexual attraction I have for you any more than you understand yours for me,' she swept on. 'Since we're being brutally honest here, till yesterday I never even *liked* you, let alone fancied you. It was weird, the way I started having these wicked thoughts about you.'

'What kind of wicked thoughts?' he asked her.

Vivienne shook her head. 'I…I've tried to work them out because they don't make sense. All I know is that I want you to make love to me. Very much so.'

Jack did his best to stay cool. Despite dying to put her words to the test, he suspected that if he wanted any kind of relationship with Vivienne—as opposed to just a quickie—then he needed to show some sensitivity to her present, highly vulnerable state. If he rushed her into bed right at this moment—there *was* a king-sized one in the nearby master bedroom, he recalled—she might regret it afterwards. At the same time, the temptation to do just that was almost irresistible.

'Hell, Vivienne, you shouldn't say things like that.'

'Why not? It's true. Crazy, perhaps, but true.'

He didn't like the 'crazy' bit.

'Kiss me, Jack,' she begged. *'Please.'*

Oh God, he thought as his groin twitched painfully. 'If I kiss you, I won't stop at kissing,' he told her bluntly.

She didn't say a word, just closed her eyes and parted her lips in the most provocative fashion.

Jack groaned, then pulled her back into his arms— hard—his head swooping down at the same time.

It was not a tender or loving kiss. It was rough and ravaging, his hands lifting to hold her face solidly captive so there was no escape from his merciless assault on her mouth.

Not that she tried to escape; Vivienne moaned her surrender the moment his lips crashed down on hers. Her body melted against his, the soft swell of her stomach pressing against his erection. This only inflamed Jack further, his teeth nipping and tugging at her lips until they felt swollen and hot. She gasped when he ran his tongue over their burning surfaces, moaning when at last his tongue darted deep into her mouth.

Jack's gut tightened when her lips closed tightly around him, sucking him in even deeper. He immediately started imagining what it would be like when she did that to other parts of his body. Which she would at some stage, he was sure. Although a cool character on the surface, Vivienne was obviously a wildly passionate woman underneath. A woman who liked sex and needed it. The perfect candidate to become his lover. Or even girlfriend, if that was what she wanted. He didn't much care, as long as he could have her in his bed on a regular basis.

When he tore his mouth away from hers, she moaned again, her green eyes glazed when they opened to stare dazedly up at him.

'Don't say a word,' he bit out. 'I'm not stopping altogether. Just till I get a couple of things straight.'

She didn't say a word. He suspected she was almost beyond talking, a fact he found rather flattering.

'I don't want this to be just a one-night stand,' he said. 'Or should I say, a one-day stand. I like you, Vivienne. Very much so. I want more from you than that. Tell me now if this idea doesn't appeal to you, then I won't start making plans for afterwards. If you say you don't like me enough to consider a relationship with me, then after this once, we'll have to go our separate ways. Because once we cross this line, sweetheart, there will be no working together unless we're sleeping together.'

Jack hoped Vivienne didn't see his ultimatum as a form of sexual harassment, or even blackmail. He was just telling her as it was. He wasn't her boss. Yet. But by God he wanted to be, especially in the bedroom.

Hot images danced in his head of her obeying his every command and demand; of her going down on him wherever and whenever he wanted; of her being tied naked to various pieces of furniture, totally at his mercy. All silly fantasies, he suspected. Because, as passionate as Vivienne seemed to be, she wasn't the submissive type. Though who knew? Maybe she would enjoy being dominated in the bedroom.

His earlier fierce arousal, which had subsided somewhat with his talking, came back with a vengeance.

'You don't need to give me your answer right now,' he ground out to a still silent but flushed Vivienne. 'Afterwards will do.' Unable to wait another second, Jack swept her up into his arms and headed for the master bedroom. When his sunglasses fell off the back of his head in the process, he didn't bother to stop and pick them up.

CHAPTER TEN

VIVIENNE'S HEAD WHIRLED with conflicting thoughts as she clamped her hands around Jack's neck and burrowed her face into the base of his throat. What remained of her sense of decency demanded that she stop him right now. She liked Jack somewhat better than she had, but to have sex with him wasn't right—surely?

But the voice of decency wasn't nearly as powerful as the voice of desire. It obliterated and overwhelmed all objections with its promise of excitement and pleasure. Jack's impassioned kiss had given her a taste of what was to come. Not just excitement and pleasure, but abandonment and satisfaction. The kind of abandonment which she'd always secretly craved. The kind of satisfaction which she'd never really enjoyed.

Somehow, Vivienne knew that in Jack's arms she would become a different woman from the one who'd kept her virginity until she was twenty-one, and who'd remained a shy, timid lover in the years since that first, uninspiring initiation into sex. With Jack, she would be wild and wanton. Maybe even wicked. Already her lips were opening to kiss his neck. Though it wasn't a kiss for long, more of a slow, sensual sucking at his skin, her heartbeat quickening at the sheer audacity of her action.

When he groaned and tipped his head to one side,

her mouth clamped him more tightly, as if she were some rabid vampire.

This time he wrenched his head away before setting her down abruptly in the middle of a large room, which was devoid of all furniture except for a huge bed, which looked new, its striped red-and-white bedding totally at odds with the pale blue shag-pile carpet and faded floral wallpaper. The air in the room was a little musty but surprisingly warm, probably because the sliding glass doors which led out onto the east-facing balcony would have caught the morning sun. Jack left her to go over and open one of those doors before turning and shaking his head at her.

'Do you have any idea what kind of teasing I'll get at work with a love bite on my neck?' he said, and rubbed at the spot on his neck that she'd been ravaging.

Vivienne tried to summon up some shame but it seemed she was beyond it. 'I can't imagine any of your employees daring to tease you.'

Jack chuckled. 'In that case, you don't know men very well.'

'Perhaps not,' she murmured, the thought occurring to her that she didn't know herself very well either. Certainly not this new uninhibited self, the one who was much more daring—and a lot more exciting—than the Vivienne she was used to.

'Not to worry,' Jack said and took off his jacket, tossing it onto the carpet with typical male nonchalance. 'I'll wear a shirt with a collar for a few days. But please,' he added as he stripped off his T-shirt, 'try to confine that sexy mouth of yours to areas of mine normally covered by clothes.'

'Yes, boss,' she said as she ogled his quite magnificent male body. His shoulders were impressively broad, his arms bulging with muscles, his chest superbly sculptured and nicely tanned with surprisingly little body hair, just a smattering of curls in the centre, plus a narrow line of them arrowing down past his six-pack, ending at his navel. His hips were slender but his thighs looked massive in those tight jeans.

So did something else…

Vivienne had always thought she would never be attracted to a big man; that their sheer size would intimidate her.

Well, guess what, Vivienne? You were dead wrong!

Her breath caught when he snapped open the waistband on his jeans, her heartbeat suspending as he ran the zip down.

'Why aren't you getting undressed?' he threw over at her as he peeled off his jeans, revealing a huge bulge in his black underpants. 'Don't tell me you've gone all shy on me. Come now, Vivienne, you and I both know that the uptight image you project at work is not the real you at all. You're hot stuff, sweetheart.'

Vivienne certainly felt hot at that moment. Her face flamed as she gulped then sucked in a much-needed breath.

Jack smiled a decidedly smug smile. 'Ah, I get it. You like to watch. Fine by me,' he said, and took off his remaining underwear.

Oh my… And she'd thought Daryl was reasonably well-equipped.

Compared to Jack, Daryl was… Well, he just didn't compare! No wonder Jack wasn't shy about showing off his body; he was incredible, Vivienne thought as her admiring gaze ran over him once again from top to toe.

'You *do* like to watch, don't you?' he said as he reached for his discarded jeans and extracted his wallet from the back pocket. 'Can't say I'm much of a watcher. But with you, lovely Vivienne, I'm going to make an exception.'

Vivienne was taken aback when, after taking a condom out of his wallet and tossing the wallet back down on his jeans, Jack walked over to the bed. He stretched out on top of the duvet, dropping the small foil packet he was holding onto his chest before looping his hands behind his head and acting for all the world like he wasn't stark naked with an erection the size of the Eiffel Tower.

'Okay,' he said, 'I'm ready to watch. Take your clothes off. But very slowly, please. I want to savour every moment.'

When she just stood there, dry-mouthed and motionless, he shot her an intense look. 'Come now, Vivienne, what are you waiting for? You know patience is not one of my virtues.'

When she hesitated further, her new, wicked self started whispering in her ear.

Yes, Vivienne, what are you waiting for? You want to take your clothes off for him. You know you do. You want to see him look at your breasts the way he did yesterday. You want to see those hard blue eyes glitter with lust for you. More than anything, you want to abandon every inferior feeling you've ever had about yourself when to comes to sex. Jack thinks you're hot stuff. Then be hot stuff, girl. It's now or never!

Her hands still shook as she took off her jacket slowly—very slowly—the way Jack had ordered. She hated the thought of dropping it on the floor, such an action going against Vivienne's compulsion to keep everything neat and tidy. But, since there weren't any chairs in the room, she really had no option. In a weird kind of way, actually letting the jacket drop from her fingers onto the carpet produced a strangely liberating buzz. By the time her hands went to the top button of her shirt, Vivienne was surprised to see that they were no longer shaking. Her breathing had quickened, however. Not from nerves; from excitement. She watched Jack's eyes as she flicked open each button. They weren't on her face, of course. They were riveted to her chest.

It did bother Vivienne slightly that she was wearing a white cotton minimiser bra rather than the kind of lacy half-cup push-up number Jack was probably expecting. After all, he'd made it clear he believed that underneath her cool, career-woman surface she was a seriously sexy babe, the sort of woman who would wear seriously sexy underwear.

As much as she liked that idea, Jack was, unfortunately, mistaken. All she could hope for was that he wouldn't care once she took the darned thing off. He'd obviously liked the look of her breasts yesterday so she wasn't shy about showing them off to him. Frankly, she no longer felt at all shy. Amazing!

His eyes remained glued to her chest whilst she peeled her blouse back off her shoulders and let it flutter down to the floor. His expression didn't change at the sight of her cotton bra, though Vivienne was quick to remove the less-than-flattering garment from her body. Now his eyes narrowed, his lips parting slightly as he drew in a ragged breath then let it out slowly. Finally, his eyes lifted to her face.

'Has anyone ever told you that you have the most beautiful breasts in the world?'

'No,' she replied truthfully. Daryl had said how beautiful she was all the time, but he'd never singled out her breasts for his compliments.

'I find that hard to believe. They are incredible. I

could look at them all day. But I'd infinitely prefer to touch them.' he said as he removed his hands from behind his head.

Vivienne's nipples responded to his declaration of intent by standing to attention in the most flagrant fashion. Obviously they wanted to be touched as much as Jack wanted to touch them. She removed the rest of her clothes in one brisk movement, thereby hiding her rather unflattering white cotton briefs. On top of that, it didn't allow time for her mind to fill with negative thoughts about her wide hips or soft stomach, or the many other physical flaws which worried her from time to time. Jack might think her breasts perfect but not all men liked full breasts, or hourglass figures.

Her first serious boyfriend—the insensitive creep—had told her that he actually preferred skinny girls. But he'd *loved* that she was a virgin. Needless to say, their relationship hadn't lasted, and Vivienne had taken some considerable time before she'd risked her heart—and her body—a second time.

Fortunately, she didn't have to worry about her heart this time, since she wasn't in love with Jack.

'You are one seriously beautiful woman,' he said thickly, his hot gaze reflecting his admiration. 'Now get yourself over here, Vivienne. I've done enough watching for one day.'

Never in her life had Vivienne felt as sexy—or as excited—as she did at that moment.

'Coming, boss,' she said in a low, sultry voice, sashaying over to stand at the side of the bed.

Jack looked her slowly up and down with a decidedly lascivious gaze. 'Mmm. I like it when you call me that.'

For some weird and wonderful reason, she liked calling him that too. Strange, when normally she found his bossy ways extremely irritating.

'Okay, Vivienne,' he went on. 'Take this condom here and put it on me. I don't think I can manage after that wicked striptease of yours.'

Vivienne wasn't sure that she could manage, either. She'd never put a condom on before. But no way was she going to tell him that. Any self-respecting sexually experienced woman should be able to slip on protection with their eyes closed. 'Truly,' she said with just the right amount of droll exasperation as she picked up the foil packet and ripped it open the way she'd seen Daryl do. 'Are you sure this will fit?' She stared down at the small circle of rubber.

Jack sighed. 'Here. Give it to me.'

She happily handed it over. 'Yes, boss.'

'Truly,' he said, copying her earlier droll tone to a tee.

When she laughed, he did too.Their eyes met, her heart squeezing tight as her stomach flipped over. The old Vivienne might have imagined there was more going on between them than just sex. The new Vivienne knew exactly what was causing her physical responses. Her eyes dropped to where Jack was expertly rolling the condom over the full length of his amazing erection, her mouth drying as she tried to imagine how it would feel inside her.

'I hope you like being on top,' Jack said once protection was completed. 'I don't usually like to hand over control, but I don't dare touch you at the moment. You've driven me to the brink. So help me out here. I'm feeling decidedly fragile.'

Vivienne gnawed at her bottom lip. What to say? If she confessed she didn't care for that position, he would think she was lying. Vivienne swallowed, telling herself firmly that she could do this. It wasn't rocket science. And she *had* done it before. Briefly. A couple of times. *Just climb up onto the bed. Now throw one leg over him. Don't think about what he can see. Just kneel up over him. Yes, that's the way. Now take him in your right hand.* Heavens, he *was* big. *What if he doesn't fit in you?*

But he did—deliciously so—sliding into her with shocking ease, Vivienne holding her breath as she lowered herself slowly down till she was sitting on him, his swollen sex filling her in a way she'd never felt filled before. She closed her eyes so that she could savour the blissful sensation, breathing out whilst rocking back and forth at the same time.

His groan startled her, her eyes flying open. He was lying there looking tortured, his breathing ragged, his hands curled into white-knuckled fists by his side.

'Stop moving like that, for pity's sake,' he ground out.

Vivienne was shocked at how much she liked his being close to losing control.

'But I want to move,' she purred, and did so, rising and falling upon him with a slow, sensual rhythm.

He didn't groan this time. He swore, then reached for her, grabbing her shoulders and throwing her roughly round and under him. Now she *couldn't* move, his hands and his weight pinning her to the bed.

'I should have known you wouldn't do as you were told for too long,' he growled. 'You're too strong willed.' He smiled a devilishly sexy smile.

Vivienne couldn't believe it when her own lips curved upwards in a saucy smile of her own. 'Maybe I prefer it this way.'

'Mmm. Now *that* I don't believe. Women of your obvious experience *never* prefer the missionary position.'

Vivienne tried not to laugh. But it was rather funny, given the limited range of her sexual experience.

'Do you always talk this much when having sex?' she asked him.

'Only when I need to get my act together. I've never been fond of ending a good thing too soon. It would be especially disappointing on this occasion, when I might be relegated to one time only.'

'Oh, I don't think that's very likely, Jack,' she said, green eyes glittering up at his. 'I can't imagine not wanting at least seconds from a man of your rather… obvious attractions.' Lord, but was it really her saying that? Talk about wicked!

'Well, that's good to know, Vivienne. But, just in case you change your mind afterwards, we're going to do this the way *I* prefer.'

Vivienne gasped when he abruptly withdrew, her mind spinning when he turned her over, wrapping one of his huge arms around her waist as he scooped her up on all fours.

Dear heaven, she thought dazedly.

As personally inexperienced as Vivienne was in the many sexual positions possible, she wasn't ignorant. She knew exactly what Jack was going to do. She could feel him right behind her but she couldn't see him, her wide eyes seeing nothing but the wallpapered wall above the bed. There was no question of resisting him, not once he re-entered her, and certainly not once he took hold of her breasts and started moving inside her. Immediately, any rational thinking shut down, her desire-laden brain making all her decisions for her, demanding that she move with him, her hips rocking back and forth in a frantic rhythm, her body searching for release from the almost torturous tension building up inside her.

Vivienne had never understood the concept of pain being closely linked with pleasure. But she understood now, even more so when Jack started squeezing her already burning nipples. Just when Vivienne thought she could not bear the sensations any longer, Jack removed his hands and pressed her upper body down onto the bed, the position emphasising her raised hips and bottom, her face flaming with a heady combination of embarrassment and excitement. When he stopped moving, she moaned in frustration, her buttocks clenching tightly together as he caressed them with long, slow, circular strokes of his very big hands.

'Do you like this?' he said thickly as his hands caressed her sensitive flesh. She tried to feel shocked but all she felt was a dark, delicious pleasure.

'Yes,' she choked out.

'Another time, then,' he said, and took hold of her hips once more. This time he thrust faster and deeper, Vivienne struggling to stay silent the way she usually did during sex. She tried muffling her moans in a nearby pillow, but in the end she could not contain the animal sounds which escaped her lips. Her moans became groans, her fingers scrunching up great handfuls of duvet as her whole body spun out of control.

She came with a rush, her release as fast as a balloon bursting. One moment she was suspended in a type of erotic agony, the next all that dreadful tension was gone, replaced by great waves of pleasure washing through her, pulling her one way then another, like the tide. She bit her lip to stop herself from crying out. Jack didn't bother with such niceties, roaring out his satisfaction as he held her tight and shuddered into her for an incredibly long time.

By the time he finally finished, Vivienne's own incredible orgasm had just faded away, her limbs succumbing to a languor which would have seen her flopping face down on the bed if Jack hadn't been holding her up.

Slowly, and with surprising gentleness, he withdrew then lowered her onto the bed where she closed her eyes and sighed the type of sigh she'd never sighed before. It contained nothing but total sexual satisfaction.

'Don't go away now,' he murmured, and dropped a kiss in the small of her back.

She would have laughed if she'd had the energy.

Vivienne vaguely heard the sound of a toilet flushing and water running. Was he having a shower? she wondered.

It was her last thought before sleep claimed her.

CHAPTER ELEVEN

JACK DIDN'T REALISE Vivienne was sound asleep until he came back from the bathroom. She didn't reply to his telling her he was going to go down the road to buy some supplies, and was there anything particular she would like to eat.

Poor darling, he thought as he looked down at her luscious but unconscious form. She was obviously exhausted, not just from the sex but from everything else she'd endured lately. Best let her sleep, at least for a while.

Very quietly Jack put on his clothes and left the room, making his way to the nearby kitchen, where he rifled through the various cupboards and drawers till he found paper and a pen. Writing Vivienne an explanatory note, he returned to the bedroom where he propped the note against her pile of clothes, careful not to look at her lest he be overcome with desire for her once more. Time enough for those seconds she'd mentioned after they'd both had some lunch.

Not that he had any intention of stopping at mere seconds. Or of letting Vivienne say no to becoming his lover on a more regular basis. Anyone could see what Vivienne needed at this point in her life. Besides, being kept busy with work, she needed a man who would make mad, passionate love to her as often as possible; who would make her see that her life wasn't over just because she'd been dumped by some fortune-hunting bastard.

Jack believed he was that man.

He'd even offer his friendship, if she wanted it.

Jack frowned at this last thought, recalling how Vivienne had said earlier that she'd never liked him all that much. He wondered why that was. Still, that had been *before* she'd got to know him. And he wasn't just referring to their getting to know each other in the biblical sense. They'd actually talked to each other more in the last two days than in all the years Vivienne had worked for him. He'd certainly confided more to her than he had to any other woman. He'd even told her about his mother's lover! Jack liked it that Vivienne hadn't been judgemental about anything, especially his decision not to marry and have children, saying he had the right to live his life as he saw fit.

She was like him, in a way, practical and pragmatic, with a sensible head on her shoulders. Except when it came to that Daryl creep. Of course, dear old Daryl had obviously been clever, saying and doing all the right things to get Vivienne hooked. No doubt he'd thought he was on to a good wicket, until a better one had come along. Or so he'd mistakenly imagined. The fool had no idea what he was getting into, marrying Courtney Ellison. Still, they were a well-matched pair, both totally without morals or consciences. Vivienne didn't realise how lucky she was, not to have married a man like that.

Jack was about to leave the room when there was a sound from the bed. For a split second, he thought Vivienne had woken up. But she hadn't. She'd just rolled over and curled herself up in the foetal position, moving her peach-like bottom into a highly provocative curve. Jack suppressed a groan, then very carefully lifted up the end of the duvet and placed it over her. Unfortunately, it only went as far as her waist, leaving her upper half on show.

As he stared down at her, Jack's mind went back to that moment when he'd taken her on all fours, her lush breasts cradled in his hands. He recalled how she'd moaned when he'd squeezed her nipples; how she'd rocked back and forth on her knees, slapping her buttocks against his hip; how she'd cried out when she finally came. Jack couldn't remember being with a woman who'd come as hard as she had. It had felt incredible, being inside her at that moment.

'Better not think about that right now,' he muttered to himself and hurried downstairs, locking the front doors behind him before climbing into his car and driving off. Time enough for such thoughts after he'd had lunch; his stomach was telling him it was eating time. Jack remembered passing a small shopping centre on the way here where they were sure to have everything he would need for the rest of day.

Vivienne woke to the sound of silence, plus the realisation that at some stage Jack had covered her with the bottom half of the duvet. Sitting up, she glanced around the empty room, looking and listening for evidence of where he might have gone to. There were no sounds coming from anywhere nearby, other than some distant chirping of birds. Surely Jack wouldn't have left her alone in the house? Alone and naked.

A shiver ran down her spine.

It was then that she saw the note. Swinging her feet over the side of the bed, Vivienne reached down to pick it up, sighing with relief as she read his message. Not that she seriously imagined Jack would run out on her. Why would he, when he no doubt thought he'd now solved two problems with one Vivienne? His need for an interior designer, plus his need for a sexual partner. After the act she'd just put on for him in bed, he would naturally conclude she would agree to whatever he wanted.

But it hadn't been an act, had it? Vivienne accepted with a degree of confusion. She'd been genuinely swept away with desire and passion for the man. She'd enjoyed everything they'd done together, thrilling to her new, uninhibited self. As for that mind-blowing orgasm… A girl would have to be insane not to want more of those.

Why was it, Vivienne puzzled, that she'd never experienced anything like that with Daryl? After all, she'd been madly in love with the man. But not once had she been carried away in bed the way she had been with Jack. Not once had she come with *Daryl* inside her. Surely it couldn't just be a question of size? She didn't believe that. After all, she'd been panting for Jack before he'd taken off his clothes. She'd been panting for him back in the restaurant yesterday, for pity's sake!

It was all very perplexing.

The sound of a car roaring up the steep driveway sent Vivienne into a momentary panic. As wildly uninhibited as she'd been during sex with Jack, no way did she want him walking in on her still in the nude.

Scooping up her clothes, she raced over to the door which she presumed led into a bathroom. And, yes, it *was* a bathroom…in a fashion.

'Oh, lordie, lordie, lordie!' she exclaimed, laughing.

Vivienne did know that, in theory, pink and black bathrooms had been all the rage at some stage last century but she'd never actually seen one. Talk about hideous! Shaking her head in wry amusement, she closed the door behind her. After using the black toilet and washing her hands in the pink vanity basin, she quickly dressed. She was finger-combing her hair in the large but chipped wall mirror when there was a sharp rapping on the bathroom door.

'You in there, Vivienne?' Jack called out.

'Er…yes; I'm getting dressed,' she said, feeling suddenly awkward with him, not to mention embarrassed. It seemed the old Vivienne was rearing her uptight head once again.

'I've bought us some food,' Jack said as he opened the door and walked straight in.

'Don't you believe in knocking?' she said sharply.

He looked taken aback. 'I thought I did.'

'Well, yes, but you should still wait till I invite you to enter.'

'Mmm. Your mood seems to have deteriorated since I left. I dare say you're mad at me for not staying to give you those seconds you wanted. Sorry, beautiful, but aside from the condom issue I'm afraid men of my size need constant refuelling.'

Vivienne wished he hadn't mentioned his size. Or her rather brazen statement about having seconds. The wanton hussy who'd said those things suddenly seemed to have disappeared, which bothered her. Because she liked that hussy. She liked her a lot. All Vivienne could hope was that once Jack started making love to her again—which he would, sooner or later—she'd turn back into that exciting new Vivienne again.

Not that she'd entirely reverted to the old Vivienne, the one who'd been taken in by the likes of Daryl. That seriously pathetic creature was gone for good!

'So, what do you think of the bathroom?' Jack went on.

'What? Oh yes, the bathroom. It's seriously awful.'

Jack chuckled. 'Wait till you see the others. The worst is all brown with a yucky olive-green spa bath in the corner.'

'Good Lord.'

'The kitchens are slightly better, as long as you like pine. Speaking of kitchens, that's where I left the food. I'm afraid it's just hamburgers, fries and Coke—but I figured, who doesn't like hamburgers, fries and Coke?'

Once again, he didn't wait for her to reply, just took her hand and led her from the bathroom, out through the bedroom and down a short hallway into a large country-style kitchen where, yes, pine was the order of the day. There were pine cupboards as well as pine benchtops, and three pine stools lined up at the pine breakfast bar. Not that it mattered. Vivienne felt pretty sure that Jack would want the whole interior of this house stripped bare and totally redone.

'Have a seat,' Jack said, pulling out a pine stool for her before picking up one of the others and carrying it round to the other side.

When she frowned at his action, he smiled over at her. 'Have to keep my distance till I've eaten,' he said. 'I can't think about sex and eat at the same time, and every time I get close to you, beautiful, I think about sex.'

Vivienne could not help feeling flattered by his re-mark, though his calling her beautiful all the time was beginning to grate. 'I find that hard to believe,' she said somewhat tartly.

His smile widened. 'Come now, Vivienne, you don't fool me for a minute with that act of yours. Now, eat up and stop pretending you don't want to get back to bed as quickly as I do.'

Vivienne opened her mouth to say something more, then closed it again. Because Jack was right. There was no point in denying it. No point in saying anything at all! So she reached for the food and started eating.

Neither of them spoke as they each consumed their hamburger, which was more delicious than any hamburger Vivienne had ever eaten—king-sized and truly mouthwatering, with the kind of ingredients you only got at a small café. The fries weren't half bad, either—golden and crispy with just the right amount of salt. As for the Coke… Vivienne sighed with pleasure as she washed the meal down with her favourite drink. The only fault she could find was that Jack hadn't bought Diet Coke, opting instead for the full-strength variety.

'Do you realise how much sugar is contained in this one small bottle?' Vivienne said after downing all of it.

'Not enough to send a rocket to the moon,' Jack replied. 'But enough to spark lift-off in yours truly,' he added with the wickedest smile, his blue eyes glittering with sexual intent at the same time.

Vivienne struggled to act cool under an immediate quickening of her heart. Although she wasn't about to play hard to get—it was a little late for that—she didn't want to appear too easy. Or too eager.

'I thought you'd give me the grand tour of the house first,' she said, casually picking up one of the paper serviettes which came with the meal and dabbing at the corners of her mouth.

'Then you thought wrong,' he said.

Vivienne glowered at him. This was why she'd never liked working for Jack. He was far too bossy. It was always his way or the highway. She used to have to put up with it when she was an employee of Classic Design. But she didn't have to put up with it now.

'Don't I have any say in the matter?' she asked with a toss of her head.

He looked taken aback for a second. But then he smiled. 'Of course you do. Far be it from me to force you to do anything you didn't want to do. I have too much respect for you for that. So which would you rather do, Vivienne? Look around this house for a dreary hour or so, or go have some more fantastic fun in bed?'

Vivienne sighed. 'You are a clever, conniving devil, do you know that?'

He grinned. 'I'll take that as a compliment.'

'Then you'd be wrong!'

'You mean you're opting for the grand tour?'

She shook her head at him. 'You know I'm not. But that doesn't mean I'll always do whatever you want.'

'Are you sure about that?'

She wasn't. But no way was she going to admit it. 'The trouble with you, Jack Stone, is you are way too used to getting your own way.'

'I have to confess I like being the boss, especially in the bedroom.'

'I gathered that already.'

'And I gathered you liked it that way.'

Vivienne rolled her eyes. He really was terribly arrogant. And super-confident when it came to sex. She wondered if that was due to his impressive equipment, or wealth of experience. Whatever the reason, Vivienne had no intention of letting him run this show entirely.

'As a modern woman living in the twenty-first century,' she said coolly, 'I expect that any sexual relationship we have will be conducted as equals.'

'Fair enough,' he said.

'There will be rules involved,' Vivienne stated firmly.

His eyebrows arched. 'What kind of rules?'

Vivienne had absolutely no idea. It was time to im-
provise. And quickly. 'Firstly, you will always use a
condom.' No way was she going to tell him she was
on the pill.

'You won't have any argument with me on that
score,' Jack said. 'That's why I went out and bought
a dozen.'

'A dozen!' she exclaimed, stunned at the thought he
might use so many during one short afternoon.

Jack shrugged. 'Better to be safe than sorry. Besides,
what we don't use today will keep till tomorrow.'

Vivienne blinked. 'What do you mean, tomorrow?
Surely you have work to do tomorrow? I know you,
Jack. You're a workaholic.'

'True. But there's always after work. I thought I'd
take you out somewhere swanky in the city for dinner,
then back to my place for afters,' he added somewhat
salaciously.

'You really are incorrigible,' Vivienne scolded, despite secretly looking forward to being his afters tomorrow night. 'Rule number two is that you *ask* me, Jack,
not just tell me.'

'Oh. Right. Okay, would you like to go out to dinner tomorrow night?'

'Maybe. I'll give you my answer later.'

'Nope. That won't do, Vivienne. I have some rules
of my own—the main one being, if and when I ask
you something, I get a straight answer. Because I'm a
straight kind of guy. I won't play word games. So is it
a yes or a no?'

Vivienne rather liked it that he wouldn't let her muck
him around. At the same time, she wasn't about to say
yes every time. 'It's a yes to dinner. You'll have to ask
me again tomorrow night about afters. I'm not sure how

I'll feel about more sex so soon after today.' And what a load of crock that was!

He looked hard at her, and then he smiled. 'Fair enough. Any more rules?'

'I...I...can't think of any more right now. But I reserve the right to add to the list if something important occurs to me.'

'Same here,' Jack said as he reached into the plastic bag which lay next to him and retrieved the box of condoms he'd told her about. 'Okay, now that I know your rules and we've finished eating, I'll ask you again. Very politely. Do you want a grand tour of the house first, or more sex?'

Vivienne swallowed. She knew what she wanted to say but simply could not bring herself to say it.

Jack rose from the stool, ripping the cellophane off the box of condoms as he walked around to her. 'Of course, there is a third alternative,' he said, his eyes holding hers. 'We could combine the two.'

Vivienne just stared up at him, her tongue no longer working.

He reached out to run a tantalising finger around her slightly parted lips. Vivienne gasped when he sent that finger into her mouth, her head spinning, as suddenly she was that new Vivienne again, with all her wild, wanton boldness. Her lips closed around his finger, her green eyes glittering as she began a slow, sensual sucking.

'I take it that's a yes,' he said thickly.

CHAPTER TWELVE

'WHAT DO YOU think you're doing?' Vivienne said sharply when Jack picked up her camera and pointed it in her direction. Vivienne was lying back on one of the desk chairs, dressed in nothing but her white blouse, looking sinfully sexy with only one button done up.

'I'm taking a photograph of my beautiful new girl-friend?' he said.

'But I'm half-naked,' she protested, sitting up and pushing her hair back from her face. 'And…and my hair is messy.'

He laughed. 'Don't be silly. You look gorgeous.'

'I'm serious, Jack. I don't want you taking any photos of me like this. And I'm not your new girlfriend. Not really. We're lovers, that's all.'

Jack tried not to scowl. He should have been pleased that Vivienne wanted to restrict their relationship to a strictly sexual one. It was exactly what he'd thought he wanted. But after spending the whole day with her, he realised he wanted more from her than that.

'I wouldn't have asked you out to dinner tomorrow night if I wanted us to just be lovers,' he insisted. 'I like being with you, Vivienne. And talking to you. And not just about work-related matters. I want to spend time with you out of bed as well as in it. I would have thought that was obvious by now.' They hadn't spent the entire afternoon having sex. Between times they'd discussed the refurbishment of the house, whilst Vivienne had retrieved her camera from the car and taken photos of everything.

'I like spending time with you too,' she said. 'But—'

'So what's the problem?' he broke in, and put the camera down. 'Too soon after Daryl, is that it?'

Vivienne stared up at him. To be brutally honest she hadn't given Daryl a thought all afternoon. But now that Jack had brought him up, Vivienne wondered again if Daryl's dumping her so cruelly was the reason behind her amazing change of character. Maybe her turning into Vivienne the Vamp was really just a revenge thing. Or a rebound thing. Or something equally self-destructive.

Common sense demanded she step back from this whole situation for a while until she could think more clearly. All that great sex today seemed to have addled her brain, because agreeing to become Jack's girlfriend at this stage could be a foolish move. Rather like jumping from the frying pan into the fire.

Yet, despite all that common sense reasoning, she still *wanted* to agree. Quite desperately. It was one thing to say no to his taking candid photographs of her; she'd always hated having her photograph taken. It was quite another thing to say no to more sex with him. Which was what would happen if she refused to become his girlfriend. Jack was not the kind of man who warmed to rejection. He'd probably take back his offer of this job as well.

Of course, she could always make an alternative suggestion…

The idea which popped into her head was truly

wicked. But oh so tempting, her heart quickening as the audacious counter-proposal formed in her brain. Hopefully, Jack would agree. Oh, surely he would. He was a man, after all. And what she would be proposing was every man's fantasy.

Her mouth still dried with what she was about to suggest.

'For pity's sake say something, Vivienne,' Jack finally snapped. 'You must know how much I detest indecision.'

'I do too,' she threw back at him. 'So, yes, it's way too soon for me to consider being any man's girlfriend.' *Especially one who's already admitted to being emotionally bankrupt,* she thought, but didn't say. 'I'm not even keen on thinking of us as lovers. You and I both know that love has little to do with what we've been doing today. I'm not in love with you any more than you are with me. But there's no denying I love having sex with you. More than I would ever have thought possible.'

Vivienne could not help but notice this last statement of hers didn't go down too well. But Jack had claimed he liked honesty and she was only being honest.

'I dare say you might be shocked by what I am about to suggest...'

'I doubt anything you say now is going to shock me, Vivienne,' he said very drily. 'So suggest away.'

Vivienne buttoned up her blouse then took a deep breath before going on. 'Firstly let me say I would very much like to do this job,' she began, waving her hand up at the façade of Francesco's Folly. 'But, as you yourself said, it would be impossible for us to work together now without sleeping together. So, for the duration of this project, I would like to become your mistress.'

His head snapped back, his eyebrows arching at the same time. 'I guess I was wrong. You *have* shocked me. So, exactly what kind of mistress did you have in mind? The kind who dresses in shiny black leather and carries a whip?'

'Don't be silly,' she retorted.

'In that case, you must mean the kind I install in a flash apartment with all the bills paid, in exchange for which I get to do whatever I like to you whenever I like to do it.'

'I'm not that kind of girl, either.'

'That's a relief,' Jack said.

'I just meant the kind of mistress who's kept a secret. I don't want anyone and everyone knowing that we're sleeping together.'

'Why not? It wouldn't bother me if people knew.'

'Well, it would bother me.'

'Why?'

'Because it would lead to questions from friends and family that I don't want to answer.' Not that she had much of either. But Jack did.

'You're worried they might think badly of you,' he said. Quite intuitively, Vivienne thought.

She stood up. 'Yes, of course,' she said. Aside from how soon it was after Daryl, everyone she knew thought she didn't like Jack. They'd wonder what had come over her. They'd probably think she'd lost it.

Jack frowned. 'You wouldn't have to worry about that if you became my girlfriend.'

'But I don't *want* to become your girlfriend, Jack,' she said, feeling both irritated and frustrated with him. 'I just want to have sex with you, okay?'

Once again Jack looked none too pleased with her. 'Okay,' he bit out. 'Where?'

'What do you mean, *where*?'

'Just exactly that. Where are we going to do it? Not your place, I gather—or your good friend and neighbour Marion would twig, and then you'd have to answer those questions you don't want to answer. So that leaves my place, or a hotel room.'

Jack was taken aback when Vivienne blushed. Lord, but she was full of contradictions. In truth, he didn't know what to make of her today. Same as himself; why wasn't he happy with her mistress idea? Why was he trying to needle her? Nothing made sense to him any more. No, he knew *exactly* what was bugging him: his ego had been dented. His considerable ego.

Get a grip, Jack, he lectured himself sternly. *You're onto a good wicket here. If you don't stuff it up, that is. Think of the positives: all the sex you want with none of the complications. No clinging. No commitment. No having to say you love her. Exactly what the doctor ordered. So put aside your emotions and take a more pragmatic approach to Vivienne's offer which, if you think about it sensibly, was really rather exciting.*

'Obviously that idea doesn't appeal,' he said, trying hard not to sound sarcastic. 'Maybe you should rethink the idea about my getting you that flash apartment. I can afford it and it would solve the "where?" problem.'

As much as Vivienne was tempted to say yes—it *would* solve the 'where?' problem—she could see that such an arrangement went against her highly independent nature. Not to mention her conscience. She didn't want to feel Jack was *paying* her to have sex with him.

'Like I said, Jack, I'm not that sort of girl. Look, I have an alternative suggestion which I think would work well for both of us.'

Jack smothered the sigh which threatened to escape his lungs.

'Okay,' he said. 'Fire away.'

CHAPTER THIRTEEN

'THAT'S THE BEST news you could have told me,' Marion said.

They were sitting having morning tea in Vivienne's kitchen, Marion having dropped in to see how things had gone with Jack the previous day. Naturally Vivienne hadn't told Marion the whole rather shocking truth, just that she had accepted Jack's offer to redesign the interior of Francesco's Folly, as well as her plan to live at the place whilst the job was being done. Though that wouldn't be happening until contracts were exchanged in a couple of weeks.

Jack had seemed somewhat at odds with her live-in idea at first, until she'd pointed out that he could come visit her there every weekend, leaving him free during the week to concentrate on work. She'd boldly stated that she would be worth the wait, promising to be at his sexual beck and call for those two days. By the time Jack had dropped her back at her place late last night, he'd warmed to the idea, especially after having tested out what she meant by being at his sexual beck and call…

Vivienne, by then on the other hand, had been bombarded by a host of second thoughts. But she didn't voice them out loud, her sated body not having had second thoughts at all. She'd slept like a log last night and had woken feeling marvellous, any lingering qualms easily pushed aside.

Already she was looking forward to seeing Jack again tonight. He'd promised to take her somewhere discreet, although he'd argued that their having dinner together could easily be explained away as a business dinner. She was, after all, going to be working for him.

And under him. And on top of him, he'd added wickedly.

Vivienne struggled to contain the heat which flooded her veins at the memory of all Jack had demanded of her yesterday. Positions which she supposed weren't all that shocking, but which she'd never experienced before, let alone enjoyed. She was well aware of the woman being on top, but had never thought of it being done with the woman's back to her lover. But, oh...she'd loved it that way. Loved riding him with her hands clasped around the rungs of the brass bed-end. Loved it that she could not see him watching her. That way, she'd been able to lose herself in her pleasure, uncaring of anything but the gathering of tension deep within her body. Had she screamed out loud when she'd come? Yes. Yes, she had. She was sure she had.

Oh God.

Vivienne swallowed.

'Now I can go away next week without worrying about you,' Marion was saying.

Vivienne blinked. 'What was that? You're going away?' she asked a bit blankly.

Marion shook her head at her. 'I thought you might have forgotten, what with everything that's happened. I'm going to Europe for a holiday, remember? London first to visit some of my long-lost rellies, then over to

Paris, and then I'm going for a cruise down the Rhine. Be gone nearly six weeks. You've no idea how much I'm looking forward to it. It's been a long time since I had a decent holiday like that. But none of that for now. Tell me more about this house Jack bought. What's its name again?'

'Francesco's Folly.'

'Sounds rather romantic.'

Vivienne laughed. 'It's nothing of the kind,' she said, thinking that she would never associate that house with romance. Just sex, along with lust and uncontrollable passion.

Vivienne suddenly frowned. How odd. They were not words which she'd ever associated with herself. She'd never fallen in lust before or suffered from un-controllable passion. But she was definitely in lust with Jack Stone. And yes, when she was in his arms, she became uncontrollable with passion. She could hardly wait for tonight to come.

'I have some photos of it, if you'd like to look at them,' Vivienne offered. Perhaps unwisely, as it turned out. Because she couldn't look at the various rooms without thinking of what they'd done in them, espe-cially that spare bedroom with that old brass bed in it.

'It's going to be a big job,' Marion said. 'You'll be away for weeks. Maybe even months!'

'Possibly,' Vivienne agreed, all the while thinking she didn't care how long it would take.

Marion gave her one of her rather sharp looks. It was hard to put something over on Marion. She was very good at reading between the lines.

'I was somewhat surprised by Jack Stone,' she said. 'He wasn't nearly the ogre you've painted him out to be. I rather liked him.'

'Yes, well, he can be quite nice when he wants something from you,' she said drily. Which was very true.

'He's also better looking than I thought he'd be,' Marion added.

'He's passable, I suppose,' Vivienne said offhandedly as she sipped her coffee.

'More than passable. But then, he's my type. I've always liked manly men. My Bob was a manly man,' Marion said in that wistful tone which warned Vivienne Marion was about to get maudlin over her long-dead husband. Normally, Vivienne didn't mind listening to Marion's memories of happier times, but not today. She didn't want to hear about what true love felt like. And she didn't want to think about lost loves.

Her phone ringing at that point was a blessed distraction until she picked it up and saw it was Jack calling. From the frying pan into the fire, she thought as her heart started racing and her head worried about Marion twigging what was going on between them.

'Hello,' she said, deliberately leaving out Jack's name.

'And hello back,' he said. 'Did you sleep well? I know I did.'

Vivienne could see Marion looking at her with curiosity in her eyes.

'It's Jack,' she mouthed, as though it was nothing.

'How nice of you to get back to me so quickly about the door,' she said aloud to him.

Jack got the message straight away. 'Ah…you have someone with you. Marion, I presume?'

'Wow, that *was* quick,' she said and he laughed. 'So I can expect the man to come with the new door tomorrow,' she went on in a matter-of-fact tone. 'What time?'

'Well, certainly not at seven in the morning,' he said.

'You'll be too wrecked to get up that early after what I have in mind for you tonight.'

Vivienne swallowed convulsively as she struggled not to blush. But, oh, the heat which immediately flooded her body at his highly provocative words...

'Noon will be fine,' she said, amazed at how cool and calm she actually sounded. Who would have imagined she could be such a good actress? 'Thank you, Jack. And thank you again for offering me such a wonderful job. I'm looking forward to it.'

He laughed again. 'Not as much as I am, Miss Cool. Now, as much as I am enjoying this titillating conversation, I have to go now. Work calls. I'll pick you up at seven tonight. And don't wear anything too sexy, if you want to pass it off as a business dinner.'

Vivienne opened her mouth to reply but he'd already hung up. Which was just as well, with Marion listening avidly.

'Fine,' she said into the dead phone. 'Thank you again. Goodbye.'

'I think he likes you,' Marion said straight away.

Vivienne put her phone back down on the table before answering.

'What makes you say that?'

'Feminine instinct. I mean, he could have employed any competent interior designer to do up this house of his, but he came looking specifically for you.'

As much as there was a part of Vivienne which was flattered by the truth in Marion's statement, she wasn't about to fall victim to thinking Jack had had anything but work in mind when he'd come in search of her the other day. What had happened between them was as unexpected to him as it was to her.

'Yes, well, he knows my work, doesn't he? He knows

I'll do a good job.' *And you'll give him good head at the same time,* came the truly wicked thought.

Vivienne still could not believe how much she liked doing that. It was a mystery all right. But Jack's motivations weren't a mystery. He was a typical man who could enjoy sex without having his heart involved. Yes, he liked her, but he didn't care for her to any great degree. He certainly didn't love her. And she was strangely comfortable with that. Sleeping together whilst they worked together was as much a bonus for her as it was for him. She refused to feel guilty about it any more. Or to continue to worry that she was on some kind of perverse rebound trip.

'I'm still not convinced,' Marion said. 'And you know what? I think you like him back.'

Vivienne smiled at her. 'Hard not to like a man who brought me flowers then gave me such a dream job.' *Not to mention countless orgasms.* 'But you're right. I do like him a lot better now than I did.'

'Hmm. He's single, isn't he?'

'Yes. And wants to stay that way.'

'Does he have a girlfriend?'

What to say to that? 'Yes, he does,' she said at last. Impossible to use the word 'mistress'.

'Oh. Pity. What's she like, do you know?'

'Not really. I've only met her the once.' Yesterday, when she'd been suddenly transformed into Vivienne the Vamp.

'Is she blonde?'

'No. A redhead.'

'Oh. Like you. Beautiful? Sexy?'

Vivienne shrugged. 'I dare say Jack thinks so.'

'But you don't.'

'She's okay, I guess. She's a working girl. A designer,

like me. Jack met her through work.' Lord, this word game she was playing was getting a bit complicated. Vivienne wished now she hadn't started it.

Marion snorted. 'I suppose she's hoping he falls in love with her and marries her in the end.'

Vivienne almost laughed, because nothing could have been further from the truth. But she could hardly say that.

'I suppose so,' she said. 'Most women want love and marriage.' *But not me. Not right now, anyway. I just want lots of great sex. With Jack.*

Marion was frowning. 'If she's a designer, why didn't Jack ask her to redecorate Francesco's Folly?'

Vivienne had to think quickly. 'I guess he didn't want her to get ideas about it becoming their future home together. Jack told me yesterday that he bought it on impulse when he was up that way, looking for land for a retirement village. I think he wants it as his secret hideaway.'

'I see,' Marion mused aloud. 'Yes, I see. Jack's really not going to marry her then, is he? Poor thing. She's going to get her heart broken if she's not careful.'

No, I won't, Vivienne thought with a stab of surprising certainty. *What I'm doing with Jack has nothing to do with my heart. It's not a love affair. It's a fling; that's all it is. A strictly sexual fling.*

'She's the sort of girl who can take care of herself,' Vivienne said firmly as she stood up and carried the now empty mugs over to the sink. Which was true— most of the time. She'd been taking care of herself for as long as she could remember. Not by choice, by necessity. Independence and self-sufficiency had become an ingrained habit. So had emotional toughness.

Until she'd met Daryl, that was. He'd wormed his

way under her skin and through the hard shell she'd encased her heart in. Her love for him had made her act in ways which were uncharacteristic and unwise. Being with him had made her weak. And blind.

Jack had been right when he'd said it was a good thing that she hadn't married Daryl. It was. He would have been a horrible husband, and she a pathetic wife. His betrayal still hurt when she thought about it. But not as much as it had. Perhaps because she didn't think about it as much any more.

'You're thinking about Daryl, aren't you?' Marion said intuitively from where she was still sitting at the kitchen table.

Vivienne turned from the sink and looked over at her friend. 'Who?' she said with brilliant nonchalance.

Marion laughed. 'Now, that's a step in the right direction.'

CHAPTER FOURTEEN

JACK JUMPED OUT of his Porsche at twenty past seven, annoyed that he was late picking up Vivienne. He hated being late, especially tonight. But one couldn't always control the traffic. He hoped she wouldn't be angry with him.

Her smiling face when she opened the door was reassuring.

'You're late,' she chided him. But gently.

'There was a breakdown on the bridge,' he explained. 'Sorry.'

'No need to apologise. I understand. I'll just get my purse and lock up.'

Perversely, Jack felt irritated by her casual acceptance of his tardiness. If she'd been looking forward to tonight as much as he was, she would have been more upset. But of course, she wasn't emotionally involved with him, was she? He was just a male body to her. A bed partner with whom she could play erotic games. She didn't want to be his girlfriend. She preferred the role of mistress. It was stupid of him to want more from her when it was obvious she was incapable of giving him more at this time in her life. He should just take what he could get and, when the time came, walk away.

Clenching his teeth hard in his jaw, Jack determined

to treat her the way she wanted to be treated—as nothing more than a sex object. A plaything. His own personal *Penthouse* Pet. There would be no pity for her. Or mercy.

Which meant dinner would definitely not be lingered over. He wanted her back in his bed as soon as possible.

So, as she walked back down the hallway towards him, he let his eyes travel slowly over her from top to toe, not bothering to hide his lecherous intent. She hadn't obeyed his command not to dress sexily, he noted, which puzzled him slightly. If she didn't want anyone to guess at the true nature of their relationship, she should have worn something less…provocative.

Her dress was purple, a wrap-around, figure-hugging style which showed off her hourglass shape in a way which did little to dampen his desire for her. Her hair was up, but in a softly sexy style, with tendrils hanging around her lovely face. She was wearing more eye make-up than usual, making her green eyes look huge. As for her glossed lips…they looked downright wicked. And then there were the earrings, long crystal drops which drew the eye down to her impressive cleavage.

'I told you not to wear anything sexy,' he said brusquely once she was close enough to touch.

She shrugged her slender shoulders. 'I decided a mistress wouldn't go out with her lover looking dreary.'

'True,' he said, and without asking her permission swept her into his arms and kissed her.

Vivienne only resisted for a second or two, and then only because of shock at his sudden move. This was what she wanted, after all—to be in his arms again. To feel the heat of his flesh pressed hard against hers. And his body *was* hard. Hard all over.

Soon, she didn't even want to go to dinner. If he'd

pushed her back inside and into her bedroom, she would not have objected.

If only she hadn't dropped her keys onto the wooden floorboards.

His head lifted abruptly at the clattering sound, giving her a wry look before bending down to pick them up. Vivienne clenched the offending hands as she tried to regain control over herself. Her face felt hot and her whole body was in danger of imminent meltdown. She could not speak. Could hardly think. After straightening, he took a closer look at her and smiled a smile which she couldn't fathom. Was it amusement curving his lips? Or some strange kind of satisfaction?

'I'll lock up for you,' he said.

She just stared at him, her head slowly clearing from the fog of passion which had been clouding her normally sharp brain. Not for the first time, she wondered why Jack aroused her so easily to a level of lust which was both overpowering and overwhelming. One kiss and she was his again. Instantly. Being his beck-and-call girl was never going to present a problem. Because she wanted to do everything with him, and for him.

Sexually speaking, that was. She especially liked it when he was masterful with her. When he was demanding. When he took without asking. How strange was that? She'd always hated domineering, arrogant men. Yet she didn't hate Jack. If truth be told, she liked him even more than she'd admitted to Marion. She was also finding him more handsome than she ever had before.

Of course, he was dressed more smartly than usual tonight in a dark grey suit, white shirt and a blue tie the colour of his eyes. A man was always improved when wearing a suit, she thought, especially suits as well-fitting as Jack's. It gave him an air of urbane sophistication which she hadn't seen in him before. She'd always thought of Jack as a rough diamond; he was anything but rough in that extremely elegant suit.

He turned and caught her staring at him.

But he didn't say anything, just handed her the keys and took her arm, leading her outside.

It was cooler than she'd expected after the warmth of the day. Vivienne ground to a halt before they reached the pavement.

'I think I should go back and get a jacket,' she told Jack. Her dress did have three-quarter sleeves but the material was thin.

'Absolutely not,' he replied firmly. 'No covering up for you tonight, beautiful.'

Vivienne winced. 'Would you mind not calling me that? I really don't like it.'

His facial muscles tightened. 'What shall I call you, then? Sweetheart? Honey? Surely not darling? That doesn't seem to befit a mistress.'

Vivienne's hand clutched her purse tightly within angry fingers. 'Why are you acting like a jerk all of a sudden?' she threw at him.

He glared at her for a moment, then sighed, his face softening. 'You're right. I am acting like a jerk. Blame it on male ego. I'm still smarting over your not wanting to be my girlfriend for real.'

Vivienne was tempted to give in and say, *okay, I'll be your girlfriend for real.* Because she didn't like to think he was angry with her. But she seriously didn't want to do that. She knew she would regret it afterwards if she gave in.

'You seemed happy with our arrangement when you dropped me off last night,' she reminded him tautly.

'Besides, I thought a strictly sexual relationship would be right up your alley.'

'So did I.'

'Then what's your problem?'

Yeah, Jack, what's your problem? For pity's sake, get a grip.

He shrugged. 'No real problem. But perhaps you could compromise a little and go out with me occasionally. On a proper date, that is.'

'That's what I'm doing tonight, isn't it?'

He laughed. 'You and I both know that tonight's dinner is just foreplay, not a date. Hell, I took one look at you in that dress and instantly decided to reduce the meal to only one course. You're going to be my dessert, gorgeous. Can I call you that—gorgeous?'

'If you must,' she said, struggling to keep her own desire in check.

'Good. So let's stop this useless banter and be on our way. The quicker we get there and eat, the quicker we can leave.'

But it didn't turn out quite that way. Shortly after they were shown to a table in the small Italian restaurant Jack had booked in nearby St Leonards, his phone pinged.

'Sorry,' he said as he whipped the infernal thing out of his pocket. 'Have to have a quick look to see. It could be family.'

As much as Vivienne admired Jack's devotion to his family, she wished he'd left his phone at home—like she had. But she supposed that was being irrational. And more like a girlfriend's thinking than a mistress's. A mistress would not object to her wealthy lover doing anything at all, even answering text messages when he was at dinner with her.

Jack's frown as he read the message aroused Vivienne's curiosity.

'Something wrong?' she prompted.

He put the phone back in his pocket. 'No. Not really. It was an invite to an engagement party next week.'

'Oh? Who's getting married? Family or friends?'

'Neither. It's the daughter of a business acquaintance. A very wealthy business acquaintance.'

'So you're probably wise to attend.'

'I'm not sure that would be wise. I might punch out the groom-to-be.'

Vivienne was taken aback. 'Why on earth would you do that?'

His smile was very droll. 'His name is Daryl.'

The waiter bringing the bottle of wine Jack had ordered stopped Vivienne from saying or doing anything at that precise moment that she would regret. It also gave her a minute or two to gather herself, and her thoughts.

It was only natural, she accepted once she could think properly, that Frank Ellison would invite Jack to Courtney's engagement party. Jack had, after all, built Frank's harbourside mansion, the same one she had decorated last year. Had she received an invitation too? Vivienne wondered. She doubted it. As much as Frank might be ignorant of Daryl's very recent engagement to another woman, Courtney certainly wasn't. Or was she? Maybe the girl didn't know he'd been engaged when they'd started seeing each other.

Vivienne suppressed a sigh. She didn't want to think about Daryl any more, or the new life he'd made for himself with Courtney Ellison. She'd moved on and, although his actions had hurt her badly, she was feeling better now. Much, much better.

By the time the waiter poured the wine, took their

dinner orders and departed, Vivienne knew what she had to do.

First she lifted her glass of chilled Chardonnay to her lips and took a deep swallow. Then she locked eyes with Jack over the rim and said in steely tones, 'I presume your invitation says "and partner"?'

Jack had an awful feeling he knew what was coming.

'Yes,' he answered warily.

'In that case, I'd like to come with you.'

He *knew* it! Jack sighed his frustration. 'I really don't think that's a good idea, Vivienne.'

Her eyes turned mutinous. 'Why?' she snapped.

'Because you don't know what and who you're dealing with,' he shot back just as sharply.

'Yes I do. I'm dealing with a two-timing bastard who's been allowed to get away with his disgusting behaviour up till now,' she said, doing her best to keep her voice low so that the other people in the restaurant didn't overhear. 'He lied to me when he broke off our engagement. Claimed he hadn't been unfaithful, that he was doing the honourable thing by leaving me before sleeping with his new love. And I actually believed him at the time! My God, I can't believe I was such a gullible little fool where that man was concerned.

'The moment I saw those photos in the paper, I should have gone after him and told him what I thought of him. I should have made him suffer a little, even if it was only discomfort at the distress he'd caused. This is the perfect opportunity for me to confront him. Look, for all I know, Courtney Ellison might not even know about his engagement to me. Daryl could have lied to her as well. I want to make sure she is well aware of what kind of man she's planning to marry!'

'There's no chance in hell that Courtney doesn't

already know everything about you, Vivienne,' Jack stated with bald honesty. 'Trust me when I say that Daryl being engaged to you would have added to his attraction for her. Seduction is her favourite game. She went after me big time when I was building her father's house and cornered me in one of the home's ten bedrooms one day, as naked as a jay bird.'

Vivienne's eyes had gone wide, showing Jack how shocked she was, her reaction to such behaviour underlining to him that she would never do such a thing. This strictly sexual fling she was having with him…it was definitely out of character for her. She was the kind of girl who would usually want marriage and children, not the role of mistress.

'Heavens!' she exclaimed, shaking her head. 'And did you…did you…?'

'No. I wouldn't touch Courtney Ellison with a barge pole,' he ground out.

Was that relief he saw in her eyes? He sure hoped so. Because that would show that she genuinely liked him, the way he liked her.

'You don't want to be around people like that if you don't have to be, Vivienne,' he went on. 'They're bad, greedy, soulless people. You're way too good for them. Like I said, you're much better off without someone like Daryl in your life.'

'I dare say what you've just said is all true. But, on a personal level, I need to show Daryl that I've survived. That he didn't destroy me. If I go to their party with you, it will be the perfect revenge.'

All the breath left Jack's lungs at the word 'revenge'. God, but that actually hurt. He leant back in his chair and studied her for a few moments. 'Is that all I am to you, Vivienne?' he asked quietly. 'An instrument of revenge?'

'What? No, no, of course not. How can you possibly say that after all I've done with you? None of that was revenge. It was…it was… Well, it was just lust,' she finished, her face flushed and flustered.

'Just lust,' he repeated, not feeling particularly happy with that little phrase either. Though it was a lot better than revenge.

'Jack, trust me, I am over Daryl, and our sexual relationship has nothing to do with him.'

'Can't say I'm convinced, but I'll take you to the party if that's what you really want.'

'That's what I really want,' she told him.

'In that case, I have one proviso.'

'What?'

'Once you've shown your face and had your say, we leave straight away. I have no intention of spending my leisure time with people like that. I'd much rather be somewhere else. With my gorgeous mistress,' he added, then smiled at her.

CHAPTER FIFTEEN

JACK'S WICKEDLY SEXY smile did things to Vivienne which were even more wicked. It constantly amazed Vivienne how quickly Jack could turn her on. A moment ago, her mind had been focused on what she would say and do at Daryl's engagement party. A split second later, she could think of nothing but being with Jack, her body liquefying as various erotic images danced in her head.

Time to go to the ladies' room, she decided, making her excuses just as the waiter arrived with a plate of delicious looking herb-and-garlic bread.

'Don't be too long,' Jack said as he reached for a slice. 'Or this will all be gone.'

She wasn't long. Just long enough to cool her overheated body, and to change her mind about going to Courtney Ellison's engagement party. It surprised Vivienne to find that she cared about Jack's feelings more than her own need to confront Daryl. She hated Jack thinking that she was using him for revenge. Because she wasn't.

'You'll be pleased to know,' she said as she sat down again and reached for one of the two remaining slices of bread, 'that I've decided not to go to that party after all.'

Jack did not seem as pleased as she thought he'd be.

'Oh? And why's that?'

'You obviously don't want to take me. And I don't want to risk spoiling what we have together.'

His eyebrows lifted.

'Look, Daryl's dead and gone as far as I'm concerned,' she went on firmly. 'Let's leave him that way.'

Jack didn't believe that for a moment. Darling Daryl wasn't dead and gone in Vivienne's mind. He was still there, influencing everything she did. His dumping her so cruelly for another woman was undoubtedly one of the reasons she'd jumped into *his* bed. Maybe not out of revenge, but there had to be an element of rebound in her actions. Okay, so there was lust, too—though Jack preferred to think of it as passion and need. Vivienne was obviously a highly sexed girl who enjoyed making love in all its forms. No doubt she'd always had a very active and imaginative sex life with Daryl.

Damn it all, but he didn't like thinking about her doing the things with that bastard that she'd done with him!

Still, her being so darned sexy was one of the things he liked about her. That and her undeniable strength of character and courage. If she really wanted to go to that party then who was he to say no?

'I appreciate your concerns, Vivienne,' he said. 'And I love it that you don't want to risk spoiling our relationship.' *Such as it is,* he thought ruefully. 'But I've had a few moments to think about the situation from your point of view and I now believe it *would* be a good idea to go to that party. Otherwise, you'll never have closure on the matter. You need to have the opportunity to tell your ex what you think of him. And prove to yourself that you're not a coward,' he added for good measure.

He'd surprised her. No doubt about that.

'Then you're happy to take me?'

'Absolutely. Ah, here's our dinner.'

Vivienne had actually forgotten what kind of spaghetti Jack had ordered, her mind having been elsewhere when they'd first arrived at the restaurant. Fortunately, she was not a fussy eater and she loved Italian food. The plate of spaghetti marinara placed before her was a huge serving, with a wide variety of seafood as well as the fish pieces: mussels; prawns; scallops; calamari.

'Goodness!' she exclaimed as she picked up her fork. 'It'll take me all night to eat this.'

'I sincerely hope not.'

Vivienne's stomach did a little somersault. She knew exactly what he was referring to and the thought excited her unbearably. Dear heaven, she was turning into a sex addict. She had to do something, *say* something to get her mind off the subject.

'Jack,' she said abruptly.

He swallowed a mussel with relish before looking up at her. 'Yep?' he said, and dabbed at his mouth with a serviette.

Oh, God. Why did he have to do that? She stared at his somewhat hard mouth and thought of the pleasure it gave her. *All* of it: lips; teeth; tongue. But especially his tongue. She could feel it now, licking, stabbing, sliding inside her.

The heat her thoughts evoked made her squeeze her thighs and buttocks tightly together. Dear heaven, she almost came then. Putting down her fork, she straightened her spine against the back of the chair, forcing herself to get a firm grip on her wayward flesh.

'I was wondering if you'd heard anything more about Francesco's Folly today?' she asked, always having found work a welcome distraction when her emotions threatened to get out of hand. 'Do you know when I might be able to move in there and start work?'

'Good news there. Things should be finalised by the end of next week. You can move in as soon as you like after that.'

'And my contract?'

'I'll draw one up for you before that. Which reminds me—I've contacted a builder I know who's going to do the actual work. He's reliable and has lots of contacts in the area. Knows all the local tradies and building suppliers. I've been wondering, since you'll be living on site, if you'd take on the job as project manager as well as interior decorator? I'll pay extra, of course,' he added, and forked in another mouthful of seafood.

'How much extra?'

He smiled. 'Lots.'

'Okay,' she said with a shrug which belied her crippling sexual tension. Talking about work hadn't distracted her at all!

'Good. Now, eat up. Nothing worse than cold pasta.'

She did her best. But her appetite still lay elsewhere. She watched Jack tuck into his meal with relish whilst only picking at hers. She did eat the seafood, the pasta part remaining untouched. And she did drink the wine. Most of the bottle; Jack told her he never had more than one glass when driving. By the time Jack pushed his own empty plate aside, the alcohol had driven out any feelings of nerves, leaving her with nothing but the most dizzying need.

'Not hungry?' he said as he wiped his mouth again with his serviette.

Vivienne swallowed the last mouthful of wine. 'Not really,' she said.

'Do you want anything more to drink? A Cognac? Coffee?'

'No, thanks.'

He looked hard at her, then nodded.

'Fine,' he said, and waved the waiter over.

Five minutes later they were out in the very cool night air, Vivienne shivering as Jack took her elbow and steered her towards the small car park behind the restaurant. His Porsche was parked over in a dimly lit corner, next to a red Mercedes.

'You must be cold,' he said, walking quickly.

Vivienne wouldn't have been as cold if she hadn't felt so hot. She frowned when he steered her round to the driver's side into the small gap between the car and a solid wooden fence.

'This'll have to do,' he said gruffly, and pushed her back up against the car door. 'I can't wait till we get back to my place, Vivienne. You must know that. Drop that bag and kick off your shoes,' he ordered her in a low, gravelly voice.

She did so, then stood there, still shivering, with her back against the car whilst his hands scooped up under her skirt and yanked both her panties and tights down in one rough movement. They joined her bag on the ground.

'Hold your skirt up to your waist,' he commanded.

She did so, shocked by her blind obedience to him. She heard voices nearby, but she knew she wouldn't drop her skirt. Not unless he told her to. Which he didn't. He just stared at her, then touched her between her quivering thighs, pushing them aside, then delving into the hot, wet core of her sex. She moaned softly, then not so softly. Thank God the voices had gone, because the whole world could have come to watch her and she would not have stopped.

She was perilously close to coming when he stopped and dropped to his knees before her. With a strangled cry she spread her legs wider, her knees bending slightly to give his mouth better access to her by then desperate body. The feel of his tongue stabbing mercilessly against her throbbing clitoris was more than she could bear, and she was unable to smother the tortured cry of release which immediately erupted from her panting mouth.

The next few seconds were a blur. Vivienne was thankful for the car's support or she might have sunk to the ground. She wasn't aware of Jack's actions, having squeezed her eyes tightly shut against the shattering storm of her climax. Just when she thought she might live, she felt Jack enter her, then surge upwards. Her eyes shot open and she stared into his flushed face. His eyes were wild, his mouth twisted, the urgency of his own need very obvious.

When he lifted her up she automatically wrapped her legs around his hips, her hands letting go of her skirt so that she could wind her arms around his neck. Her dress fell down over them like a curtain. Not that what they were doing was subtle. Anyone walking by would have known instantly what was happening.

He groaned as he ground slowly into her, his hands kneading her buttocks at the same time.

But she didn't want him slow. She wanted him hard. And fast.

'Faster, Jack,' she urged, squeezing him tightly with her insides.

'Bloody hell, Vivienne,' he muttered, taking a bruising grip of her hips before grinding into her with a power which took her breath away. He came almost as quickly as she had, shuddering into her, groaning his satisfaction. Vivienne didn't mind that she was left still wanting. Jack's pleasure was enough for her at the moment.

She began to shiver when he lowered her to the ground, the heat of the moment giving way to the chill of the night.

He shook his head at her. 'We're mad. You do know that, don't you?'

'Yes,' she agreed shakily. 'Quite mad.'

'Anyone could have come.'

'I didn't care.'

'I know. Neither did I. Come on, let's get you into the warmth of the car. You'll catch your death if we stay out here.'

'Well, there's one consolation,' he added wryly, once they were under way with the heater going full blast.

'What's that?' she asked somewhat dazedly. She was, quite frankly, still a little off the planet.

'I had enough of a brain left to use a condom.'

'Yes. Yes, I noticed that,' she said. But only after he withdrew. She hadn't during the act. She'd been off in another world. It was just as well she was on the pill. Being with Jack had made her uncharacteristically reckless. He wasn't much better. They were mad, all right. Mad for each other. She almost told him then that she was on the pill because of course it would be better, not having to worry about protection all the time, especially if they were going to have spontaneous sex at any given moment. Which seemed on the cards. His desire for her was as strong as hers for him. But being on the pill only protected you against pregnancy, nothing else. She couldn't see Jack as a man who took silly risks, but who knew?

'What are you thinking about?' he asked her when they stopped at a set of lights.

'Nothing.'

'Come now, Vivienne, I know you too well. Your mind is never empty.'

She stared down at the bag in her lap which was bulging from where she'd stuffed in her cotton panties. The tights, she'd left behind since they'd been ruined when Jack had ripped them off her. Finally, she looked up and over at him.

'I was thinking I'm going to go out tomorrow and buy myself some seriously sexy underwear,' she invented. 'As long as you promise not to destroy it, that is.'

He smiled a wicked little smile. 'Sorry. Can't give you any guarantees on that. You bring out the beast in me.'

'I do?'

'You know you do.'

'You bring out the same in me,' she admitted. 'I'm not usually like this, you know.'

'What do you mean?' he asked straight away.

Vivienne wished she hadn't said that. For how could she tell him that she'd never before done a tenth of the things that she'd done with him? He probably wouldn't believe her. Either that or he'd start asking her questions, questions she didn't have answers for. She didn't want to think about why she was so different with him. She just wanted to live in the moment. To say and do whatever she wanted with him. To be wild and wanton and, yes, even downright wicked.

She smiled a saucy smile. 'I mean, I don't usually have sex in car parks. But it was fun, wasn't it?'

His smile was wry. 'It wouldn't have been fun if we'd been arrested.'

'Can you get arrested for that?'

'I would imagine so.'

'Have you ever been arrested?' she asked, happy to change the subject from herself onto him.

'Not as yet.' The lights went green and he drove on towards the bridge. 'You're coming back to my place for the night, aren't you?'

'What…the whole night?' She hadn't been expecting that. But instantly, it was what she wanted to do. To sleep with him naked, all night, where she could touch him at will, kiss him all over, whenever and wherever it took her fancy.

'You have a problem with that?' he said when she remained silent. Little did he know the thoughts going on in her head, or the instant need gripping her flesh. 'I could drop you home first thing in the morning on my way to work. You could sneak in like a naughty teenager before Marion wakes up and spots you.'

'Marion never wakes up till around ten,' she told him, her matter-of-fact tone hiding the escalating desire firing her blood once more. 'Not when she's doing the two-to-ten shift. She doesn't get home till nearly eleven, and she's always dog tired. She never knocks on my door till late morning.'

'That settles it, then. You're staying the night.'

'If that's what you want,' she agreed, hugging her excitement to herself.

Jack glanced over at her and wondered what she'd been really thinking back at the lights. He wasn't a mind reader—especially where women were concerned—but he doubted she'd been thinking about underwear shopping.

Vivienne was an enigma all right. Always cool on the surface, but underneath, very hot to trot, a classic case of fire and ice. His stomach lurched when he thought of how she'd urged him on back in that car park.

'Faster, Jack,' she'd said in a voice unlike the one she used when working. Or even just now, here, in the car. There'd been nothing cool, calm and collected about that voice. It had been wild!

He felt the sex between them now would be even better, knowing he had all night. He could take his time with her. Make her wait more. Make her see the rapture in elongated foreplay. There was something infinitely satisfying about long, slow lovemaking where the emphasis was not so much on coming but on sensual experiences. He would stroke her back with gentle hands, massage her bottom with oil and caress her beautiful breasts. He would make her sigh with pleasure. He wanted to satisfy her more completely than she'd ever been satisfied before.

'Now what are *you* thinking?' she asked.

Jack turned to smile at her. 'I was thinking that you don't need to buy any new underwear. Because, from now on, you won't be wearing any.'

Her blush startled Jack. Why on earth, he wondered, would the girl who'd just done what she'd just done blush at the idea of going without her underwear? It didn't compute. She was an enigma all right. A woman of contradictions and contrary behaviour.

Take her apartment, for instance. Why was it furnished in such a stark way when her professional designs were never like that? Vivienne had a reputation for creating warm, comfy interiors which appealed to people. It was why he always hired her to do his show units and villas, because her décor made them sell. There had to be reasons for why she'd chosen to decorate her own place in such a soulless fashion; deep, personal reasons. Jack suspected it had something to do with her family background, which obviously hadn't been very happy. She'd sounded stressed when she'd talked about her parents. She hadn't been all that forthcoming, either. Most of the women he'd dated in the past were eager to talk about themselves, launching into detailed life stories without too much encouragement.

Of course, he wasn't *dating* Vivienne, was he? He was just sleeping with her. For now, that was. Jack hadn't abandoned his idea of her becoming his girl-friend for real. He'd just put it on the back-burner for a while.

One day, in the hopefully not-too-distant future, she would see that it would be good for her to date a guy like him: an honest, straightforward, straight-down-the-line type of guy who didn't lie or cheat and who could show her a good time, in bed and out, without any false dec-larations of love and till-death-do-us-part commitment. Just the thing she needed after getting tangled up with El Creepo. And, when she finally realised that having an easygoing boyfriend would be good for her—*and* once she got her trust back in men—he would find out all that she'd been hiding from him.

Meanwhile, he would give her exactly what she wanted. Which was fine by him, because quite frankly, right at this moment, it was just what he wanted as well.

CHAPTER SIXTEEN

'IT'S AMAZING HE could find a door to match your old one,' Marion said as she looked at Vivienne's new bathroom door. 'Amazing that the man came on time to do it as well,' she added.

'Jack said all his contractors come on time,' Vivienne said, very happy with the door. It had even been painted the same colour, Bert explaining that he'd taken a scraping of the paint when he'd come to look at it the first time. It had only taken him half an hour to remove the old door and put in the new one. Marion had dropped in once she'd seen Bert drive off.

'In that case I'll certainly be giving Jack a ring if ever I want something fixed. Tradies give me the willies, the way they're never reliable.'

'I know what you mean. Jack won't tolerate workers who are late, or unreliable, or don't do things up to his high standards.'

'Hmm. A difficult man to work for, then,' Marion said.

'Difficult. And demanding,' Vivienne agreed. 'But fair.'

'Still, make sure you get a proper contract with him. You can't be too trusting, even if Jack is normally a fair man. He might try to get you to do this job under the table, so to speak. You know, cash in hand. There's no security in that. Where money is concerned, even the fairest man might be tempted to take advantage. And you're vulnerable at the moment, Vivienne, even more vulnerable in the coming weeks without me around to warn you to be careful. Jack didn't get to be as successful as he is without being a bit ruthless on occasion.'

'Don't worry. I won't let him take advantage of me. But, might I remind you that you never warned me about Daryl?'

Marion sighed. 'I have to confess that Daryl took me in as well, the handsome devil. He was an accomplished charmer all right. Though, looking back, I suppose he was always too good to be true. Too ready with the compliments, if you know what I mean.'

'Yes. Yes, I certainly do know what you mean,' Vivienne said, recalling how over the top he'd been in his praise of her. Not just her looks but other things, things which she knew weren't true. But she'd lapped it up all the same, thinking he was praising her out of love, imagining that he'd been *blinded* by loved, whereas in fact *she'd* been the one who'd been blinded.

Jack, on other hand, was thankfully light on the compliments. Yes, he'd called her beautiful and gorgeous at times, but that was par for the course with men who wanted to have sex with you. And, yes, when in bed he did say nice things about her body. Especially her breasts and her bottom. But he didn't rave on at length, for which she was grateful.

What he did at length—last night especially—was make love to her. Impossible to call it anything else this time, Vivienne conceded Jack had showed her that sex with him didn't have to be kinky or quick or in unusual places and positions to be stunningly pleasurable. He'd surprised her with how long he could spend on fore-play, caressing, admiring and gently exploring every inch of her body before finally entering her, where he rocked gently back and forth, kissing her every so often, bringing her ever so slowly to climax in the most satisfying way.

Then, after a short rest during which they'd lain in each other's arms and talked about what plans they had for Francesco's Folly, he'd made love to her again. Once again he'd been in no hurry, remaining still inside her for ages whilst he'd played with her breasts and told her how lovely they were, and that he could stay doing what he was doing for ever. Which was what it seemed like he did, in hindsight.

Vivienne knew she should have been exhausted today. Instead, she felt more alive than she ever had before. She could hardly wait to see Jack again tonight.

'I have to go get ready for work,' Marion said, breaking into Vivienne's thoughts. 'Now, forget all about dastardly Daryl. He's not worth thinking about. See you tomorrow, love.'

Marion's advice reminded Vivienne of her decision to go to Daryl's engagement party. Once again, she no longer felt as strongly about doing so. If truth be told, Daryl was fading from her mind. Yes, it still stung, what he'd done. And yes, he didn't deserve to get away with it scot free. But would she really have the gall to confront him at his engagement party? It *would* take courage; she could see that now. Jack hadn't wanted her to go at first, then he'd said he did. Something about closure—he was probably right. She supposed she could do it, with him by her side. He wouldn't let anything horrible happen to her. Of that Vivienne felt confident. He was a man who could be relied upon.

Vivienne reached out to pull the bathroom door shut, pleased that it didn't stick the way the other one had. She smiled. Oh, yes, Jack could be relied on. She wondered if she should text him, tell him that the door man had come and done a splendid job. Yes, of course she could. He wouldn't mind. But she wouldn't ring. He'd told her he didn't like to be rung when he was at work, not unless there was an emergency. Which there wasn't. But she did so want to contact him. It would be like touching him. She did so like touching him. With a shiver of remembered pleasure, she hurried out to the kitchen where she'd left her phone.

'Marion says I'm to make sure I get a proper contract with you,' Vivienne told Jack later that night. They were in his very nice bed in his very nice apartment, lying in each other's arms in a state of post-coital bliss. 'She says I'm not to let you take advantage of me, and then she warned me that you must be ruthless to become as successful in business as you have.'

Jack's eyebrows lifted. 'And do you agree with her? About my being ruthless?'

'Not really. No, I don't think you're ruthless. You are a tough man to deal with on a professional basis, but fair. And I told her so. You'll be glad to know, however, that I didn't inform her that on the personal side you're a bit of a softie.'

Jack laughed. 'That's not what you said a few minutes ago. You said I was hard as a rock.'

She gave him a playful slap on his magnificent chest. 'Don't be silly. You know what I mean. I was talking about the way you love your family, especially your mother. A man who loves his mother couldn't be bad.'

'Really? I seem to recall reading somewhere that Hitler loved his mother.'

She glowered up at him. 'You just made that up.'

He faked a shocked expression. 'You don't think I read?'

'I didn't say that.'

'I'll have you know I read all the time. Only yesterday I picked up a copy of *Playboy* at a building site and read it from cover to cover. *Very* interesting articles in that magazine.'

Now it was Vivienne's turn to laugh. 'I'll bet. No seriously, do you like to read? Because I do. Very much.'

'Can't say it's my favourite pastime,' he admitted.

'I couldn't be without a book. I read every night before I go to sleep. Or I used to,' she added, thinking she hadn't read a word since she'd started her relationship with Jack. He left her exhausted naturally after their passionate nights together.

'If that's the case, how come you don't have bookshelves crammed with books in your place? Or do you keep them all under your bed? I haven't been in there yet.'

And neither will you, Vivienne thought with a spurt of panic. She didn't want to be with him in the same bed she'd shared with Daryl. A small part of her was still afraid that if she did that she might revert to being the same pathetic bed partner she'd been with him, something which still occasionally bothered and confused her. If she'd loved Daryl—truly loved him—why hadn't she been more passionate with him? Why hadn't she enjoyed sex with him the way she did with Jack? There was no making sense of it. Really, there wasn't.

'I don't keep the books I read,' she told Jack in answer to his question. 'I buy a couple at a time from a local second-hand bookshop and when I finish reading them I return them and get two more. No point in keeping them after I've read them, is there?' she said, and glanced up at him.

Jack shrugged. 'I don't know. You could always lend them to friends. Doesn't Marion read?'

'Yes, but not the kind of books I read. She likes romance and I like crime.'

'I see,' Jack said. 'I like watching crime shows on TV,' he ventured.

'I do, too. Which ones are your favourite?' she asked, and they talked at some length about their favourite programmes, Jack discovering that Vivienne liked shows which mixed crime with relationships, not just crime itself.

'So you do like some romance in your stories,' he said at last. 'Just so long as it's not *all* romance.'

'Yes. Yes, I suppose that's true.'

'Now, you told me earlier that you were driving Marion to the airport on Saturday, is that right?'

'Yes.'

'What time?'

'Around one. Her plane goes just after three.'

'And will you stay with her till the plane leaves?'

'Yes, I thought I would. I couldn't let her go off alone.'

'Yes, of course. I'm not complaining. I'm just trying to work out the weekend. I was originally going to suggest we drive up to Francesco's Folly on Saturday and stay the night but that's not very practical when you probably won't be back from the airport till after four. I'll go visit Mum instead on Saturday whilst you're busy. Then I'll take you out somewhere special for dinner that night. If you want to go, of course,' he added, adhering to her rule that he asked her first. 'Then, if you like, you could stay the night here and we could head north first thing Sunday morning for the day. What do you say to that?'

'Sounds wonderful,' she agreed whilst privately worrying that it sounded like she was becoming more like a girlfriend than a mistress. Dinner out somewhere special. Sleeping over afterwards—not that that was new—and then all day Sunday together. Still, as long as they kept their relationship secret then she supposed it didn't matter how much time they spent together. It was important to Vivienne, keeping their sexual relationship a secret. She didn't want people to think she was a fool, jumping from the frying pan into the fire. After all, Jack was never going to marry her. He'd made that clear up front. Still, if she didn't do something silly like fall in love—again—then there was no reason to worry that she might get burnt by him.

'Good,' Jack said in a satisfied tone. 'Now, I think it's time for seconds...'

CHAPTER SEVENTEEN

'IT'S NOT LIKE you to visit on a Saturday,' Jack's mother said over lunch the following Saturday. He'd rung her the previous night, saying he'd drop in around noon, and she'd told him to stay for lunch.

Jack forked one of the baby beets into his mouth before answering. God, but he did love salads, though he hated making them himself; hated cooking all round. He wondered briefly if Vivienne was a good cook. He imagined she would be. She was good at most things, that girl. Maybe he would ask her to cook him a meal one night, though not in that antiseptic kitchen of hers. Damn, but he wished he could find out why she was so clinical when it came to her own flat's décor.

'Couldn't make it tomorrow,' he explained. 'I'm driving up to Francesco's Folly to see the place again.' He'd told her all about the place during his previous night's phone call. As had become her habit lately, his mother wasn't as surprised as he thought she'd be. In fact, she seemed suspiciously pleased, though that could have been because he'd said she and Jim could go there for romantic weekends once it was finished.

'You'll have to take me up there one day soon,' she suggested.

'I'd rather not till it's refurbished. Actually, I'm not

going alone tomorrow. I'm taking up the designer I've hired to do the interior decorating. She's a girl who's worked for me often, doing my show homes and villas.'

'What's she like, this designer you've hired?'

'What do you mean?'

Eleanor did her best to adopt an ingenuous expression. She knew from past experience that Jack didn't like her questioning him about the women in his life. Something told her—some feminine instinct, or possibly motherly instinct—that this girl might be different. 'Well…er…is she young? Old? Plain? Pretty? The usual questions.'

'I'm not sure how old Vivienne is. Late twenties, I guess. And I'd call her attractive rather than pretty. She does have lovely green eyes, though. And a great figure.'

Aha! So he'd noticed her eyes and her figure. And what a nice name: Vivienne. Classy.

'Single?'

'Yep. Though she was engaged till recently. To some fortune hunter who dumped her for Courtney Ellison. Frank Ellison's daughter, you know? The mining magnate.'

'Yes, I know who you mean. How awful for her, Jack. She must be devastated.'

'She's better off without the likes of him.'

Was that jealousy she heard? Or just dislike? Jack detested men who cheated, and he had a strong sense of responsibility and integrity. He would make some girl a wonderful husband. One day.

'Does Vivienne think that?' she asked quietly.

Jack frowned into his plate. Did she finally? One might have thought so when she was panting beneath him. Or when she lay naked in his arms, satiated from another of their nightly sexathons. But, to be brutally honest, Jack still wasn't sure if Vivienne's wildly wanton act in bed wasn't just that. An act. Not that he thought she was faking her orgasms. Hell, no. No one pretended that noisily.

'Possibly not,' he replied to his mother's question. 'But hopefully she will soon.'

Jack knew as soon as he said 'hopefully' that it was a mistake.

He glanced up to find his mother looking intently at him.

'You like this Vivienne, don't you?'

Jack saw no point in denying it. 'Yep,' he said succinctly, and stabbed a spear of asparagus.

'And does she like you back?' his mother persisted.

'Yep,' he said.

'Are you sleeping with her?'

Jack put down his fork with a sigh. 'Mum. Truly. I'm thirty-seven years old. Who I sleep with is none of your business.'

'You're my son and your relationships will always be my business. It's not as though I'm going to start nagging you to settle down and get married, am I? Though I would if it would work. For what it's worth, I've always thought you'd make some lucky girl a great husband. And you'd be a great father as well, so there!'

Jack rolled his eyes, then went back to eating his salad.

'What if she falls in love with you, Jack? She might, you know. On the rebound.'

Jack scowled. 'Look, she won't fall in love with me, our relationship isn't like that. We're just having fun, no complications and nothing that serious.' Jack said the words, knew they were true, but for some reason he suddenly found himself wishing it were otherwise.

'Oh, Jack, physical intimacy often leads to a deepening of feelings for a woman. It's hard to be intimate with a man and not become emotionally involved. And what if you fall in love with *her*? Have you thought about that?'

Jack practically ground his teeth in exasperation. He should never have told his mum about his relationship with Vivienne. Vivienne was so right: it was best to keep this kind of relationship a secret.

'Don't be silly, Mum. I don't do love.'

She laughed. 'You don't *do* love, Jack. It just happens.'

Jack ignored her.

'I'd like to meet this Vivienne.'

Jack slammed down his fork again. 'Mum, our relationship is not that serious. You don't need to meet her and I don't think she would appreciate it either. Vivienne and I are both completely relaxed about our relationship and there will be no falling in love from either of us!'

Eleanor sighed. He really could be very difficult. Of course, Jack might proclaim that he wasn't falling in love with this Vivienne girl, but perhaps he didn't know that was what was happening to him yet. But it was. She'd heard the jealousy in his voice when he'd been talking about Vivienne's ex. On top of that, this was the first girl he'd ever actually told her about in years. That had to mean something.

'Okay, I'll stop bothering you about her,' she said at last.

'Good,' Jack snapped. 'Now, I'd like to finish my meal, if you don't mind.'

CHAPTER EIGHTEEN

'HOW DID THE visit with your mother go yesterday?' Vivienne asked Jack shortly after they took off for the drive up to Nelson's Bay the following morning. 'I forgot to ask you last night.'

In truth, she'd been looking forward to being with him so much by Saturday evening, having not seen him the previous day, that she hadn't been able to focus on anything but how much she wanted him. Dinner out had been a trial and she could hardly remember what she'd eaten or what they'd talked about. It had taken a lot of control for her not to do outrageous things to him during the taxi ride back to Jack's place after dinner—he hadn't taken his car, saying he wanted to have a few drinks—especially after he'd kissed her, slipping a hand up under her skirt at the same time. She'd read about women who went down on men in the back of taxis but had always thought it utterly outrageous. But she'd been tempted. Oh, so tempted.

She shivered as she recalled how close she'd been to coming as Jack had stroked her through her panties. He'd withdrawn his hand—the knowing devil—before she did, leaving her desperate with wanting. She recalled how annoyed she'd felt at how unaffected *he* had seemed at the time. But that had just been pretence on his part. He'd shown her within seconds of closing his apartment door that his desire for her had been just as great. He'd taken her up against that door, not bothering to undress properly.

That he hadn't used a condom only sunk into them both afterwards, Jack profusely apologetic whilst she'd just been shocked, not worried so much. After all, she *was* on the pill. Which she confessed when she saw how upset he was. For the rest of the night, Jack hadn't used protection, assuring her that she was safe from any other kind of health hazard. It had been wonderful not having to bother with protection, not to mention deliciously pleasurable.

Jack glanced across at Vivienne before replying. 'Good,' he said. 'She made my favourite salad for lunch. By the way, I told her about buying Francesco's Folly, and that I'd hired you to do the refurbishment. *And* that I was bringing you up here today to look at the house,' he added, omitting the fact that his mum had asked to meet her.

'Oh? Didn't she think that was odd?'

Jack shot Vivienne a frown. What was it with women that they often jumped to the right conclusions? That mysterious feminine instinct perhaps.

'I don't see why she should. Like I said, I explained the situation. How you've worked for me before. Many times.'

'Maybe so, Jack, but this is Sunday, not a work day.'

Jack shrugged. 'She knows I often work twenty-four-seven. It's nothing new. If you want something to worry about, then how about us going together to that engagement party next Saturday night? The paparazzi are sure to be hanging about and we might get our photos snapped. How are you going to explain that to people if our picture gets in the Sunday gossip columns?'

Vivienne hadn't thought of that. But, once she did, she wasn't overly worried. 'I doubt that will happen. We're not celebrities, Jack. You keep a low public profile and I'm a nobody. They won't be taking pictures of us.'

'Just thought I'd warn you.'

'Fine. I'm warned. Now, can we talk about something else? I don't want to think about next Saturday night. I'm not keen on going but I *am* going, and that's all there is to it. I aim to approach it the same way I do the dentist.'

'What do you mean, the way you approach the dentist?'

'I hate going to the dentist. Silly, really, since the dentist I go to is very gentle. The first time I went to him, though, I hadn't been to the dentist in over ten years. I was so nervous during the days leading up to my appointment that when I got in the chair I almost threw up.

'Anyway, he gave me some gas and a couple of injections and it didn't hurt at all. After that, I started going every six months for check-ups but I still used to feel sick for days beforehand. Finally, I got a grip on myself and decided it was a waste of my nervous energy to worry till I was actually sitting in that chair. I trained myself not to think about it during the days leading up to my next appointment. Though I do allow myself a short burst of nerves when I'm actually in the chair. I'll do the same with that engagement party— I'll think about it when we're walking up the steps of Frank Ellison's mansion.'

'No kidding,' Jack said in a droll tone. 'And I'm the Queen of England.'

Vivienne shrugged. 'Okay, so I might have to give it *some* thought beforehand. I have to buy a dress, for starters. No way am I going to show up looking daggy. Did the invitation say black tie?'

'I think so. Yeah.'

'In that case, it's a tux for you and an evening gown for me. Do you have a tux?'

'I'll get one.'

'You can rent them, you know.'

'I do know that, Vivienne. I'm not a total Philistine. But I always prefer to buy rather than rent. So why did you leave it so long between dental visits?' he asked, finding it strange that such a perfectionist would neglect her teeth like that.

'What? Oh, I…um…that wasn't recently. It was ten years ago, when I was seventeen. After Mum and Dad's divorce, Mum just didn't take me. And I didn't think about it, not till I was in my final year of high school and I got this dreadful toothache.'

'But why didn't she take you? Couldn't she afford to, was that it?'

'No. She had the money. She…she… Oh, it's very complicated, Jack. Please, I don't like talking about those years. I survived and my teeth are fine now. See?' And she flashed an impressive set of pearly whites at him.

Jack only had to look into Vivienne's haunted eyes to know that she might have survived—physically speaking—but she'd been left with some lasting emotional damage. Reading between the lines, he worked out that her mother must have become seriously depressed after the divorce. Divorce was like a death to some women.

He recalled how depressed—and useless—his own mother had been after his father had died and it had taken her years to bounce back. It sounded like Vivienne's mother had never bounced back. Instead, she'd neglected her only child. Very badly, by the sound of things.

Jack would have pried a little more into her background but a quick sidewards glance showed that she'd brought the shutters down, her expression closed and bleak. Jack decided to change the subject.

'We might actually have to do some work up here today, Vivienne,' he said.

She turned happier eyes towards him. 'Oh? What kind of work?'

'Nothing too strenuous. But I want to make up our minds which way to tackle the renovations. Whether we just tart up what's there or go the whole hog and rip out walls.'

'I definitely won't be advising that you rip out any walls, Jack. The floor plan of the house is great. It's just what's *in* the rooms which needs ripping out, especially the bathrooms and kitchens. The bedrooms just need new paint and carpet. And furniture, of course. Plus all those hideous curtains will have to go. Perhaps you could think about double glazing on the windows. And tinted glass, of course. Keep out the glare of the morning sun.'

'Wow. You've really been giving this some thought, haven't you?'

'Well, I had nothing to do all Friday, so I thought I should get started.'

'Good girl.'

'I can't wait to move in. I was thinking next Sunday. Provided you get my contract ready before then, of course,' she added, somewhat cheekily.

'Next Sunday will be fine. And we'll definitely get your contract drawn up and signed this week.'

'Good.'

'Now, you sure you won't find it too lonely up there?'

Vivienne shook her head. 'I'm used to living by myself, Jack,' she said.

Another enigmatic comment. One which he would have liked to explore, but decided not to. Not yet.

'To tell you the truth, I'm looking forward to it,' she added.

In a way, so was Jack. Because he couldn't keep up with what he'd been doing this past week for much longer. He'd found it hard to concentrate on work after making love to Vivienne half the night every night. He was a very hands-on builder and he wasn't as young as he used to be. He'd been glad he had an excuse not to see her on Friday night, giving him the opportunity to recover. Though sleep hadn't come as easily as it did when he was in bed with Vivienne. Sex was a wonderful sleeping tablet, no doubt about that.

But he really did have an important job to complete in the coming weeks, finishing off a block of units, with a killer deadline built into his contract. He couldn't afford to slack off, or let his men slack off. They took the lead from him, he'd found. He knew he wouldn't be able to resist being with Vivienne whilst she was in Sydney but it would be another matter once she was living in Francesco's Folly. He could hardly drop in every evening. He would miss her but it would make the weekends even sweeter. He could just imagine how he would feel by the time he arrived on a Friday evening: more than ready for her to be his beck-and-call girl, that was for sure.

Spots on his windshield brought a frustrated groan. He hated driving in the rain. Especially heavy rain, which was exactly what he was contending with half an hour later. Their usual stop at Raymond Terrace was a respite, but not long enough to last out the rain. It was still pouring when they both ran for the Porsche and dived in.

'I hate this kind of rain,' Jack grumbled. 'Makes a builder's life hell. Puts you behind, big time.'

'You don't have to worry too much about the rain with Francesco's Folly, though,' Vivienne said. 'Most of the work is indoors.'

'True. How long do you think it will take? I'd like it all complete before Christmas.'

'That depends, I guess, on how reliable this builder is you've hired.'

'He's very reliable. And if he isn't, I'll rely on you to crack the whip.'

Vivienne laughed. 'I thought I told you I wasn't that kind of girl.'

'Maybe not in the bedroom, but you're quite formidable at work. Don't forget, I've seen you in action. You always want everything done just so.'

'You ought to talk!'

'We're two peas in a pod, then, aren't we?'

They glanced over at each other, their eyes laughing.

So Jack was surprised when a strange wave of bleak emotion suddenly washed through him. His gaze swung back to the road ahead, his eyebrows bunching together in a frown.

'You do like me now, don't you, Vivienne?' he asked.

His question startled her. Then worried her. Because

it forced her to face the fact that she liked him more and more with each passing day. How long, she wondered, before liking—combined with lust—turned to love? Another week? A month? Six months? Vivienne feared that by the time the refurbishment of Francesco's Folly was complete she would be in much too deep where Jack was concerned. Yet she'd known what she was doing, getting involved with him. He hadn't hidden the fact that he didn't want marriage and children; that he wasn't looking for 'forever' love. Just friendship and fun. He hadn't lied to her. Ever. Which was what she liked about him most of all.

'Very much so,' she said truthfully.

When Jack's heart actually swelled with happiness, his mother's words came back to haunt him.

You don't do *love, Jack. It just happens.*

Dear God, he thought. But not altogether unhappily. Which was perverse. He'd always believed he didn't want to be bothered with the whole love and marriage scenario, especially the children part. He'd wanted freedom from any more responsibility. But when love struck—as it obviously had—you actually wanted to embrace such things. He could think of nothing more desirable than being married to Vivienne and having children with her. How amazing was that?

Amazing, but also problematic. After all, she didn't love him back, did she?

'That's good,' he said, somewhat distractedly. 'Look, the rain's stopped.' Which was just as well. Jack doubted that Francesco's Folly would look as marvellous in the rain. And he wanted it always to look marvellous. Wanted Vivienne to fall in love with the place, as well as with him. It might take time but that was all right. She wasn't going anywhere fast. She'd be signing that

contract to work for him till the refurbishment was complete. That gave him several months to achieve his goal,
though Jack suspected he would need every single one
of them.

CHAPTER NINETEEN

SHE'D LIED TO Jack about being able to control her nerves over the party. Come the following Saturday morning, she woke with an already churning stomach which quickly worsened once it hit her that D-day had finally arrived: Daryl Day.

She hadn't spent last night at Jack's apartment, because she had an early appointment at the beauty salon just down the road from her own flat. Normally, she enjoyed the couple of hours she spent there every six weeks or so, having her hair trimmed, shampooed and blow-dried, after which she usually had a pedicure and manicure. The owner of the salon, a lady in her early forties, was a bright and breezy conversationalist who made all her clients feel better for their visit to her salon. But nothing was going to make Vivienne feel better that morning.

'What colour do you want on your nails?' the girl asked.

'Red,' Vivienne replied, thinking of the red evening gown which was hanging up on the front of her wardrobe. It was too long to hang inside, and had cost her a bomb. 'A bright, dark red.'

'This one is very popular,' the girl said, holding up a bottle of dark red varnish that had a shimmer in it.

'It's called Scarlet Woman. There's a lipstick to match, if you'd like to buy it.'

Vivienne suspected the girls got a commission if the clients bought some of their products. Usually, she didn't say yes to their offers, preferring to buy her hair-care products and cosmetics online. But this time she said yes to the lipstick. She might not feel confident about tonight, but by golly she was going to look it!

The expression on Jack's face when she opened her door to him at eight that evening was gratifying, even if the butterflies in her stomach had by then reached epic proportions. She was also grateful for the distraction of how fabulous he looked in his black-tie outfit. Not just tall, dark and handsome, but very sophisticated.

'Heavens, Jack!' she exclaimed before he could say a word about her. 'You do scrub up well. And that tux is amazing. It looks like it was made for you.' Which it did, fitting his broad-shouldered physique to perfection with not a wrinkle anywhere. She'd half- imagined he might look out of place in formal clothes but she was wrong.

He smiled. 'It was, actually. I couldn't find anything off the peg to fit me so I had no alternative. And might I say the same about your outfit? Red suits you.'

Strangely, it wasn't a colour she'd worn before. She'd always thought it too in-your-face. But in-your-face was the look she was going for tonight, the red having extra impact because the material had a glitter effect, similar to her lipstick and nail varnish. The style of the dress was not her usual style either, being *very* tight. And, whilst it had long sleeves and a high neckline, the back was cut very low, along with a split in the back seam from the hem up to her knees—possibly put there so the occupant of the dress could actually walk.

'You look like you've stepped out of one of those glamorous movies they used to make in the old days,' Jack said. 'Especially with your hair done that way.'

Vivienne's hand lifted to pat the jewelled comb which anchored one side of her hair back from her face, the other side waving down over her shoulder in the way, yes, the movie stars of the forties used to do their hair.

'You really like it?' she said, her voice a wee bit tremulous. Those butterflies were acting up again.

'What's not to like?' Jack replied. 'You look good enough to eat and you know it, so don't come that coy nonsense with me. If ever a look was designed to make an ex-fiancé feel regret and his new fiancée feel jealous, then you've nailed it tonight. I just hope you won't regret it yourself.'

'Why should I?' Vivienne shot back with a surge of sudden defiance. 'I've done nothing to regret.'

'Not yet. But just remember if you fire bullets at people they just might fire some back. But it's too late now. Cinderella is going to the ball.'

Vivienne rolled her eyes. 'I can't see Cinderella wearing a dress like this, can you?'

'Not quite,' he said, and eyed her up and down with a decidedly sexual gaze.

'In that case we're well matched, because you're far from Prince Charming,' she threw back at him. 'Come on, let's get going. The sooner we get there and I say what I have to say, the sooner we can leave.' *And the sooner those butterflies will stop their infernal wing flapping!*

Jack didn't say another word till they were on their

way. Fortunately, when he did speak, it wasn't about tonight.

'Are you all packed and ready for the big move north tomorrow?' he asked.

'Of course,' she replied. 'I'm a very organised person. Everything's already in the boot of my car.'

'I'll drive over to your place in my car around nine and you can follow me up in yours.'

'All right. Do you have the keys to the house?'

'Not yet. We'll have to pick them up on the way. I've also organized for the builder to drop by around one, so that you can meet him. His name's Ken. Ken Struthers.'

'Fine.'

'Are Daryl's folks going to be there tonight?'

Vivienne was taken aback by this abrupt change of topic. 'What? No, no, he's estranged from his family.'

'How come that doesn't surprise me?'

'He said they weren't very nice people. He was put into a foster home when he was only ten.'

'And you believed him?'

That brought Vivienne up short. She sighed. 'Yes, I did at the time. More fool me. But don't worry, that fool has been well and truly put to bed. Daryl could tell me the world was round now and I wouldn't believe him. I despise the man and I aim to tell him so. Like you said, Jack, tonight is all about closure.'

Jack glanced over at Vivienne just as her red-glossed lips pressed hard together in a determined pout.

Oh dear, he thought. It was going to be a difficult night.

CHAPTER TWENTY

SECURITY AT THE Ellison mansion was tight; Jack had to be checked off at the gates as a guest on the guard's list. He even had to show the guy his driver's licence, which rather underlined Vivienne's statement that neither of them had easy-to-recognise celebrity status. There weren't paparazzi obviously lurking about the gate; there was a helicopter hovering which might have been filled with photographers, but more likely more security. Frank Ellison was paranoid when it came to protecting his patch and his privacy.

As he was directed to one of the multitude of parking spaces available in the huge grounds, Jack experienced a measure of pride at how magnificent the house looked at night, lit up by the literally thousands of lights Frank had commissioned him to build in everywhere: the façade, the roof, the garden, not to mention each of the two-dozen stone steps which led up to the impressive entrance.

'Is this the biggest house you've ever built?' Vivienne asked him as he guided her carefully up the steps, his hand on her left elbow.

'By far,' he replied. 'I presume this is the biggest house you've decorated as well.'

'Absolutely. It took me over six months, even with lots of help.'

'Building the house took two years.'

'I can imagine. I hope you made plenty of money out of it.'

He grinned over at her. 'Heaps.'

'Good,' she said, and there was that determined look again.

Once they reached the massive front porch, with only the equally massive front doors separating them from the party inside—you could hear the music from outside—Vivienne sucked in sharply and squared her shoulders.

'It's not too late to change your mind,' Jack said quietly by her side, even as he reached to ring the doorbell.

But it was already too late; both doors flung open before his finger connected with the buzzer.

And there stood Frank Ellison, as huge as his house. Around sixty, he had a large, florid face, and an even larger stomach.

'I told them to keep these damned things open,' he boomed before noticing his new arrivals. 'Jack! You came. I'm so glad you did. And who's this stunning creature by your side?'

He hadn't recognised Vivienne, Jack realised. Of course, she did look different from how she did in her work wardrobe.

But still...

Vivienne thought it was typical of the man that he didn't recognise her. He'd rarely spoken to her during the months she'd worked on this house. They'd only ever had one decent conversation when he'd actually looked at her, and that was the day he'd come to Classic Design to hire their services.

'Money's no object,' he'd said. 'Just make sure everyone else knows that. I want the place to look like it's owned by royalty. Or a filthy-rich sheikh. You got that, girlie?'

She'd got it. And she'd delivered. The place was seriously palatial, from the Italian marble floors to the exquisite furniture—all genuine antiques—the air of opulence enhanced by the seriously expensive artwork hanging on every single wall.

'It's Vivienne, Mr Ellison,' she said with a cool smile. 'Vivienne Swan. I was the interior decorator for this house. Don't you remember me?'

He didn't look embarrassed in the slightest. 'Yes, of course I remember you. I just didn't recognise you in that smashing red dress. So, you and Jack are dating, are you? I didn't realise that when he told me you were the best interior decorator in Sydney. A somewhat biased recommendation, eh, Jack?' he said, with a 'nod nod, wink wink' grin. 'Not that you didn't do a fabulous job, girlie. Actually, both of you did a fabulous job. I couldn't be happier with the finished product. Couldn't be happier tonight all round, with my daughter finally finding herself a bloke man enough to put a bun in her oven. And then to actually agree to marry her!'

Vivienne realised in that instant that Frank Ellison had no idea she'd once been engaged to his daughter's fiancé. He obviously didn't recall her being with Daryl at their house-warming party. He'd probably been too busy impressing his other celebrity guests that night to notice her, or who she was with.

Which was fine by her. She hadn't come here to have a go at Frank Ellison.

The arrival of other guests at that moment had Frank

telling Jack and Vivienne to go inside and mingle whilst he turned his attention elsewhere.

'He doesn't know you were engaged to Daryl,' Jack muttered to her as they walked under the huge chandelier which hung from the ceiling of the massive marble-floored atrium.

'No,' she agreed. 'Maybe Courtney doesn't know, either. Come to think of it, I wasn't wearing an engagement ring when we came to Frank's house-warming party. Daryl had asked me to marry him but I…er… he…um…hadn't bought the ring yet.' No way was she going to admit in front of Jack that she'd eventually bought her own engagement ring. That would be just too humiliating for words. 'She probably only knows what Daryl told her, which would be a pack of lies.'

Jack's laugh was dry. 'Courtney knew about you, Vivienne. I'd put my money on it.'

As if on cue, the girl herself, resplendent in a cocktail dress which made Vivienne's gown look demure, came undulating up the three steps which separated the foyer from the huge sunken living room. Her dress—obviously a one-off made for her—was black and strapless, the beaded bodice cut so low across and between Courtney's impressive and possibly enhanced breasts that it only just covered her nipples. The skirt was black chiffon, flaring out from just under her bust, effectively hiding her baby bump, and ending with a handkerchief hemline which flowed around the girl's ankles, their slender shape shown off by the highest, slinkiest, sparkliest shoes Vivienne had ever seen. Even more sparkly were the exquisite diamond earrings hanging from Courtney's lobes.

Much as she tried, she could not fault the girl's face, with its perfect skin, cutely turned-up nose and pouty mouth, though Vivienne did wonder how much was natural and how much was owed to the skills of a top plastic surgeon. After all, her father wasn't even re-motely handsome, so she hadn't got any beauty genes from him. Obviously they came from her mother, who-ever she was. Frank Ellison had had lots of wives, and they'd all been good-looking. Men like that didn't marry plain women. Even so, Courtney's long mane of creamy blonde hair definitely wasn't real—those dark roots were a dead giveaway—though it did suit her. One could not deny that Courtney Ellison was a very sexy creature all round; Vivienne's admiration for Jack went up a few notches at his having resisted her advances.

Daryl trailed several paces after his fiancée, sip-ping a glass of champagne, not having noticed Vivi-enne as yet. He was looking back over his shoulder at a striking brunette who was smiling invitingly after him. Leopards didn't change their spots, Vivienne re-alised ruefully as her gaze swung from the brunette back to her ex.

There was no doubt Daryl was elegantly handsome in his black dinner suit and bow tie, but not nearly as impressive as Jack. As he made his way slowly across the expansive lobby, Vivienne began to see the weak-ness in Daryl's features, and foppishness in his walk. She even found new criticism in the way he wore his hair, the streaked blond locks flopping onto his fore-head in a style way too young for a man in his thirties.

It pleased Vivienne that she no longer felt one ounce of unhappiness, or jealousy, or envy, over the situation. If anything, she felt a little sorry for Courtney, having Daryl's baby. He would make a horrible father.

'Jack!' Courtney gushed, and reached up to give him a slightly too-long kiss on the cheek, at the same time throwing Vivienne a sharp glance, as though trying to place her. 'How lovely to see you again. Thank you so much for coming. And thank you for the lovely present you sent.'

Vivienne's eyebrows arched. He'd sent them a present?

'My mother always says a girl can't have too many irons,' Jack said with a brilliantly straight face whilst Vivienne suppressed a gasp. He'd sent her an *iron*, this billionaire's daughter who'd never ironed a thing in her life?

Courtney looked startled, betraying that she'd had no idea what he'd actually sent. There were probably myriad unwrapped presents piled high in one of the myriad bedrooms.

Daryl finally caught up with his fiancée, only to see his *ex*-fiancée standing in front of him.

'My God!' he exclaimed, his voice thin and high. 'Vivienne!'

Courtney's blonde head jerked back as she stared at Vivienne, then Daryl, then Jack.

'Is this some kind of cruel joke?' she demanded to know, her porcelain-like cheeks flushing with anger.

'Not at all, Courtney,' Jack replied as smooth as silk. 'Daryl's moved on, and so has Vivienne. She and I have become…good friends. There's no hard feelings over your stealing her fiancé, are there, Vivienne?'

'None at all, darling,' she replied, glad when Jack didn't bat an eyelid at her endearment. She'd decided on the spur of the moment not to bother tearing verbal strips off Daryl. Just being here with Jack by her side was the best revenge. She could see Daryl was shocked, and most put out. And so was Courtney, which meant she'd known about her all along. She might not have recognised her, the same way her self-absorbed and self-centred father hadn't recognised her. But she had known. Suddenly, Vivienne didn't feel sorry for her at all. She was getting what she deserved: Daryl as a husband, with all his vanity, greed and selfishness.

'You did me a good turn, Courtney,' Vivienne added with a brilliant smile as she touched Jack tenderly on the arm.

Courtney's blue eyes darkened appreciably. 'Really,' she bit out.

Her father joining them rather stopped any further conversation on the subject.

'Don't stand around in the foyer, folks,' Frank said expansively. 'Let's go down to where all the food and wine are being served. I would be totally miffed if you didn't taste some of the specialities I ordered in, Jack. And you too, Vivienne. Caviar from Russia and truffles from France, not to mention several cases of their best champagne. Nothing like champagne.'

The next half hour went quite well—which meant without anyone creating a scene—with a none-the-wiser Frank plying Jack and Vivienne with champagne and caviar, whilst Courtney eventually took Daryl off somewhere, hopefully to have a lover's spat. Vivienne wasn't blind. She could see that Courtney was totally miffed. Vivienne was glad that she'd gone to so much trouble with her appearance. She knew she looked good.

Frank finally left them alone and they wandered out onto the massive back terrace, Vivienne happy not to have to make further chitchat with the kind of people Frank courted: all rich snobs who thought they were better than everyone else, just because they could afford habourside mansions and more than one Picasso.

'So I'm darling now, am I?' were Jack's first words as they strolled alongside the well-lit, Olympic-sized pool. There was no one else around. A pool party, it was not, though there were several portable heaters dotted around for warmth.

'Sorry. I couldn't resist. I thought it was a better revenge, his believing I'd moved on almost as quickly as he had. You didn't mind, did you?'

Of course I minded, Jack thought. But it was impossible to say so. Stupid, too. 'Not at all,' he lied. 'I thought you conducted yourself brilliantly. Much better than you saying things you might regret. Dignity is always the best policy.'

'I thought honesty was the best policy.'

'That too.'

'In that case, I want to tell you how much I appreciate having you by my side tonight, Jack. I can honestly say you are more of a man than Daryl could ever be.'

Jack's heart lurched in his chest. Hopefully, it didn't show on his face how much her compliment meant to him. Because, despite her voicing admiration for him, he knew that Vivienne still wasn't ready yet to fall in love again.

'That's sweet of you to say so…darling,' he added with a cheeky smile, determined to keep a light note to the evening. 'I presume you don't want to leave yet?'

'I don't think we should,' Vivienne answered, despite really wanting to. 'Frank might be offended, and he's not a man you should offend. I don't care for myself but he'd be a dangerous enemy for you to have, Jack.'

'I don't give a damn about Ellison. I'll survive without his patronage. But if you like we'll stay a while and stick it to Daryl some more.'

'Good idea. Now, I simply *have* to go to the ladies'. All this champagne. Wait for me here, would you?'

Handing Jack her now empty glass, she turned and made her way slowly back inside.

Jack watched her go, thinking how classy she was. The kind of woman a man would be lucky to marry.

He sighed, then wandered over to the nearest outdoor setting where he put down the two champagne glasses. He was about to turn and walk back towards the house—he'd made up his mind to collect Vivienne and leave—when he saw Daryl slink out of the pool house, hurriedly doing up his trousers. A sexy-looking brunette followed, giggling and sorting out her own dishevelled clothes. When Daryl saw Jack watching them, he said something to the brunette, who hurried off whilst Daryl sauntered over to Jack with a smarmy guilt lurking in his heavy-lidded eyes.

'It's not what you think,' came the cliché.

'Why should you care *what* I think?' Jack returned coldly.

'I don't. I just don't want you to make trouble for me and Courtney.'

'I don't give a damn what you do, mate. Just keep away from Vivienne.'

Daryl laughed. 'I won't be going back there, mate. Trust me on that. She's too screwed up for me. Not only a tidy nut but bloody boring in bed. Lord knows what you see in her. Great body, though. I'll give her that.'

Jack gritted his teeth. Hard. There was only so much a man in love could take. His right fist shot out before he could stop it, connecting with Daryl's decidedly soft stomach with the force of a jackhammer. Daryl made a whooshing sound as he doubled over, all the air rushing from his lungs like a pricked balloon. And then he did something even better than collapsing at Jack's feet. Clutching his stomach, he stupidly tried to straighten up, staggering backwards to the edge of the pool before falling, arms flailing widely, into the water.

He didn't scream, thank goodness; he possibly didn't have enough air left in his lungs. Though he did manage some spluttered expletives once he resurfaced, by which time Vivienne had returned from her trip to the toilet.

'What happened?' she asked Jack on sighting Daryl floundering in the water. 'Is he drunk or what?'

'He hit me!' Daryl spluttered.

'He deserved it,' Jack replied coolly.

Daryl finally made it over to the side of the pool. 'I'll get you,' he threatened. 'I'll tell Frank you assaulted me and he'll ruin you.'

Jack immediately strode over and bent down to grab one of Daryl's hands, crunching his fingers painfully whilst whispering in his ear at the same time. 'You say a single word and I'll tell Courtney all about the brunette I saw you with in the pool house just now.'

That shut him up, especially when Courtney herself made an appearance, also wanting to know what had happened.

'Just an accident, babe,' a sodden Daryl said after Jack hauled him out of the water. 'I bent down to wash my hands and overbalanced. No great drama.'

'But you've ruined your nice new suit!' she wailed.

'For Pete's sake,' he threw back at her, his temper obviously fraying. 'It's just a suit.'

Jack could see the beginning of a nice little argument there. Which was almost as satisfying as hitting the bastard.

'Come on, Vivienne,' he said, and took her arm. 'Let's go home.'

'What did you mean by he deserved it?' she whispered as Jack steered her swiftly back inside the house, across the living room and up the steps to the foyer. 'What did he say to you to make you hit him?'

'Later, Vivienne,' he told her, not sure what reason he would give. Because what Daryl had said would hurt Vivienne and Jack didn't want to do that. Okay, yes, she was excessively tidy, but to call her screwed up was insulting. As for her being boring in bed… What planet was Daryl from to call her that? Vivienne was anything but boring in bed. It was all decidedly odd.

Fortunately, Vivienne held her tongue till they were in the car and safely away. But he should have known that female curiosity would soon get the better of her.

'I can't wait any longer, Jack,' she said when he pulled up at a set of lights. 'I'm dying to know what happened between the two of you. And I want the truth, the whole truth and nothing but the truth.'

Jack winced. 'Are you sure about that, Vivienne?'

'Positive. Look, I just want to know what he said to make you hit him. I've been thinking, and I presume it was something bad about me.'

'Not that bad,' he said.

'But not too complimentary. Out with it, Jack. No lies now. And no watering down. Give it to me straight.'

'Okay,' Jack agreed, seeing that it really was the only way. On the plus side, he could then ask her some questions he'd always wanted to ask. 'He said you were a tidy nut and boring in bed.' He decided to leave out the 'screwed up' part.

He glanced across in time to see her blush fiercely.

'I see,' she said stiffly. 'Well, I guess he was only telling the truth.'

'Don't be ridiculous,' Jack snapped. 'Okay, so you are a bit uptight when it comes to clutter, but that's hardly a crime. As for being boring in bed… Well, you and I both know that's a bald-faced lie,' he added, try-ing to bring a smile to her face.

It didn't.

The lights went green and Jack roared off, upset that the evening looked like it was ending badly.

'I'm not going to let you go all quiet on me, Vivi-enne,' he said firmly when she just sat there in silence. 'I want to know why Daryl said you were boring in bed. Because it doesn't make any damned sense to me.'

CHAPTER TWENTY-ONE

VIVIENNE KNEW BY the look on Jack's face that nothing less than the truth would satisfy him. Which was fair enough, she supposed. She just hoped he wouldn't jump to conclusions over why she'd been different with him sexually. She didn't want him to think that it was because she'd been falling in love with him, or that this process had probably started long before she was aware of it. For how could you not fall in love with a man who'd come to your rescue with flowers and a fascinating job when you needed it most? A man who'd saved your life and held you close, then made love to you endlessly with a passion which had been as healing as it had been wonderful?

But the coup de grâce was the way Jack had stood up for her tonight. Oh…the satisfaction she'd felt when she'd discovered he'd flattened Daryl, and then when he'd said 'he deserved it'.

Jack was her hero, her knight in shining armour. The man she loved. Truly, really loved. What she'd felt for Daryl had been nothing more than a mirage.

But she could not tell Jack that. If she did, he would run a mile. And she couldn't bear that. He might never love her back but she could not voluntarily do anything to lose him. So she would tell him other things. Not lies, exactly, but not the total truth.

'Could this wait till I get home and out of this dress?' she said.

He frowned. 'This isn't some kind of procrastinating ploy, is it, Vivienne? Because I aim to get some answers. Don't go thinking you can avoid it by seducing me.'

Vivienne blinked. Now *there* was a thought! Not the right one, however.

'Don't be silly,' she said. 'I'm just uncomfortable, that's all. This dress is dreadfully tight.'

Jack knew she was stalling but he didn't say anything further, just drove her home and helped her out of the car and inside, where she fairly bolted for the bedroom, telling him she wouldn't be long.

He sat down on the black leather sofa, his determination to get answers deepening with the time she took to emerge. When she finally did, she was wrapped in the same fluffy white dressing gown and slippers that she'd worn on that fateful day he'd come here to hire her less than two weeks ago. He suspected she wasn't wearing anything underneath this time, either. Or not very much. She'd taken the jewelled comb out of her hair, he noted, and spread her hair out onto her shoulders in sexy disarray. As much as she looked good enough to eat, he resolved not to be swayed or distracted from getting those answers he wanted.

'You want coffee?' she asked.

'I wouldn't mind,' he said, standing up and following her out to the kitchen which was as clean and clutter free as always. Seeing her place again—he hadn't been inside there lately—underlined the fact that her tidiness *did* verge on obsessive.

'I still don't have much food to offer you,' she said,

and turned from the kettle to give him a small, some-what wry smile. 'Someone's been taking me out to dinner every night.'

'Lucky you. But I don't want any food, Vivienne. What I do want is for us to talk.'

Vivienne sucked in a deep breath, letting it out slowly as she turned and carried the two mugs of black coffee over to where Jack was already sitting at the kitchen table.

'First things first,' he said. 'Let's go back to Daryl's "boring in bed" accusation. I'm presuming, from what you said, that you weren't the same with him that you are with me. Is that right?'

'Well...um...yes,' she admitted with a small shudder. 'If you must know, I haven't done most of what I've done with you with him.'

Jack's male ego might have been flattered if he didn't still worry she might have been indulging in some kind of crazy act with him, brought on by Daryl dumping her. 'Why was that, do you think? Were you just pretending to be sexy? Acting out some role with me?'

There was no doubting her shock. 'No! I never acted with you, Jack. Never. I loved everything I did with you. I...I'm not sure why I'm so different with you. I just was, right from the start. You made me feel things that Daryl never did. I still don't quite understand it myself. I just know that I love having sex with you and I wouldn't give it up for the world.'

Jack liked the sound of that. 'We do have great chemistry together,' he said. 'Now, whilst we're having an honest chat, do you think you might tell me why your place looks like it does? I don't mean the tidiness part so much. I'm talking about the starkness of the décor. Because let's face it, Vivienne, it's just not you.'

Vivienne's first instinct was to clam up about that. But then she realised that, if she couldn't tell the man she loved, who could she tell?

Still, it wasn't going to be easy. Not that she thought Jack would be judgemental: he'd had some experience with emotionally fragile mothers so he would understand better than most.

She sighed. 'I will have to go way back to the years before my dad left us…'

'I'm listening,' Jack said gently. He could sense her reluctance but wasn't about to let her off the hook.

She looked at him for a long moment before going on. 'Have you ever watched that show on TV about hoarders?'

'I have, actually. Once or twice.' Jack was about to add that he'd been totally disgusted and revolted by the state of some of the houses those people lived in when he stopped himself short.

Vivienne sighed again. 'I can see by the look on your face that the penny has dropped. Yes, my mother was a hoarder.'

Jack wasn't shocked so much as sad. For Vivienne. What kind of childhood would she have had if she'd been forced to grow up in the kind of filthy place he'd seen on that show?

'I see,' he said. And he did. He could imagine that the children of hoarders would either grow up like them or become diametrically opposite. It certainly explained why Vivienne had an obsession with cleanliness and clutter in her own home.

'So is that why your father left in the first place?' he asked.

'Yes. He couldn't bear it any more.'

'Was she always a hoarder?'

'No, not at all. I remember when I was little, Mum always kept the house beautifully. But after my baby brother died—he was only a week old—she became very depressed. Some days she couldn't even get out of bed.'

'Didn't your father take her to a doctor?'

'She wouldn't go.'

Jack nodded. 'So that's when the hoarding started?' he asked.

'Yes. Not only wouldn't she get rid of all the things she'd bought for the baby but she started buying more: clothes. Furniture. Toys. Like Brendan was still alive. We could have outfitted half the babies in Australia with what she bought. She used to go shopping every day, till one day she suddenly refused to leave the house. After that, she discovered online shopping.'

'So your house wasn't dirty, just full of baby clothes?'

'It was dirty too. Impossible to clean rooms when they're full of stuff. There wasn't a room in the house— or a surface anywhere—which was free of things. The kitchen too. Even the sink. In the end, we lived on take-away. The delivered kind.'

'So that's all you ate? Pizzas and rubbish like that?'

'Yes. For a long while. But when I started high school and realised I was getting fat, I put my foot down and demanded healthier food. But Mum wasn't interested in cooking and the kitchen was a disaster area. I tried cleaning it up when I came home from school but the job became overwhelming.

'In the end, I negotiated moving into the master bed-room which had an *en suite* and enough room for me to set up my own small kitchen. Just a microwave and toaster, really, and a small bar fridge which Dad had left behind in his den. I got Mum to give me an allowance from the money Dad sent so that I could buy my own food and clothes. When I was home, I lived in just that room and let the rest of the house go to pot. Of course, I couldn't have any friends over for sleepovers, so I didn't have any close girlfriends till I left school and moved out. No boyfriends, either, of course. By then, I wasn't large on social skills where the opposite sex is concerned. I was a virgin till I was twenty-one, which I dare say is some kind of record these days.'

'I would say it is for someone as beautiful as you. Which you are, Vivienne, inside and out. And brave too. That is a terribly sad story. But you survived, and for that I have nothing but admiration for you. So how long ago was it that your mother had her heart attack?'

Vivienne grimaced. 'She didn't actually have a heart attack. She tripped over the stuff she'd piled up on the stairs, fell down and broke her neck. I warned her that she'd have an accident in the house one day but she wouldn't listen. Of course, after I moved out, things got much worse. The stairs were chock-a-block with things. Not just baby things now, other stuff she didn't need: shoes. Handbags. Lamps. Ornaments. Silly things. When she didn't answer the phone one evening—I used to ring her every night—I came over and found her body at the foot of the stairs.'

'Oh, Vivienne. That must have been dreadful for you.'

'It was,' she choked out, the memory still having the power to upset her. She'd loved her mother, despite everything. Not that she'd ever felt loved in return. Maybe that was why she'd been so susceptible to Daryl. Because he'd told her he loved her all the time; had even made her believe it. That was what had devastated her the most, to find out his declarations of love had been nothing but a lie, right from the start. At least Jack didn't lie to her. She respected that. When she glanced up and saw the concerned look on his face, she smiled a small, sad smile.

'It's all right, Jack,' she said. 'I'm not going to cry. Frankly, in a way, Mum's dying was a relief. Let's face it, she'd been wretchedly unhappy for years and years. I'm surprised she hadn't committed suicide before that. She often threatened it. Anyway, after the funeral I hired a rubbish removal company to clear the house out, then I hired industrial cleaners to clean it from top to bottom. I couldn't bear to do anything in there. It hurt too much to even look at it. Once it was fit to sell, I auctioned it off. I wanted it gone and I didn't care what price I got for it.

'Strangely enough, it sold for an amazingly good price. The agent explained that, despite its slightly dilapidated state, the house was in a prime location and the block of land was large. I got enough money to buy this place and have it totally renovated, with enough left over to attract the likes of Daryl. Till he met someone seriously rich, of course,' she added.

Jack's fingers tightened around the handle of his coffee mug when he heard the bitterness in her voice. How long would it be before she got over that creep? He felt reasonably confident she no longer loved Daryl, but that kind of betrayal was hard to forget and impossible to forgive. It also made a person reluctant to trust.

Patience, Jack, he lectured himself. *Patience.*

'Like I've already told you several times, Vivienne: you're better off without the likes of him. You're still a young woman. You have your whole life ahead of you.' *With me,* he was dying to say but couldn't. Not yet. 'Plenty of time to get married and have children, if that's what you want. Meanwhile, you can afford to be selfish for a while. Do things that give you pleasure. Live for the moment. You're looking forward to making over Francesco's Folly, aren't you?'

Her bleak eyes actually lit up. 'Oh yes.'

'Though, I must insist, I want the decorator I usually have and not the one who did *this* place, thank you very much,' he said bluntly.

She laughed. 'Fair enough.'

'And just think, on top of the pleasure and satisfaction you'll get from doing a brilliant job, you'll have *me* all to yourself every weekend. That can't be too bad, since you like having sex with me so much. And, let's face it, I'm going to be randy as hell after not seeing you all week. You won't be able to keep up with me.'

Vivienne smiled. 'You should know better than to challenge me, boss. I am competitive by nature. And obsessive to boot. I can guarantee you'll be the one to cry for mercy before I do.'

'I have only one thing to say to that, missy.'

'What's that?'

'Bring it on.'

CHAPTER TWENTY-TWO

VIVIENNE WANDERED THROUGH the upstairs apartment, turning on all the lights—it got dark early in the winter—and checking that everything was just so. She'd decided on finishing this area of Francesco's Folly first whilst she lived in one of the downstairs apartments. It was the easiest part to change, but it had still taken close to two months to complete, mainly because some of the furniture she'd ordered had taken six weeks to arrive. But she was extremely happy with the results and she thought Jack would be too.

She hadn't let him see any of it yet, teasing him that it was all black and white and horribly minimalist, with nothing but black leather, glass furniture and fake Picassos on the walls.

Vivienne could not wait for Jack to arrive tonight, because tonight was the big reveal. She felt as excited as a kid on Christmas morning, glancing at her watch as she hurried downstairs and along past the pool to the balcony which was closest to the driveway. It was nearly six. He would be here soon; he usually left Sydney around three. Friday afternoon traffic was tricky, though. He sometimes got held up getting out of the city, or on the motorway. But if that was the case he would ring her and let her know he was running late, and she'd received no such call this afternoon.

He was very considerate that way. He also brought her the most gorgeous bunch of red roses every Friday, which she found so sweet. It made her hope that his feelings for her were gradually becoming as strong as her feelings for him. Then, one day, he might decide he didn't want to stay a bachelor for ever; that marriage and children and a life here at Francesco's Folly was what he wanted after all.

But she didn't let her hopes get too high. Jack was still very passionate with her. Their weekends together were wonderful, but a few times lately she had caught him falling oddly silent and looking off into the distance. They would often sit and share a bottle of wine on the balcony on a Saturday afternoon. Last weekend, when she had asked him what he was thinking about, he'd said nothing much. Just life. It was an odd answer for him. Odd for him to sit and think like that. He wasn't overly keen on thinking.

Vivienne could not help but worry that he might break off their relationship once Francesco's Folly was finished. It was a depressing thought, but one which she refused to entertain too often. For now, she was happy. Or as happy as a girl could be under the circumstances. Still, she was careful not to do or say anything which might spoil the rest of their time together. She never told him that she loved him, even when the words were in danger of tripping off the end of her tongue—especially when he was making love to her. She always bit her tongue and said something else. Or nothing at all.

Her heart lifted as it always did when she saw headlights turn into the driveway at the bottom of the hill. Jack was home. Safely home.

Whirling, she ran inside so that she could be there, waiting for him when he came in. She didn't run all the way to the front door. That would have been too needy. Too clingy. She went to the kitchen, ostensibly to check that the curry she was making was fine. Which, of course, it was. She always cooked for him on a Friday night, knowing he would be too tired after his long drive to take her out anywhere. Besides, she liked to conserve his energy for other things.

'Honey, I'm home,' he called out as he walked in, one arm full of red roses as usual. And a bottle of champagne in the other.

'Is this to celebrate the big reveal?' she said, beaming.

For a split second, he hesitated to answer. And then he bent to give her a brief peck on the lips. 'But of course. What else?'

Why, she wondered, did his voice sound so odd, as though he was disappointed about something? Had she said something wrong? Done something wrong?

'I made your favourite curry,' she raced on as she put the bottle of champagne in the fridge. When she turned, she found him arranging the roses in the vase which was always at the ready on the pine counter. 'You know you don't have to buy me flowers *every* week.'

'But I like to,' he said, and smiled at her. 'Come on, best show me Francesco's apartment before we do anything else. I know that's what you want to do. You've been talking about nothing else every night this week. But be warned, if I don't like it, you're in big trouble.'

'Oh dear,' she said with mock worry, because she was sure he was going to like it.

He did. In fact, he *loved* it, even the fact that she had had all the walls stripped back and painted white. Not a stark white, however; a soft off-white which had a hint of cream in it. It was the perfect backdrop for the furniture she'd chosen: Mediterranean style pieces made of richly grained wood, which gave the place the kind of solid but warm feel she'd seen in pictures of Tuscan villas she'd sourced on the Internet. The deep plump sofas and chairs she'd chosen for the living room were covered in soft linens in warm colours: creams, fawns and a buttery yellow, with the occasional splash of olive-green thrown in. The fireplace remained, its once-heavy wooden surround replaced by Italian marble made in a warm brown shot with gold streaks.

The two *en suite* bathrooms and kitchen were white, of course, but she'd used the same brown marble on the counter tops and dual vanities. The fittings were gold—though not real gold—evoking quality without being over the top. The living areas were tiled in large cream tiles, with thick rugs dotted here and there for warmth and colour. The carpets in the bedrooms were sable, which went well with everything.

What pleased Jack the most—and consequently thrilled Vivienne—was her choice of artwork, both for the walls inside the apartment and the art gallery on the top landing. Not originals and not worth a fortune, either: prints of famous landscapes and seascapes, which definitely looked like things he would recognise: beautiful beaches and graceful sailing boats. Stately mountains and picturesque valleys. Their frames were expensive, however. Some were gilt, some shabby-chic white, depending on where they were positioned.

'You like, boss?' she said cheekily when he just stood staring at one seascape for a long time. It was hanging over the fireplace in the living room, and was of a spectacular beach on a rugged coastline.

'Too much,' he replied.

'How can you like anything too much?' It was a peculiar thing to say.

He didn't answer her, just turned away from the picture abruptly and strode across to the sliding glass doors which led out onto the balcony. He reefed one back and stepped out into the cold night air, going over to where the rusted and broken railing had been replaced by clear panels of toughened glass. Vivienne followed him out there, unsure what was happening here. He stood at the railing for a long time in silence before turning and facing a by-then shivering Vivienne. Inside was air-conditioned, but outside was now very chilly.

'I'm sorry,' he said abruptly. 'I thought I could do this but I can't. Not any longer.'

'Do what?' Vivienne asked, suddenly feeling sick to the stomach.

'Wait…till Francesco's Folly is finished.'

So this was it, she thought despairingly. He was going to break it off with her.

She wanted to scream that she wasn't ready yet. That she needed longer with him.

But then she realised that no amount of time would ever be enough. If he didn't care about her the way she cared about him, then what was the point of delaying things?

'So what is it you're trying to say, Jack?' she said, desperately trying to hide her wretchedness. 'You don't want me any more? Is that it?'

His eyes widened, his head jerking back. 'Good God, woman, nothing could be further from the truth. Not *want* you any more? I want you every minute of every day. I love you, Vivienne, so much that not being able to say the words is slowly killing me. I can't play this game any more. I thought I could wait till you fell in love with me before I said anything but I find I can't. Seeing this place tonight…this absolutely glorious place…I don't want to ever live here by myself. I want to live here with you. As husband and wife.'

'Husband and wife?' she choked out.

Jack could see that he'd shocked her but nothing was going to stop him now that he'd opened his mouth and said something. 'Yes, I know I said I didn't want to get married and have children,' he raved on. 'But that was before I fell in love with you, Vivienne. Love changes things. It makes you want more. And, yes, I know it's probably still too soon for you. But do you think you might possibly come to love me one day? You already like me, I know, and you like having sex with me, so loving me is not such a big leap.

'I promise you that, if you marry me, I will do everything in my power to make you happy. I will never cheat on you. Never. And I'll give you anything you want. You can have a hundred children, if that's what you want. No, wait…perhaps not that many…but two or three, or even four, I would consider. Three is not a good number. Yes, four would be good. So what do you say, my darling, beautiful Vivienne? Would you at least think about it?'

She didn't say a single word. She just stared at him, then burst into tears.

Oh God, Jack thought frantically. What did that mean? Was she happy or sad?

Naturally, he gathered her into his arms—*naturally*—holding her against him till the weeping subsided to the occasional hiccup. By which time Jack was frozen to death standing out there in the wind.

'I think we should go inside,' he said and steered

her back into the living room, shutting the door behind them.

'I'm sorry,' he said unhappily. 'I shouldn't have said
anything. I told myself to be patient but I'm not a patient
man. Now I guess I've ruined everything.'

'No no,' she denied hurriedly, her green eyes glistening as she stared up at him. 'You haven't ruined
anything.'

'I haven't?'

'Jack, I've been in love with you for ages.'

'You have?'

'Yes. I didn't want to say anything either, because I
was hoping you might fall in love with me in the end.
And, yes, of course I'll marry you, my wonderful, marvellous, adorable, darling Jack.' And she reached up to
lay two warm hands against his still-cold cheeks.

It was weird, Jack thought, that happiness could
make a grown man cry. He struggled to blink away
the moisture which suddenly pooled in his eyes. But
it was no use. This was one battle he would not win.

And then it was *her* hugging *him*, telling him over
and over how much she loved him. They cried together,
then kissed, then laughed at each other, calling each
other silly fools for not being honest. After that, they
went downstairs and opened the champagne to celebrate their happiness before heading back upstairs to
cement their love the way couples had been cementing
their love since time began.

The curry wasn't eaten till later that night. Much,
much later.

CHAPTER TWENTY-THREE

IT WAS EARLY summer, three weeks before Christmas. The sky was clear and blue, the air warm and the bride very beautiful.

Not that his Vivienne was ever anything short of beautiful, Jack thought as he held both her hands and looked deep into her lovely green eyes.

They were standing on the same balcony where it had begun all those months ago. The marriage celebrant stood with his back to the view whilst the guests gathered on each side of the bride and groom to witness the ceremony. Not that there were all that many guests. Aside from Jack's mother and George, there was only Marion and her new English husband, Will, along with Jack's two sisters, husbands and children. Of course, Jack's family already adored Vivienne. But who could not? She was a genuinely lovely person.

Jack had bought her an engagement ring the very next day after his proposal, a large baguette diamond with emeralds on the shoulders to match her eyes. But they'd waited till Francesco's Folly's refurbishment was actually complete to get married.

Painted white now, with a new terracotta roof, it sat on top of its hill, standing out like a sparkling jewel, surrounded by the lush green of the surrounding bushland. Inside, the rest of the house was totally trans-

formed. Vivienne had given full rein to her design
skills, not making any silly compromises just because
she would be living there permanently now. It seemed
that telling him about her mother's hoarding had somehow freed her of the anxiety which she associated with
clutter, though she still wasn't fond of rooms being over-
furnished or overdone. Less was sometimes more, she'd
told Jack.

As for colour schemes, she obviously preferred neutral
colours, with just splashes of accent colours. She had let
her head go a bit with the two apartments downstairs, despite still sticking to her base of white walls, white kitchens and white bathrooms. But there was a lot more colour.

Because children would be occupying the rooms,
she'd selected leather lounges and chairs as they were
more easy care. And nothing pale: reds and blacks.
She'd also used black granite on the various counter
tops instead of the brown marble that she'd used upstairs. Again, saying she was thinking of the children,
she'd had several bookcases built in to the living rooms
to accommodate toys, knick-knacks, photographs and,
yes, the odd book or two. Not that children read that
much anymore, Jack realised. It was all games consoles
and tablets. Jack had been pleased when Vivienne had
bought herself a bookcase recently to go in the living
room upstairs, a lovely old antique one which was now
overflowing with thrillers, none of which Jack had read.
Though he kept meaning to.

Vivienne had never returned to live in Sydney, selling her Sydney apartment to Marion and Will. For a
bargain price, Jack thought. Not that he cared. He had
plenty of money. They'd decided that once the house
was finished Jack would divide his time equally between here and Sydney until he could wind up his business down there and start another building company up

in the Newcastle area. Vivienne had already set up her own website for a boutique design business, and was receiving quite a few offers of work. She hadn't wanted to try for a baby until they were married—and Jack aimed to get onto that project asap. He was really looking forward to becoming a dad—more than he would have thought possible.

Vivienne giving his fingers a squeeze brought him back to the moment at hand.

'We're now man and wife,' she said with a soft, sweet smile. 'You can kiss me if you like.'

He kissed her while everyone clapped.

'So where were you when the ceremony was taking place?' she whispered after his lips lifted enough for her to speak.

'I was thinking about making you a mother tonight.'

'It doesn't always happen as quickly as that, Jack. We might have to wait months.'

Vivienne was right. She didn't become a mother that night. Though she did fall pregnant early in the New Year. With a boy.

As for Francesco's Folly, it was always a happy home, full of laughter and love. Eventually, Jack and Vivienne had four children: two boys and two girls. Vivienne continued to work, though only part-time. And Jack? He gave up being a workaholic and devoted a lot more time to his family. His mother never married George. But they were still happy, living next to each other and going on endless holidays together. Jack's two sisters and their families often came to stay, especially at Christmas, when all the cousins would have a great time together, having barbeques and going to the beach. In fact, lots of people came to stay with them at Francesco's Folly.

Marion and Will. Even Nigel and his wife. It was that kind of house.

Sometimes, on a balmy summer evening, when Vivienne sat on her favourite balcony sipping a deliciously chilled white wine and drinking in the glorious view, she imagined Francesco up in heaven looking down at her and feeling very content that his lovely home was being lived in and loved. And it was in those moments that she would thank God for saving her from disaster all those years ago and sending her a man like Jack to love.

Her life was not perfect. Whose life was? But it was very good. Very good indeed.

* * * * *

BRING IT ON

BY
KIRA SINCLAIR

When not working as an office manager for a project management firm or juggling plot lines, **Kira Sinclair** spends her time on a small farm in north Alabama with her wonderful husband, two amazing daughters and a menagerie of animals. It's amazing to see how this self-proclaimed city girl has (or has not, depending on who you ask) adapted to country life. Kira enjoys hearing from her readers at www.KiraSinclair.com. Or stop by www.writingplayground.blogspot.com and join in the fight to stop the acquisition of an alpaca.

I want to dedicate this book to my wonderful editor,
Laura Barth. not only is she a joy to work with, but
her strengths are a perfect balance for my weaknesses.
She helps me write the best book possible.
Laura, here's definite proof that together
we can figure anything out. Thank you!

1

"IF ANY MAN CAN SHOW just cause why this man and this woman should not be joined in holy matrimony, let him speak now or forever hold his peace."

Lena Fuller's stomach rolled as if she'd just gorged herself on junk food and then gotten on the worst roller coaster. Was it her imagination, or was every person inside the church holding their breath?

No, wait, that was just her.

But she wasn't imagining that everyone was staring at her. Although she supposed wearing a wedding dress made that a given.

She looked across at the man she was marrying. Wyn Rand. Flawless features. Aristocratic D.C. family. Challenging job. Limitless future.

Wyn was the perfect man for her. Nothing like the men her mother had paraded through her childhood. He respected her and appreciated her intelligence. He didn't treat her like a piece of meat, assuming the only thing she was good for was warming his bed.

All of her friends were jealous that she'd snagged

such a wonderful man. So why were the butterflies threatening to break through her stomach in a replay of *Alien?*

Her eyes drifted from Wyn with his pearly-white smile and confident gaze to the line of men standing diagonally behind him. Her gaze skipped purposely to Colt Douglas, one of her best friends.

He was three back in line, put there because she'd asked Wyn to include him in the wedding party. Wyn had never liked Colt, although Lena still didn't understand why. But Wyn had reluctantly acquiesced because it had been so important to her. She wanted—needed—Colt standing beside her on this important day.

She wasn't sure what she was looking for, maybe a smile of encouragement or a calm certainty she couldn't seem to find inside herself. It definitely wasn't the intense, laser-sharp stare Colt leveled at her. Nor the beginnings of a frown as the space between his brows wrinkled. Lena felt an answering pucker pull at her face.

No, wait, she should be smiling.

"I object." The small voice behind her quivered, but everyone heard the words anyway.

And suddenly Lena could breathe again.

Wyn's shocked gaze morphed into a glare that he directed somewhere over her shoulder. Something in the back of the church clattered loudly against the stone floor. The preacher sputtered, "Excuse me? I—I've never actually had anyone object."

No, probably not.

The preacher looked at her with a befuddled expression, as if she could tell him what to do next. As if this happened to her on a regular basis.

"I can't let you do this, Lena. I'm in love with Wyn. We've been having an affair for the last two months." Mitzi, her youngest aunt's oldest daughter, raced from the line of bridesmaids to stand between her and Wyn.

Lena focused in on her cousin's face. Peaches-and-cream beautiful, her eyes sparkling with the innocence of youth. An innocence she had no doubt this girl was about to lose. Wyn's mother was not going to be happy, and the woman was connected enough to make Mitzi's life hell. Lena tried to dredge up some sympathy for her but couldn't.

She watched mutely as Wyn attempted to pull Mitzi out from between them, to make her disappear, as if he could make the problem go away.

He hadn't even tried to deny it. And deep down, Lena wasn't surprised. Wyn didn't ask forgiveness of anyone…especially his future wife. Former future wife.

Mitzi leaned forward, straining against Wyn's hold. "I'm so sorry."

Yeah, right.

"I didn't mean for it to happen, Lena, honest. I ran into him at a club one weekend. We had a few drinks. One thing led to another."

Despite the shock and pressure suffusing her chest, Lena's own temper began to break through. How could this all be happening? On her wedding day.

"If you tell me he slipped and his dick fell into your vagina I'm going to strangle you."

A nervous titter went up from the congregation

beside her. Lena shot the entire mob a glare. Several of
them stirred, the century-old wooden pews creaking
beneath the weight of their guilty consciences.

"Mitzi, shut up." The first words Wyn bothered to
speak and they were seriously less than helpful.

Around Lena chaos finally erupted. A cacophony of
noise reached out to grab her. Pain burst through her
chest when she looked into Wyn's eyes and realized that
it was true. Guests talked to, at and above each other,
making it difficult to pick out single voices from the
crowd.

Her mother's high-pitched squeal, "I always said
your daughter was a whore," joined her aunt's "At least
she isn't a stuck-up snob who thinks she's better than
everyone else."

Lena cringed at her aunt's words. She was not a snob.
She just preferred not to associate with her mother's
family. Frankly, they were all cut from the same self-
absorbed, overly emotional cloth and she just didn't
have the energy to deal with them. Putting up with her
mother was draining enough.

Two of her cousins, Barley and Matthew, grabbed
Mitzi's arms and tried to pull her away from the mass
of people pouring up onto the steps of the sanctuary.
Lena's best friends had rounded on the poor girl, their
faces livid as they yelled at her for ruining Lena's wedding. And through it all, Wyn wouldn't let Mitzi go.

Lena stood in the center of it all, the motion and
noise rushing past her, completely ignored.

Lena stared at her cousin. Nineteen. The girl was at

least eight years younger than Wyn. And in maturity and experience, he was light-years ahead.

A red haze filtered across Lena's vision. She closed the few steps that had separated her from Wyn and hauled back and slapped him. "Bastard."

Wyn looked stunned. Unfortunately, the livid red handprint across his cheek did nothing to dampen his perfect New England aristocratic good looks. For that, she hauled off and slapped him again.

Spinning on her heel, Lena tried to walk away, but the crowd of people pressed in around her. Her mother. Her cousin. Her best friends. Wyn. Wyn's mother. The people who moments ago had ignored her in favor of yelling at each other suddenly wouldn't let her leave.

Their fingers plucked at her. Someone stepped on her train. The dress had cost her six months' salary but had been worth every penny. She'd dreamed of what she would wear on this day ever since she was six, and the reality had been perfect. *Had* being the operative word.

The nasty sound of ripping satin and tulle made her cringe and the ping of crystal beads as they hit the marble floor made her want to scream. Her body jerked, straining against the phantom hold. And then she was blessedly free.

People, flower petals and sequins trailed in her wake as she raced down the aisle. She stumbled on the torn train, stopping long enough to scoop up the material and throw it over her elbow.

God, she must look a sight.

Her veil clouded around her face, obscuring her

vision and irritating the hell out of her. Lena reached
up, yanked the thing off and threw it at someone as she
flew by.

"Don't do anything rash, Lena. I'm sure you can
work this out, dear," Diane, Wyn's mother, yelled
behind her. The woman must really be panicked if she
was willing to make that kind of public declaration.
Diane was the perfect D.C. wife who spent her days
organizing charitable events but didn't have an identity
outside of her family and husband. Her face was frozen
in place by too much Botox. Her hair was pulled back
so tightly Lena wondered how the woman didn't have a
permanent headache. And even on this day, her trademark single strand of pearls draped across the conser-
vative neckline of her plum-colored dress.

That was what she'd almost signed up for. Relief
washed over her.

But it was short-lived. Everywhere she looked there
were people. Family, strangers, friends, enemies. All
crying, yelling and full of pity.

She couldn't take it. It was all too much.

Pressing her hands over her ears, Lena looked for a
way out.

She was halfway across the church when a calm in
the center of the storm appeared. Colt stood beside the
heavy wooden doors at the back of the church. His long
and languid body was propped against the elegantly
carved frame, both hands shoved into the pockets of
his tux pants, one ankle crossed over the other as if he
was just hanging out there, waiting.

He wasn't yelling. He wasn't freaking out.

She met his eyes, beautiful calm green eyes, so familiar and friendly. No pity or sorrow or anger or anything else, just Colt.

Relief pulsed beneath her skin, along with the urgent need to get out.

Her heels clicked against hard stone as she hurried toward Colt. Skidding to a halt, she looked into his eyes and said breathlessly, "Take me home."

"GET ME OUT OF THIS THING," she growled the minute her apartment door closed.

Not waiting for Colt to do as she'd asked, Lena craned her arms behind her, scrabbling at the tiny row of buttons running down the length of her spine. She struggled, twisting, trying in vain to reach them all and rid herself of the mountain of satin she'd crushed into the tiny passenger seat of his Porsche. That car definitely had not been made to hold two people and a wedding gown.

Brushing her fingers out of the way, Colt said, "Let me," and finished the job for her.

The slight tremor in her hands did not go unnoticed and Colt fought the urge—once again—to drive back to the church and beat the shit out of that sorry excuse for a man she'd almost married. The only thing that stopped him was knowing Lena wouldn't want him to make a scene. She hated drama. Never wanted to be the center of attention. While it would definitely make him feel better, it wouldn't do her any good.

He just hated to see her upset.

The bottom button had barely popped free before

she was pushing the voluminous mess off her shoulders and down her body. Pulling at the slip beneath, she left the lump of satin behind. Miraculously, it retained its shape, a sad white bell of material with a hole where her body should have been.

She blew out a sigh of relief, pushing the swell of her breasts against the edge of the full-length bra that skimmed over her hips and waist. Colt tried to ignore the way his mouth went dry, telling himself it was a normal male reaction to any woman undressing in front of him.

This was Lena. They'd been friends since they were kids. And if he'd occasionally woken from erotic dreams about her in the past, he told himself that it was simply the pitfall of having a female friend. Men thought about sex all the time, right? It was inevitable that his brain would put two and two together eventually.

Lena disappeared down the hallway. Deciding not to follow, Colt went into the kitchen and filled a wineglass from the open bottle he found in the fridge. It was the same bottle that had been there when he'd visited three months ago on his way to film a piece in Spain. He remembered because he'd come from Alaska where the frigid temperatures had played havoc with the film equipment. He'd brought the bottle with him, picking it up in the airport. He could no longer recall which airport it had been, they all started to look the same after a while.

Colt shook his head, hoping the wine hadn't spoiled. Yelling down the hall, he asked, "What now, Lee?"

She stuck her head around the corner, her bare shoulders just visible and her lips twisting into a crooked line. "I have no idea," she said before disappearing again.

Taking a sip of the chilled wine, he stopped in the open doorway of the kitchen, leaning against the jamb. The place was definitely bare. Lena had spent a lot of time and energy filling her apartment with things that mattered. It had been comfortable, warm and welcoming. This place had always been her pride and joy.

Boxes were stacked in the corner. He could see the neat labeling from here and knew she probably had a master list tucked into a binder cataloguing which box held what. The whole thing was depressing.

Lena returned wearing an oversize T-shirt and a pair of black leggings. Her hair, previously arranged into a twist that had probably taken hours, was now piled haphazardly on top of her head, tufts sticking out in every direction. In that moment she reminded him so much of the young girl he'd met so many years ago.

They'd both been ten the summer Lena and her mother moved into the estate next door. They'd become fast friends, inseparable. She'd spent more time at his house than hers, blending seamlessly into his family. His parents had treated her like one of their own.

When she'd left nine months later he'd been so upset. His parents had given Lena a laptop so they could keep in touch. And they had, building a friendship on emails, phone calls and brief visits here and there that had lasted through distance and time.

He hadn't seen that carefree girl in a very long time.

He wasn't sure when she'd disappeared—probably when her mother was dragging her all over the world. Or maybe after his parents' fatal accident. His life had been falling apart and she'd been holding together the pieces for him. Or possibly while he was rushing from one corner of the globe to another, working his butt off trying to prove his talents as a photographer and documentarian were more important than his bank account and family name.

Sure, he could have bought a production company and hired himself to direct any film he wanted, but that wouldn't prove he had the skills to make it on his own.

Staring at Lena, he wondered what else he'd missed in the months and years they'd been separated. And whether he could have prevented the debacle at the church if he'd been here more than a few days at a time.

Closing the space between them, he held out the wine he'd poured for her. With a sad smile, she took a long swallow. Cradling the glass against her body, her mouth twisted over the rim. "I think it's going to take more than some wine to fix this one."

Unfortunately she was right, and her family would likely descend at any moment. "This probably isn't the best place to hide. Maybe you should get away for a few days?" he suggested. "Let things die down a bit before you have to deal with everything."

"I can't afford to go anywhere. I spent all my savings on the dress." She gestured halfheartedly to the pile of satin still sitting behind them in the entranceway.

"What about the honeymoon?"

"Wyn paid for it," she said slowly, drawing out the

words as she apparently turned over the idea. "But I've got all of the travel documents."

For the first time since he'd walked into the church, Colt felt a genuine smile tug at his lips. "Even better. Where was he going to take you?"

A spark flickered in her eyes for just a moment as she told him, "To a secluded Caribbean resort off the coast of St. Lucia. It's supposed to be upscale, adults only. I was really looking forward to it."

"Well then, I think it's the least the bastard owes you."

"No, I can't. Besides, I wouldn't want to go by myself. That would just be…depressing."

"So take a friend."

Lena's head cocked to the side as she studied him for several moments. "What are you doing for the next week?"

"No, I didn't mean me," he sputtered.

"Why not? I haven't seen you in forever. The last time you were in town hardly counts. You were so jet-lagged you spent half your time sleeping."

Colt could see the hope in Lena's eyes. He hated to disappoint her. "I was hoping to be in Peru to film a documentary about an exciting archaeological find, but the producer chose another director."

"I'm so sorry, Colt. I know you really wanted to land that one. Why didn't you tell me when you found out?"

"You were all wrapped up in the wedding plans. Besides, it isn't important. Something else will come along. It always does."

He tried to hide his disappointment, but probably

failed miserably. The job was perfect, everything he'd been working and waiting for. A great opportunity, an interesting subject and a challenging location.

Lena didn't seem to pick up on his lie, though; she was understandably preoccupied with her own disappointment.

"So there's no reason you can't go with me. Come on. Fruity drinks and lounge chairs on the beach. Sleeping late, five-star meals. You know you want to."

He opened his mouth to say no again, but as her eyes went misty with unshed tears, Colt realized it was a losing battle. When she said, "Please, Colt, I need you," it was the final nail in his coffin.

"Fine." He sighed, and tried to ignore the tremble of her bottom lip when she wrapped her arms around his body and squeezed tight.

"Thank you," she whispered against his skin, her nose buried in the crook of his neck.

Her breath tickled and something thick tightened in the back of his throat. He ignored it.

He held her, knowing what she needed right now more than anything was a friend. But the moment was interrupted when a loud knock sounded on the door.

"Lena, let me in." A man's voice boomed through the closed door.

Colt didn't have to ask who was on the other side. The stiffening of Lena's muscles beneath the circle of his arms said it all.

Jerking away from him, she faced the door, but didn't actually move to open it. "Go away, Wyn. I don't want to talk to you right now."

"Fine, but your mother gave me your suitcase."

Lena cursed under her breath. "Of course she did. Remind me to thank her." She rolled her eyes and grimaced. "Right after I kill her."

Shaking her head, Lena headed for the door. Colt reached out to stop her, but she was too fast. "You don't have to let him in."

"I do if I want any clothes to wear on the island. I wonder how long it took my mother to realize she could hand Wyn the perfect excuse to make me see him."

Not long, Colt guessed. The woman was flighty, but she was also calculating. From everything Lena had told him about her childhood—which wasn't much— he'd gathered her mother had spent her entire life moving from man to man—and dragging Lena behind her. Her only valuable skills seemed to be charming and wheedling her way into whatever she wanted.

The minute Lena opened the door, Wyn pushed past her. However, he slammed to a halt the minute he saw Colt. With a dark scowl on his face, he said, "What's he doing here?"

Colt knew Wyn had never liked him, but then the feeling had been mutual, so he didn't exactly hold that against him. What he did have a problem with was the way he'd treated Lena.

She deserved better.

"Give me one good reason. That's all I need," Colt promised in a calm and even voice, taking a menacing step towards him.

Lena inserted herself in the middle, splitting a hard

stare between them. Tension simmered as they both glared across the top of Lena's head.

"Stop it, both of you."

Wyn took a step forward, but she planted her hand hard into the center of his chest, stopping him in his tracks. The minute her palm collided with him, she recoiled. A knowing smirk touched Colt's lips and he enjoyed the way Wyn's mouth tightened into a hard line.

"Thanks for returning my suitcase. You can go now."

Wyn tried to reach for her, but she scooted backward, straight into Colt. For a minute she jerked the other way, but as soon as her mind caught up and she realized he wasn't a threat, she leaned gratefully against the solid line of his body.

"Lena, we need to talk," Wyn said, grinding the words out between clenched teeth.

"I have nothing to say."

"Okay, then just listen."

"I don't want to hear it. All I want is for you to leave."

"Look, we still have the honeymoon. Why don't we go away? See if we can fix this. I mean, see if I can fix this."

Lena shook her head, sadness clouding her eyes. Colt wanted to rush to her defense, to stand between them both and defend her, but he realized she didn't need his help. She was perfectly capable of handling this on her own. She'd always been a strong woman—it was something he admired about her.

"I'm not going anywhere with you. I am, however, taking the trip that you promised me. I think it's the least that you owe me. A chance to get away, sort through some things. Maybe after I get back I'll be ready to talk to you, but don't think for a second that means I'll ever take you back. I experienced enough dysfunctional, toxic relationships with my mother. I have no intention of falling into one myself."

A hard glint entered Wyn's eyes. He wasn't happy, but then there wasn't much he could do about it. What did it say about Colt that he delighted in seeing the other man thwarted?

"What if I just show up?"

"I wouldn't do that if I were you. Besides, I'm not going alone. Colt is coming with me."

Wyn's body bowed tight with anger. Colt had no doubt that it was barely in check. Taking a deliberate step forward, Colt drew Wyn's glittering gaze.

"I always knew there was something more between you two."

Lena let out an exasperated sound, as if this was ground they'd covered more than once and she was sick of traveling it. "How many times do I have to tell you? There's nothing between us. Hell, I barely see him. Don't paint me with your brush just because you're feeling guilty at being caught."

Wyn's teeth ground together. Colt could hear them from where he stood several feet away. If the man had come here to beg forgiveness, he certainly had an ass-backward way of doing it. But Colt had no intention of pointing that out.

"Fine. Enjoy your trip." Looking Colt square in the eyes, Wyn said, "I hope you get sunburned."

Colt delighted in being able to smile at him and promise, "Don't worry about me. I never burn. And I swear I'll keep Lena good and covered up. Or even better, out of the sun altogether. I wonder what else there is to do on a romantic tropical island besides swim?"

2

THE LAST TWENTY-FOUR HOURS had been hell. Sure, Colt had upgraded them both to first class but a delayed flight, two hours sitting on the tarmac, a missed connection and nine hours in the Atlanta airport were not how she'd envisioned the trip beginning. Of course, nothing about the past day had happened as planned.

But they were here now and that was what mattered.

The island was about forty-five minutes by ferry from St. Lucia. The ride over had been amazing—bright blue sky, therapeutic sunshine and a brisk tropical breeze that had helped to clear the jetlag cobwebs from her brain.

When Wyn had told her he'd booked them at Escape, Lena had checked the place out online. The resort, the only thing on Île du Coeur, had a volatile and romantic history. The small island had originally been a cocoa plantation but had been turned into a boutique resort about fifty years ago. It had been renovated, added onto, changed hands multiple times and let fall into disrepair until the current owner had purchased it almost three years ago. The place was now billed as an adult-only tropical retreat. Small and intimate, lush and seductive, perfect for a honeymoon.

Apparently, there was a local legend to the name of the place. *Île du Coeur* literally translated meant Heart Island. Supposedly, everyone who visited found their heart's desire—whether it was what they were looking for or not. Lena had her doubts, but she had to admit that it was a great marketing angle.

Lena had been surprised that Wyn had sprung for the most expensive bungalow at an already pricey resort. The man came from money, but he was very careful about how he spent it. His frugal nature was one of the things that had attracted her to Wyn in the first place. Considering where she'd come from, that quality had been extremely important to Lena.

Her mother had been...erratic. Hell, she was still unreliable. Using her ethereal beauty and fragility, she'd spent her life conning a succession of men into taking care of her. But the arrangement was never permanent. It had been a good year if Lena didn't have to change schools more than once. And that was assuming her mother actually enrolled her. Sure, she'd lived in Europe, Brazil, D.C., New York and possibly every state in between, and she'd hated every last second of it. Except for those few months with Colt and his family. That was the only time she'd ever felt that she belonged.

All she'd ever wanted was to find someplace permanent, to grow some roots. Someplace that wouldn't change in the middle of the night when the wife discovered the mistress, and Lena and her mother were thrown out on their ear.

The only contact she'd ever had from her father was the monthly check that provided the only steady income they had. Unfortunately, it wasn't enough to keep her mother in the lifestyle she preferred. Lena had often wondered if her mother had gotten pregnant on purpose, just to ensure money would come from somewhere. She'd never been brave enough to ask. Probably because she'd been afraid of what the answer might be.

Normally Lena wouldn't have been one to splurge on unnecessary luxuries, but whatever Wyn had spent on the honeymoon had been worth every penny.

The island was gorgeous, just what she'd expected. Lush colors—green grass, red, pink and yellow flowers, rough brown trunks of towering palm trees and clear turquoise water—surrounded her. The pebbled path leading from the pier to the main building wound through perfect landscaping. She could hear laughter and music floating on the warm sultry air.

The grand facade of the plantation house greeted them. Antique wood and faded walls lent an aura of old-world charm and history that just couldn't be faked. A larger more modern building rose up behind the house. No doubt it had been added at some point to expand the hotel space.

Lena spun on the path trying to take it all in as Colt held the door open for her. Ducking beneath his outstretched arm, she scooted past. The minute her body brushed against his, an unexpected tension stole into her limbs. It wasn't the first time she'd had this kind of reaction to Colt, although it had been a while. She groaned inwardly. Why did the physical reaction always have to blindside her? It was nothing. Chemistry. Shaking it off, she tried to focus on the lobby.

Polished wooden floors, hand-carved molding and period fabrics covering the chairs all gave the space an air of authenticity that immediately charmed her. From across the room a cheerful woman with friendly eyes asked, "Checking in?"

Lena nodded, the first genuine smile she'd felt in days on her face. "Lena Fuller."

"Rand," Colt's deep voice rumbled behind her.

She whipped her head around to look at him. "What?"

"I imagine they'd have you listed under Rand, not Fuller."

Lena wrinkled her nose. "I suppose so."

"Oh, are you the Rands?"

"No—"

"Not rea—"

The cheerful woman spoke over their words, moving away as she said, "We've been expecting you, although we thought you were arriving on the earlier ferry. Let me get Marcy for you, she'll be handling everything while you're here."

Not only was she friendly, but fast. The woman disappeared, leaving Lena standing at the vacant counter, her mouth hanging open, unsaid words stuck in her throat. Colt tapped his finger on her chin and she snapped her jaws shut, ignoring the rush of heat that blasted through her face.

A small woman burst through the doorway behind the wooden counter. Beautiful pale hair fluttered around the sharp angles of her face. She carried her shoulders in the straight line of a drill sergeant, telling Lena that she was definitely in charge.

Marcy stuck her hand out and Lena automatically grasped it.

"Welcome to Escape. I'm Marcy."

She reached for Colt's hand. "It's nice to finally meet you in person, Wyn. Of course, I'll be working with you both this week, trying to keep everything flowing smoothly."

"Working?" Lena's mind raced, but she couldn't make sense of what Marcy was saying.

"The production crew arrived yesterday and set up this morning. We were under the impression you'd be arriving earlier, but I suppose things happen when you're traveling."

Lena found herself apologizing, although she wasn't exactly sure why. Normally, hotels didn't care when you checked in and none of the literature she'd read about Escape indicated there was a strict policy. "We missed a connection."

"No matter. We're on a tight schedule, but we've adjusted things accordingly. The team would like to start immediately with some romantic shots during your welcome dinner this evening once you've settled."

The fireball glanced down at the tiny gold watch wrapped around her slender wrist. "Your reservations are at seven so that gives you a couple hours to settle into your bungalow and unpack." With a smile that was more perfunctory than welcoming, she asked, "Any questions?"

"Yes, what are you talking about?" Lena stared blankly at Marcy. It was as if she was speaking another language, one Lena knew she should understand but didn't.

"The photo shoot." The other woman's eyes glanced behind her at Colt before returning to Lena again. "Surely Wyn explained everything to you."

Colt cleared his throat. "Perhaps you could do us both a favor and go over it again."

An expression of disbelief and irritation flitted across Marcy's face, but she looked at Lena and explained. "Wyn and I have been working on a marketing campaign for Escape. When we started throwing around the idea of featuring a couple, he had the brilliant suggestion that we use you both as a real example of a loving couple honeymooning on our beautiful island."

"Why would we want to spend our honeymoon posing for an ad campaign?"

Marcy's brow wrinkled as her frown deepened. "Because you aren't paying for the vacation." She shot another nasty look across at Colt. "He really didn't tell you any of this?"

"No, no, he didn't."

"I'm going to kill him." Colt's words were low and she thought Marcy hadn't actually heard them. He started to turn, but Lena grasped his arm and held him there beside her. His biceps flexed beneath her hand. When had he gotten so strong?

"Where do you think you're going?"

"To catch the first ferry so I can kick his ass. He could have stopped us or told us, but he didn't. Don't worry, I'll be back before you know it."

Frowning at him, she said, "That isn't funny," before directing her attention back to Marcy who now looked just as confused as Lena had been moments ago.

"Marcy, there's been a mix-up."

"You aren't Lena Rand?"

"No, yes, I mean I'm Lena but—"

"Are you telling me that if we don't go through with the photo shoot that we can't stay at the resort?" Colt raised his voice to drown out the rest of her words.

"Yes. No. Why would you want to back out now?" Marcy's gaze bored into Colt's. "You signed a contract, Wyn."

"Um, I didn't get married and this isn't Wyn," Lena blurted out. She almost felt sorry for Marcy as her eyes widened with shock before narrowing into slits.

"What do you mean this isn't Wyn? What the hell is going on?"

Lena swallowed, realizing it was the first time she'd had to say out loud what had happened since leaving the church. "Let's just say that Wyn decided he preferred my teenage whore of a cousin."

Marcy blinked owlishly and then waved her hand in Colt's direction. "Then who is this?"

"A friend," she said, before realizing just how that might sound.

Marcy's eyes narrowed just a little more as she took

in the sight of Lena, unmarried Lena, with Colt towering over her in that way of his.

Lena launched a preemptive strike. "No, seriously,
we're just friends. When the wedding fell apart Colt
was there. I had the honeymoon, or what I thought was
supposed to be a honeymoon, and we hadn't seen each
other in a very long time." Lena realized she was rambling but couldn't seem to stop herself. "He travels.
He's a director. He makes documentaries all over the
world."

"Well, isn't that nice for him," Marcy said, looking
unconvinced.

"How much would a week here cost, Marcy?" Colt
asked, filling the pregnant silence. Which was a good
thing because who knew what might come out of Lena's
mouth if she opened it again.

"We reserved the honeymoon bungalow for Wyn, the
best location on property. An entire week there would
cost $8,595. Not including tax."

"It's a private island. How can there be tax?" Colt
asked.

"We have to pay the mainland for use of their util-
ities, municipal resources and the ferry service. But
price isn't the problem."

Tension poured off Colt in waves. Lena could feel it
tightening the muscles in her own back. He was frustrated, angry and ready to kill someone; the only problem was that the target for his anger was an entire ocean
away. Normally, she wasn't a violent person, but if Wyn
had been standing next to them, she most definitely

would have let Colt have at him. She was getting angrier and angrier with her ex-fiancé by the minute.

"Then what is the problem?" she asked.

"We're booked solid. I don't have another available room for four days. I have a contract with the production company, a deadline with the ad agency and an internationally distributed travel magazine. I don't need more paying guests, I need a couple to photograph for our ad campaign."

With a dismayed glance behind her, Marcy looked at Colt. She wasn't sure why. It wasn't his job to fix the mess Wyn had created.

"So basically, you're saying our choices are to agree to appear in your photo shoot and get a free vacation or leave?"

For a moment, Lena thought she saw a glimmer of panic and regret flash through the other woman's eyes, but before she could pounce it was gone.

"Look, I'm sorry, but I'm stuck between a rock and a hard place. You're both attractive. You'd make a great couple for our ad campaign. If you're willing to do the work, I'd be happy to give you the same agreement I offered Wyn. Free room, food and amenities in exchange for your cooperation with our photography team."

Lena looked around her at the charmingly elegant lobby. Outside the windows she could see the beckoning water and almost hear the lap of the waves as they hit the sand.

She didn't want to leave. Not yet. Her life back home was a shambles. She wasn't ready to face it. The resort was beautiful. She'd been looking forward to staying.

"I suppose it could be worse," she said, looking back at Colt and raising one eyebrow in reluctant surrender.

"How?"

"I could have actually married Wyn."

A laugh rumbled deep in Colt's chest. Lena was close enough to feel the vibrations and found an answering smile touch her lips.

"I suppose it would be an adventure. How much work could it possibly be? We're here…" His voice trailed off. Even he seemed reluctant to turn around immediately and leave. And considering what an ordeal it had been to get here, Lena didn't blame him. The thought of getting back on a plane right now was not appealing. Especially when she had sandy beaches and a crystal-clear sea stretching invitingly in front of her.

Marcy's relieved smile was hard to miss. "I guess the only question that remains—since you insist that you're not a couple—is can the two of you pull off looking like honeymooners for the cameras?"

"Please. I've spent most of my adult life behind the camera, plotting angles and setting up shots. I think I can handle being in front of it."

Without any warning, Colt grasped Lena's upper arm and spun her around to face him. She wobbled a little, until his arms around her body steadied her. What was he doing?

Laughter still lingered in the back of his bright green eyes. A soft smile touched his mouth, curving his lips even as they parted, moved closer. Lena found her own lips drifting apart. What was *she* doing?

He bent her backward over his arm, making the

room and her equilibrium tilt. His mouth claimed hers in a devastating kiss. She had a moment of shock when her body went rigid, but it was quickly overwhelmed by a radiating warmth that melted through her bones.

He didn't devour her as some men had a habit of doing. He gently persuaded her to open to him, constant pressure and reassurance that he wouldn't push beyond what she was comfortable giving.

After several seconds…or maybe minutes, he slowly, smoothly, pulled her back upright and let her go. The world tilted around her for a few seconds.

Her lungs burned. She took a deep breath to fill them back up again, but instead of the tropical scent permeating the lobby, all she could smell now was Colt. A masculine scent that always made her think of sandalwood.

What the hell had just happened?

"Satisfied?" Colt's voice was smooth and poised. Unaffected. While Lena wasn't sure she could actually form coherent words. She blinked, trying to clear her vision and the shift her world had taken.

She'd always known he was a good kisser. While he never kept a girl around long, she'd had occasion to mingle with a few of his conquests. They'd always been quick to sing his praises, as if they had some shared knowledge. No one ever believed her when she said they'd never slept together.

Marcy arched an eyebrow, pursed her lips and considered them for several seconds. "I suppose that settles that. Welcome to Escape."

3

WHY HAD HE KISSED HER?

It had seemed like a harmless thing to do at the time—take a little dig at Marcy and show her she had nothing to worry about—right up until the moment his lips had touched Lena's. He'd expected it to be light, quick, unimportant. Somehow between the idea and the execution, it had all gone wrong. Instead of something theatrical, he'd found himself really kissing her.

He'd pressed in slowly and asked her for more. And she'd given it. He wasn't sure what was more shocking, his reaction or hers.

The gut-deep wrench of yearning had come out of nowhere. Left him breathless and reeling. It'd taken everything he had inside to let her go. To pretend nothing had happened. Nothing had changed.

But it had.

He'd known her for sixteen years. When they were children it had been easy, connecting mostly through emails and phone calls. They'd skipped the awkward exploration of teenage years because she was always so far away. And while they'd both gone to college in D.C., they'd been at different schools. They'd seen each other more often, but not every day. They'd always lived separate lives and it was easy to continue to do that even in the same city.

And then his parents had died and he'd…floundered. His brother had tried to fill the void, but he had a young family to take care of. Lena was there for him, and he'd needed her so much. Needed the steady support of their friendship. It was the only thing that had felt real and solid when the rest of his life had spun out of control.

D.C. had become a constant reminder of the parents he'd lost. The family home. His brother, sister-in-law and newborn niece. He'd begun taking jobs, going anywhere as a way to escape it all. However, the work had quickly become important to him for other reasons. He enjoyed the challenges that came with difficult projects and the transient lifestyle that allowed him to move from place to place, constantly experiencing something new.

Ahead of him on the path, Lena's bright voice floated back to him. "Ooh, they have snorkeling. Maybe Marcy will let us do that one afternoon."

It was a fluke. That was all. This was Lena they were talking about. They'd studied together, shared pizza, razzed each other about horrible taste in movies, spent hours on the phone when he called from faraway places. She'd been there for him during the worst possible moments of his life.

She'd been the first person at the hospital the night he'd crashed his car going one-twenty down a back-country road. She'd tried to talk him out of skydiving, base jumping and extreme rock climbing. But when he'd refused to listen, she'd been there to bandage his cuts and smack the back of his head. Ultimately, she was the one who shook him out of his grief over losing his parents and convinced him he needed to get back to living.

Lena was important.

Sure, they rarely saw each other now—for the past five years he'd been wandering the globe trying to make his mark as a filmmaker—but their friendship was easy. They could go weeks or even months without talking, but when he did pick up the phone, it was as if they'd spoken the night before.

He didn't want to lose that. He needed her grounding influence in his life.

Gritting his teeth, Colt determined to ignore the firestorm of hormones raging inside his body until it went away. She'd just been jilted, for heaven's sake. The last thing she needed was to deal with his wayward lust. And really, that's all it was. A quick reaction based on a bad decision. He'd been so busy on his last job in Kenya that he hadn't had time to blow off steam.

Eventually, it would subside and things would go back to normal. Until then, he could fake it.

"Ooh," she said again, stopping short on the path. Skidding to a halt, he barely missed colliding with her.

She looked up at the tiny bungalow Marcy had assigned them, although he supposed *tiny* was a relative term. As a permanent residence it would never have done. But as vacation spots went it was pretty amazing.

The outside was made of warm, polished wood that gleamed beneath the late-afternoon sun. Lena pushed open the solid door, revealing the dark interior. Cool air leaked out to touch Colt's skin. Before that moment, he hadn't realized how hot it was here.

Their bags, along with an itinerary Marcy was eager to get started on, were to be delivered shortly. In the meantime, they had nothing to do but explore their temporary home.

Lena was busy wandering around the edges of the room, looking through the windows and squealing about their private infinity pool on their secluded patio.

All he could see was the single king-size four-poster bed that dominated half the room.

Eventually, Lena made her way over to it. She bounced down onto the mattress, the comforter bunching up around her and the pillows toppling haphazardly behind her.

"One bed, huh. Wanna draw straws?"

"Please. You're welcome to take the couch if you don't trust yourself in the same bed with me," he joked, a smile plastered to his still-pulsing lips.

She snorted. "It's my honeymoon. If anyone's sleeping on the couch, it's you." She flopped onto her back, her arms spread wide across the entire length of the bed. "It would be the gentlemanly thing to do."

"You've known me for how long?"

"Long enough."

"So you know better than to accuse me of being a gentleman."

"True enough." She laughed. Sitting up, she looked across at him.

"Why did you do that?"

He thought he knew what she was talking about, but part of him hoped he was wrong. "Do what?"

Her mouth took on a serious slant. "Kiss me."

He shrugged. "It seemed like a good idea at the time."

Awkwardness, never present before, settled between them. He realized that he should probably apologize. Or maybe promise her he wouldn't do it again. But the words didn't form.

"Well, um, let's try to avoid having to do that again."

"Well, hell, I've never gotten any complaints before." He exaggerated his words, pulling his face into a mock scowl, trying to restore the equilibrium they'd lost. "Was kissing me such a hardship?"

"I didn't say that."

"You enjoyed it."

"I didn't say that, either," she exclaimed, rolling her eyes.

"Anyway, I don't think Marcy will require that kind of commitment. From either of us." He hoped.

"Maybe not, but I'd really like to avoid having to explain to everyone what happened. I'm here to forget about the wedding, and I'm afraid these photo sessions will cause a stir. Maybe we should just pretend that we're actually married."

Well, he definitely hadn't expected this. But, now that he thought about it, her suggestion made sense. If he were in her position, he wouldn't want to have to retell the story over and over, reliving the painful experience.

"All right," he agreed slowly. "I have a problem with outright lying, but I don't mind letting people think whatever they want."

"Thank you," she said softly.

A knock at the door signaled the arrival of their luggage and put an end to their conversation. Several minutes later, he found himself outside walking slowly around the rim of the pool while Lena got ready for their first assignment—a romantic dinner, according to Marcy.

He just hoped he could get through the night without doing something he'd regret. Like kissing her again.

AWKWARDNESS HAD SETTLED around them again. The restaurant was elegant and romantic, which probably didn't help the situation. Decorated in soft blues and greens that complemented the untamed tropical beauty outside, the dining area had an undercurrent of sensuality and sophistication. It was the sort of place a man took a woman he was planning to seduce, Lena thought.

Her eyes strayed sideways to Colt as the maître d' led them through the restaurant. Colt's hand settled lightly on the small of her back, guiding her through the maze of tables. Her muscles tightened beneath his touch, making her feel even more unsettled.

Colt had touched her a thousand times. Hadn't he? Her body had never responded this way before. Had it?

Lena thought hard. Maybe. When they were both in college, there'd been some faint wisp of attraction.

But it had gone away, to be replaced by deep affection. Which meant more than a fleeting physical attraction that could burn out and die. Right?

She'd seen it time and time again growing up. Her mother would gush over the latest man in her life. Her cheeks would be pink, her eyes would glow. But three months later there would be yelling and crying. Until the next man and the next place. If Lena had learned anything from watching her mother, it was that sexual attraction never lasted and was hardly the foundation for a good relationship.

Oh, she liked sex just as much as the next woman, but she'd always looked for more than a spark. Which is what she'd thought she'd found with Wyn.

The sommelier approached their table and introduced himself. "Marcy has arranged for a flight of excellent wines to accompany your dinner this evening." Twisting the bottle he'd held against his arm, he presented it to Colt for his inspection. "This is our best champagne, compliments of the house in celebration of your marriage."

Colt, who had leaned forward, sprawled back into his chair. The tip of his shoe nudged against her foot. Lena drew her own feet back underneath her chair. Two days ago, heck two hours ago, it wouldn't have bothered her. But something had changed. An awareness of him as a man had sprung up seemingly out of nowhere.

Oh, she'd always thought he was an attractive man. With his rugged good looks and the well-defined muscles his dangerous hobbies had given him, any woman would be hard-pressed to argue. Colt had an air about him, an adventurous spirit that made you think you'd never be bored while he was around.

But she didn't want adventure, never had. She wanted a man who would settle in one place, build a solid and stable life for her and their children. Colt didn't fit that bill. Yet another reason she'd never thought of him in a romantic or sexual way.

"Didn't you hear? We're not—"

Lena kicked him with her sandal-clad foot, stubbing her toe and shutting him up in one fell swoop. Grimacing, she said, "Colt, behave."

"What would be the fun in that?" he asked, mischief glinting in his eyes. She'd seen that look before, many times, and it usually heralded some harebrained scheme that she wanted no part of—such as jumping out of a perfectly functioning airplane.

There were many things about Colt that she liked. He was a good friend, always there for her when she needed him. But there was plenty about him that she just didn't understand, and she had convinced herself a long time ago she never would.

She shot Colt a warning look for good measure as the sommelier poured. Lena gratefully accepted her glass. Taking a sip, she let the chilled bubbles tickle her nose and cascade down her throat. "Mmm, this is good." It was light and fruity, sweet on her tongue. She took another sip. And another.

Looking at Colt, she smiled. Candlelight flickered between them, casting shifting shadows across his face. She wanted to reach out and run the pad of her finger over his skin. Her smile vanished and her eyes darted away. What was she thinking? She lifted her glass and drained it.

Colt palmed the bottle from the waiting bucket and asked, "More?"

The playful mask he'd been wearing slipped and for the first time Lena realized he was worried about her. The space between his eyebrows wrinkled and his lips pulled tight into a straight line.

"I'm fine," she said.

Colt shrugged, the dress shirt he'd put on pulling tight against the broad expanse of his shoulders. "If you say so."

She was halfway through her second glass, on an empty stomach, when Marcy appeared at her elbow.

"All settled in?"

Lena looked up at the other woman, at the strained smile that stretched her lips but didn't touch her eyes.

"Yes, the bungalow is lovely."

"I'm so glad you're pleased."

Marcy plunked something that made a metallic twang onto the table. The plain gold bands rattled for a moment before settling against each other. "I noticed you didn't have rings. We'll need them for the photographs."

Lena stared at the rings. Without looking at her, Colt reached for the bigger one, slipping it onto his finger.

She swallowed, picked hers up and slid it snugly against the princess-cut diamond already on her finger. She'd been wearing the engagement ring for so long she'd forgotten it was there. Now, however, it felt all wrong, and she wished she'd left it back in D.C. Both bands sat heavy against her skin. She didn't want either of them, but when Marcy let out a sigh of relief, Lena dropped her hands into her lap, her naked right covering her left.

With a wave of her hand, Marcy pulled over a man with a camera draped across his neck. Lena had wondered when the three-ring circus would start.

"This is Mikhail. He's going to be the photographer this week. The photo shoot was supposed to be organic, catching a real honeymooning couple as they explored all the resort had to offer. We were hoping to use candid shots. Obviously, that might be a little difficult now."

"Why do you say that?" Colt asked.

Marcy shot him an incredulous look. "Well, for starters, you're both sitting as far away from each other as possible without being at separate tables."

Colt's lips dipped down into a frown. Lena took in their positions and realized Marcy was right. A hard glint entered Colt's eyes. Slapping his hand down onto the table, his open palm waited expectantly as he said, "Give me your hand."

Reluctantly, Lena placed her hand in his. His fingers brushed against the pulse at her wrist, sending it skittering. A warm heat that had nothing to do with the alcohol she'd drunk suffused her skin.

Colt's eyes changed, going from hard to soft. He pulled their joined hands closer, forcing her to either let go or press her body against the biting edge of the table.

She'd left her hair down and it fell around her face, somehow closing the rest of the restaurant out and training her focus solely on him. Colt leaned forward, meeting her halfway across the table. His tongue licked across his lips, drawing her attention to his mouth. She'd never bothered to study it before. Or maybe it had been intentional avoidance. But since he'd used his mouth against her...

It was sensual, wide. The dip in the center of his top lip flared out in a way that made her want to close the gap between them and suck it into her own mouth.

Something flared in the back of his eyes. An awareness and intensity she'd only ever seen him focus on someone else.

She leaned closer. The candle burning between them flickered with the breeze from their joined breaths.

What was she doing?

Her teeth clinked together and she pulled back. He reluctantly let her hand go. His palm scraped slowly against hers. Her nerve endings pulsed and flared, sending unwanted signals all through her body.

Lena put her hands in her lap and rubbed her palm, trying to stop the ripple effect. It didn't work. The damage was already done. She blinked, feeling sluggish, disoriented and sorely out of her element.

"Better?" he asked in a low rumbling voice that sent shivers down her spine.

Without thought, Lena nodded, and then realized Colt was no longer looking at her but up at Marcy.

"Uh-huh," Marcy uttered before clearing her throat and jerking her gaze away. "Mikhail, we'll try the candid shots tonight."

Marcy flicked them one more calculating glance

before melting away from their table. Lena thought she heard the other woman whisper, "Wine. Lots of wine," to their sommelier as she passed, but she couldn't be certain.

Lena looked across at Colt and for the first time in their friendship had no idea what to say. Luckily, the salad course arrived and saved her from having to come up with something.

Her mouth watered at the crisp greens, strawberries, candied nuts and light citrus dressing their waiter placed before her. She was grateful for something to occupy her hands...and her mouth.

But apparently Colt wasn't as desperate for the distraction. He took a few bites and then set his fork down. Instead of eating, he watched her. Several times she picked up her napkin and blotted her lips for fear that the dressing was dribbling down her chin. She was already on edge and he wasn't helping any. She was about to tell him to knock it off, but he spoke before her.

"Why did you want to marry Wyn?"

Surprised by his question, she sputtered for a few seconds, unsure what to say. They'd never really talked about her relationship with Wyn before. She didn't know why, but there was some tacit agreement between them. He didn't tell her about the women who flitted through his life and she rarely mentioned Wyn when they spoke.

It felt weird to be talking with Colt about him now, but he'd asked. She tried to remember exactly what it was about Wyn that had mattered. Her brain felt fuzzy and the only thing she could come up with was, "Because…he was good to me."

"Not because you loved him."

"Of course I loved him," Lena protested.

Colt shook his head. "I don't think there's any 'of course' about it. You haven't even cried."

"I hate crying in front of people. You know that," she scoffed, dismissing his statement without really even thinking about it.

"Maybe. But I watched you up on that altar. You were so pale I was worried you might faint. Right up until the minute your cousin objected and then color flooded your cheeks. You were shocked, possibly angry, but that was relief I saw all over your face."

Lena looked at him, the pleasant buzz that had entered her blood lessening just a little. Was he right?

"You're upset because things didn't work out the way you wanted them to. Maybe you're even embarrassed that it fell apart in front of so many people." Colt paused. "But you aren't heartbroken."

He was wrong. Wasn't he? "How is heartbroken supposed to look, Colt? Am I supposed to be inconsolable? Sobbing in my bed surrounded by spent tissues? Please. I've seen that scene before, more times than I care to count."

Her tongue felt loose, unhinged. Even as she said the words, she realized she was sharing more with him than she meant to. More than she'd ever said before. To anyone. "Do you know how often I scraped together the pieces of my mother and tried to put them back together? How many times I had to beg and plead with her just to get out of bed? After every man—there were plenty and they all left—she'd spend days, weeks, sometimes months inconsolable and incapable of doing anything. Especially taking care of a child."

She glared across at him, years of conviction radiating from her eyes. "I refuse to be like her. I will not let a relationship devastate or control me like that. So, yes, I'm upset. Wyn and I were supposed to have a life together. He betrayed me in the worst possible way. With my cousin. Excuse me if I'm not handling the situation the way you expected me to."

Colt's eyes were round with shock. His silence slammed down between them and the minute it did Lena regretted her words. It was obvious that he'd gotten way more than he'd bargained for.

Their food hadn't even arrived, but that didn't matter. Lena wasn't hungry anymore. In fact, she needed to get out of there before she said even more. Lena scraped her chair against the stone floor and walked toward the exit.

Colt called her name. The photographer cursed.

She ignored them both.

4

COLT HEARD THE MAN CURSE, too, and couldn't have agreed more. How was he to know his question would hit a sore spot? They were supposed to be friends, right?

Lena had seen him at his absolute worst. When he'd crashed his car, she'd been the one to sit by him in the hospital. He'd told her things about his life that he'd never shared with anyone else. She'd seen him cry, moan with pain and had supported him even when she thought he was making unwise decisions.

How could there be part of her life he knew nothing about? Why had she never told him how bad her mother had been?

Thinking back on those months she'd lived next door, he realized they'd rarely gone to her house. When he'd asked, she'd almost always had an excuse. Sure, he'd only been ten, but why hadn't he picked up on that? And why, in all the times that they'd talked since then, had she not shared her pain? Heaven knew he'd dumped plenty of his own worries on her small, capable shoulders.

The table teetered, silverware, china and glass clinking ominously, as he bolted after her.

Tropical heat and guilt slapped him in the face as he pushed outside. Colt ripped at the buttons on his shirt, trying to release the noose that had apparently slipped around his throat.

He found her halfway across the resort, standing alone on the deserted beach. Moonlight streamed over her, making her look fragile. Her body curved in on itself, her arms hugging her waist. She shouldn't be sad. Not here. Not because of him. This was a place for fun and adventure. For laughter and the excitement of discovering something new.

He touched her arm, and she turned around, looking up at him with sad eyes that glistened with unshed tears. Another shock of guilt kicked through his system.

He hadn't meant to make her cry.

With a sigh, Colt gathered her into his arms and pulled her tight against him. Something deep inside him stirred at the press of her soft curves into his hard body. He ignored it.

"I'm sorry," he whispered into the crown of her hair.

Her body was stiff, her muscles tight. After several minutes, she relaxed. The emotion that had been swirling within her subsided, he could feel it slip away.

Melting into him, Lena let him take the weight of her body. His own muscles relaxed, the tension that had whipped through him easing as he realized she wouldn't hold his careless comments against him.

After several minutes she pulled away and Colt let her. She looked up at him again, calm and collected, the Lena he recognized and remembered. He was glad to see the sadness gone.

"It's not your fault," she said.

"Maybe not, but I didn't help."

Lena's lips twisted. "No, but I can't fault you for telling the truth. I knew something was wrong. Deep down, I knew. I just didn't want to admit it. Everyone was so excited. Jealous. Everyone told me how perfect Wyn was. What a wonderful husband he'd be. How lucky I was to find a great man who just happened to be heir to a fortune."

"But it didn't feel right."

Lena turned away. Reaching down, she flicked off the sandals protecting her feet. They fell to the sand with a muted plop. She walked a few steps barefoot. Colt did the same, letting his own shoes topple crookedly beside hers.

The sound of crashing waves shushed gently between them. In the distance Colt could hear the rumblings of laughter and dance music from somewhere on the island. Sometimes, like now, it was hard to remember they weren't the only people here.

"It felt right at first," she finally responded. "Wyn was sweet. We worked together for at least six months before he asked me out. I'd look up from my notes during company meetings to find him watching me instead of paying attention."

"You don't have to toe the line when daddy's in charge."

Lena reached over and shoved him. The unexpected reaction had him teetering sideways for a moment before regaining his balance.

"That isn't nice, Colt. Wyn's very good at his job."

"Yeah, so good he managed to weasel his way into a free vacation with a client."

"I was flattered."

"You were hunted, like a lion stalks an antelope. I only met the man a few times, but it was enough to realize he was charming and focused and untrustworthy."

Lena twisted, the heel of her foot grinding into the sand with the force of her motion. "Why the hell didn't you say anything?"

"Because it wasn't my place." Colt had thought about it, once, but realized he had nothing to back up his gut instinct. "I thought maybe you'd just think I was being overprotective. Playing the big-brother card or something."

A strangled sound that could have been anything from incredulity to embarrassment burst from Lena's mouth. "You're hardly my big brother."

"True. You were serious about Wyn though, and I figured he must have some qualities I couldn't see. If he'd loved you, I could have lived with it."

"But, obviously, he didn't."

The question he still had was whether she'd ever loved Wyn. Colt didn't think so, but he wasn't going to make the same mistake twice, so he wouldn't ask again.

"So, yes, in the beginning it felt right. And by the time it didn't I was in too deep. The wedding was months away and I convinced myself that it was just jitters."

Silence stretched between them. Colt had no idea what the right response was and he was afraid to say the wrong thing again.

After a few minutes Lena said, "Jeez, we're a pair. I stay in a relationship I shouldn't, and you can't stay in one more than five minutes."

"Hey, I last a hell of a lot longer than five minutes," he joked. "But I don't want to have a relationship longer than two weeks," he argued. "Too much work. Besides, I like variety in my life."

Lena grimaced. "So try a different cereal in the morning. Seriously, Colt, you need to grow up."

"When did this turn into a discussion of my short-comings?"

"I like talking about yours better than analyzing mine."

Colt laughed.

Silence stretched between them, only this time there was comfort and familiarity to it. Colt reached for her again, wrapping his arm around her shoulders and pull-ing her into his body. Together they stared out across the Caribbean Sea.

The jungle far behind them rustled. An animal howled in the distance. And Lena groaned quietly. "What does it say about me that I'm more upset at losing my job than my fiancé?"

"It says that you're practical," Colt said, unable to hold back a smile. Because that described Lena to a T.

"I actually think it says I'm a coward. But, dammit,

I liked my job. I was good at it and I put several hard years in at Rand Marketing."

"You are good at your job, which is why you'll be able to find something else. Graphic designers are in demand. You'll land on your feet."

"I'm pissed that I have to land at all."

"Think of it as an opportunity then. To find something better. Or maybe to work on your jewelry for a while."

He'd been upset when she'd told him she'd given up her craft. Especially because that decision had come months after she'd started dating Wyn, and Colt couldn't help but think the man was partly responsible for Lena's decision. He couldn't remember how many nights he'd watched her string together beads, bend gold wire and produce the most breathtaking and original pieces.

"You know, my sister-in-law still tells me that the earrings I gave her are the best birthday present she's ever gotten. She wears them all the time."

"I'm glad she likes them."

Colt stared up into the night sky. Stars twinkled down on them, so bright and yet too far away to touch. This conversation was beginning to feel the same way. They'd had it before, but nothing ever changed. "You're an artist, Lena, don't you long for an outlet?"

"I have an outlet. Graphic design is art."

Colt held in a snort. Maybe, but it wasn't her passion. He dropped the subject though because he knew it wouldn't get him anywhere.

"The sand's still warm." Lena looked down at her

feet, wiggling her toes in deeper. Her dark red toenails peeked out, making him want to join her in the childish gesture. Playing in the sand was something he hadn't done in a very long time. Not since his parents had died five years ago and he'd stopped joining his brother's family at the beach house.

At first, the memories had been too painful. And then it had just gotten easier to make excuses. He was out of the country. Working. Tired. Standing there with his feet pressed deep into the sand, he couldn't remember the last time he'd actually seen his brother, sister-in-law and niece. He talked to them on the phone occasionally, but he was slowly coming to realize that might not be enough.

Even the few days or weeks he'd managed to see Lena over the past couple of years had left chinks in their relationship he hadn't even been aware of. If he'd been home more, seen what was happening with Wyn, maybe he could have helped Lena avoid this mistake.

She looked over at him, a calculating expression on her face. Her eyes narrowed, and for a second he thought she was going to bring up something else he wouldn't like. Instead, she said, "Wanna race?"

He blinked, his mind trying to swiftly change gears.

Without waiting for his answer, Lena bolted for the edge of the water, leaving nothing but a spray of sand in her wake. Her happy chuckle as the waves rolled across her toes was a heck of a lot better than the sadness she'd been fighting a little while ago.

Walking slowly behind her, Colt enjoyed watching as she played in the surf. Wispy clouds passed slowly across the moon, playing peek-a-boo with the light. She twirled, her dress floating out around her body and a spray of water splashing across his face.

He thought it was an accident—until she did it again. And he couldn't let that go without retaliation. High-stepping out into the surf, Colt scooped water with both hands and threw it in her direction.

He could hear her sharp intake of breath as it rained over her. Her dress was quickly soaked, sticking to her skin. Colt had seen her body before. She'd lain out in the sun at his pool. Often enough for him to know she preferred bikinis to anything else. He'd always known she was beautiful.

But tonight, she was more than that. She was sensual and seductive without even realizing it. Her eyes sparkled. Her skin glowed. She darted in and out of the surf, taunting him, the only problem was the game he suddenly wanted to play with her had nothing to do with innocent fun.

Her foot twisted on something beneath the surface of the water. Colt watched as the expression on her face went from pleasure to panic in the space of a heartbeat. Lunging forward, he caught her, picking her up and turning toward shore.

Her arms wrapped around his neck. Her body, wet and warm, pressed against his. She looked up at him, licking stray droplets of water off her lips. His groin tightened and an answering need burst open inside him.

He growled deep in his throat, unable to stop himself. He leaned forward to claim the lips that she'd left open in invitation—intentional or not, he didn't care.

Lena's eyes went round. He felt her breath stutter against his chest. Before he could follow through, she twisted in his arms, struggling against him.

What was he doing?

Ripping his hold open, Lena dropped to the ground. The spray of her feet touching the surf landed halfway up his chest. Before he could say anything—apologize yet again—she was darting away. She didn't even stop to pick up her sandals, instead bypassing them for the fastest route back to the resort.

Some beast inside told him to run after her, to pursue her and catch her and have her right now. He ignored it, choosing instead to turn his back on the temptation. A flash of light caught Colt's attention.

Mikhail, standing several feet away, partially hidden by the jungle, stared at him with one eye. The upraised lens of his camera covered the other.

Colt's hands clenched into fists. "How long have you been there?"

"Long enough," Mikhail said, lowering his camera to let it settle heavily around his neck.

Colt wanted to make some biting retort, to expend the bubbling energy rushing through his blood. Mikhail seemed as handy a target as any.

But he didn't. Rationally, he knew the other man was simply doing his job. If the roles had been reversed, he probably would have done the same. Work was everything, and the final product held priority. He was simply not used to being on this side of the camera.

Colt had to admit that he wasn't sure he liked it. Especially if the camera—and the man wielding it—were going to be capturing things he didn't want recorded. It was one thing to pretend an attraction in front of the camera because they'd agreed to do it. It was entirely another for the camera to capture a real attraction that Colt didn't want and had no idea what to do with.

The camera didn't lie. For once, Colt wished that it would.

LENA FEIGNED SLEEP, screwing her eyes tight and burying her head into the mound of pillows when Colt returned. He'd stayed away long enough for her to rush through her nightly routine. She'd had to dig past the honeymoon negligees at the top of her suitcase for the pair of yoga pants and a tank top buried beneath. Seeing those tiny scraps of silk and lace on the heels of what had happened on the beach didn't do much for her peace of mind.

While Colt sorted quietly through his own bag, Lena fought another flash of desire. Clamping her thighs together to lessen the awakened tingle, she tried not to move beneath the covers. She had no idea what to say to Colt.

Had no idea what had really happened.

Well, obviously he'd almost kissed her. Or had she almost kissed him? She couldn't be certain. The first one, in front of Marcy, had meant nothing—for her or for him. It was playacting, and she was adult enough to go with the flow. The fact that her body had reacted was her issue to deal with. It was chemistry. Nothing more.

Now that she thought about it, she and Wyn hadn't

exactly been burning up the sheets over the past several months. Initially, she'd chalked up their lack of sex to the pressure of the wedding. They were both busy, at home and at work. Perhaps it should have been her first clue that things weren't quite right. Either way, when Colt kissed her she'd thought her dormant libido had simply chosen a bad time to rear its head.

But tonight was different. It wasn't for show. The need pulsing through her body had nothing to do with biological functions and everything to do with Colt. She'd wanted *him,* not just a male body.

It had been real. And if she wasn't mistaken, he'd felt the zing too. Which almost made it worse. How long had he wanted her? she wondered. Always? Or was this as new for him as it was for her?

What if it was simply biological for him? Romantic setting, candlelit dinner, wet clothes and close bodies.

It scared her, this unexpected reaction to Colt.

She came close to jumping in surprise when the far side of the bed dipped down with the weight of his body. She wanted to protest. The words were on her lips, although something inside her swallowed them instead of letting them out. She was supposed to be asleep.

Besides, objecting to him sleeping beside her would reveal too much. She'd have to explain why they—two grown adults, friends—couldn't share a bed without it turning sexual.

Settling on his side, his back to her, Colt let out a tiny sigh. His body rubbed against the sheets. The rasping sound suddenly seemed very intimate.

Lena lay there, listening to the steady rise and fall of his breathing. She felt her own lungs synchronize with his. The sheets that had minutes before seemed cool and comforting were suddenly smothering, cocooning them together. She wanted to fling them off, but couldn't. His heat melted into her. Her body twitched, fighting to snuggle closer.

Colt dropped off within minutes. She envied him that ability to sleep wherever. She also resented that he wasn't fighting the same urges that kept her tossing and turning.

She was going to look awesome in the morning. She knew the camera added ten pounds. She wondered what it did with bags beneath the eyes.

Several times during the night Lena awoke to find her body curled tightly against Colt's. Once her leg had been thrown across his thighs. She'd quickly rolled back onto her side of the bed only to wake again with her derriere snuggled into the cradle of his thighs and his hand cupped possessively around her breast.

As if the physical contact wasn't bad enough, the dreams that had interrupted her sleep in the first place were almost worse—filled with frustrating shadows and tempting heat. Her mind certainly had no problems conjuring up exotic and tantalizing ways Colt could pleasure her.

Even now, close to dawn, her body hummed with a level of sexual frustration she hadn't felt since her teenage years. She didn't like it. It made her feel out of control, possessed by her own desire.

She would not let it rule her. Especially with Colt.

They had too much history to throw everything away on a fling. He was important to her, which also made the whole thing more complicated. She already loved him. Add sex and there was the strong possibility she would fall in love with him.

And that would be terrible. Their friendship worked because they didn't have expectations. Colt called when he called. He came into town when it was convenient. He was a nomad and liked it that way.

She just couldn't live like that. The thought alone made her want to break out in hives. She'd moved enough in her life and didn't want to do it again. In fact, she'd been dreading moving from her apartment into Wyn's. She'd put it off until the last possible second. Her apartment had been the first home she'd ever had. She'd bought it with her own hard-earned money and could admit she'd been reluctant to give up that sanctuary.

No, bottom line was that she and Colt would make a terrible couple. They might enjoy a few days rolling through a sexual fog, but when it cleared they'd both realize it was a mistake.

They hadn't done anything that couldn't be forgotten. Better to stop things now before they went further.

5

LENA WAS GONE when Colt woke up. Just as well, since
he was sporting a rather obvious erection and probably would have done something stupid—like capture
her mouth again—if he'd woken up next to her. However, when she hadn't returned a little while later, he
began to worry.

As if on cue, some animal let out a screech from the
jungle.

Several frantic minutes of searching led him to a
thatched hut down the beach. If he hadn't seen her red-
tipped toes peeking out of the structure he probably
would have missed her.

"There you are. I've been looking for you everywhere," he said, his words sounding slightly accusatory even to his own ears. He tried to soften them with
a bright smile. Something in his chest twisted for a
moment before letting go, releasing a tension he hadn't
been aware of until it was gone.

Her eyes were slightly unfocused when she looked
up at him. He might have wondered if she'd already

started in on the fruity drinks, but as he watched, her eyes cleared. She looked around, slowly taking in her surroundings as if seeing them for the first time.

"What time is it?"

"Almost nine. I expect Marcy will be hunting us down soon."

Lena shrugged. "I hope she has something fun planned."

Colt crouched in front of her, his feet digging into the sand. He noticed she had a pile of shells and smooth stones in front of her. Some were whole. Some were broken. But all held a sort of wild beauty that came only from nature.

She'd arranged several—handpicked he'd bet— into a descending swirl that echoed the pattern of the shells themselves. The subtle shift of color gave the piece a feel of inherent movement, like sunlight filtered through water.

"That's beautiful."

Her hand fell on top, crushing the middle shells deeper into the sand and marring the perfection. "It's nothing. My version of doodling."

Colt frowned, but didn't argue. Lena pushed up from the ground, forcing him to move back if he didn't want to get knocked over. She ran her hands across the seat of her shorts, cleaning off the sand. Some stubborn grains clung to her legs. Colt thought about reaching down and brushing them away but caught himself just in time. The last thing he needed was to feel her smooth skin beneath his fingers, not if he expected to get through the day without embarrassing himself.

"I'm hungry. Any idea where we could get breakfast?"

They were rounding the curve of the beach heading back to the civilization of the resort when Marcy appeared before them. Her steps were quick and purposeful. Mikhail trailed behind her at a more sedate pace.

"There you are. We need to get started."

Lena's stomach growled and she and Colt glanced at each other, sharing a smile. The awkwardness that had settled over them disappeared. Colt let out a sigh of relief, feeling back on solid ground for the first time since he'd kissed her.

They walked around the resort, posing for photographs at various spots along the way. It was easy, comfortable, to wander around, laughing, touching, teasing each other. After a few hours—and a quick stop at the breakfast buffet—they ended up at the pool.

The midafternoon heat had set in and they were both starting to wilt. Changing into the bathing suits Marcy provided them was a welcome relief.

Mikhail set a scene with towel-draped lounge chairs, sweating glasses of some tropical drink and abandoned books sitting open at the foot of their chairs. For the next thirty minutes they worked, moving where Mikhail told them, smiling on cue, the temptation of the pool just a few feet away almost cruel.

A crowd of people gathered around them, not overtly gawking, but definitely watching as Mikhail put Colt and Lena through their paces.

"I think I'm melting," Lena mumbled through a smile that was looking more fake by the second.

Her skin was flushed, glistening beneath the sun. His eyes raked down her body. He couldn't help it. The turquoise bikini she'd put on revealed more of her than he'd seen in a very long time. Her flat stomach, pert little breasts, long legs…

Colt swallowed. A hard need twisted through him and his body stirred. Lena's eyes sharpened. Her lips parted. She leaned closer to him and suddenly the heat was absolutely oppressive.

"That's great, guys. We're done. Marcy needs you later, but for now you can enjoy the pool." Mikhail dismissed them, turning to his equipment and leaving Colt floundering once again.

He did not like the sensation. Never in his entire life had he been this out of his element with a woman. Hell, he was known for his love affairs. They were short, intense and satisfying for all parties involved. Easy.

Nothing about Lena was easy. If she'd been anyone else, he would have seduced her last night and been done with it. It wouldn't be the first vacation fling he'd ever had.

But it was Lena. And she deserved so much more than a fling.

She wanted permanent. The white picket fence, kids and a dog. And he knew that wasn't something he could give her…even if he'd been inclined to try.

Sex was not supposed to be this complicated.

He was just about to suggest they both jump into the water—if for no other reason than it would cover up the temptation of her body—when a woman popped up at the end of their chairs.

"Y'all are the honeymooning couple they're taking photographs of, aren't you?" The perky little blonde had a wide smile and friendly eyes.

Lena looked across at him as if to say *save me.*

"Uh, yeah, they're photographing us."

Without an invitation, the blonde plopped her rear onto the end of Lena's chair.

"I thought so. I think y'all have the bungalow next to ours. I saw y'all come in yesterday." The girl leaned closer to Lena, mock-whispering as if they'd been friends forever, "We're honeymooning, too. I'm so glad the wedding hoopla is finally over. I wanted to elope, but Daddy insisted on throwing a big party." She sighed, rolling her eyes. "The things we do for our parents, right?" An indulgent smile belied the martyr act she was playing.

Lena stared at the other woman. Colt's lips twitched with humor at seeing her speechless. The chatty interloper didn't seem to notice Lena's lack of participation in the conversation, she just breezed right on.

"Where are my manners?" She giggled, sticking out her hand, first to Lena and then to him. "I'm Georgia Ann but everyone just calls me Georgie."

"Quit bothering these nice people, Georgie." A man walked up, dark-haired, young, an apologetic expression on his face. But the minute his eyes landed on his wife, that expression disappeared, replaced by a sort of adoration that Colt found fascinating. "Georgie's never met a stranger in her life."

"Guilty as charged." She smiled. Colt realized that Lena was now smiling, too. There was something about the woman's friendly, infectious attitude that was too hard to resist. Like a tractor beam, she pulled you in. "This is Wesley, love of my life." She stared up into his face, her eyes twinkling with a brightness that hadn't been there moments before.

They might have been sickening, if the love they shared hadn't been so obviously genuine.

Lena looked across at him, her eyes wide. Colt shrugged. They'd leave eventually.

Wesley's hand dropped onto Georgie's shoulder. She leaned back against him. "We're thinking about hiking into the jungle tomorrow. We hear there's a beautiful waterfall. What are y'all doing?" Without waiting for their answer, she bounced against the chair, looked up at Wesley and said, "I have an excellent idea."

"Uh-oh" was his response, despite the fact that a smile stretched across his face.

Turning back to them, she grabbed Lena's hand. "Why don't y'all come with us? It'll be fun. We can bring a picnic, bond over horror stories of the wedding. My aunt Millie gave us the ugliest lamp you've ever seen. I think she pulled it out of her attic. I swear the thing has got to be fifty years old if it's a day. It'll probably catch our house on fire."

Lena shot Colt a panicked look. "I think we have—" she started.

Wesley shot him a knowing expression. "Take my advice and just say yes now. It'll be less painful that way."

Georgie piped up, "I won't take no. Leave everything to me." Scooting up from her chair, she began to walk away, still talking. "We'll meet you outside your bungalow at ten sharp. I'll pack the picnic."

The excuse Colt was going to use lay useless on his tongue as the couple rounded the other side of the pool.

"What just happened?" Lena asked, flopping back into her chair.

"I think we're going on a picnic in the jungle tomorrow."

Lena blinked. "What if Marcy needs us?"

"I suppose she'll just have to get over it. Or maybe she could get us out of the picnic."

Lena looked across the pool to where Georgie and Wesley had settled back into their own lounge chairs. Georgie waved. Lena lifted her hand in a half-hearted response.

"I don't think even Marcy could stop her. I'm exhausted just listening to her."

"Hey, on the bright side, we get to see the waterfall."

"And on the dark side, they think we're married."

"I thought that was what you wanted."

"Sure, but I didn't think we'd be spending time with anyone but Marcy and Mikhail who already know. I figured if we talked to anyone it would only be for a few minutes and then it would be over."

Colt looked across at Georgie and Wesley and felt a grimace turn his lips. They were so happy and in love they would surely pick up on the fact that he and Lena weren't. "We could always explain."

"Horror of horrors. I can just hear Georgie's gushing sympathy right now." She looked over at him, a pained expression on her face. "I don't think I could take that.

It was bad enough dealing with the chaos at the wedding."

"Then I guess if we can't get out of it we'll be married. That doesn't sound so bad, does it?"

Her eyes sharpened with a deep intensity that he didn't quite understand. Slowly, she answered, "I suppose not."

LENA HAD NO IDEA what they were doing. All they'd been told was to disappear for a while and to return to their bungalow at eight sharp. Obviously, Marcy's next photo shoot had something to do with their room. Fine.

In the meantime, she and Colt had finally managed to get into the pool. The water had been heavenly. They'd skipped the dining room in favor of fattening fried foods at the snack shack. The atmosphere was completely different, which was a good thing. The last thing she needed was another romantic meal with Colt. Playing around in the pool had been bad enough.

Grabbing his ankles to dunk him in. Her fingers grazing across the tight wall of his abs. His body sliding against her beneath the water. Lena gulped, squeezing her eyes shut and hoping the building storm of awareness would disappear, like the monster that couldn't hurt her if she couldn't see it.

The problem was it was still there, eyes open or closed.

The more time they spent together, the more aware of him she became. Lena was beginning to worry that ignoring her stirring emotions wasn't going to be enough. They were getting more powerful, more demanding.

She needed to get hold of herself and her libido. The problem was she no longer trusted that she could actually control either one. And she was starting to question why she needed to—why couldn't she have him?

A shiver raced down her spine as she remembered the exquisite pleasure of his body rubbing against hers.

"Are you cold?" Colt asked from behind, his palm landing gently at the small of her back.

Ripples of awareness continued through her body like rings from a stone hitting a pond. She wanted him to go on touching her forever, which was why she shook off his hold and said, "No, I'm fine," tossing a smile over her shoulder to take the sting of her rebuke away.

They rounded the corner in the path to see Marcy waiting for them, the door to their bungalow standing wide open behind her.

Marcy swept them inside and with a grand gesture of her arm, indicated the single room.

It had been completely changed.

The couch and end tables had been removed, along with the small table and chairs in the eating nook. The beautifully carved wooden bed had been placed in the center of the room, and draped with gauzy white material that fluttered on an easy breeze. Someone—probably Marcy—had flung open every door and window, letting in the scent of tropical flowers and the salty tang of the sea.

Drippy, mismatched candles had been placed across

the few remaining surfaces—a faux mantel, the kitchen counter and even the floor.

There was no question, this was a seduction scene taken directly from the most romantic and unforgettable movie she'd ever wanted to see. And Marcy clearly expected her to star in it. With Colt. Lena swallowed and waves of heat washed across her skin. Anticipation mixed with dread. Her worst nightmare and hottest dream all mixed into one.

Colt spun slowly in the center of the room. "Someone's been busy," he drawled, leaving to interpretation whether his words were complimentary or derogatory.

Lena narrowed her eyes, studying his face, trying to figure out what he thought about all of this. Was he horrified? Or, possibly, intrigued?

"We aim to please," said Marcy, grasping Lena by the elbow and pulling her along behind her. "I have several outfits for you to choose from. Whatever you're most comfortable in is fine with me."

"What kind of outfits?" Colt asked, his voice going dark.

"Nothing like that," Marcy admonished. "We're not going for salacious here. We want a few romantic shots highlighting the private bungalows that are available to our couples."

Marcy pushed Lena into the bathroom, closing the door behind her. The wood creaked as she leaned against it. With trepidation, Lena took in the row of soft, filmy fabrics Marcy had lined up for her. She had to admit that considering where they were filming, the choices could have been worse. Not a bustier or padded bra in the mix.

Lena reached for one, a pale pink color that probably wouldn't look great with her fair skin. But it was so soft beneath her fingers. She reached for another, this one dark red. Lena was afraid it would make her look as though she was trying too hard. She liked the black gown with lace edging, but it just seemed too stark somehow.

The final one had drawn her eye immediately which was why she'd saved it for last. To say that it was blue was somehow wrong. It was, but it had an iridescent shine to it that captured every shifting shade from the water outside their door. It was light and dark and bright and soft all at once.

It was perfect.

Slipping it on over her head, Lena felt as if she were wearing water instead of silk. It was longer than she'd expected, skimming just above the curve of her knee. The spaghetti straps might have left her feeling exposed, but the neckline was cut high enough to cover her cleavage so that helped. As far as lingerie went, it was enticing but not revealing.

Lena looked at herself in the mirror and felt a flutter of nerves, anticipation and hope deep in her stomach. She was…sexy. It wasn't that she'd never thought of herself that way. She had. Just not with Colt waiting in the other room. Taking a deep breath, she headed out.

The sun had begun to sink as they'd come into the bungalow. Now it was almost completely down, just the rim of gray, gold and pink at the edge of the world brushing the room with a soft, romantic glow.

Colt's eyes were bright as they slowly perused her body, taking in every inch of her. Her skin tingled and tightened. Lena shifted, trying to find some way to relieve the pressure that was mounting inside her.

His intensity was unnerving. She'd never seen this side of him. Lena wanted to back away, to pretend that none of this was happening. Instead, she found her feet moving slowly toward him, as if drawn by a gravitational pull she couldn't see, but definitely felt.

Thank God Marcy broke the spell by clearing her throat. Embarrassment at forgetting they weren't alone flamed up Lena's face and body.

"Mikhail, what do you think?"

The photographer joined them in the middle of the room. He looked over at Lena for several seconds. "Lena, what do you think of being on the bed, with Colt in the background?" The other man was warming to the vision only he could see.

"With her almost blurry and slightly romantic?" Colt asked.

And apparently Colt saw the same thing. Gone was the devouring expression from moments before, replaced by a studied gaze as he contemplated what the lens would see. It had been a very long time since Lena had watched him work.

During college, his camera had been like an extension of his hand, always present and subject to being pulled out at a moment's notice. Walks around the city had turned into photojournalism sessions. Heck, on occasion that lens had even turned on her. She wondered if he'd kept any of the photographs of her from years ago.

"Exactly." The two men walked off for several paces, their heads bent together as they talked about shutter speed, light and exposure—things Lena didn't fully understand. With nothing better to do, she climbed up onto the mattress.

She felt like a fool, stretched out across the cream silk sheets, which were not the standard Escape issue. Considering the price this bungalow rented for, they should be.

"So, what's the story?" Marcy leaned against one of the posts at the foot of the bed, her eyes friendly and curious.

"What do you mean?"

Lena shifted, using the pretense of arranging her legs and the silk gown to avoid looking into Marcy's eyes.

"There's more going on with you two than meets the eye."

"I told you, we're old friends."

"Please. I've spent the last two years managing a resort that specializes in selling sex—tasteful and romantic sex but sex nonetheless. I know chemistry when I see it. He couldn't keep his eyes off you when you walked out here. And the minute you stepped through that door he was the first thing you wanted to see."

Lena's eyes were drawn across the room to Colt. She couldn't help herself even though it was a dead giveaway.

"It's...complicated."

"Isn't everything?" Marcy asked. "He is beautiful," she added, her eyes cataloguing Colt in a purely academic way.

Lena was used to women staring at Colt, calculating whether he was available and if she was competition. There was absolutely no interest in Marcy's gaze.

"Athletic, with enough little-boy charm and mischief to make him approachable," Marcy analyzed. She leveled a pointed look at Lena.

"He moves around a lot. No roots. Anything we start would be short-lived and when it was over our friendship would never be the same."

"That's assuming it ends."

"It would. Colt doesn't form attachments."

"Except to you."

"I told you, we're just friends," Lena protested.

"Isn't friendship an attachment?"

"It isn't the same."

"But it's something. More than he's had with anyone else, I'd hazard. It's easy to dump someone you don't really like, harder to walk away from someone who's already important."

For no good reason fear swamped Lena. Her mouth felt dry and gritty, as if she'd swallowed sand. A bone-deep chill washed over her and her hands began to tremble.

That was exactly what she was afraid of. If she gave in to this and he walked away, could she survive? For the first time in her life, she understood how her mother had found herself repeatedly ruled by her emotions. They were too overwhelming to ignore.

Even though she knew giving in would be a mistake.

"Everyone ready?" Mikhail asked, interrupting Lena's little panic attack. She wanted desperately to say no, to rush out of the room, away from Colt, from temptation, from inevitable heartache. But she didn't. She couldn't. Not with Colt standing in front of her, a concerned expression on his face.

"Are you okay?"

She swallowed, the lump of sand in her throat refusing to budge. He moved closer, reaching for her. Lena scooted away, knowing if he touched her right now she would erupt into an inferno of demanding need neither of them could control.

Unable to speak, she nodded. And hoped it was enough.

6

"Lena, can you look a little more longingly at Colt? Extend your lines. You're yearning for him. Trying to get him to come to you, to join you."

Mikhail had been barking orders at Lena for the last twenty minutes, clearly not enamored with her performance. Colt had no idea what was going on with her. She'd gone from relaxed and enjoying the process this afternoon to uneasy and awkward. Maybe the gown was making her uncomfortable, although she hadn't appeared so when she'd walked out in it. She'd looked sexy, confident in her allure as a woman. Besides, the bikini she'd worn earlier had covered far less.

Colt bit down on the inside of his cheek to keep from snapping at Mikhail. He realized the photographer was just trying to get the picture he needed. But the more he barked at Lena the stiffer she became. She wasn't a natural model. She was beautiful, poised and self-contained, not an exhibitionist who relished displaying herself and her emotions for the world to view.

"This isn't working." Mikhail dropped his camera to his side with a huff of frustration.

"If you'd stop growling at her then maybe you'd get what you want." So much for trying not to interject and make things worse.

"Do you have a better idea?"

As a matter of fact, he did. "Can we clear everyone else out?"

Marcy began to sputter in protest, but one look from Mikhail seemed to stop her in her tracks.

"Sure." It took exactly five minutes for Mikhail's assistants and Marcy to clear the room. By the time they were gone the sun had completely sunk and the lighting was actually better—darkness outside and romantic, flickering lights inside. Mikhail took the opportunity to fiddle with the light stands in the corners, adjusting for the changes.

Lena flopped back against the jewel-toned pillows piled high at the headboard, her arm flung across her face. "When will the torture end?"

"Torture?" Colt asked, walking around the headboard to stand above her. The gown covering her shimmered in the shifting light, making it look as if her body undulated beneath the thin layer of silk. A sharp spike of need lanced through him. His fingers curled into his palms to keep from reaching for her.

But he couldn't stop himself from moving closer. Placing a knee on the bed beside her, he enjoyed the way she rolled toward him, her hip bumping against the inside of his thigh.

Even as he bent above her, words he hadn't meant to

say fell from his lips. "The only torture has been watching you writhe around on this bed and not being able to touch you." His words were guttural, primal, pulled from a place deep inside him that he didn't want to acknowledge but couldn't seem to contain.

She gasped, her eyes widening as she looked up at him. He watched her swallow, the long column of her throat working.

"Then touch me," she whispered, the words pulled from her body as reluctantly as his had been. He heard the hesitation, understood it.

But couldn't seem to do the right thing.

Her features were taut. Her eyes glittered, possessed by the same driving need that pulsed inside him. It was new, startling, tempting.

Colt slowly reached for her, running a single finger down the exposed curve of her arm. Her skin was so soft.

Her breath hitched. He heard the sound, saw the catch as her chest rose, paused and finished the climb.

In the back of his brain Colt heard the click of the camera, but this time he didn't let it matter. Nothing could distract him from Lena.

Her lips parted in anticipation. His finger continued over the slippery silk that covered her body. He brushed the side of her breast and watched in fascination as the nipple, so close he could have reached out and touched it, puckered and jutted towards him.

He stopped at the curve of her hip, pressing his curled fingers into the mattress for balance. He loomed over her, expecting that at any moment she'd come to her senses and tell him to stop.

But she didn't.

Instead, she arched beneath him, exposing the long, slim line of her neck. Her hair, darker in the low light, fanned out around her. He wanted to bury his fingers in the thick mass, use it to hold her to him.

The gown she was wearing pulled tight across her chest. He was sure there was some name for the neckline, probably something tantalizing and provocative since it tempted him with the curve of her flesh beneath the slick material. He didn't know what it was though, and frankly didn't care.

Her eyelids drooped heavily over mesmerizing blue-gray eyes. She was a temptress, pulling him in and making him forget why he shouldn't have her.

His lips drifted across her skin. He licked at the pulse point pounding against her throat. He breathed her in, consuming the scent of her as it swirled around them both. Dark, mysterious, feminine.

He latched on to her skin and sucked, drawing a sigh of pleasure from her as she surrendered to whatever he wanted.

What he wanted was her.

With an answering growl, Colt dove in and claimed her lips. She opened for him as he pushed inside. This kiss was completely different from the one they'd shared before. It wasn't soft and persuasive. It was fire and heat and devouring desire. It was demanding and yearning and the release of denying what he wanted.

In the back of his mind red warning lights were

flashing, but he was too far gone to care. His hands were rough as they pulled her to him. His fingers tore at the silk covering her body. He needed to feel her. Touch her. Own her.

Make her his…

The loud slam of the door had him shooting up and off the bed.

But she wasn't his.

Lena looked up at him, a mixture of embarrassment, horror and desire swamping her eyes. Her chest, now barely covered by the slip of soft fabric, rose and fell in halting time to his own uneven heartbeat.

He'd almost made a huge mistake. He liked things casual. He never slept with anyone he truly cared for, which made it easy to walk away.

He couldn't walk away from Lena. Once Pandora's box was opened there would be no going back.

And that scared the shit out of him.

Backing slowly toward the door, Colt couldn't pull his gaze from Lena's. Not even as he fumbled behind him for the knob and slipped out into the comforting darkness.

A KNOCK ON THE DOOR HAD LENA bolting up in the bed. Her hair hung limply into her bleary eyes. She pushed the mop away, clearing her vision, and then regretted it when the bright morning sunshine speared straight into her brain. Squinting, she mumbled a curse and stumbled for the entrance to the bungalow.

To anyone else it probably appeared as if she'd been on a five-day bender. The reality was that she'd gotten barely a few hours' sleep, and those had come in random snatches between crazy nightmares and erotic dreams—both featuring Colt.

She had no idea where he was, but he definitely hadn't shared the bed with her last night. If he was the one on the other side of the door it was entirely possible she might kill him.

Somewhere during the night she'd gone from relief that he'd had the forethought to stop what they'd started, to anger that he'd walked out without a word, to worry that he'd do something stupid such as hike into the jungle in the middle of the night and fall off a cliff.

The pounding increased, joined by the cheerful sound of Georgie's drawl. "Wake up, sleepyheads. We've been waiting on y'all for a half hour."

Lena's right eye began to twitch, but she opened the door anyway.

Georgie leveled a knowing, conspiratorial look in her direction as she brushed past into their bungalow. "Someone had a fun night."

Lena self-consciously patted her hair, trying in vain to smooth out the knots.

"Honey, you look like you've been rode hard and put up wet. At least tell me the ride was worth it." Georgie took in their bungalow. "Well, this is...interesting. A little different layout than ours." The frown on her face said she wasn't impressed.

"Marcy moved everything around. We had a photo session last night." Lena couldn't stop the hot flush that burned her skin at the memories. A stinging heat settled between her thighs and she shifted from one foot to the other, trying to find relief.

"Where's Colt?" Georgie asked, her puzzled eyes looking around the space as if he might pop out from beneath the kitchen sink.

Lena opened her mouth to tell a lie—although she wasn't sure which one—but the dark rumble of Colt's voice stopped her.

"Right here," he said, leaning against the open doorway out to the patio and private pool. Had he been out there the whole time?

Arms crossed over his chest, he lounged there, looking for all the world like a relaxed—sated—groom. His wide chest was naked, a tempting V of hair running in an arrow down his body to disappear beneath the lowriding band of his jeans.

Lena swallowed, her mouth suddenly dry and useless. Colt's eyes flashed for a moment as they ran over her body, rekindling what he hadn't been willing to finish last night.

Lena's hands crumpled into fists at her side, although she wasn't sure who she wanted to use them on more—Colt or her unruly libido.

Georgie reached out to pat her arm, grinning slyly. "Don't worry, sweetheart. Looks like someone has enough stamina for both of you."

Colt's lips twitched. Lena's eyes narrowed in warning. Clearing his throat, he said, "Why don't you give us time to get ready, Georgie? We're obviously running a little late."

"Twenty minutes," she said, swinging a perfectly

manicured nail to point at both of them. "Or we're leaving without you."

"Promise?" Lena muttered beneath her breath. It was Colt's turn to flash *her* a warning glance, ushering Georgie out with promises that they'd be there.

Not waiting for him to return, Lena went into the bathroom and rummaged through her toiletry bag until she found some aspirin. Thanks to her restless night, her brain felt as if it was trying to push straight through the top of her skull. Not bothering with water, she swallowed the tablets dry and then regretted it when Colt asked, "Everything all right," and the chalky lump stopped somewhere in the middle of her throat.

Pushing past him, she made a beeline for the fridge and the Diet Coke Marcy had stocked there. Popping the top, she swallowed several gulps.

"Slow down," he said, propping his hip against the counter, pulling the edge of his worn jeans down far enough that she could see the jutting tip of his hip. She gulped some more, tearing her eyes away from his body.

"Caffeine. I have a headache."

Colt frowned. "Maybe we shouldn't go."

A few minutes earlier, Lena would have jumped at the chance to back out of spending hours on end with little miss sunshine. But as her eyes strayed to the bed still sitting in the middle of the room, she realized there were worse ideas in the world.

Like being alone with Colt. With chaperones she was less likely to throw herself at him like a wanton hussy.

Besides, the alternative was whatever Marcy had

scheduled for the day, and frankly, after last night she was afraid to find out what that might entail.

Pretending for the camera had gotten seriously complicated. She no longer knew what was fake and what was real. Where her friendship with Colt ended and her attraction began.

Part of her was grateful Colt had put a stop to things last night. But most of her was just frustrated.

Yeah, putting people between them was probably the intelligent choice.

She reluctantly said, "No, I want to go. Wild jungle, tropical waterfall, sounds like a great way to spend the day." Unfortunately, her tingling body reminded her there were plenty of more enjoyable ways to pass the time.

TREKKING THROUGH THE JUNGLE was not exactly what he'd had in mind. Although, after last night, what he had in mind was out of the question. It had taken everything inside him not to grab Lena and throw her down on the looming bed this morning.

Getting out of the bungalow and away from temptation had seemed like the best plan.

Ahead, Georgie and Wesley walked hand in hand through the jungle. The path was barely wide enough to accommodate them, probably meant for single file hiking. But that didn't deter them. Colt noticed they were always touching. Nothing major, the brush of his hand across her back or her arm around his waist.

His palms itched to reach for Lena, to pull her next to him just to know that she was there. Instead, he let her walk a few steps in front. The hem of the tiny shorts she'd put on barely covered the bottom swell of her ass. Colt couldn't pull his gaze away, constantly hoping for a bigger glimpse.

It was making the whole situation more difficult. Hiking he could handle. Hiking with a raging hard-on was far from enjoyable. Although, he had to admit the view was damn nice and more than worth the discomfort.

Without even looking behind her, Lena said, "Stop staring at my ass."

Colt probably should have felt guilty for being caught. He didn't.

"How'd you know I was looking?"

She peered over her shoulder, raking him with a laser gaze. "Because I can feel it."

His entire body tightened. His veins pulsed, too small to contain the quick shot of desire.

"You're the one who walked away, Colt. Don't get me wrong, I'm glad. It would have been a mistake. But you can't leave like that and then stare at my ass like it's the first bite of the best meal of your life."

She shot him another glance, this one a little darker with promise. "It isn't fair."

What wasn't fair was having her prance around in tempting clothes without expecting a reaction.

"I'm a man, Lena. What do you want from me?"

She stopped on the path, spinning to face him. "I don't know anymore," she said, the harsh words carrying an air of reluctant honesty.

Colt stepped into her space, toe-to-toe. He towered

over her. He had to admire the way she tipped her head
back and stared straight into his eyes, defiant and determined to stand her ground and not let him—or their
situation—intimidate her.

Deep in her eyes he saw the same emotions he was
fighting against. Confusion. Awareness. Fear, hope,
heat.

They were in over their heads, but he realized at least
they'd drown together. Maybe there was a way for this
to work, for them to release the energy building between them, without ruining what they already had.

There was a term for it, right? Friends with benefits.
He'd never understood the appeal until now.

"Admit it. You wore those shorts on purpose."

Her eyes widened and she gave a little shake of her
head, the motion sending her bangs into her eyes. With
a gentle brush of his fingers, he pushed the hair back
so that he could see her expression. Her eyes flared at
the simple connection, her pupils contracting.

He could tell she wanted to look away. But, just like
him, she was caught in the moment and couldn't let go.
"Maybe."

His thumb stroked down the line of her cheek to her
jaw. Her lips parted, giving him an unobstructed view
of her little pink tongue. He wanted to reach inside and
stroke it with his own.

And he might have, if they hadn't been reminded
they had company by Georgie's amazed exclamation.
"It's so beautiful!"

In that moment he heard the shushed roar and wondered if it had been there the whole time.

"Hurry up, y'all." Georgie's voice floated down the path.

Lena had already turned to follow. Colt rushed to catch up with her. This time when the urge to run his hand along her spine hit, he didn't tamp it down. Instead, he reached for her and relished the way her muscles jumped and her body pressed into his touch.

They broke through the trees a few minutes later. The waterfall was beautiful, with an untouched quality that Colt knew couldn't be real. There was a path cut straight to it after all. They weren't the first humans to visit here. Heck, probably not even the first this week.

"Look at this place. It's gorgeous," Lena breathed.

Colt walked into the clearing that surrounded the pool where the water from the falls collected before it broke through the rest of the jungle in a quiet line. He was struck by how calm the water was, especially considering that it was tumbling over a cliff twenty feet above them to churn over large boulders and rocks just a few feet away.

How could something so violent turn so calm within such a space? Mother Nature truly deserved respect for her awe-inspiring beauty.

Lena walked up beside him. Her arm brushed against his and a shock shot through his body, stronger than anything he'd ever experienced before.

"Look at those colors. What I wouldn't give to be able to capture them in a stone or a shell or a piece of glass." Colt heard the same awe in her voice that was expanding his chest.

"Why don't you?"

"Because I can't. No stone or glass could produce

something so pure and vibrant. There are just some things that can't be replicated and I refuse to create a cheap imitation."

Her integrity was impressive, but something he'd always known she possessed. She expected a lot from herself and the people around her. Which made it worse when those people failed her as her mother and Wyn had.

Colt had the sudden urge to protect her, to make sure nothing ever hurt her again. But he, more than anyone, realized that wasn't possible. No one could stop the inevitable.

All you could do was minimize your exposure and protect yourself as best you could.

"Soups on, y'all," Georgie called out. She'd been busy spreading a blanket beneath the soaring trees. An array of food sat in sealed containers. She'd even brought real silverware and plastic plates.

Colt shot Wesley a commiserating look. The poor bastard had packed it all into the jungle. Wesley shrugged. "My baby prides herself on hospitality."

"I do know how to throw a party, don't I?" she asked, with a proud smile.

The four of them settled onto opposite corners of the blanket. Wesley speared a bite of broccoli salad off of Georgie's plate. She swatted at his hand, but followed the empty gesture by offering what was already on her fork.

They all seemed to settle into a comfortable companionship. Lena managed to steer Georgie away from the topic of their wedding whenever the other woman wanted to hear details, although he did catch her fiddling with the gold band around her finger several times. They talked about their lives, it turned out Georgie was a counselor at an elementary school and Wesley had just taken over running his family's car dealership.

They were fascinated by all the places Colt's job had taken him.

"That'll be so much fun for a while. Moving around, seeing new places, experiencing new things." Georgie looked up at Wesley with a sad smile on her face. "I envy y'all that flexibility. Wesley's a bit tied down."

"I told you I'd quit tomorrow if that's what you want me to do."

"I don't." She patted his leg, leaning into his body. "I'd rather have boring and ordinary with you than exotic without you."

Lena made an incredulous sound that she quickly turned into a cough.

"Let's cool off," Wesley suggested. They all made quick work of cleaning up. The water was cool and refreshing, washing away the heat of the hike. Even as he tried to behave himself, Colt found his hands and mind straying to Lena.

Despite the friendly atmosphere, a pulsing undercurrent ran between them every time their gazes caught and held. It was torture, having her so close and knowing he couldn't do anything about it.

7

SOMEWHERE IN THE LATE afternoon the four of them drowsed beneath the sun. Filtered through the canopy of the trees above, the light was washed out and soft against their skin.

Lena pretended to settle, although she was too restless to actually get comfortable.

Between last night and this morning something had changed. She could see it in Colt's eyes, the way he watched her. He no longer tried to cover up the interest she could now see clearly. Instead, he tortured her with it, letting his eyes roam across her body the way she wanted his hands to touch her.

In the water, he'd teased her, letting his hand brush across her sensitive breasts before pulling away. His fingers had slid up the smooth expanse of her thigh only to disappear before giving her what she wanted.

She'd tried to play the same game, but he was too fast.

Beside her, Colt shifted. Pushing soundlessly to his feet, he walked several paces away, paused long enough to scoop up the pack he'd brought, looked over his shoulder at her, and then continued past the water to disappear into the cool shadows of the jungle.

She had a decision to make. She could follow him, finish what had been building between them. Or she could stay on the blanket, yearning twisting her insides into knots, and walk back to the resort frustrated and disappointed.

The second option held absolutely no appeal.

As Lena pushed to her feet, Georgie raised her head and looked over.

"Don't wait for us," Lena whispered.

Georgie gave her a drowsy, knowing smile but didn't say anything. Instead, she laid her head back onto Wesley's shoulder, snuggling deep into his arms.

On silent feet, Lena followed Colt into the jungle. She softly whispered his name, but he didn't reply. She moved farther, letting the gigantic trees and thick underbrush swallow her. Not even the rush of the waterfall could penetrate the dense growth around her.

She was about to turn back, certain she must have gone in a different direction from Colt, when his hands wrapped around her waist.

She let out a surprised squeak which Colt's devouring mouth immediately swallowed.

Surprise mixed with adrenaline, but even as her mind raced to catch up her body was already melting into him. His arms wrapped around her, lifting her up onto her toes and crushing her against him. Their tongues warred, sucked, played. His hands wandered. It would have been so easy to just let the moment take her and deal with the consequences later. But that wasn't who she was.

Pulling away from him, Lena drew in a deep breath. Colt didn't take the hint, instead latching his mouth onto the sensitive side of her neck. Her knees buckled and he caught her, scooping her into his arms.

Carrying her a few feet, Colt laid her onto the silvery surface of an emergency blanket. It crinkled loudly beneath her body.

"Where did this come from?" she asked.

"I was a Boy Scout. 'Always be prepared.' This pack has been all over the world with me and it's always ready."

He dropped to his knees beside her, adding his own rustling to the muted sounds of the jungle around them. In this moment, it was easy to believe they were the only people in the entire world.

He leaned over her, ready to pick up where they'd left off, but Lena stopped him, pushing her hand between them. Her fingers connected with his lips and even that shot a tiny spark through her blood. But this was important.

"What changed?" she asked, hoping with every fiber of her being that she liked his answer.

He drew back from her, rocking onto his heels. "I don't know."

That wasn't what she wanted to hear. Pulling her legs beneath her, she was ready to get up and walk away, but he stopped her.

"I'm tired of fighting it, Lena. I've wanted you for days. Probably longer, if I was honest with myself. It was easy to ignore when we were continents away. I'd come home, feel a little buzz when we were together, and leave again. I'd convince myself it wasn't real. Or I'd stay away long enough to forget it."

"I was so easy to forget?"

He bent down, pressing his forehead to hers, whispering, "No. But I don't want to change what we've already got." He pulled back, looking into her eyes. A shadow of something clouded the bright green surface.

"I think it's too late for that. The minute we stepped onto this island it was inevitable."

"I can't promise you anything."

She swallowed, recognizing exactly what he was telling her. Nothing that she didn't already know. They had two completely different lives that only intersected on occasion. He was the worst possible man for her, but apparently that didn't mean anything to her wayward body.

"I don't remember asking you for a promise. What I want is for you to make me feel. To make me forget. To give me everything you've got for however long we have. At the end of the week we'll both go back to our separate lives. Like we always do."

Knowing what to expect should help keep her heart uninvolved. Sex. That's what this was. Nothing more.

"You're sure?" he asked, one last time. She probably should have taken the escape hatch, but she really didn't want it.

"Absolutely," she said, wrapping her arm around his neck and drawing him back down to her. "Love me. Now."

His eyes blazed. With a growl, he reached for her, rolling their bodies until she was draped across him, her soft curves sinking into his hard planes. She expected his hands to be rough, for him to tear at her clothes and skin and hair, to want to devour her as much as she wanted to be devoured.

Instead, he gently scraped the hair back from her face, staring up into her eyes for several moments. His eyes were sharp, missing nothing. With all of her clothes still on, somehow he managed to make her feel naked. Exposed. The intensity she could have handled, but this soul-deep exploration made her want to squirm.

Colt knew her better than anyone—including Wyn—and she realized she was about to share the only part of herself he hadn't already seen.

As if he'd read her mind Colt spoke, his gravel-roughened words brushing against her skin. "You're beautiful and he's an idiot."

She tried to capture his mouth, to cut off the words so that she wouldn't have to think about them, but he wouldn't let her.

"I don't want to talk about him while I'm having sex with you."

He rolled them, the unexpected motion leaving her breathless and slightly disoriented when the world stopped spinning around them.

"Who said anything about sex? *Sex* implies something raunchy and quick. Nothing about this is going to be quick. I'm going to touch every inch of you. Drive you mindless. Before I'm done you'll be begging me to let you come."

The secret muscles deep inside her body contracted at his words. She felt the slick proof that he could make good on his threat between her thighs. Lena squirmed, trying to relieve some of the pressure, but it didn't help. Nothing would.

"What if I make you beg first?" she asked, reaching between them. Her fingers had barely brushed against the tantalizing ridge of his erection before her hands were captured and stretched above her head.

"Maybe later."

She wanted to protest, but couldn't. Not with his mouth annihilating hers, stealing what coherent thought she had. The only thing left to do was feel.

He kept her locked there, at his mercy, as his mouth consumed everything it could touch. Pushing her thighs wide, he settled his own hips into the cradle there. The hard length of his erection pressed into the weeping center of her sex. Layers of clothing separated them, keeping what she really wanted so close but so far away.

As he worked slowly across her skin, stopping to suck and lick at pulse points she hadn't even known she had, he kept up a steady, torturous rocking motion. The hard heat of him rubbed against her, too light to bring her any sort of relief. It wasn't long before her head was thrashing between her upstretched arms, her eyes closed tight against the unforgiving edge of frustration.

Only when her body burned so hot she thought it might implode did he let go long enough to tug her clothes away. Any time she'd allowed herself to think about this moment, there had always been a tinge of anxiety. They'd been friends forever, but he'd never seen her naked. Would he be disappointed?

In reality, she was too consumed to worry about anything but the relief only he could give her.

Her eyes, gritty with need, watched as the sharp edge of his gaze scraped down the length of her body. Her back arched, begging him to put her out of her misery. Her breasts felt heavy and swollen. The tight nipples ached to feel the pebbled surface of his tongue caress them. The insides of her thighs were wet with desire, waiting, weeping, for him to finish this.

After all her blustering bravado, it didn't take long for her to beg. "Touch me. Please."

He did, this time leaving her hands free to return the favor. She reached for his clothes, tearing frantically until they finally fell away. Her hands shook as they skimmed down the warm expanse of his chest.

He was so solid beneath her touch, drawn tight with the same tension that whipped through her own body. The muscles beneath her fingers quivered. The further they dipped towards his sex the harder they leapt.

Her fingers feathered down the length of his erection and his entire body jerked. A low animal rumble ripped through his chest. She'd meant to play, to torture him the way he was making her mindless, but that intention disappeared the moment he sucked the tip of her aching breast deep into his mouth.

Her breath backed into her throat and the world around her blurred. Her fist closed tight around him, a reflexive reaction to find an anchor in the storm. He was hot and heavy in her hand.

Her palm slipped up and down his smooth weight. He felt wonderful and she could imagine the exquisite pleasure of him filling her deep inside. Her own hips pumped in unison with her motions, mimicking what she wanted.

Lifting her legs, she wrapped them around his waist. Her heels pressed into his flanks, her hand guiding him to the center of her need.

"Wait," he said, the single word garbled almost beyond recognition. She whimpered in protest as he fought against her hold on him. Until she realized he was reaching into the magic backpack, removing a shiny foil packet.

"Condom," he uttered, tearing into the packet and rolling the latex over his sex. She watched as the long, throbbing vein that ran the length of him disappeared beneath the opaque surface.

Grasping her hips, Colt pulled her back beneath him. The weight of his body pressed her into the blanket, grounding her in a way she'd never realized she wanted. Her body felt hot and light, ready to break apart into pieces and disappear. Colt was the only thing that gave her substance. Surrounded by wild jungle, he was the only thing that felt real.

Reaching down to spread her folds, his fingers slipped and slid, hitting her clit and making her arch against him. Cool air brushed across her exposed skin and her muscles contracted in anticipation.

Colt slid inside, slowly, deliberately, the heft of his sex stretching her. Filling her up. She gasped. Lifting her knees, she widened her thighs, taking all of him that she could.

Their eyes locked. Something deep in her chest tightened, something scary. But it was too late to go back now.

"Don't think we won't be talking about why you just happen to have condoms in that backpack," she whispered, trying to distract herself.

A broken chuckle erupted from his body. She could feel it everywhere, the vibrations echoing through where they joined. "Later." His mouth grabbed hers and he said again against her lips, "Much later."

The frenzy, held at bay for far too long, finally broke free. Their bodies slapped together, over and over, each trying to pull and push one last ounce of desire from their joining. Lena sunk her teeth into Colt's shoulder. The salty tang of his skin exploded across her tongue. His fingers dug into her hips, lifting her higher as he pounded in and out of her.

Lena's body bowed. Every muscle froze and then exploded into a quivering mass of delirium. Pleasure tore at her, breaking her into pieces and leaving behind a shell of what she'd been before.

Colt joined her, yelling so loudly that a bird in the branches above them startled. Flying away, it rained indignant squawks down on them. Lena barely heard them, focused as she was so totally on the rolling aftershocks that rocked through her body.

Deep inside, she could feel the speeding pulse where she and Colt joined. Collapsing beside her, Colt gathered her in his arms. She was coherent enough to realize they were shaking, his entire body quivering with long-denied release.

She had no idea how long they lay there. She should probably be feeling something. Panic maybe. Or remorse. Perhaps guilt. But she felt none of those things. She felt…right. As if there was nowhere else in the world she'd rather be than right here, tucked against Colt, satisfaction still rushing through her muscles.

Exhaustion stole across her. There would be plenty of time for regret. *Later,* she thought, and snuggled deeper.

COLT BOLTED AWAKE. Where was he? It took him a minute to remember. The jungle. With Lena. She stirred beside him, still asleep.

Sitting up, he looked around and cursed. Darkness had fallen, although a weak, watery light still managed to filter down through the canopy of leaves above them. It couldn't be all that late. Here, surrounded by dense trees, the light disappeared early. The jungle thinned closer to the resort. If they hurried, they might be able to make it out.

He didn't want to think about Lena's reaction if they couldn't. While sleeping out in the open didn't bother him, he was pretty sure it wouldn't be her first choice. Not when there was a soft, comfortable bed waiting for them.

If he hadn't been such a lust-fogged idiot.

"Lena, get up. We have to go," he whispered gently.

"Hmm," she mumbled and rolled onto her side. Thirty seconds later she sat straight up. Eyes wide, she looked around them. Her body sagged as she frowned. "Well, shit."

Colt chuckled. Her reaction could have been worse. Holding out her clothes he said, "As much as I hate to say this, you need to get dressed."

While he'd been gathering her clothes, he'd pulled his own on. Reaching down, he grabbed his pack. Zipping open a side pocket, he pulled out his cell phone. Illuminating the dark screen confirmed what he'd already feared, no signal. Who needed a cell tower in the middle of the jungle?

Apparently, they did.

At least the phone's display told him what time it was. Later than he'd hoped but earlier than he'd feared.

Scraping her hair away from her face, Lena said, "What now, Boy Scout?"

"We might be able to hike out of here. If we can get to the waterfall, the jungle won't be as dense. There's still enough light that if we find the path back to the resort we'll be fine."

"And if we don't?"

"Then I guess we sleep outside."

Lena's mouth twisted into a grimace but she didn't protest. Instead she gestured forward. "Lead the way, Lewis."

"Lewis?"

"If we're going to be forging our way through the jungle I get to be Clark."

Colt just shook his head. Most of the women he'd dated would be having hysterics by now. Not Lena. Nope, hysterics were a waste of time.

"I don't suppose you have a flashlight in there." She gestured to the pack he'd thrown across his shoulder. Lifting his hand, he showed her that he'd already pulled it out.

"What about a four-course meal?"

"Sorry, out of luck. But I promise to feed you the minute we get back to civilization."

"You'd better." She mock-glared.

Grasping her hand, he pulled her directly behind him. "Stay one step back. The darker it becomes the easier it'll be to get separated."

"Why do you get to go first? What if I want to lead?"

"Who's the Boy Scout?"

Her mouth crunched into a straight line. Her eyes blazed with indignation. Colt cut off the argument he could see coming. "Besides, this way you won't get hit with any stray branches."

And he'd be able to tackle any danger head-on, protecting her the best he could. If anyone was going to step off a cliff or startle a wild animal it was going to be him. He'd gotten them into this mess and if anything happened to her...

His chest constricted. His lungs fought to pull in enough air. Something seriously close to panic suffused his entire body. Clenching his hands into fists, Colt deliberately banned the thought from his mind.

They were fine.

8

Darkness settled well and truly around them. The space that had seemed enchanting, lush and romantic just hours before quickly took on a sinister cast. Gone was the gentle sunlight filtering through the canopy of the trees. Instead, dim moonlight barely broke through, only to completely disappear before touching the ground.

Lena was cold, tired and hungry. The jungle was supposed to be hot, but apparently not at night. She fervently wished for the sun, not only for light but also for warmth. Wrapping her arms around her body, she really wished she'd worn longer shorts.

They walked silently, the only sound between them the rustling of the dry leaves and branches beneath their feet.

Something startled beside them. The bush to Lena's right erupted and a large bird, its multicolored feathers muted by the darkness, flew straight at her.

She screamed—it was a reflex she wasn't proud of,

but there it was—and ducked. The thing almost grazed the top of her head, her hair swirling in the wake of its passing. Angry sounds echoed back as it settled into the branches of another tree behind them.

Lena's hand covered her chest, hoping that the pressure would keep her heart from escaping along with the bird.

Colt was there beside her, his hands running over her body looking for any sign of damage.

"I'm fine," she croaked through a tight throat. Frowning, she tried again, "I'm fine, just startled," and was happy to hear no hesitation in the words this time.

Although her legs still felt a bit wobbly. Colt wrapped his arm around her waist and pulled her up. Lena was grateful for the support, but knew it couldn't last. Locking her knees, she said, "Look, admit it, we're stuck out here for the night. We need to find some shelter and stop wandering around aimlessly over unfamiliar terrain."

The flashlight Colt had trained towards the ground bounced up to hit his face at an eerie angle. It highlighted the sharp contours of his jaw and cheekbones, leaving large sections of his face in shadow. It made him look…austere, a word she never would have used to describe him before now.

"No, the path has to be close. If we can find it we can follow it out."

The flashlight between them flickered ominously.

Lena looked pointedly down. "We need to conserve battery power."

Colt's face tightened. "It isn't safe out here. I need

to get you back to the resort before something terrible happens."

Lena frowned. What the hell was wrong with him? Colt was usually the most levelheaded person in a crisis. Driving one-twenty down a country road might have been the stupidest thing the man had ever done, but getting himself out of the car, calling 911 and then applying his own tourniquet to his broken and bleeding leg before he passed out had taken nerves of steel.

Colt was a problem solver. A Boy Scout for heaven's sake.

Maybe she wasn't the only one who'd been scared out of her skull by that bird.

"Don't they teach you to stay put when you get lost? Besides, the only thing I'm in danger of is twisting my ankle because I can't see where I'm walking. It's late, Colt. I'm tired. We need to find someplace to sleep and then hike out in the morning."

She watched as his eyes roamed her face. No question, he wasn't happy, but even before he opened his mouth she knew she'd gotten through to him.

"All right. I remember seeing a cave behind the waterfall. I've been hearing the rumbling for the past few minutes. We'll find the cave, make camp and then leave at first light."

Lena's eyebrows beetled. She didn't hear anything. Taking a step sideways, she moved out of the shelter of Colt's body and finally heard it. His tall frame had apparently been blocking the sound.

"Great. Lead on."

Twenty minutes later they broke through the line

of trees surrounding the pool. Somewhere along the way they'd circled around, coming out about thirty feet closer to the falls than where they'd both left the clearing. No doubt they'd spent some of the past few hours walking parallel to the falls instead of directly toward them.

"Remind me to give you a compass for Christmas," she quipped. "You can keep it with your stash of condoms."

"Don't worry. I'll have one delivered from the mainland tomorrow."

"Why? We coming back out here?"

Colt spun suddenly on his heel. Lena collided with him. His arms steadied her even as they pulled her closer.

"Not on your life." His eyes blazed, not with passion but with determination and fire. His fingers gripped her upper arms, digging almost painfully into her skin. She tried to move, but realized she couldn't even wiggle. "Promise me you'll never do something like this again."

"Like what? Go hiking? Have a picnic? Get lost? I can promise you I'll try."

Colt's jaw worked back and forth, his molars grinding tightly against each other.

Lena took a slow step closer and said quietly, "Colt, let go. You're hurting me."

His hands burst away from her body. She rocked slightly, surprised by the sudden loss of his support.

Spinning away, he raked his hands through his hair, leaving it disheveled and standing on end. "I'm sorry," he said, still facing away. "I'm just…worried. I can't believe I let this happen!" he roared.

She was finally beginning to understand.

"You let this happen?" she asked slowly. "I don't remember you being the only adult in this situation. Why are you to blame for us getting lost?"

Spinning back to her, he barked, "Because you're my responsibility."

That had her back up within seconds. "No, I'm not. I'm responsible for myself and have been for years, you idiot." Lena stalked closer, jabbing a finger into his chest. With each step she took forward, he took one back. "I don't remember blaming you for this predicament. Or wailing like some helpless female."

"I didn't mean…" he sputtered, backtracking nice and fast…straight into the water. One second he was standing in front of her, the next he was sprawled in knee-deep water, his eyes round and bright with surprise.

Lena's first reaction was to jump in after him. Uncaring that her shoes were now soaking wet, she splashed into the water and crouched down beside him. "Are you okay?"

She reached for him, tugging uselessly at the weight of his body. Instead of answering, he reached beneath her arms and toppled her into the water beside him. The water was shockingly warm, the pool shallow enough to have heated through from the sun.

They grappled in the water, each trying to get the upper hand. She knew it was useless, but refused to give up without a fight. After several minutes, Colt ended up above her, her legs pinned down by the weight of his hips and her arms held loosely in his hands.

He grinned down at her, wicked and mischievous.

"Great, now my clothes are soaked. I don't suppose you have a spare set in the pack?"

"Sure," he said. "For me."

"You're going to have to share. I'm already cold, and wet clothes won't help."

He ground his hips slowly against her, making a warm ribbon of need wind slowly through her body.

"I'm sure we can come up with a better way to keep you warm."

"Oh, yeah," she countered, arching her back and pressing the wet globes of her breasts against the warm expanse of his chest.

Desire, strong and hard, zinged between them. She wanted him again. She wanted to feel him moving inside her, stretching her body and filling her up. She wanted to touch him, taste him and learn what she could do to make those little growling noises erupt from his throat again.

And here was as good a place as any. Reaching between them, she wiggled her hand closer to the burgeoning ridge of his cock. But she didn't get there in time.

Instead, Colt pushed away from her. Drops of water rained down around her as he stood, reaching to help her up after him.

"I was talking about building a fire," he said, a teasing grin playing at the corners of his mouth.

"Bastard," she grumbled, suppressing her own smile.

She took a step away, but Colt pulled her back, jerking her into his arms and stealing her breath with a kiss. She went under, happily, letting him take whatever he wanted. Opening herself, body, mind, soul to him.

The clearing around them was quiet. And while the jungle they'd hiked through had seemed dark and dangerous, the waterfall and pool somehow held a tinge of magic. Even the massive roar of the water as it crashed over the edge only reminded her what the power of letting go could provide—deep, reverberating pleasure.

Maybe being lost wasn't so bad after all. Not if she was lost with Colt.

Lena was all ready for round two. Who needed an emergency blanket when the sandy shore beneath their feet was available? She tried to wiggle away from Colt, to work her hands between them enough so that she could fill her palms with the rolling waves of muscle that crossed his tight abs.

But instead of reacting to her touch, Colt stilled. It was unnatural, his sudden and complete lack of motion. Even his lungs stopped sucking in air.

Lena looked up into his face. "Colt?" His arms tightened, but his gaze was no longer focused on her.

Turning her head slowly, Lena followed his line of sight and nearly screamed.

"Don't move," he whispered.

A large cat, black as the center of the jungle, crouched across from them.

"What is that?" she whispered.

"Jaguar. I think."

It was lapping up water from the pool, somehow

managing to never take its stalking, steady gaze off them. It paused, the whites of its eyes flashing as if realizing it was no longer the only one watching.

Even from this distance, Lena could see the powerful muscles of its flanks. They quivered, as if gathered in readiness to spring at any moment.

"I wonder if it's hungry," she whispered wryly.

It stared at them. Lena could count the seconds by the racing thud of Colt's heartbeat next to her own. The cat's dark pink tongue licked, lightning-fast, over its maw.

"I don't think that's a good sign," Colt rumbled.

Lena felt the tight coil of Colt's muscles as he braced for fight or flight. A bolt of awareness—ill-timed and seriously unhelpful—blasted through her body. She jerked against him, unable to stop herself from the bone-deep reaction. Colt felt it, his body stirring against hers.

As if sensing their distraction, the cat took that moment to disappear. They caught the flash of tail as it slipped into the jungle. If they hadn't known it was there, the twitch could have been just a shadow.

Galvanized into motion, Colt set her away, pulling her out of the water behind him. Her body protested the loss of his heat, but she understood. He was in a flurry, gathering sticks, leaves and moss. Pushing the mess into her arms, he went back for more, this time searching for larger chunks of wood.

She assumed the paraphernalia was for a fire. He proved her right when he directed her across the pool toward the waterfall and said, "We'll build a fire at the entrance. It'll keep us warm and keep that guy away."

A shiver of a different sort raced up her spine.

Her waterlogged shoes sunk into the sand at the bottom of the pool. The closer they got to the falls the harder it became to lift each foot.

Colt stopped in front of her. With a curt "Wait here," he disappeared through the wall of water protecting the entrance to the cave.

A protest sputtered on Lena's lips even as she realized it was pointless. Stupid man. If he encountered something dangerous in there he'd be fighting alone.

Wrapping her body around the fire-starting materials to keep them as dry as possible, she followed behind him.

She let out a gasp as the water washed down over her back. She might already be wet, but the water cascading down was much cooler than that of the collecting pool.

The place was dark. Lena looked around, frantically searching for the telltale shine of Colt's flashlight.

"Colt," she yelled.

There was no answer.

She tried again, lifting her voice and spinning around in the dark cavern. "Colt!" The only thing that came back was an empty echo.

"DAMMIT, I TOLD YOU to stay put."

Colt tried to ignore Lena's jump of surprise as he walked up behind her. After sweeping the cave to make sure it wasn't already occupied, he'd switched off the flashlight and let his eyes become adjusted.

His heart had pounded every second they'd been separated, but leaving her alone outside had been the lesser of two evils. Without knowing what was inside the cave, bringing her with him had been too much of a risk. The confined space wouldn't have provided many options for escape or fight.

As it turned out, the cave was empty. The ceiling at the front opened high above their heads, but it sloped downward to connect with the floor about twenty yards back.

For the first time since he'd awoken to find the jungle darkening around them, Colt let out a sigh of relief. At least here they'd be safe until morning.

Lena's eyes shimmered through darkness, twin beacons of light that pulled him closer. The smell of her, wild and wet, slammed through him. The primitive urge to have her, to prove to himself that she was unharmed and safe, overwhelmed him. He jerked her forward, crushing her against his body. The heat of her singed his skin. He swore he could hear the sizzle as the water on his skin turned to steam.

Her breath whooshed out to tickle across the damp cotton of his shirt. His arms wrapped around her, plastering her to him as tightly as their wet clothes clung to them.

His heart pounded against his rib cage like an angry bird fighting to get out. He was certain she must be able to feel it, too. His teeth ground together in the back of his mouth, a last-ditch attempt to find some shred of control.

Somewhere in the back of his mind, Colt realized he was heading for disaster. Out here, something dark inside him had been released—the urge to protect and dominate, to claim what was his and to never let it go.

It was a side of himself he wasn't completely enamored with but couldn't seem to fight. Not with Lena standing in front of him, the dark centers of her eyes watching, waiting, the low guttural words of her taunt egging him on. "Take me."

With a growl of surrender—to her, to himself, to whatever this was—Colt erupted around her. He claimed her lips in a frenzy of passion. His tongue plundered her mouth, but she met him thrust for thrust, scraping and jabbing and asking for more.

She sucked him deeper inside, so far that he could feel the vibration of her mewl of approval.

His hands scraped against her scalp, burrowing in her hair and angling her mouth so he could get more of her. His arm wrapped around her back, lifting her up off the floor so she had nowhere else to go but to him.

She didn't fight against the tempest blowing between them. Instead, she opened to him, giving everything and taking even more in return. What they'd shared before had been slow and tender, the final capitulation of two people who'd cared about each other for a long time. This was a scrabbling fight for the ecstasy only they could give each other.

Her legs, left with nothing else to do but dangle, found purchase around his waist. She arched into his hold, rubbing the heat of her sex against his throbbing erection.

Colt fought the sensation that he was drowning, swamped not only by his emotions for Lena, but by her unquestioning surrender and trust in him. Trust that he would keep her safe.

A cloud of passion wrapped them together, blocking out everything else. All he wanted to do was feel her, taste her, absorb her into his body so he'd never forget this moment of possessing her. In the days and weeks to come, when the inevitable happened and they returned to their real lives, he'd still have this memory to take with him into dark, lonely nights.

And he was bound and determined to make the most of it.

Oblivious to everything except his need for her, Colt stumbled backwards until Lena's back connected with the rough stone wall. She arched against him, letting out a tiny sound. He tried to pull away, but her fingers scrabbled against his shoulders and a low growl of protest vibrated between their lips.

Her legs gripped him tighter, her ankles digging mercilessly into his back to bring him closer.

He pulled back long enough to look into her eyes, deep, dark and smoldering. Her thigh muscles squeezed around him, raising and lowering her body in a caress that nearly drove him to his knees.

The feel of her, wild and restless in his arms, was something he'd never allowed himself to want. And now, he was sorely afraid he'd never get enough.

Ripping at the hem of her shirt, Colt tore it up over

her head and threw it into the yawning mouth of the cave behind them. She took the opportunity to do the same with his. The wet plop of his shirt against stone was somehow satisfying.

Her soft lips settled against his skin. He felt as if he were on fire, but the heat of her tongue as it licked across his throat was still hard to miss. She pulled at him, sucking him inside and sending sheets of lightning dancing across his skin.

His own mouth clamped hard and fast around the begging center of her breast. She tasted sweet—like tropical fruit after a cool rain—as he rolled the tight nipple beneath the swell of his tongue. Intoxicating, that's what she was.

Colt ran his hands up the length of her thighs, trying to find a way in beneath the taut cloth of her shorts. He could feel her damp center pressed against him, taunting him with the promise of wet heat. He wanted it, but he didn't want to let her go.

Finally, with a growl of frustration answered by a peal of feminine laughter, Colt tumbled them both to the hard stone floor.

She arched into his waiting body, and he relished the heat as they collided. Skin on skin, their damp bodies clung. She reached between them, opening the catch on her shorts. He hissed as the back of her hand caressed the bulge of his erection, a torturous caress that was hardly enough.

Her lips curved into a smile she failed to suppress. "Witch," he breathed against those lips before he nipped gently at the corners, punishing them for their taunt.

Together, they rolled across the floor, an undulating mass of legs, arms and heated bodies. Somewhere in the middle of the melee they managed to push their remaining clothes out of the way. Colt's legs were hobbled, tied together by the material neither of them could be bothered to deal with. Lena's shorts dangled from one ankle, the one she managed to wedge high up his hip.

They came to rest, Colt's back propped against the wall, Lena straddling his lap. Her thighs were spread wide, feet propped behind him, the swollen flesh of her sex open and waiting. He wanted to taste and touch, to explore every inch.

Colt reached between them, slipping his fingers deep into the heat of Lena's body. She gasped, contracting around the invasion. Her hips surged forward, pulling him deeper.

Her head fell back in abandon. His fingers flexed, widening her channel and pushing against the force of the tension building inside her. Slowly, he dragged them back out again to the very edge. Her whimper of protest quickly morphed into a moan of pleasure when he slammed in again.

He tortured them both, watching as her body took him over and over again. The slippery evidence of her desire coated his hand. She quivered around him. He could practically feel the crank of tension as it twisted inside her. She was so close.

His cock throbbed with an insistent demand that he was powerless to ignore. Pulling his hand from her body, he swallowed her protest with his mouth. Grasping her hips, he pulled her up and brought her down onto his hard length.

She screamed with pleasure, the echo reverberating around them tenfold. He surged beneath her, driving every last inch into her welcoming depths. The feel of her muscles contracting, trying to hold him in place even as he pulled out for another thrust was exquisite.

Skin on skin, they crashed together over and over again. Rough rock bit into Colt's back. Lena's fingers bored into his shoulders, trying to find a purchase. Her face pressed into the crook of his neck, each panting wail of her pleasure bursting deep inside his chest.

He felt her fall, knew the moment her body let go. The rolling waves of her release started deep inside, ripping up his shaft and quaking through her entire body. Colt felt the answering surge start at the base of his spine, an explosion of ectasy that had the world around them going even blacker.

The increasingly powerful swells of bliss left him breathless, floundering, as they washed repeatedly across him. His arms tightened around Lena, holding her to him. She was the only solid thing in the universe.

She collapsed onto his chest, her body limp and spent. Part of him relished knowing he'd done that to her, brought her that kind of devastating pleasure.

Above him, her chest continued to heave, fighting to catch her breath. Aftershocks burst through her body, making her quiver and contracting her walls around his spent sex. It felt right, this connection they'd found deep in the heart of the jungle.

And then he realized what they'd done.

"We didn't use anything," he said through a dry throat.

"What?" she mumbled sleepily against his chest.

Panic shot through him. "We didn't use a condom."

9

LENA TRIED TO SIT UP, to move away from Colt and what they'd just done, but the steel bands of his arms kept her tight against him. She could still feel the pulse of him buried deep inside her. She wanted to be upset—with herself and with him—but she couldn't be.

They'd both gotten carried away, neither of them taking time to think rationally.

Panic rushed through her blistering and hard. *She* hadn't thought rationally. She knew better than to let hormones and emotions overwhelm her that way.

But, apparently, that was difficult for her to do with Colt around. He broke through all of her barriers, pulling at pieces of her she'd never wanted to admit existed. No one, no man, had ever made her feel so deliriously out of control.

And the fact that she'd liked it just made it that much worse.

Colt stirred beneath her, picking her up and gently placing her onto the cool floor. He towered above her, staring down with shuttered eyes. She really wished she knew what he was thinking, but she couldn't read him. Not now.

Pushing up to her own feet, Lena crossed her arms over her breasts. She realized it was a pointless gesture, but she did it anyway.

"I'm on the pill."

"Oh," he said, his voice flat. "That's good."

Turning on his heel, Colt silently gathered the branches they'd brought in with them. Reaching into his pack, he pulled out a box of matches. The tiny flare of light hissed through the quiet cave.

Lena shivered. Gathering her clothes, she was about to pull the damp material over her head when Colt stopped her.

"Spread them out over here to dry." Reaching back into the pack again, he pulled out a T-shirt and handed it to her. Their fingers brushed, and the now-familiar sizzle of need flashed up her arm. Colt jerked his hand away.

And she mourned for the sense of closeness they'd shared a few minutes before.

"We also had blood tests for the marriage license, if that's what you're worried about."

Fire caught, stuttered and then flared between them. Colt pulled on a pair of nylon gym shorts that must have also come from the pack. Across the flames, his eyes flashed. Something quick, hard and bright, but before Lena could figure out what it was it was gone.

"It never crossed my mind, Lena. I know you better than that."

"Maybe, but Wyn was certainly promiscuous enough for all of us."

"Something tells me that sex wasn't on your agenda for the past few months."

What the heck was that supposed to mean? "How the hell do you know that?"

He stepped closer, the red-orange glow of flames washing across his bare chest. His voice took on an intimate timbre. "Let's just say, you don't respond like a woman who's been well-satisfied."

For perverse reasons she didn't understand even as she said it, she countered, "Wyn is a great lover, thank you very much."

Colt's lips twitched, not with humor but something far darker. "I'm sure your cousin would agree."

She drew in a breath, as if the barb had actually connected with her chest.

"What about you? How many lovers have you had in the last year? Ten? Twenty?"

"I like sex."

"You may like it—and I'll be the first to admit you're pretty damn good at it—but that doesn't make you a god among men. What it makes you is pathetic and lonely. When's the last time you had a real relationship, Colt? Not some one-night stand but something meaningful? Something built on a level beyond the physical?"

Colt's mouth thinned and he took another menacing step toward her. Instead of taking the hint and backing away, she moved closer, going toe-to-toe.

"You don't know what you're talking about."

"The hell I don't. I watched you self-destruct after you lost your parents. And when that didn't cure the pain, you shut everyone out of your life."

"You're still here."

She scoffed. "Please. I get random phone calls. A long weekend here and there. That's not a relationship, that's convenience."

"That's my job!" he hollered, his voice rising with frustration that matched her own.

How had they gone so quickly from total bliss to this?

"A convenient excuse, Colt. You immersed yourself in your work, using it as a barrier to distance you from everyone and everything that matters. You insulated yourself in the hopes that it would keep you from being hurt."

She saw pain flash across Colt's face and immediately regretted her words. They were true, but that didn't give her the right to throw them at him like expletives.

Reaching for him, she tried to apologize. "Colt, I'm sorry." He shook her off.

Closing the conversation completely, Colt said, "We'd better get some sleep while we can."

Spreading the emergency blanket out on the cave floor, he lay down, gesturing for her to join him. She was surprised when he wrapped his arm around her waist and pulled her tight against his chest.

Tension still clung to his muscles; she could feel the hard coil of them pressing into her back. But he was touching her. At the moment she'd take what she could get.

Squeezing her eyes shut, Lena tried to will her body and mind to sleep, but it didn't help. After a while, she thought he must have dozed off. Until he whispered, "I was..."

"Worried."

"Scared."

Lena realized that sometime while they'd lain there, wrapped together, the tension had left his body. He'd relaxed behind her, his voice sounding drowsy and thick.

"Not sure I'm ready for that responsibility. Tiny little thing dependent on you for everything. Too fragile." The steel band of his arms pressed against her lungs. She didn't think he knew what he was doing. "Bad enough you almost got hurt."

She wanted to argue with him, to protest that she'd come nowhere close to getting hurt. But she realized it wouldn't do any good. Not just because he wouldn't have listened, but also because he was already asleep.

"OH, THANK GAWD," greeted them when they exited the jungle the next morning. Waking at dawn hadn't been difficult since the hard stone floor hadn't made a very comfortable bed.

Georgie, tears glistening in her eyes, broke through a group of people who'd gathered at the head of the path. Throwing her arms around Lena's shoulders, the petite blonde squeezed her hard before pushing her away. "You scared us half to death."

Wesley appeared behind her, gently pulling her away.

Marcy came next, two tall men Lena had never seen before quick on her heels. She wore an expression that was probably meant to intimidate, but Lena was too happy to see Marcy's efficient face to pay attention.

"What happened?" she asked, her stern tone ruined by the tremor of relief she couldn't hide.

The men, one with hair as dark as the jungle had been, the other bright and blond, followed her. The dark-haired one studied them both, his sharp gaze missing nothing. He didn't speak, but there was no missing the air of authority that clung to him.

The blond, who looked as if he should have a surfboard tucked beneath his arm, put his hand on Marcy's shoulder. Lena wasn't sure if it was in warning or support, but either way she didn't let it sit there long. Shaking him off, she asked, "Are you both all right?"

"We're fine," Colt answered.

"Tired and hungry, but no worse for wear. We… um…got distracted."

A titter went up from the crowd that had gathered behind Marcy and her mystery men.

Colt spoke up when embarrassment made Lena's words falter. "Before we knew it, dark was falling. We couldn't get out so we camped in the cave behind the waterfall."

"You two are damn lucky," the tall blond interjected.

Colt just nodded his head.

"Well." Turning on her heel towards the gathered group, Marcy clapped her hands and said, "It looks like we won't be needing your help after all. Everyone can return to his or her previous schedule."

There were several shouts of "Glad you're back" and "Happy you're safe" as the group broke apart and melted away.

Wesley pulled gently at Georgie's elbow, trying to get her to follow him down the path. She reluctantly did, yelling over her shoulder, "You have to tell me everything when you're feeling better. I was so worried."

Left with Marcy and the men, Lena felt exhaustion envelop her. It had been a long, emotion-filled night.

The blond man stepped forward, finally introducing himself. "I'm Simon, the owner. This is Zane, our head of security." The other man jerked his head up in silent acknowledgment of the introduction, but didn't bother to speak.

"If you need anything, let Marcy know. If you'll excuse me, I need to get back to my office. I'm glad to know you're safe."

Without waiting for their response, the men spun on their heels and disappeared. Marcy stared after them, a frown tugging at her mouth. Looking back at them she said, "I'm sorry for Simon's abrupt departure."

"No, really, it's fine," Colt said. "We're actually very tired. We could probably sleep for the rest of the day."

Marcy's frown deepened, digging grooves between her eyebrows. "Well, we already lost all of yesterday. When I realized you'd slipped away I rescheduled several things for today. I suppose we could push most of them to tomorrow." She studied them for several seconds. "Would you feel up to something tonight?"

Lena looked across at Colt. He shrugged.

"All right. We'll be ready tonight," she offered. After all, it was their fault the photo shoot was so far behind.

"Excellent. I'll send Mikhail to get you around seven. Come hungry," Marcy said, her eyes sparkling.

Together, Lena and Colt stumbled across the resort, pausing long enough to change out of their rumpled clothes before falling into bed. She couldn't speak for Colt, but she was asleep almost instantly.

SEVERAL HOURS LATER, Lena stirred awake, arching her body in a stretch before she even opened her eyes. Colt watched her, as he'd been doing for the past several minutes.

Sometime yesterday Marcy had returned their bungalow to its former state, including putting the standard-issue cotton sheets back on the bed. The crisscross pattern had imprinted into Lena's skin, marring her cheek in an endearing way that made him want to kiss her, slowly and deliberately.

Had it only been yesterday that he'd first claimed her? It seemed like days, years ago, instead of less than twenty-four hours. But thinking about their brief history made him realize they hadn't made love in a bed. Nice, comfortable mattress, soft sheets, no bugs or birds or leaves or rocks.

The insatiable exhaustion was gone, replaced with a languid awareness. And suddenly he wanted to push her deep into that plush mattress and leave the imprint of their joined bodies there. Reaching toward her, Colt brushed his fingers gently down her spine. A smile curved her mouth, but her eyes stayed shut.

His lips feathered against her bare shoulder, the tiny strap of the gown she'd thrown on slipping down her arm. She rolled over into his arms, her bleary eyes opening to reveal the unhurried heat that smoldered there.

She hummed deep in her throat as his fingers trailed lightly over her chest. The soft material of her gown slipped across her skin beneath his touch, arousing them both. A single fingernail snagged on the telltale tent of her peaked nipple.

She pushed into him, silently asking for more.

But before he could give it to her, a loud knock sounded on the door. With a curse, Colt looked at the clock and realized it was already six. How could they have slept the entire day away?

Another knock sounded at the door. Colt yelled, "We have an hour." A chuckle was the only response.

While he wasn't looking, Lena had scooted off the other side of the bed. He tried to reach for her, but she twisted away. "No way, buddy. You might not care what I look like in these photographs, but I do. I haven't showered since yesterday. I fell in a pond, slept on the ground and desperately need to condition my hair."

"You look beautiful," he countered.

"Said the man sporting the rather impressive erection."

Lena's lips twitched. Colt looked down, although it wasn't as if he needed proof. He could feel the pulsing ache all the way to his toes. In that split second, she slipped into the bathroom, cutting off any thought of him following inside when the lock clicked loudly behind her.

Colt wanted to be upset, but couldn't muster up the energy. The wait was worth it when she emerged a half hour later, her skin glowing beneath the warm earth tones of the dress she'd put on.

Colt would have reached for her then, but the shake of her head stopped him. Not to mention the pointed finger she leveled at the still steamy bathroom. Being surrounded by the scent of her shampoo while he showered was torture of the highest degree.

A low, steady strum took up residence deep in his blood. It was relentless, this need for her that had settled into his bones. No matter how many times he had her, he wanted her again. Immediately, as often as possible. He was beginning to fear that need could never be met.

For the first time since he'd convinced himself he could have her, he wondered what would happen when they left. He'd promised himself they'd go their separate ways, but what if he couldn't do it? What if one week with her wasn't enough?

"You almost ready?" she called, cutting off his line of thought before it took him someplace he didn't want to go.

Walking outside together, they were greeted by Mikhail, who grinned knowingly. Colt felt the urge to knock the expression right off his face, but fought against it. Instead, they followed him down a path and out onto the beach.

A white canvas tent had been set up along the deserted stretch. Colt could hear the laughter of other guests farther back toward the resort, but here the place had an untouched, primitive quality that appealed to him.

Beside him, Lena twined her arm through his. He could feel the way her whole body quivered. He wondered if she was nervous and then realized nerves had nothing to do with it when she looked up at him. Her eyes glowed with anticipation, excitement and a knowing expectation that he had every intention of fulfilling at the first opportunity.

Mikhail slipped ahead of them. Colt held the flap open so Lena could enter. Marcy, Mikhail and his crew waited.

He had to admit that Marcy had gone above and beyond the call of duty. The tent was made of lightweight canvas. Even if she'd had it up all day, it wouldn't have absorbed as much of the sun as some other fabrics might have. Piles of pillows were thrown around the intimate space that centered around a low table barely a foot or two off the ground.

A sea of silver-covered dishes sat on the table, waiting to be revealed. He wondered what was inside and figured he'd find out soon enough. He expected stuffed grape leaves and dripping baklava. Instead, when someone from the crew stepped forward, she exposed trays of tropical fruit, shrimp, oysters, skewers of chicken and beef with sweet-smelling chili sauce and an assortment of finger-size desserts that made his mouth water.

Lena dropped to her knees in front of the table, staring in wonder at the spread before her. Looking over her shoulder at the woman standing at the entrance to the tent, she said, "Marcy, you didn't have to go to all this trouble."

"Yes, I did. The shot has to be perfect. I want to feature it in a two-page spread."

Some of the wonder disappeared from Lena's eyes and Colt wanted to admonish Marcy for ruining the moment for her.

Apparently realizing what she'd just done, Marcy took a step forward, reaching out to Lena. "I'm sorry, that didn't come out the way I meant it to. I didn't do this just for you, but I do want you to enjoy it. I've seen some of the preliminary pictures. Trust me, you've earned it. They're amazing and people will be flocking to Escape in no time because of them. I owe you."

Lena smiled up at the other woman. "Well, this is certainly a great way to start. This is wonderful, Marcy. You've thought of everything."

Even double-layering a soft rug across the bottom of the tent so that neither of them would end the night rolling around in the sand. For that, Colt was eternally grateful.

"I try." Marcy's cheeks flushed with satisfaction. "I'm going to let Mikhail get to work. He has instructions to leave you alone once he's got what he needs."

Colt dropped to the pillows on the opposite side of the table thinking about how perfect this was and hoping Mikhail would finish quickly.

Mikhail entered as Marcy left. He surveyed them both, asked Lena to angle her legs differently and positioned Colt's shoulders more squarely toward the camera. But on the whole, he seemed satisfied with the scene.

Colt looked down at the food and realized for the first time that there weren't any utensils. Everything on the table was designed to be eaten with their hands. Marcy really had thought of everything.

Shaking his head in awe, Colt reached for a morsel of something and held it out toward Lena. She paused for a second, reaching for her own bite, but instead leaned against the table and opened her mouth. She sucked the food from his hand, her pink tongue licking across the underside of his fingers. His eyes narrowed as a spike of need stabbed straight through him.

Picking up a shrimp, he reached for her hand, closed her fingers around it and brought it up to his own lips. Two could play that game. He relished the way her eyes flashed as his tongue lapped the sauce from her fingers. He practically swallowed the thing whole, grateful it was small, so that he could chase a drop as it slipped down her wrist.

"So good," he breathed against her skin. He licked across the sensitive veins there, enjoying the way her fingers curled and her pulse jumped.

In the background, Colt could hear the whir of the shutter and the click of the button as Mikhail caught shot after shot. He ignored the other man, instead focusing solely on Lena and building the tension and desire between them.

He slipped around the corner of the table, moving closer to her. She was up on her knees, leaning toward him, waiting for him to feed her something else.

He picked up a pastry shell filled with a spiced rice mixture. Tipping it to her mouth, he waited for her to take a bite. The crunch of the broken shell echoed through the space, but his eyes were drawn to the curve of her neckline and the dark hollow between her breasts. A few grains of rice had slipped free, rolling down her skin to disappear.

Colt leaned forward, ready to dive in after them but Mikhail's loud throat-clearing stopped him. Instead, Lena wiggled her body and dress till the stray grains fell free. He had to admit watching her gyration was almost as good as retrieving them himself.

They fed each other, drank sweet wine from crystal flutes and laughed at the mess they both made of the beautiful meal. Their fingers grazed, their bodies touched and while they started out on opposite sides of the table Lena was soon practically sitting in Colt's lap.

Colt wasn't sure when Mikhail left. He was aware of the man's departure in some foggy corner of his mind because at that moment he'd been freed to do everything that he wanted, no longer obligated to hold back in deference to the audience or the lens. When he'd left, Mikhail had had the foresight to close the single flap to give them some privacy. Colt was glad the other man had thought of it, because he was too far gone.

One hunger slaked and another stoked so high that both of them feared being consumed by the flames. They pushed back from the table and rolled together onto the pile of soft pillows.

Lena's dress twisted around her thighs. He wanted

to see her, all of her, spread out before him. Lifting her up into his arms, he peeled the garment from her body.

His breath backed into his throat when he realized she wasn't wearing anything beneath. All night, she'd been naked under the thin layer of fabric and he hadn't known it. He was still sane enough to realize perhaps that was a good thing. If he had known, he might not have been able to control himself long enough to let Mikhail get what he needed.

"What have you done with my practical Lena?" he asked as his fingers glided down the smooth expanse of her inner thigh.

Her eyes smoldered, an intensity that drove deep down into his soul and twisted. "I didn't put on any panties, Colt. It's not like I organized a bra-burning or chained myself to the door of some industrial giant. I figured why bother if they were just coming off."

His lips trailed across the dip of her stomach, his tongue swirling into her navel. "There she is."

"What's wrong with practical?" she stuttered as his knee nudged against her own. He relished the view of her swollen flesh as she opened for him.

"Nothing," he growled. "Practical is good, especially if it makes touching you easier."

The heady scent of her arousal swirled around them. He took a deep breath, holding it inside so he could remember this moment forever.

With one hand he parted her folds, sinking in and swiping his tongue across the warm surface of her sex. She tasted like heaven, and he wanted more.

She bucked beneath him, pressing against his mouth.

She was so hot and wet. Her sex burned around the invasion of his tongue as he drove relentlessly in and out. His lips clamped tightly over the jutting nub of her clit, sucking hard in a way that had breath bursting from her body in frantic pants.

Before he could spear a finger inside and suck her to orgasm, she reared up beneath him, bucking him off. Colt sprawled backward into the pillows. Lena rose above him, the tangled mass of her dark mahogany hair running riotously down her back.

Her eyes smoldered. A tempting smile teased across her lips. Colt tried to sit up, but a single hand on his shoulder pressed him back down.

"My turn," she said, pressing her mouth to the flat plane of his stomach. Colt enjoyed the happy leap of the muscles where she touched. Her mouth slid close and his cock jumped.

She laughed, a low-throated sound that had air brushing torturously across him. She didn't keep him suspended in misery long. Her tongue quickly followed, licking slowly from tip to base. Her hand teased across the swollen orbs below as she sucked him deep into her throat. The moist heat was maddening, but not nearly as perfect as being buried deep inside her body.

She slid back and forth and he let her play, until he couldn't take anymore. Pulling her away, he spun them both, pressing her hard into the soft floor.

"Please tell me you were practical and brought condoms," she panted.

Her nails scraped down his chest, leaving red welts as he reached behind her to grab the condom he'd stuffed into the pocket of his pants. She flicked one of his erect nipples, making his stomach contract with pleasure.

Snatching the packet from his fingers, she tore through the foil. The combination of her warmth and the tight latex as she rolled it down over his aching cock had him hissing through his teeth.

He pulled from her grasp. Spreading her thighs wide, he plunged deep inside. She was so hot and ready, welcoming. Her gasp of pleasure blasted through him even as her sex wrapped so tightly around him that he could barely breathe.

"Oh g-god…" she stuttered as he moved inside her.

He pulsed in and out—quick, shallow, deep. Lena's head thrashed against the pillows. Incoherent whimpers fell from her parted lips. Her hips pumped, grinding against his.

One second she was straining, reaching for the same exquisite moment as he was. The next she was wild beneath him. Her body, poised on the edge, flew apart. Bucking, quaking, sobbing, her orgasm was more than he could take. Her milking muscles gripped him in a hard fist, refusing to let him go.

The power of his own release crashed over him in warm waves, blocking everything but the feel of her from his brain. Each time was stronger, better, more powerful than the last, than anything he'd experienced before.

How was he ever going to live without this? Without her?

Lena collapsed beneath him. Her legs and arms

sprawled uselessly. He had just enough brainpower left to realize he was going to crush her. Rolling them both one last time, he draped her spent body across his.

Her hair spilled over his chest and her nose buried deep into the crook of his neck. She burrowed against him, as if she were trying to get inside his skin as the last and only joining they hadn't actually been able to accomplish.

And he was happy to have her there. As close as they could possibly get.

Colt wrapped his arms around her and held on. He didn't want to let her go.

But he would have to. Because everything ended, even this.

10

A BRIGHT BEAM OF SUNLIGHT sliced across Lena's face, pulling her from the most delicious dream. Sometime during the night they'd stumbled back to their bungalow. Grumbling, she cursed their preoccupation and lack of foresight—neither she nor Colt had thought to draw the curtains.

"What time is it?" Colt croaked out, his head buried beneath a pillow.

Squinting against the glare, Lena rummaged on the bedside table until the bright red numbers on the clock came into view.

"Nine."

Colt sat bolt upright in bed. "Crap! We have to get ready."

Lena frowned at him. "Ready for what?" If her memory served, they didn't have anything planned until later in the day. She had to admit that while she'd been a little trepidatious about the whole photo-session thing, it actually hadn't been that bad.

A smile Lena couldn't hold in stretched across her lips. Especially last night…

"I have a surprise," Colt said, his lips and words brushing across her naked shoulder.

She narrowed her eyes. "You know I don't like surprises." Her whole life, *Surprise!* was usually followed by *We're moving to*…fill in the blank. L.A., Chicago, London, Geneva, Bangkok, whatever. No, she didn't appreciate surprises. The word alone had the ability to send dread and panic through her body.

"You like *my* surprises."

"When have you ever surprised me?"

"That time I showed up on your doorstep when I was supposed to be in Kenya."

Oh, yeah. She did remember that. The first year out of college had been difficult for her. She'd hated her job writing bad copy for a third-rate marketing firm. Her apartment had sucked and no one in the building seemed interested in making new friends. She'd been lonely, but had tried to hide it from Colt whenever he managed to call. He'd been so excited about the project he was working on.

That conversation, she must have failed miserably because two days later he was on her doorstep, a bottle of wine in one hand and a fistful of movies in the other. Granted, he'd brought shoot-'em-up, world-destruction, epic adventures instead of chick flicks. But spending those two days together had made a huge difference in her disposition.

A few months later she'd gone to work at Rand doing

graphic design—what she'd wanted to be doing in the first place—met Wyn and everything had changed.

For the first time, Lena wondered what would have happened the next time Colt came home if she hadn't been dating someone. That weekend, something had felt different, but she'd convinced herself it was all the changes in her life, not how she felt about Colt. Would all the sparks flying now have erupted then?

"Okay, so I reluctantly give you the opportunity to surprise me. But I retain my right to balk at any time."

"Trust me, you won't." With a mischievous glint running through his bright green eyes, Colt scooted off the bed, grasping the covers and dragging them with him.

The entire knot—comforter, sheets, pillows—fell with a plop to the floor leaving her totally naked. Two days ago she probably would have squealed, made some ineffectual attempt to cover up and then quickly disappeared. Today, she simply stretched, arching her body toward him.

"No fair," he growled, his eyes going dark and dangerous as they traveled up the length of her body.

A heavy heat settled low in her belly. "You're the one who took the sheets."

"As much as I'd like to call you on this bluff—"

"No bluff."

"We're already late. Put on a swimsuit, grab a wrap and a towel and meet me outside in fifteen minutes."

"Where are you going?"

His hot gaze scorched across her skin again. "Out, before I say to hell with it and climb back into that bed with you."

"I wouldn't mind."

"You would if you knew what we were doing."

Colt didn't exactly disappear. Instead, they managed to get ready together with only one or two brief delays when they got too close to each other and good intentions were overwhelmed.

He made a fruitless attempt to cover her eyes—Lena patently refusing to submit. They walked to the opposite side of the resort, Lena becoming more and more confused when they passed the pool, the beach and even the main hotel building. They were on the path toward the dock before realization struck.

"We're taking a boat ride?"

Colt answered, "Maybe." Although when they rounded the corner in the path it became obvious they were.

The boat—although she hated to use that term since it appeared big enough to carry twenty people—bobbed softly on the swells of a calm sea. A man, she assumed the captain, lounged against the tall wooden post the bow was tied off to.

"Welcome," the man said as he took Lena's hand and helped her aboard.

Once they were on, the captain went to the helm, which sat high above the deck. Beneath it, there was an open doorway and a set of stairs leading down into a dark, pleasant hold. Lena peeked far enough inside to see a small galley, table and banquette, and in the back, a wide bunk built straight into the side of the ship.

Spread across the surface of the table were several masks, fins and bent rubber tubes. Lena had never been snorkeling before, but she'd seen pictures of the equipment.

"We're going snorkeling?" she asked, spinning on her heel and ramming straight into Colt's chest.

His arms automatically wrapped around her, pulling her tight against his body.

"You said you wanted to go."

She'd made the comment once in passing, and he'd remembered. Reaching up on tiptoe she placed a quick kiss to the underside of his jaw. "This is very sweet."

He leered at her in an exaggerated gesture that made her smile widen. "I'm sure we can come up with a way for you to repay me."

Smacking him playfully, Lena twisted out of his hold and headed straight for the table. "Okay, so explain to me how all this works."

Lena was glad that she didn't get seasick as the boat bounced over the waves. After a few minutes below deck, they brought everything above, settling into the seats at the bow so that they could look out. Dolphins joined them, jumping playfully alongside the boat, keeping pace as they raced into open water.

The water was crystal clear and she was actually getting excited about the prospect of snorkeling. The captain explained that they were heading out to a sunken ship he promised would be teeming with a rainbow of fish. She had to admit that Colt's surprise was a good one. Touching in a way that made her heart constrict and race all at the same time.

This was the sort of thing a man did for his lover. And she could get used to being spoiled. The problem was it wasn't real. This experience, this week—they weren't real. She tried to keep reminding herself of that, but it was becoming harder and harder to do.

She had no idea what was going to happen at the end of the week. Whenever she let herself think about it, a sharp pain shot through the center of her chest.

But she refused to let her worry about tomorrow ruin today.

The boat powered down and the captain released the hydraulic anchor. Once they were secured and the only thing visible for miles around, the captain switched modes and became their snorkeling guide.

Colt, obviously comfortable around the equipment, sat silently and listened to the instructions their guide provided. They went over safety and signals. After practicing a couple of times on deck, she and Colt dove off a platform at the back of the boat and into the water. Their guide remained with the boat.

It took Lena a couple of tries to get the hang of diving beneath the surface without choking on the water that poured into her open breathing tube. But it didn't take long before she was cruising after Colt, who raced back and forth as if he were born with fins and gills. She knew that he was certified in scuba, but she was amazed by how natural he seemed in the water.

The sunken ship was nothing like she'd expected, nothing like the *National Geographic* specials she'd seen. The dark pieces of wood were hard to distinguish, covered in centuries of barnacles, sand and underwater debris. Once Colt pointed out what she was looking at, it became easier to distinguish the edges of the broken ship from the rock and reef around it.

It was cool to think that she was looking at a piece of history. However, it was a little creepy, as well, and she quickly abandoned the site to follow a school of brightly colored fish as they swam close to the surface.

She should have signaled that she was going up, but she knew Colt would have insisted he follow her. He was enjoying his exploration of the ship and she didn't want to ruin his experience. It just wasn't her thing.

Lena went up to clear her snorkel and simply floated with her face in the water staring at the vista below. It was easier up here—she could breathe regularly, and didn't have to worry about swallowing a mouthful of water. She could still see the pink, blue, green and yellow fish as they swam in and out of the ship and reef below.

She kept Colt in sight, watching as he moved down, over and through the ghostly timbers of the ship. He was beautiful, a sleek bullet cutting through the water, coming up for air every couple minutes.

She had no idea how long she stayed there. Her back, no longer covered by the water began to heat, but she didn't move. It actually felt good, a nice contrast to the cool water. Fifteen, twenty minutes later, Colt came barreling around the distant corner of the ship, heading straight for the surface. And her.

His gaze locked with hers through the wavy plastic of their masks. For a moment she thought she saw panic but as he got closer she convinced herself that she must have been wrong because all she saw in his clear green eyes was desire.

He shot through the surface of the water beside her, spraying droplets across her hot back. She lifted her face out of the water just as he reached for her and pulled her into his arms.

His snorkel dangled beside his face, caught in place by the connecting strap on the mask he'd shoved to the top of his head. Lena pushed up her mask as well, spitting out the bulky mouthpiece so that she could smile at him.

"Where did you go?" he asked.

His arms were cool as they touched her sun-warmed shoulders. She shrugged. "I like it better on the surface."

"I wish you'd told me you weren't enjoying this."

"Who said I wasn't? I like snorkeling just fine. I'm just not as experienced at it as you. You were having fun." She leaned closer into his embrace, mock-whispering as if she didn't want anyone around them to hear. "Besides, I enjoyed watching you."

Colt laughed. His teeth flashed in the sun and an answering bubble of happiness grew inside her.

The day was perfect. His arms were around her, his smooth skin sliding against hers. He didn't kiss her or caress her or turn up the dial on the desire that constantly simmered beneath the surface whenever they were together now.

Instead, he simply held her close as they bobbed together in the waves, enjoying the pleasure of the shared moment. Lena realized these stolen hours were the best of both worlds. The ease of their friendship had somehow melded with the passion they'd found.

And that bubble burst as she realized she loved him.

It slammed into her with enough force for her to lose her breath. No, no, no. How could she have let this happen? She wasn't supposed to fall for him.

Her legs jerked up in the water, her body curling around itself and the pain and fear rippling inside her.

"Are you okay?" Colt asked, his eyes, just moments ago glittering with the excitement of discovery, were now cloudy with worry.

Somewhere Lena found the strength to nod and give him a sickly smile that she knew was nowhere close to normal. But it was the best she could manage right now.

"I think I have a cramp." Lena reached down for her calf, rubbing the phantom pain.

What was she going to do? She'd promised him this would be no strings attached. She'd promised herself she wouldn't allow emotions and hormones to rule her decisions.

And, really, that was still possible. So she loved him. Hadn't she always? Sure, the emotion had somehow grown and changed, but she could deal with that.

At the end of the week, he would leave and head for whatever adventure came next. She'd go home, start circulating her résumé and try to find another steady, stable job as a graphic designer. Her skills were in high demand. And a few months from now, out of the blue, he would call.

And by then, maybe, she'd have figured out a way to deal with the inevitable pain.

Why had she fallen for Colt? The worst possible man for her to want. A nomad of the highest order, who didn't even bother ordering cable because he wasn't home long enough to watch it.

He was her opposite in every possible way. The craziest thing she'd ever done was deciding to buy her apartment even though she only had ten percent instead of the recommended twenty saved. He threw his body off the side of mountains, trekked into distant jungles, experienced exotic cultures. And enjoyed every second of it.

They would be terrible for each other. She couldn't ask him to give up that part of his life—his career, his dreams, the very fabric of his identity—anymore than she could change who she was and what she needed.

Dammit, she wanted to scream.

Somehow she managed to get back into the boat, although she didn't remember doing it. Colt insisted they eat lunch in the galley, to keep her pale skin out of the sun as much as possible. The dark, cool interior was far better than the bright sunlight outside. Beneath the stark sunshine, he might have seen more than she wanted him to.

She tried to recapture the enjoyment of the day, but couldn't seem to do it. At one point Colt suggested they head back, but that only added guilt to the mix she was struggling against. He'd gone to so much trouble to make her happy…even if it could only be for this one day.

Finally, the captain came down and said, "It's time

to start heading in. Marcy told me to have you back at two on the nose."

Together, they went to sit at the bow again. Lena curled her legs up onto the cushion beside her. Draping an arm around her shoulders, Colt pulled her closer against his body and leaned down to capture her lips.

The kiss was hot, as they all were with Colt, but there was a softness beneath it as well. Tears she desperately wanted to hold in stung the backs of her eyes. She let her eyelids slide shut to hide them.

She wanted the heat they'd shared the night before. She wanted to be consumed so that she could forget, for a little while anyway, what was eventually going to come.

Well, she supposed, there was one bright spot. Unlike when her mother had been overwhelmed by disappointment and despair, there was no one else in her life to be caught in the crosshairs of her devastation.

No, Lena clamped down hard on the inside of her cheek, ignoring the metallic tang of blood as it welled into her mouth. She refused to be that person. No matter what happened, she would not let this crush her.

When it was over, she'd tell Colt goodbye. And go on with the rest of her life. And find exactly what she was looking for.

If she could figure out what that was anymore.

THEY HAD JUST ENOUGH TIME to shower, change and get ready for Marcy's next assignment—a ballroom-dancing lesson followed by a party so that everyone could practice their newfound skills.

Lena was beautiful, as always. She'd dressed in a black strapless sheath that hugged her body and made his mouth water. She'd taken the time to pile her hair high on her head, mahogany curls cascading down to brush against the nape of her neck. Colt's fingers itched to sweep them away, to palm the curve of her neck and kiss her senseless.

He resisted, barely.

She'd been out of sorts since they'd gotten back into the boat this afternoon. He couldn't pinpoint what was wrong, but something definitely was. He'd asked, but she'd given him a quick—too quick—answer that she was fine.

He didn't believe her.

Perhaps his surprise hadn't been such a good idea after all. When they'd first reached the boat, she'd seemed excited. Even in the water, she'd been laughing and smiling, enjoying herself.

Now she was silent and distant. And he wasn't used to that. Aside from the details of her childhood, he was under the impression that they'd shared everything. In the past, he would have teased her until the truth spilled out. But this wasn't the past and the dynamic of their relationship had changed.

He no longer knew how to handle her. He was terrible at relationships, which was one reason he tried desperately not to have them. They were work. He had to consider someone else's feelings, wants and needs.

No woman had ever been important enough to deal with that headache. The difference was, with Lena, it didn't feel like a headache. He was genuinely worried about her. If she was upset, he wanted to help.

But he couldn't force her to talk to him.

They walked across the complex, entering the main resort building for the first time since checking in. A friendly girl greeted them, directing them up two floors to the ballroom at the end of the hallway.

Walking into the room, Colt had the sudden feeling that he'd stepped back in time a couple hundred years. The space was huge.

Floor-to-ceiling windows ran the entire length of one side, interspersed with French doors that led onto a full-length balcony. Through the glass Colt could see the scrolling ironwork that ringed the space. It looked as original to the structure as the hardwood floors, crystal chandeliers and period wall sconces.

Ornately framed artwork graced the walls. Depictions of scenes from Victorian ballrooms echoed what the current residents must have assumed took place inside the ballroom. Touches of the modern—Mikhail's light poles, a large rolling cart with sound equipment and the updated wiring that allowed for electrical lights—left him with a sort of distorted reality.

A small group of people were gathered at the far end of the room. Probably twenty or thirty total. There were two or three older couples, perhaps empty nesters enjoying their newfound freedom. The way they joked with each other, laughing and teasing, twisted something sharp inside him.

They reminded him of his parents. Before the accident his father had just retired, selling the business he'd spent all of his life building. His parents wouldn't get to enjoy those quiet years together and that made him sad.

Even now, years later, the pain of losing them was still so sharp. It would surprise him sometimes, coming out of nowhere, regret and loss tightening an ever-present band across his chest. Maybe if their deaths hadn't been so sudden, or if he hadn't lost them both at once. But Colt didn't think that would matter. He missed his mother's indulgent smile and his father's high expectations, and he always would. Losing them was the most difficult thing he'd ever had to deal with. And he never wanted to experience that kind of grief again.

Colt was locked somewhere inside the demons of his own past when a squeal shattered the moment.

Separating from the group, Georgie rushed up beside them, wrapping her arms around Lena and giving her a big hug. It didn't seem to register with her that Lena did little more than pat her on the back before trying to extricate herself from the other woman's grasp.

"What have y'all been up to since yesterday?" Georgie asked with a sly wink and a big white smile.

"Snorkeling," Lena said, looking around her, probably for the emergency exit.

Before she could find it, Marcy and Mikhail entered the room, followed by a striking couple who seemed to glide across the floor with effortless grace.

Marcy stopped in front of the gathered group. Putting on her straightest Manager smile, she said, "We're all excited to welcome you to our couples' ballroom class. I hope you're enjoying your stay at Escape. Please let us know if there's anything we can do to enhance your experience. Everyone enjoy the class."

The man stepped forward, his eyes running expertly over the crowd. "I'm Tony and this is my partner Sara. Our only rule is that everyone must have fun tonight. Does anyone have a request for which dance we learn?"

Behind them, Georgie's light, lyrical voice shouted, "The Lambda." Everyone chuckled at her mispronunciation of *Lambada*. Wesley groaned, but as Colt turned around to look at him, he noticed the man's arms were wrapped tightly around his wife.

Tony said, "Maybe we should start with something a little easier. How about the Tango?"

A general sound of acceptance rose from the group.

Marcy stepped up beside Tony and addressed everyone again. "Mikhail is going to be photographing one of our couples." She pointed toward them. Lena squirmed beside Colt as every eye in the place turned to take them in. "You might have seen them around the resort this week. They're going to be featured in an upcoming ad campaign and magazine spread. Mikhail's going to attempt to keep everyone else out of the shots because we value our guests' privacy. Rest assured we will be obtaining your permission if you appear in any of the photographs. In the meantime, just pretend that he isn't here."

Colt knew from experience that that was easier said than done. There was nothing like a camera to make the shyest person outgoing and the most flamboyant person retiring. People seemed to change, although now that he stopped to think about it, Lena hadn't.

With a clap, Tony and Sara began the class. Colt, who'd taken ballroom lessons as a child, immediately picked up the hold that he remembered. Lena, on the other hand, turned out to have two left feet. He honestly never would have guessed it. She was fluid and sensual in bed. But on the dance floor, her arms and legs moved as if her knees and elbows had been frozen in place.

"Lena, can you look a little more…relaxed?" Mikhail asked as he spun around them.

She grimaced. "I don't think so."

Mikhail sighed and dropped to his knees, setting up for an elongated shot that would minimize her stiffness in the final product. Colt admired the man's adaptability.

Georgie and Wesley wedged their way beside them. The two were obviously no strangers to a ballroom floor. Colt would wager she'd insisted on six months of classes before the wedding. He wondered, as practical and detail-oriented as Lena was why she hadn't done the same.

"Didn't you and Wyn take lessons for your first dance?" he asked, forcing her backward in the basic step.

"No. We weren't going to have a traditional first dance."

"I bet that went over well with Diane."

Lena stumbled, unable to keep up with the advancing steps of the dance. Colt caught her, deliberately slowing their pace.

"She didn't know," she gritted out through stiff lips.

Sara walked up behind Lena. Without any warning, she bracketed her hands over Lena's hips, making her jump in surprise.

"It's all in the hips, Lena. Loosen up and just let yourself feel the beat of the music. Slow, slow, quick, quick, slow."

Colt wanted to yell at everyone to leave her alone, but he realized that wouldn't solve anything. He was about to whisk her away, photographs and party be damned, but before he could do it, Georgie and Wesley slid to a smooth stop beside them.

Wesley had his wife bent over backward, supporting her with a lunging knee and his strong frame. Georgie's head was thrown back, her spine arched, her blond hair trailing against the floor.

Hanging upside down, Georgie looked straight at Lena and said, "Honey, it's like sex standing up. Colt, however did you get through the reception?"

He could see it coming. Colt watched as anger, frustration and something akin to pain gathered deep in Lena's blue-gray eyes. They darkened and swirled, and even he was powerless to stop the explosion.

"We did not have a reception. We did not have a wedding. We are not married!" Lena yelled, her voice getting louder with each statement, until the entire room was staring.

11

THE MOMENT THE WORDS LEFT Lena's mouth she regretted them. Georgie was speechless, something she was certain hadn't happened often in the young woman's life. Wesley pulled her slowly up out of their dip, sheltering her with his arms and body. A shocked, hurt expression filled Georgie's face. For a minute, Lena felt as if she'd just kicked a puppy. A sickly sensation that she didn't like settled thick in the bottom of her stomach.

A rather large scowl pinched Marcy's mouth. And Colt simply watched Lena, as if trying to decide what she might do next so he could formulate a plan of action.

Reaching up, Lena rubbed both hands into her eye sockets, hoping that the pressure would relieve the headache she'd been fighting all day.

It didn't work.

Colt tried to pull her into the protection of his arms, too, but she wouldn't let him. Instead, she turned to Georgie and said, "I'm sorry. I shouldn't have taken my frustration out on you."

And then she turned around and walked away.

Lena could hear the hushed murmurs as the group behind her began to discuss her outburst. She hated that, knowing she'd let her emotions get the best of her and made herself a spectacle.

It was exactly what she always tried to avoid, and the unwanted attention reminded her painfully of her wedding day.

She was so close to the edge. Volatile and unpredictable. Her entire body was overrun by chaos, and she didn't like it.

She didn't want to go back to the bungalow. It wouldn't take long for Colt to follow her and he'd want to talk about what was wrong. And she couldn't explain it…not to him. Not this time.

And that made things worse. Colt was the person she'd always turned to for help, for advice. He might have been worlds away, but she could always count on him when she truly needed someone.

This time, she didn't have that. She longed for the easiness of their friendship, the comfortable familiarity they'd always shared. It was definitely gone, overrun by her own complicated emotions and uncertainty. Lena feared they'd never find that ease again.

A blast of music ricocheted off the buildings around her. Laughter and happiness underlined the sound and right now, that was exactly what she was looking for. Something to take her mind off of everything that was going wrong.

Heading in the general direction of the noise, Lena rounded the corner in a path she hadn't been down all week and discovered a brightly lit bar. It only had three and a half walls, the center of one wall standing open to the night so guests could wander in from the beach. The thatching from the roof blew in the gentle breeze, making a rustling sound that could barely be heard above the jovial voices.

She walked inside and immediately realized she'd stumbled onto the singles' side of the resort.

Women and men were bumping and grinding on the dance floor in the center of the room. The smell of expectation and sex seemed to linger everywhere. It was clearly a pickup place.

And while she didn't feel completely right taking a seat at the bar, she realized she probably belonged here much more than she had at the ballroom party she'd just ditched. She *was* single, after all. And she supposed it was time she got used to the idea.

Although, she certainly didn't feel single. In fact, she had no interest in any of the men in the place. And there were some her single friends would definitely have drooled over.

"What can I get you?" the bartender asked. He was already pouring another drink, even as he leaned forward to hear her.

"I don't care. Something strong and sweet."

Lena downed two of the orange-and-yellow concoctions he brought her in quick succession. Her gaze swept across the crowd. Not one of the men had approached her since she'd sat down. She wasn't sure whether to be relieved or insulted.

Before she had a chance to decide, Colt slid up to the bar beside her.

"How did you find me?" she asked, without bothering to look at him.

She didn't need to. Her body had begun reacting the second he walked through the door. Her heart stuttered inside her chest and her body began to heat like an engine sitting idle waiting for the expert hand of its driver.

Damn, she thought.

That was why none of the men here mattered, because they weren't Colt.

"Process of elimination."

She looked at him from beneath her lashes as he sat down beside her. "Surely you didn't check every single building."

"Why not? You're upset and I'm your friend."

Four days ago, that would have been enough for her. But Lena feared it wasn't anymore. She no longer wanted Colt to be her friend—or *just* her friend—she wanted him to love her.

And he didn't. Oh, he cared about her or he wouldn't be sitting there beside her. But it wasn't the same. And it wasn't enough.

"I could tell all day something was off. Want to talk about it?"

No, she didn't. What she wanted to do was have another drink, to bump and grind with him on the dance floor and then make mad, passionate love with him all night.

Instead, she said, "I think it's just all finally hitting me."

"What, that you never loved Wyn?"

Lena wanted to laugh. If he'd said that to her days
ago she would have vehemently denied it. In fact,
she thought maybe she had. She would have argued
that they'd had a perfectly good relationship, even if
it hadn't been filled with passion. However, that was
before she knew what real love felt like.

It hurt. It made you vulnerable. It was bliss and fear
all wrapped up together.

"No, I didn't love Wyn."

"So why were you going to marry him?"

"Because he was there. Because he was good and
decent—or at least I thought so at the time. Because
we could have had a perfectly satisfying life."

"You mean boring."

"I mean normal. We would have bought a house together. Had a couple of kids. Chaired the PTA and sat
on the bleachers together at T-ball games."

Colt spun the bottom of his glass around and around
between his hands. Lena's gaze was drawn, to their
strength, the single scar that ran diagonally from the
corner of his thumb up over his wrist.

"And that's what you want," he finally said.

She stared down into the bottom of her own glass.
The frozen concoction had melted, the yellow and
orange mingling together. The drink had looked bright
and happy before. Now it just looked sad.

Without realizing what she was doing, Lena opened
her mouth and told Colt the truth.

"I don't know what I want anymore. I'm so confused."

"Do you have to decide tonight? Who said you had to have all of the answers all of the time?"

"But I hate being…directionless. I hate not knowing where I'm going and how I'm going to get there. I like being in control."

Colt smiled, a sort of sad twist of his lips. "I know, but life doesn't always work that way. If there's one thing I've learned traveling the world and seeing different cultures it's that life throws you curveballs. You show your character through how you deal with them."

Character. She didn't even know what that meant anymore. She'd dealt with plenty of curveballs in her life. By herself. She was tired and wondered when it would be enough.

She realized Colt was just trying to help. And the things he'd dealt with made her issues seem somehow petty in comparison. Unfortunately, he was part of the problem, and his inability to realize that made the entire conversation a little difficult. Rather than have it go in a direction she didn't want to deal with, she decided to lighten the mood.

"Great pep talk, Yoda," she groused, leaning her body into his and knocking him sideways on the stool.

"Hey." He pushed back. "I'm wise beyond my years and you should listen to me."

"Please. If I did that you'd have talked me into jumping out of an airplane so that I could prove to myself I have the strength to get through this."

"Don't knock the power of the adrenaline rush until

you've tried it. Besides, there's something about facing fear head-on that reminds us we can handle more than we think."

"I am not going skydiving. I don't care what argument you use."

They sat together in silence for several minutes, lost in their own thoughts.

Lena realized that on some level Colt was right. She'd deal with the aftermath of Wyn's betrayal because she had to. And maybe knowing she'd never really loved him would make it easier in the end.

"If I can't convince you to skydive, can I at least persuade you to come to bed?"

And she'd handle their parting, as well. Because she had to—there was no other choice. But in the meantime, she had two days left to enjoy. And there was no reason not to make the most of them.

"I'm sure something can be arranged," she said, sliding off her stool. Anticipation buzzed through her blood. It was always there, just beneath the surface, waiting.

Colt followed her as they weaved through the undulating bodies and steamy heat of the bar. She threw a teasing glance behind her and relished the way his eyes sharpened.

She managed to keep people and tables between them so that he was several steps behind as she reached the beach exit. The minute she stepped outside, she broke into a sprint.

Calling behind her, she taunted, "But you'll have to catch me first."

COLT CAUGHT HER halfway down the path. He spun her in his arms, his mouth was rough as it claimed hers, but she met him thrust for thrust. They rushed together, groping mouths and urgent fingers.

His thigh wedged between hers and the exquisite bolt of awareness that rocketed through her sex almost sent her to her knees. His commanding hold on her was intoxicating. Every step he took forward drove her relentlessly back toward their bungalow and the rising passion building inside her. That passion was quickly becoming the easiest thing between them.

She couldn't help but be aware that their retreat echoed that of the dance she'd sorely butchered. Out here, alone with him, it was effortless. She didn't have to think, to worry that she was doing the wrong thing. Even without music, her body undulated against him, eager to go wherever he might lead. Inside, surrounded by people, she'd been stiff and uncomfortable and she knew it had shown.

But she hadn't known how to fix it.

"See, you *can* dance," he whispered against her ear, pulling her chest flush against him. "You just have to let yourself feel."

Maybe it was the dark night or the drinks she'd consumed, but she found herself saying, "I can't. I don't trust it. The pulse deep inside my muscles that urges me to just let go." That thing deep inside that insisted she should take a chance and stop fighting what she really wanted. "It's overwhelming. I'm afraid to lose myself."

"Do you trust me?" he asked.

Lena pulled back. She knew in her head that the question was simple. The answer, however, was not.

"With my body? Absolutely."

Apparently he was satisfied with her answer—they burst through the bungalow door. With a well-placed kick, Colt closed it behind them.

He moved her across the floor in the mimicked steps of the dance until the backs of her knees struck the edge of the bed. She toppled over, not even trying to keep her balance. She sprawled before him.

He towered above her, staring down with those intense, watchful, all-seeing eyes. He knew her too well and she wondered if he'd caught her equivocation after all.

Lena fell back on her elbows. His knee joined her on the bed, dipping the mattress next to her hip and rolling her body against him. Her mouth was suddenly dry. She tried to swallow but nothing was there.

Somehow this moment felt more important. It wasn't the first capitulation to a startling new awareness. It wasn't a hurried tumble on the ground because they'd both been scared and worried and needed the feel of each other. Nor was it the perfectly prepared seduction complete with romantic setting.

What it was, was emotional, more so than Lena wanted. There was a connection, an understanding, that hadn't been there before. She wondered if the difference was in her, the acknowledgment of her true feelings. Or was it part of him, too?

Lena realized it was the first time they'd actually had sex in a bed. The first night had been awkward, the second she'd been alone. Then they'd been out in the cave and finally inside the tent. Anytime they'd fallen into the bed, it had been from exhaustion that immediately claimed them both.

Maybe that was the difference.

He overwhelmed her as he always did. He tugged his shirt off over his head. Lena reached for him, running her fingers across the ridge of his pecks and abs. His skin was damp.

She arched beneath him, wanting to rub against him like a languid cat. He took the opportunity to tug at the zipper that ran along the line of her body, his fingers tickling against the swell of her breast and sliding over her skin to the curve of her hip. When he reached the zipper's end, he peeled the fabric away.

Her panties and bra joined the rest. Colt was braced above her. She marveled at the strength of his arms, the ripple of muscles, as he levered himself away. She wanted him to give in and fall onto her waiting body. She wanted to feel him, all of him, against her.

Hooking her feet around his ankles, she jerked his legs out from under him. He collapsed with a whoosh of surprise on top of her.

"Why did you do that?"

Lena undulated her hips beneath him, grinding his erection against her stomach. "So I could do that."

Grasping her hips, Colt rolled them both, reversing their positions and settling her sex over his erection.

"Do that again," he ordered. She complied, sending a bolt of need straight through her body as she moved her hips against him.

"Holy sh…" His words trailed off as his eyes closed, an expression of pure rapture crossing his face. She did it again just to see that all-consuming pleasure. She relished knowing she wasn't the only one overwhelmed by what was happening.

His eyes opened again, glittering at her with an intense hunger she felt down to her bones. Rearing up from beneath her, he covered her aching breasts with his hands. Her nipples spiked against his palms. He rubbed them in circles, soothing the throbbing before teasing them into hungry peaks again.

His head dipped as he sucked one deep into his mouth. Wet heat surrounded her. Her hips jerked against him, searching for more. Her fingers fisted into the hair at the nape of his neck, holding him where she wanted him.

Lena threw her head back, exposing her throat. The world spun around her. It took her a second to realize the motion was real and not just her equilibrium being bombarded with sensations. Her back bounced softly on the bed before settling. Her feet dangled off, forgotten and unnecessary.

His mouth trailed kisses across her stomach; his fingers found the slick heat of her sex and dove inside. The invasion was sudden and shocking, but Lena wanted it so badly that she didn't care. In fact, her hips immediately tried to push him into a faster rhythm so she could find relief from the storm building inside her.

But he wouldn't let her off that easily.

He brought her to the brink of orgasm so many times she lost count. His hand. His mouth. She was sobbing, her useless fingers scrabbling against his shoulders, trying to find purchase, anything that would compel him to give her the relief she needed.

She tried to reach for him, to fill her hands with the heat of his erection, but he stopped her. Undeterred, she found other ways. The arch of her foot brushed slowly against the jutting length of his cock. He gasped and then growled. She used her calf, her knee and inner edge of her thigh.

With soft pressure, she used his own body against him, sandwiching his cock between them. The pressure of her slipping back and forth against him drove them both insane. But it still wasn't enough.

She wanted to feel him, to hold him, to taste him. To torture him half as much as he was torturing her. With the last of her strength, Lena grasped his face. Looking him in the eye, she begged, "Colt, please."

His eyes were hot, his face drawn hard by the desire whipping through both of them. He was as close to the edge as she was. Maybe closer. Lena never realized how sexy it was to have a man so enthralled with her that her pleasure made him delirious. It was intoxicating.

Colt pushed against her hold. Lena collapsed to the bed, her thighs wet with her own desire, open and sprawled. He could do anything he wanted to her and she knew she'd love every second of it.

He paused only long enough to grab the condom— not something they'd forgotten since the cave.

His knees nudged her legs open wider. Her internal muscles contracted, sensing they'd soon be filled with him. He claimed her mouth, breathing her name across her lips before he did. His tongue slipped between her lips as his sex slid home inch by inch. Her body stretched, taking him in and holding him.

Her muscles quivered against the slow pace he was setting. She wanted him to rush, to finish it, but he wouldn't. Instead, he grasped both of her hands, threaded their fingers together and locked them beside her head.

Her body arched beneath him so that the swollen tips of her breasts brushed against his chest with each deliberate thrust. He stared down at her, his gaze deep and powerful.

A swell of something so overwhelming burst deep inside. She felt vulnerable, caught there beneath him, open, delirious with passion. It was too much. This was too much.

To protect herself, Lena let her eyes slip shut.

But Colt wasn't having it. With a growling demand, he said, "Look at me."

And she was powerless to resist.

She saw more than she wanted. Revealed more than she'd meant to give. In that moment there were no barriers between them. Not her fear nor their past. Not the uncertainty of what might come nor the understanding that it wouldn't be enough.

It was just them, connected in a timeless act that united them in a way that nothing else could.

Colt thrust against her. Her breath caught as he hit the sweet spot inside. Her hips rushed to meet him. Deliberately, he drove them both to the edge, meeting and grinding and demanding more. She wanted it to go on forever, to be so completely lost in the moment that it never ended.

But that couldn't happen.

Little bursts of electricity tingled up her spine. Her sex quivered. Colt yelled her name, surging deep inside her. Every part of her lost control, surrendering to the power of the connection building between them.

12

COLT WOKE SLOWLY. He felt almost hungover, although he hadn't had enough to drink for that to be the case. Beside him, Lena was buried beneath the covers, the soft contours of her body snuggled against him.

Last night had been intense. More intimate than anything he'd ever experienced before. He'd had plenty of sex in his life, but nothing came close to comparing.

His desire for Lena was intoxicating. Not just the sexual interludes, but the moments in between. Listening to her laugh. Watching her excitement as she learned something new. Even the way they disagreed made him want her more.

She challenged him in a way that no other woman ever had.

They had two days left, and looking down at the soft glow of Lena's skin, he realized it wasn't going to be nearly enough.

Unfortunately, he had no idea how to convince her of that.

The timing surely sucked. Less than a week ago

she'd been standing at an altar ready to marry a different man. But even she admitted that had been a mistake. She'd never loved Wyn.

The question was could she ever love Colt?

Fear roiled deep in his belly. It suffused his body with a restless heat that had him kicking off the covers and pacing away from her and the bed they'd shared.

He wasn't ready for this. He wasn't ready to love Lena.

She stirred restlessly in the bed, making little protesting noises as she rolled into the imprint of where he'd just been. Letting out a sigh, she burrowed deeper, apparently satisfied with the spot that she'd found.

There was the real possibility that he might lose her. Not just the new physical side to their relationship, but the friendship they'd built across distance and years.

Colt fought the urge to rip her out of the comfort of the covers and make her promise that she'd never leave him alone. Doing that wouldn't help.

Tight on the heels of that first inclination came another. The urge to love her completely, to brand her as his in every way possible, rose up inside him. Needing some air and distance before he did something stupid, Colt threw on the first thing he came to—a worn pair of jeans—and headed out onto their private patio.

The soft blue water in their infinity pool shimmered and mocked him. They hadn't even bothered to take advantage of it, which was a shame. Maybe later, when he had his emotions in check, they could swim together. Preferably naked.

He walked around to the far side of the pool. From

that vantage point, he could see the edge of the sea in the distance. The jungle, untamed as ever, was off to his left. He stood there, staring out into the unruly beauty.

A loud ringing interrupted the silence. It took him several seconds to realize it was coming from inside the bungalow. His cell phone.

He'd almost forgotten its existence over the past several days. Racing back inside, Colt scrambled to answer it before it could disturb Lena.

"Hello," he said in a hushed tone, moving back outside.

"Colt? Is that you?" The connection was awful, loud crackling interspersed with a low hum. He should probably know who it was, but with all of the interference he didn't.

"Who else would be answering my cell? Who's this?"

"Desmond Owens with the production team in Peru."

A drumbeat picked up somewhere in his chest.

"Desmond. How's the shoot?"

"Not...great." Desmond's response crackled. "Several of the crew came down with dengue fever. The local doctors say they won't be ready to return to the field for at least two weeks. And yesterday Ryan—" the man Desmond had hired as director instead of Colt "—fell off a cliff. He's going to be fine, but he broke a leg and dislocated his shoulder. They medevaced him to the closest hospital."

"That's awful. I'm sorry you guys are having so much trouble. But I'm in the middle of the Caribbean. What can I do from here?"

"We've put the project on hold for a few days. It sets us way behind schedule and plays hell with our budget, but I just don't have another choice. I was hoping that would be enough time for you to get here."

"Get there?"

"I need you to direct."

"Direct?" Shock, excitement and a rush of adrenaline shot through his body.

This was the chance he'd been waiting for. The break he needed to prove himself. The Peru shoot was complicated. It covered an archaeological find that was set to rival that of Machu Picchu. But the film site was remote.

Just getting there involved hours on a plane, connecting multiple times. Then driving to a local village and hiking through the thick jungle to a spot that had been virtually untouched for hundreds of years. The crew had packed in all their equipment. Not to mention generators, since they'd be living and working out there for weeks.

It would be challenging, but that's what had excited Colt about the project in the first place.

"We'll work out all the details when you get here. I've already booked you a flight leaving St. Lucia this afternoon."

"Presumptuous, aren't you?"

"Desperate is more like it. I don't know anyone else who could step up and fill Ryan's shoes so well."

Colt ran his hand through his hair. The temptation was great. It was what he'd been working so hard for over the past several years.

A small sound made him whirl to find Lena standing behind him. She was framed by the doorway to the patio. Her hair was mussed, her skin still flushed from sleep. She'd thrown on a shirt that barely skimmed the tops of her thighs. She looked rumpled and sleepy.

Everything except her eyes—they were wide awake. Watchful. Somewhat wary.

"Let me get back to you."

"But we don't—" Desmond protested.

Colt cut him off. "I'll call you back in twenty minutes," he said, hanging up.

The cell sat heavy in his hand, as if it suddenly carried more gravitational pull than the rest of the world around them. And in some way, Colt supposed it did. It was the connection to everything he'd ever wanted. Five days ago he wouldn't even have hesitated.

Now he looked across the infinity pool standing between him and Lena and wondered if the space had somehow gotten bigger.

"I'm so happy for you, Colt. You deserve this job. You've worked hard for a chance like this."

He nodded.

It felt as if he had a choice. As if he had to decide between taking the job that he'd been waiting for all his life and staying with the woman that he loved. But that wasn't right.

Why could he only have one or the other? Wasn't there a way to have both?

"Come with me," he said.

"What?" Her body rocked backward as if she'd been physically struck by his words.

"Come to Peru with me."

Colt watched as her eyes widened. She swallowed hard, her throat working overtime. A war of emotions crossed her face. They moved so fast that he couldn't determine what she was thinking.

He moved slowly around the pool, but stopped when she took a single step away.

Dread, hope and an engulfing grief that he recognized but didn't understand swamped him.

"Lena," he whispered, "come with me."

He knew her answer even before she said it, the reality dawning right along with the sadness that filled her eyes.

She shook her head.

"I can't."

"WHAT DO YOU MEAN YOU CAN'T? You have nothing to go home to. No fiancé, no job. What's holding you there, Lena? Come with me."

His words hurt. And they scared her senseless. There was nothing in D.C. to return for. Her job was gone. Even if Mr. Rand didn't fire her, she couldn't continue to work for the company. It wouldn't feel right, seeing Wyn and his father every day.

Her relationship was dead. The life she'd imagined had disappeared before it'd even had a chance to start. Unpacking the boxes in her apartment was really the only thing she had to look forward to.

How pathetic was that?

But what Colt offered wasn't any better. In fact, it was worse.

"And what exactly would I do in Peru? Wash your clothes? Cook your meals? Or would my only responsibility be to make myself available whenever you weren't busy and wanted a roll in the hay?"

Colt's eyes narrowed. "Don't do this."

"Do what? Ask the hard questions?"

"Bring everything down to the lowest common denominator. Don't put a wedge between us."

She laughed, the sound ringing with bitterness. "Us? There is no us, Colt. There's now, this week. We both knew when it was over we'd go our separate ways. It's just going to happen a little earlier than we'd planned."

She shrugged, a sharp pain lancing through her chest. She resisted the urge to wrap her arms around herself, not wanting him to see her weakness.

"I will not follow you like some bitch in heat. I will not be my mother."

"What the hell does your mother have to do with this?" he bellowed, frustration and anger quickly overshadowing everything else.

"Nothing. I have a life. A job I enjoy. Pieces to pick up and put back together. My place is in D.C."

She would not leave everything behind without a backward glance for a man, not even for Colt. Part of her wanted to give in, to agree to anything he asked. It would be so easy to do.

But he hadn't offered her promises. He hadn't told her he loved her or needed her or wanted something more than an extension of the pleasure they'd found together on the island.

Maybe if he had…

But he hadn't and she refused to be ruled by her libido. With Wyn she'd had a relationship that was passionless but practical. And with Colt she'd had the all-consuming passion that clouded her brain and made her contemplate making bad decisions.

When would she find a happy medium? Someone who could give her everything she wanted and needed? Passion, happiness, a stable future and roots that ran so deep they couldn't be removed.

That's what she deserved. But at the moment, the idea of ever finding it felt foreign and unattainable.

Still, she refused to settle for something less. She refused to fall into the same trap her mother had. She refused to lose herself simply to please a man.

She refused to let the moment when Colt walked away break her.

As if realizing that his outburst hadn't helped his case any, Colt lowered his voice and quietly countered, "Everything will be there after Peru. You can deal with it all then."

"No, no, I can't. I can't put my life on hold because you're not ready to give up our vacation fling."

He reached for her, but Lena pulled away. If he touched her, she might cave. And then she'd never forgive herself.

"Go, Colt. I want you to. I know that this is the break you've been waiting for. I'm happy for you, really I am."

Colt's jaw tightened. His entire body was pulled tight. She knew he wanted to say more, wanted to come up with some argument that was sure to change her mind.

But there wasn't one. They didn't have a future. She

knew that. Better to end things now and minimize the pain as much as possible.

The loud ring of his cell blasted between them. Colt's hand tightened around it before pulling it up to look at the screen. He didn't immediately answer. Instead, he looked at her over the top of it and said again, "Come with me."

Lena swallowed, forcing back the lump of tears that was stuck in her throat. With a slow shake of her head, she said, "I can't."

Spinning away from her, Colt answered the call. She listened, unable to move away and save herself the heartache, as he did exactly what she'd told him to do and accepted Desmond's offer.

As she sagged against the frame of the door, the pain burst full-fledged through her body. *Finally* was all she could think. Here was the pain she'd come to expect.

It was over and some day she'd figure out how to deal with it. In the meantime, she refused to fall apart. No one would find her unwashed and unhappy, so weighted down by grief and pain that she couldn't get out of bed. Tissues would not lie crumpled between the layers of her bed. She would not refuse to eat for days and weeks. No one would watch her waste away, losing twenty pounds she couldn't afford in the space of a few days.

She would not let herself be held hostage by these emotions.

Instead, she sat quietly and watched as Colt went through the bungalow packing his bags. Within thirty minutes all evidence that he'd even been there had disappeared.

At the door, his hand wrapped tightly around the handle of his bag, Colt paused. He looked back at her across the intimate space they'd shared. He paused, staring at her for several seconds before finally saying, "I hope you'll be happy."

The door had barely closed before she gave in to the torrent of emotions rushing through her. Tears flowed down her face, silent and as lonely as she suddenly felt.

She'd made the right decision.

So why did it hurt so much?

13

STALKING INTO THE MAIN LOBBY, Colt headed for the receptionist's desk. There was one more thing he needed to do before he left.

"I need to see Marcy, please."

The woman behind the desk cringed away from him, letting him know that the expression on his face was probably not the best one to be wearing if he wanted to charm anyone into anything. He tried to wipe the scowl off his face, but it wouldn't seem to budge.

The woman backed away from the desk, glancing behind her to the hallway leading into the offices. "I'll go get her," she said reluctantly.

Colt was in no mood to wait.

Rounding the desk, he headed for the opening, beating her there.

"Wait, sir, you can't go in there." She tried to skirt in front of him. He'd give the tenacious little thing points for effort, despite the fact that he could have picked her up and moved her aside with nothing but his pinky finger.

"Trust me, Marcy won't mind if I find her."

"Trust me, she will," the woman answered dryly, but apparently she realized there wasn't much she could do to stop him.

Colt vaguely heard her pick up the phone and whisper into it as he disappeared into the back offices. He probably had less than five minutes before some security force came swooping down to save little Marcy. By then he knew she'd stop whoever tried to throw him out.

Sticking his head into several offices, he noticed that they were all neat, with mismatched furniture that somehow fit the homey, eclectic feel of the resort. Escape was no doubt a pleasant place to work. Although, at the moment Colt wasn't exactly harboring the warm and fuzzies for it.

A light shone out into the hallway from the last door on the right. It was early enough that he supposed no one else had made it in, but Marcy was here. Lucky for him.

Rounding the corner, he plopped down into her guest chair. Marcy did a double take, pulling her focus away from the computer screen that sat adjacent to the corner of her desk.

A scroll of color caught Colt's eye before she had a chance to minimize the screen. It was a photograph of Lena and himself.

"Colt. What are you doing here? I thought you'd be sleeping in today. We don't have anything scheduled until your couples massages later this afternoon."

"That's what I need to talk to you about." His harsh

voice had Marcy shifting in her chair, and glancing back at her computer screen, no doubt just to make sure the pictures weren't still revolving across it.

"Don't tell me you're one of those men who refuse to get a massage. You know, there's nothing sexual about it. I promise our staff is highly trained and extremely professional."

"I'm sure they are, but that's not the problem."

She frowned. "Then what is?"

"Something's come up and I have to leave."

She sputtered, at a loss for words for several seconds. Colt got the impression that rarely happened to Marcy. "But you can't. We haven't finished the sessions."

They had, although she wasn't ready to admit it yet. He'd only gotten a quick glimpse of the picture as it had flashed across her screen, but it had been enough to recognize good work. If he hadn't seen it, it might not have occurred to him to use the quality of what she already had as an argument against the need for more. But since he had...

"Show me." He gestured to the screen now displaying a generic beach scene.

"Show you what?" she asked.

"The photographs. I want to see them."

She studied him for several seconds. He assumed she was weighing her options and the potential consequences of doing as he asked. She made a move toward her screen but before she could touch it a man burst into the room. If Colt remembered right, this was the head of security they'd met the morning they came out of the jungle.

"Tina said there was a problem." The man skidded to a halt just inside the doorway. His eyes took in everything. Colt appreciated the thorough calculation used to assess the threat. No doubt he was former police or military.

"Everything's fine, Zane." Marcy gestured between the two men. "I can't remember if you two were introduced. Colt Douglas meet Zane Edwards, our head of security. Colt is part of the couple we're using for the ad campaign. He dropped by to discuss something with me."

"Tina said it was more like 'pushed in' than 'dropped by.'" The other man's eyes narrowed in consideration as they swept over Colt. He was happy that he was sitting down. Less chance Zane would consider him a threat. He was also pretty happy to notice the other man didn't have a gun tucked into a holster at his shoulder...unless he kept his beneath his black T-shirt and Colt just didn't see how the man could have hidden it.

Swiveling in his chair to face Zane, Colt decided some damage control couldn't hurt. "I apologize if I frightened Tina. I didn't mean to."

Zane harrumphed, but he let Colt's apology pass without really challenging it.

"Well, if you're certain everything's all right." Zane's eyes bored into Marcy's as if looking for some minute signal she might send.

"I promise she's not in any danger, at least from me. If you need a secret word or code or something go ahead and ask her for it. She isn't under duress."

"Honestly, Zane, I appreciate your concern but we're

fine. I'll call you if I need you," Marcy said, lifting up her cell phone from the desk where it had been lying beneath her computer monitor. "Anything else going on that I need to be aware of?"

"Not a thing," Zane said, already backing toward the door. The man's eyes swung to Colt's, his hazel gaze a bit unsettling. "I'll be keeping an eye on the hallway from the Crow's Nest."

It was clearly a warning, an unnecessary one, but he supposed he couldn't fault Zane for doing his job and doing it well. "Whatever makes you happy, man," Colt said with a shrug.

Turning on his heel, Zane disappeared almost as quickly and silently as he'd entered.

"I'm guessing he can kill with his bare hands," Colt quipped, returning his focus to Marcy.

"In many and varying ways. Part of me wishes I was daring enough to ask him for a demonstration."

"You haven't?"

"Are you kidding me? Did you see the size of his biceps? No, thank you."

Colt chuckled. Zane's appearance had managed to do one thing, if nothing else. It had defused the tension he'd carried with him into the room. He was angry and on edge, but that wasn't Marcy's fault.

"I really am sorry that I barged in here this way," he smiled at her.

She shook her head. "You truly can't help it, can you?"

"Help what?"

"That mischievous, impish charm thing that you've got going."

"I don't have a clue what you're talking about."

"I know. That's the problem." Reaching for her mouse, she started the slide show. "Here, let me show you."

His original intention was to glance through what they already had and use them to convince Marcy she had enough photographs. But the minute she flipped the screen toward him and the photos started scrolling that all changed. Photographs whizzed by, a kaleidoscope of memories from the past several days.

"Here," she said as the merry-go-round of colors stopped. A photograph from their first night at dinner popped up onto the screen. Lena was clearly uncomfortable. Her body and face were stiff and awkward.

He thought back to that night, after their first kiss. At the time he'd just assumed the whole photo-session thing was bothering her. In retrospect, he wondered if it had actually been residual awareness from their kiss that had her strung so tight.

The next photograph was of them on the beach. The tension was gone, replaced by the relaxed way her body leaned against his. Their heads were tilted together and for all intents and purposes they looked like a couple, one that shared the comfortable familiarity only achieved through time and common history.

Marcy scrolled through the photos again, flying past the rest of that evening to shots from the next day. By the pool they'd been laughing and relaxed. But there was more. Mikhail had managed to catch several candid shots. In one Lena was studying Colt beneath her lashes, stealing a glance while he wasn't looking. In another, he was devouring her with his eyes while she was focused on the pages of her book.

The sexual chemistry between them was almost palpable. Never in his life had he felt this exposed.

There was no doubt they were beautiful shots. Mikhail really was a talented photographer. If Colt had been looking at the final products through the filter of his education and experience he might have seen them in a different light.

But he couldn't separate that professional part of himself from the man who was staring at the woman he loved as she slowly moved closer and closer.

When they reached the group of photos from the night in the bungalow Colt felt heat suffuse his body. The first few obviously didn't work. But the rest were dripping with a sensuality that he didn't appreciate sharing with anyone. If he'd realized at the time, he would have kicked Mikhail out on his ass.

"Enough," he said, his voice rough and broken. He didn't want to see any more. It was too painful watching the progression of their affair knowing now how it would end.

There was one thing he knew for certain. No one could see these. They were too personal, too painful to share with the world. "You can't use those."

"Of course I can," Marcy said, her voice steady and self-assured.

"You don't understand. I can't let you use those photographs." He turned his gaze to hers. "I can't let the world see them."

"Why not? They're beautiful. The photographic evolution of a love affair."

"No, you don't understand. It's over. That's why I'm leaving."

"What?" Marcy shook her head as if hoping that some random piece would shake loose and what he'd just said would finally make sense. "What happened?"

He didn't answer, how could he when he wasn't entirely sure himself? Instead, he focused on the one problem he could solve. "I'll pay for the photographs. I'll pay for Mikhail's expenses and those of his crew. I'll pay for the week here at the resort and any extras that you arranged. I'll even pay for the new shoot you'll have to schedule to replace this one."

"But... No. I need these photographs in the next few weeks or we'll miss the deadline for the photo spread in *Worldwide Travel*."

"Then I'll pay for any rush fees required."

Marcy flopped back. The leather of her desk chair creaked with the force of her body. "What if I don't want to deal with the headache, Colt? Money can't solve everything."

"From my experience, money can solve everything. Everything except grief."

"Again, what if I refuse?"

"I'll get my lawyers involved."

"That won't do you much good. You signed an agreement."

"Maybe, but the court system is liable to issue an

injunction preventing you from using the photographs until everything is settled. That could take a while. Especially when you're dealing with multiple court systems that might have jurisdiction."

Marcy's eyes glittered and her jaw locked hard beneath her unsmiling mouth. "Where's the charm now, huh? Why are you doing this, Colt?"

"Because I can't stand the idea of her seeing those photographs and figuring out just how vulnerable I am."

"Men!" Marcy exclaimed, throwing her hands up into the air. "Would that be so damn bad?"

"I asked her to come with me." His eyes found Marcy's. He had no idea why he was telling this woman intimate details of his life that he couldn't even explain to Lena. Maybe it was the no-nonsense attitude she wrapped around herself like a shield. Or the soft center he sensed was hidden beneath. "She said no. It's over. I was the rebound guy, nothing more than an island fling."

"I'm not so sure about that."

But he was. Lena had no desire to take their affair further than this week. If she did, she would be leaving with him.

"Your call, Marcy. Do I pay for everything or contact my attorneys? And trust me, I have many who jump when I call."

With a growl, Marcy slapped the top of her desk. He heard Tina yelp out in the hallway and had no doubt Zane would be appearing again shortly. But one way or another, Colt would be gone before he appeared.

Reaching into his pocket, he pulled out his cell and began dialing.

"Fine. Stop. You win," she said.

Punching End, Colt slipped his cell back into his pocket. She didn't need to know that he'd been about to call himself. He wasn't going to bother his attorney this early, not when he already knew that he'd won.

"I'd like all digital and physical copies of the photographs, and I want them deleted from your computer so I know that they can't resurface anywhere."

Marcy narrowed her eyes but nodded.

"And if you could arrange for a private launch to pick me up at the dock, I'd appreciate it."

"The ferry will be here in a few hours."

"I didn't say ferry. I said private launch. And the sooner the better."

"It'll take at least an hour before they can get here."

"Fine, I'll wait. That should give you time to get any remaining pictures from Mikhail. And to erase the originals."

Marcy's mouth twisted in an unflattering frown. "I'll make a call."

Colt passed Zane in the hallway on his way out to the main lobby. The other man eyed Colt but didn't stop him. An hour later he was bumping across choppy seas, a bulging manila envelope tucked under his arm.

He couldn't keep himself from turning around and watching the line of the island as it receded into nothing.

LENA WANDERED ALONG the vacant beach, listening to the waves as they crashed against the sand. She'd walked along the shore many times since they'd arrived on the island.

Today it felt different. Instead of being warm and relaxing…it was lonely. Because she knew Colt wasn't lurking in the trees or waiting for her to return to their bungalow. He was gone.

Today was her last day on the island. Originally, they'd planned to take the later ferry, but Lena couldn't stand to sit here upset and alone.

She'd done the right thing. So why did it feel so bad?

Walking back to the bungalow, she threw the last few items into her suitcase and set it by the door so she'd be ready. She glanced quickly into the mirror above the sink, thinking how appropriate it was that she'd be leaving the island in much the same condition she'd come onto it—sleep deprived and miserable, with dark circles under her eyes.

The resort was beginning to bustle as sleepy guests stirred. It was late by most standards, but not for Escape. Here people indulged. How quickly she'd become used to the hedonistic pace.

She walked across the compound to the main building. Stopping at the front desk, she asked to speak with Marcy, hoping the other woman was already up and at work. The smiling clerk told her she'd be right out.

Unable to sit still, Lena walked across the empty lobby to the windows and the vista of sun, sand and waves outside. It looked beautiful. Too bad she was leaving the idyllic setting under less than happy circumstances.

"I thought I'd see you this morning," Marcy said as she walked up beside her.

"Oh?" Lena turned briefly to look at the other woman, working restlessly on the rings that still sat heavily on her finger. She spun them around and around.

"Colt came to see me yesterday."

Lena returned her gaze to the beautiful view out the window. Better than the pity she saw in Marcy's bright blue eyes.

"He's gone," Marcy said gently.

"I know. He got a call to take a job in Peru."

Marcy pulled a large manila envelope from behind her back. "These are for you. He demanded all of the copies, but I thought the least he owed you were the photographs."

Lena stared down at the nondescript brown paper and then back up at Marcy without actually touching it.

"What are you talking about?"

"He didn't tell you?"

"Tell me what?"

"Jeez, woman. Do the men in your life tell you anything? Colt bought the rights to all of the photographs."

Disbelief blasted through her and Lena turned to face Marcy fully.

"Why would he do that?"

Marcy shrugged. "You'll have to ask him, but I think it probably had something to do with keeping them private."

"That idiot," she breathed out.

"Oh, it gets better. He threatened to get his lawyers

involved and tie us up in the courts until the photo-graphs were useless to me."

"It was a bluff."

"I don't think so."

Lena threw her hands up in the air. "What are you going to do? Don't you need the photos for your ad campaign?"

Marcy's frown was genuine, along with the linger-ing pique no doubt directed toward Colt. "Yep. Colt made some suggestions for an alternative." Her frown pulled into a reluctant smile. "And damn the man for being right."

"He's a great photographer," Lena admitted. While she might be upset, she couldn't deny his talent.

"He's paying for Mikhail to stay and shoot the new photographs."

"How much is this costing him?"

"You really don't want to know. Between the photos and the cost of your stay…"

"That's got to be thousands."

"Try about forty."

Anger bubbled up inside Lena. "I'm sorry. We both agreed to this and he shouldn't have reneged." A growl of frustration and unreleased sadness rolled through her. "I'd like to strangle him."

Marcy laughed. With a pointed look, she said, "You'll have to catch him first."

They both knew that wasn't going to happen. Lena turned back toward the window. The perfect setting was easier to deal with than anything Marcy was saying.

"Colt paid for an extra day, but I'm guessing it's a waste of breath to tell you to stay."

Lena nodded.

Marcy laid the envelope on the edge of a nearby table before saying, "The ferry should be here in about twenty minutes. I'll have someone fetch your luggage and meet you at the dock."

And like that, it was all over.

Again.

In the space of a week she'd lost two men. One she'd never loved but thought she had. And one she'd never considered loving until it was too late.

Marcy's words echoed through her head, *you'll have to catch him.* Part of her wanted to do just that. To chase after him like a love-starved puppy, eager for any crumbs he might throw. A restless need suffused her body, but she refused to give in to it.

She had her own life, her own identity, and she refused to give it up. This was the right decision for her.

A tiny voice in the back of her brain said *you thought that about Wyn once, too.* But she ignored it.

Slipping both rings off her finger, she shoved them deep into her pocket. Past and present hidden away. She probably should give the band back to Marcy, but she wouldn't…. Couldn't. Picking up the envelope, Lena tucked it under her arm and headed for the dock and the journey to the rest of her life.

Whatever that might hold.

14

SHE'D BEEN HOME FOR A WEEK. In that time, she'd managed to avoid her family and had formally quit her job. Mr. Rand had tried to get her to stay, and part of her had been tempted. Fear of the unknown almost made her accept his offer.

It felt wrong to be cut adrift with no real direction. She'd worked so hard to become successful. She'd even held two jobs to put herself through college.

For the first time since she'd turned sixteen, Lena had no responsibilities. No boss waiting for her to come in. No rush projects that would require all-nighters.

And she almost wished that she had. Being busy might have helped keep her mind off Colt. She wondered what he was doing and if he missed her. Probably not, he was out in the middle of the rain forest living his dream.

She slept late and unpacked. Once or twice she wandered the city like a tourist, seeing the sites she'd never made time to visit. Finding another job was high on her list of priorities, but she decided to put it off for a few weeks. Mr. Rand had offered her a generous severance package, which meant she had some breathing room.

Since the decision to push Colt out of her life had been hers, it seemed stupid to mope. But it was difficult not to. One day after quitting, Lena pulled out the bin of jewelry supplies she'd stuck deep in the back of her closet. Dust fluttered to the ground when she popped open the lid.

Semiprecious jewels, crystals, beads, gold wire and silver stared back at her like long-lost friends.

The first night she didn't stop until her stomach growled and her fingers were so sore she could barely continue the next morning. But she did anyway.

By the end of the fourth day she had an array of necklaces, earrings, bracelets and rings. Things she was proud of. She had no idea what to do with them, but she'd figure that out.

She'd figure out a way to make this a part of her life. Lena was through sacrificing pieces of herself. She enjoyed making jewelry and that was all that mattered. Even if she couldn't find a way to support herself with it, she wouldn't ever pack it away again.

A knock on the door startled her, causing her to drop a pair of small pliers, which clattered to the tabletop, scattering a handful of the peacock-blue beads she'd been working with.

Grumbling under her breath, Lena chased after them. She was ass up with her head as far under the couch as it could go when a deep voice sounded behind her. The back of her head cracked against the wooden edge of the couch frame. Adrenaline burst through her body. Holding her splitting head, she fell into a heap on the floor and managed to spin around at the same time.

Wyn was the last person she expected to find staring down at her sprawled body.

"What are you doing here? How the hell did you get in?"

Holding a shiny gold key in front of his face he said, "I came by to return this."

"And thought you'd use it one more time?"

"You didn't answer." His eyes shifted around the apartment, looking everywhere but at her. "I was worried about you."

He'd thought she'd be inconsolable. Or worse that she'd hurt herself. She could see it in his eyes, the sheepish realization that he'd jumped to the wrong conclusion. He probably would have preferred it if she had been comatose with despair.

"Don't flatter yourself, Wyn. I'm hardly a candidate for suicide watch because you slept with my cousin."

He shifted from one foot to the other and Lena realized he was nervous. Or maybe *uncomfortable* was a better word. Good.

Pushing up from the floor, Lena dropped the few beads she'd managed to find back onto the table. She and Wyn stared at each other, both at a loss for what to say next. More than the room and her scattered jewelry supplies stood between them. And probably always had.

"What's that?" Wyn asked, pushing his hands deep into his pockets and nodding toward the mess on the table.

"I've started designing jewelry again."

"That's good. I always thought you were great at it."

That was a revelation she hadn't expected. "Why didn't you ever say that?"

"You didn't seem to want my opinion on it. You were always so independent and capable. You never asked what I thought about your jewelry, or anything else for that matter."

"That's not true."

He shrugged.

"I definitely didn't ask you to sleep with my cousin."

A frown pulled the corners of his lips down and marred the perfect expanse of his brow. "I'm sorry about that, Lena. I honestly didn't mean for it to happen. I never meant to hurt you."

She blew a deep breath out of her lungs and sank slowly to the couch. She couldn't let him take all of the blame. Yes, he'd been the one to betray their relationship, but at that moment, Lena wondered if she'd given him any other option.

"You didn't, which probably says a lot." She waved her hands, dismissing his apology. "It doesn't matter. We didn't love each other, but neither one of us wanted to say so."

He might have taken the coward's way out, but then she almost had, too. She should have listened to the jitters—they'd been trying to tell her something, but she'd been unwilling to take a risk and let what was safe and comfortable go for the unknown.

"Doesn't excuse what I did."

"No, it doesn't."

"If it makes any difference, we're trying to make it work."

Shock had Lena staring at Wyn's face. Unable to help herself, she began to laugh. "God help you. You do realize that she's almost ten years younger than you are and one of the most helpless people I've ever met."

"That's okay. I like that she needs me. Besides, she makes me feel young."

"You *are* young, Wyn."

"Yeah, but sometimes I forget that. You've met my mother, can you blame me? I was a little adult before I started kindergarten, my entire life laid out for me like a Christmas suit."

Lena shook her head. "I suppose it makes sense in a weird way. She really is the opposite of everything you probably thought you wanted."

He laughed. "She's definitely the opposite of you."

"Don't I know it."

"I've been thinking about it a lot, and maybe that's why we didn't work. We're too much alike. Mitzi challenges me, infuriates me and makes me laugh. She sees things in a different way and makes me see them that way, too."

"You don't think that'll get old?"

"Who knows, but we're going to give it a try. We might end up hating each other or we might find that we're exactly what the other needs. I ground her to reality and she makes me pick my head up and look around every once in a while."

Unexpected jealousy spurted through Lena's veins. Not because Mitzi and Wyn had found happiness together. The fact that their relationship didn't bother her was just proof that she and Wyn had made the right decision in not getting married. But she envied that they'd found each other and had a camaraderie she hadn't felt since she'd walked off that island alone.

From the very beginning, she'd had that with Colt. A sense of easiness, a connection and kindred spirit. Oh, he knew exactly how to push her buttons, but he challenged her and prodded her and made her question her view of the world. Or he had until it had all fallen apart.

Even on the island, in their most intimate conversations, what had he done? Challenged her view. Most of the people who might have gone to that island with her would have plied her with alcohol and told her what a bastard Wyn was.

Not Colt. He'd held her own feet to the fire and made her look logically at the bigger picture. The man was insightful and brilliant in a way that she hadn't really given him credit for.

Silence stretched between Lena and Wyn, neither of them knowing what else there was to say.

"You don't have to quit. If anyone should leave the company it should be me."

"Please, we both know your dad would never let you do that."

"Actually, I think he'd rather have you than me."

Lena frowned. "I'm not coming back, and even if I was I wouldn't make you leave. You're good at your job, Wyn. Most of the time."

"Well, would you at least consider freelancing for

us? You're the best graphic designer we've got. You could work from home. Take the jobs that you wanted."

She stared at Wyn as if he'd suddenly grown another head. He was suggesting something that had never occurred to her, but that was definitely intriguing.

"I'll think about it." She had to consider all the angles before making a decision. What he was talking about was going into business for herself. That took planning and preparation. Rand Marketing couldn't be her only client if she intended to make a living.

But it was definitely a possibility. And she liked the idea of having more flexibility. Of being in complete control of her destiny.

A flash of guilt crossed Wyn's face. "So…uh…how was the honey—your trip?"

Lena lifted a single eyebrow and stared at him for several seconds. "Do you know what an idiot I looked like when Colt and I arrived at that resort?"

"Well, if things had gone according to plan you'd never have known the difference."

"Trust me, I would have noticed. Marcy makes drill sergeants look like fuzzy puppies. And Mikhail, the photographer, was good at blending in, but not that good."

"So you went through with it?" he asked, surprised.

"What choice did I have? I couldn't afford that place."

"I never liked Colt—I always thought there was more going on between you—" Lena tried not to look guilty "—but I figured he'd take care of everything for you."

"Oh, he did. After the photographs were already taken."

"Something tells me there's more to that story."

If only he knew. But she and Wyn had never had the same kind of relationship she'd once shared with Colt. They'd never talked in depth about their feelings. Never really shared their worries or struggles. Until that moment it was something she hadn't even been aware of.

"Maybe."

Wyn stepped closer, holding out his hand and offering the kind of comfort he'd never bothered with before. Lena didn't accept it. Somehow it would have felt wrong. Artificial.

"I know you well enough to realize that whatever happened, you aren't happy."

"Let's just say things got complicated."

"You mean you slept with him."

Lena resented the heat that flared up her face. It was pointless and all but screamed he was right. However, she refused to confirm his suspicions with words.

Wyn shook his head. "I know I'm probably the last person who should be doling out relationship advice, but I'm going to do it anyway. You and Colt are perfect for each other. It's one of the reasons I didn't like him. Whatever happened, it can't be bad enough to ruin the bond that you share."

"You're wrong. We're terrible for each other."

"*You're* wrong. He's adventurous and exotic. You're practical and grounded. You complement each other just like Mitzi balances me."

Lena frowned.

"Trying to make it work might be risky, but would the end result be worth it?" Wyn cocked his head to the side and studied her. For the first time since they'd met, she thought maybe he was really seeing her. "Do you love him?" he finally asked.

Lean nodded.

"Then go for it. Don't give up on love, Lena. I know from experience that it's a tricky thing to find. Don't let fear or duty or what everyone else expects hold you back. You have to take what you want."

This time when Wyn reached out to her, she let him wrap his arm around her shoulder. It felt weird, having him hold her. Now that she'd experienced the connection she shared with Colt, it was obvious there was nothing here. Nothing except for the kind offer of comfort.

"I've always thought of you as fearless. You don't take no for an answer. You set your sights on something and you work tirelessly until you get it. Why would love be any different? Decide what you want and fight for it. Until you win, or until there's no breath left in your body. Either way, you'll have no regrets."

She smiled up at him. "When did you get so smart?"

He laughed, bumping his shoulder against hers. "Almost two weeks ago, when an amazing woman walked away from me and I realized I'd almost screwed up several lives because I was a coward, too scared to break free from my family's expectations."

"You've changed," she said. And definitely for the better. This Wyn, the one who was wise and insightful and understanding, was a far cry from the distant, charming man she'd been set to marry. Not that she was any more attracted to him. But this Wyn, she thought, might make a great friend.

"That's what happens when you get dropped into chaos and baptized by fire. You slipped off to a secluded island. I had to deal not only with my parents, but your mother, aunt and Mitzi, too."

Part of her wanted to grin. "I think I would have liked to see that."

"I assure you, it wasn't pretty. And I'm still paying for what I did, but that's okay."

"Oh, before I forget." Lena pulled out of Wyn's embrace and disappeared into her bedroom to retrieve the ring she'd placed in her jewelry box for safekeeping. The large diamond flashed as the light hit it, but it was the plain band sitting next to it that held her attention.

Walking back into the living room, she held the engagement ring out to Wyn. "Just promise me you won't rush into things and give it to Mitzi the minute you see her." She thought about her words, about everything Wyn had just said and the slow progression of their own relationship. "Wait. Scratch that. Maybe you *should* give it to her right away."

Wyn held out his hands, not to take what she offered, but to tell her to stop. "No, Lena, that's yours. Sell it. Keep it. I don't care. It's the least I owe you."

"You don't owe me anything, Wyn." Reaching for his hand, she turned it over, dropped the ring into his palm and curled his fingers around it. Giving him back the ring was the right thing to do. Not because it was expensive. Not because it mattered to either of them. But because it *didn't* matter and never really had. It was a symbol of the mistake they'd almost made, and keeping it around just felt wrong.

He looked up at her with a mixed expression of guilt and hope and something she hadn't seen in a long time but never realized was missing—happiness.

"I hope you can be happy, Lena."

Wyn left after she promised to give his father a call in a few days, once she'd thought about his offer to freelance. If nothing else, she might do it until she found a new job.

Wyn was gone, but his words still lingered in her head.

Was she being a coward? Was she allowing fear to rule her decisions and keep her from really living?

There was certainly no hiding the devastation she was feeling. No, she wasn't wallowing in her bed, but that didn't mean she wasn't heartbroken and upset.

She was definitely afraid. Afraid to put herself out there, to admit that she loved Colt, only to find out that he didn't feel the same. Or that they couldn't make their lives mesh. Or that he wanted something different from the future than she did.

How quickly he had dropped everything to rush off to Peru. It scared her, his ability to pull up stakes at a moment's notice. But a tiny part of her also envied him those adventures.

She had to admit that there were a few good things about her childhood, although she often had a hard time remembering them. She'd seen so many amazing things. She hadn't just taken history, she'd learned about all the ancient sites in person. There were memories, good ones, of sharing laughter and happy times with her mother. It was just that they'd been overshadowed by the helplessness, fear and uncertainty of the bad times.

But could she continue to let those bad memories and unwanted lessons dictate her future?

How did she know for sure that she and Colt couldn't make it work? She hadn't given them the chance to try.

Hell, if Wyn and Mitzi could make it work, anyone could.

That left only one thing for her to do.

Go to Peru.

COLT LET HIS EYES WANDER the dark jungle surrounding the camp. Off to the right, several of the team huddled around a campfire joking, laughing and drinking bad coffee. Normally, he'd have been right there with them enjoying the rugged parts of the job that forced him to rely on his own skills and instincts.

Not tonight. Actually, not since he'd gotten there. All he'd thought about was Lena.

How she'd turned him down. How he'd walked away.

He'd thought long and hard about what had been different between them on the island. Was it that she'd been free? Was it the romantic, sensual atmosphere of the place?

Colt didn't think so.

"I'm an idiot," he said to no one in particular.

High up in a tree, a monkey chattered back at him.

Colt strained to make out the features of the animal in the dark, but could only see the barest outline. The leaves rustled as the monkey crept closer. It was almost eerie, the way the animal stared at him, as if it expected an explanation.

For some reason, Colt responded. "I was scared. Everyone gets scared," he defended, as if the monkey could understand. He, the guy who fearlessly jumped into any new adventure, had been scared of practical, grounded Lena. Scared to take a risk and find out that she didn't love him the way he loved her. Scared to have her and lose her.

Although that had happened anyway.

And now it was worse, because he didn't even have their friendship anymore.

The night he'd gotten the call that his parents' helicopter had gone down in a forest in North Carolina, he'd been devastated. Until then, the only person he'd ever lost was his grandmother and it hadn't been a shock. But that phone call...it had floored him. He hadn't known what to do. What to think. Where to turn.

But Lena had been there. She was the first person he'd called, and she'd rushed over. He'd relied so heavily on her for emotional and moral support. And that had scared him even more. Somewhere in the haze of grief and anger that had followed, he'd convinced himself that it was better to be alone than to risk feeling the pain of losing someone he loved again.

It was easy to push everyone in his life away. Lena, his brother, sister-in-law and niece, none of them could come with him as he directed his career to far off places. Yes, part of him relished the adventure that fueled some innate need. But he could have found that elsewhere. He could have gone to L.A. or New York and found work in a more traditional setting.

But working on documentaries allowed him to slip away into the world and get lost in his art.

And he'd thought he was happy and satisfied—until Lena's life exploded in front of him. He'd been there for her—there was no question that he would be. He'd have walked to the ends of the earth if she needed him.

That kiss. That stupid, wonderful, innocent kiss had changed everything. From that moment on, his curiosity about what being with Lena might be like had become impossible to ignore. There was no more pretending or trying to shunt his desire and awareness of her away.

He loved her, had always loved her, even if he hadn't been able to admit it to himself. He'd been scared of loving her only to lose her. But he'd lost her anyway because he was an idiot and hadn't told her the truth, the reason he wanted her with him.

When he'd asked her to go to Peru, he hadn't told her the thought of living without her made him crazy. And when she'd said no, what had he done?

Used his work once more to escape from the pain. The only problem was that it had followed him, sharper than ever now that she wasn't there.

He should have told her he loved her.

The monkey began to rattle the branch that it perched on, as if upset it was being ignored. "What am I doing here?" Colt asked it. The little creature, its white face materializing out of the darkness as it leaned down, cocked its head to the side and stared at Colt as if it'd finally figured out the million-dollar question… and was still waiting for him to clue in to the answer.

He shouldn't be here. He should be with Lena. The realization was crystal clear. The monkey opened its mouth, chattering some syllables only it understood. Colt almost reached toward it but at the last minute noticed the gleaming sharp teeth in its open mouth. Instead, he backed away slowly.

Raking his gear up into a pile as quickly as possible, he began assembling what he'd need to get back out to the nearest village.

"What are you doing?" one of the camera crew asked, breaking away from the pack of people.

"I have to go home."

"Now? Colt, we're just getting started. We need you here. Desmond is not going to like this."

Colt glanced up at the group of people who'd stopped talking and were now all staring at him, a tight circle that looked almost as dangerous as the monkey he'd left behind.

"We're doing fine. I'll be back in a few days. A week at the most. You know the schedule. Continue to shoot the footage that we talked about and I'll go over it when I get back."

Thirty minutes after talking to the monkey, Colt was headed out of the Peruvian jungle and home to Lena. He had no idea what was going to happen…but it was about damn time that he found out.

15

WYN WAS RIGHT. When Lena chose to go after something, she did it with a vengeance.

Twenty-four hours following her decision to go, she was winging her way to Peru. As it turned out, she'd needed to get up to date on her vaccinations. Her doctor had even given her a rabies shot, since she thought Lena would probably end up in remote locations.

And she was right. It had taken her several hours to get in touch with Desmond. The man was difficult to track down. But he'd been happy to tell her what village Colt's team had traveled out of when she'd explained the situation.

Unfortunately, she'd arrived too late in the day and had been forced to rent a room for the night. None of the villagers she'd spoken to had been willing to make the trek into the jungle so close to dark.

Lena was frustrated. She'd come all this way only to be stopped by someone else's fear, but she couldn't really blame them. She knew firsthand that the jungle was a dangerous place after dark.

Her room left something to be desired. It was clean, although in serious need of a facelift. However, the woman who ran the place had bent over backwards to make sure she felt at home. Probably because Lena was currently the only guest.

Although she had to admit that there was something nice about sitting in a cane rocker on the screened-in front porch. The tiny village bustled with activity as the residents ended their work for the day and disappeared into their own houses. As she watched, the open-air market closed up for the night. The colorful awnings that had protected the wares were rolled up and stored for morning.

The heat might have been unbearable except for the lazy rotation of a fan high above her. The thick manila envelope lay in her lap. Packing for the trip, she'd found the photographs she'd left unopened in the bottom of her suitcase. She hadn't stopped to look at them until she got on the plane.

Her hand rested softly over the envelope, warming the paper beneath her palm. She'd been…surprised by what she'd seen. If she'd needed any more proof that she was making the right decision, it had been captured in the photographs Colt had worked so hard to keep private.

She could understand his insistence now, and appreciated his forethought. They were intimate, personal, and she had no desire to share them with the world.

Stars began to appear in the sky above her, brighter than anything she'd ever seen.

Far down the main path, a figure appeared, materializing out of the lush green brush that bordered the village. For some reason she watched, drawn to the man long before she could clearly see him.

It was obvious he wasn't local. He was taller than most of the native people she'd met and walked with a purposeful stride that seemed foreign here.

He was halfway past when she bolted up out of her chair.

"Colt," she breathed.

The screen door slapped, springing backward as she rushed through it.

Again she said his name, only this time yelling it. "Colt!"

He stopped, the sudden shuffle of his feet kicking up a cloud of dust around his ankles. He stared at her as she ran toward him, his eyes wide with surprise.

"Lena," he said, "what are you doing here?"

She wanted to launch herself into his arms. The sheer joy of seeing him was so overwhelming that she could hardly contain it. But she wasn't certain of her reception, so she didn't. Instead, she halted several paces away.

He looked good, although she had no idea what she'd expected. He'd only been gone a week.

"I came to find you."

"Find me?" he asked, parroting her words. "But I was heading back home to you."

She laughed, elation filling the sound. That was a good sign, right? All the fear and anxiety that had been riding her for the past twenty-four hours dried away to nothing.

A couple of times she'd almost chickened out, convinced that it was madness to follow him to Peru. But she'd clamped down on the doubts and told herself to get over it. It was difficult to ignore years of conditioned reactions and emotions, but for Colt she was willing to try.

Rolling up her sleeve, she showed him the tiny round bandages that covered her vaccination spots. "I even got shots."

Colt reached down and grabbed her, lifting her up off the ground and crushing her against his body. He stared down into her face. The sheer intensity in his gaze overwhelmed her, but not nearly as much as the love she could now see clearly in the depths of his eyes. Had it always been there and she'd just been afraid to accept it? Or, like her, had their days apart been enough to make him realize what they had together?

"Do you need me to kiss them and make them better?" he finally rumbled.

A welcome shiver of awareness racked her body. She wanted him to kiss her senseless, but there was plenty of time to give in to the passion pumping deep and dark inside her. They had more important things to deal with first.

"Maybe later. Why were you going home?"

"Why are you in Peru?"

She pursed her lips, wiggling in his hold and silently asking to be released. He ignored her.

"I've always wanted to see Machu Picchu," she answered.

"Huh," he grunted, obviously not convinced by her lie. "Too bad it's not anywhere close."

"Why were you leaving? I thought you had a job to do. The break you've been waiting years for."

"I do. But none of that mattered without you," he whispered.

A sense of peace stole through her body. They'd find a way to make it work.

"Good thing I've cleared my calendar, then. That way you can have your cake and me, too."

"What about your life in D.C.? Your job, apartment, friends?"

"I don't have a job."

"He fired you? What an idiot."

Lena chuckled, appreciating the heat of Colt's support. "Actually, he didn't. I quit and he offered me a severance package. And then a position freelancing for the company."

"Freelancing?"

"I'm seriously considering it. Once I've built my client base I could work from just about anywhere. Even from the middle of the Peruvian jungle."

Colt stared down at her, speechless. Finally, he licked his tongue across his lips and cautiously asked, "What, exactly, does that mean?"

"It means that I can follow you wherever you go… whether you want me there or not."

"I want you there." His mouth claimed hers in a hot, hard kiss that didn't last nearly long enough. "Always. Anywhere. I want you with me, Lena. But I'd happily settle for a little house in the suburbs of D.C. I'd settle for anywhere you wanted to be."

"Good thing for you where I want to be is with you. For now, we can gallivant around the world. Later, when we have kids, I'll want to talk about settling down and giving them some roots, but there are always summers and school breaks."

She smiled up into Colt's bright eyes and realized something that should have been clear years ago.

"All these years, I've been searching for roots. For a sense of the stability I never had as a child. Until you left, I didn't realize that having roots means surrounding yourself with people you love, trust and respect. It's about having a partner to share your life with—good and bad. It has nothing to do with one specific place."

"Well, hell, I could have told you that."

"So what made you change your mind?" she asked, snuggling tighter against his chest.

"I realized I love you. And have for years. I was too scared to admit it, to risk what we already had and open myself to the potential for more pain. It was easier to pretend that I was happy alone. I was so afraid to lose you, but by not admitting how I felt I lost you anyway."

He pulled back, making sure that she saw him when he said, "I love you, Lena, and I need you in my life."

"Well, for better or worse, you've got me."

A few minutes earlier, Lena would have claimed there was nothing Colt could say that would surprise her. She'd have been wrong.

"Does that mean you'll marry me?" he asked, his lips brushing down the side of her neck.

Lena didn't know what to say. Her heart fluttered inside her chest. Until that moment she hadn't realized that's what she'd wanted to hear. But even as she wanted to scream yes, a bone-deep need for caution welled up inside her. Old habits were hard to break.

"Maybe it's a little too soon? I mean, two weeks ago I was marrying someone else."

A wicked gleam drifted into Colt's eyes and Lena suddenly had the urge to turn tail and run. "What difference does that make? You have a dress—a beautiful dress that looked amazing on you, by the way. Bridesmaids. The groomsmen would have to change, but I bet we could have this wedding ready in no time flat. I want to make this legal, bind you to me so you can't leave."

"I'm not going anywhere."

His arms tightened around her, arching her body into his so that she couldn't help but feel the hard press of his erection lodged between them. "You better not be."

"Don't you have a film to direct or something?" she asked breathlessly.

"Yes, but that won't take forever," he answered as he bent down to taste the hollow of her throat. His hot mouth seared her skin. Her fingers dug deeper into his shoulders. "Besides, if we get married right away you can come back here with me as my wife."

Lena's head was spinning, a combination of lust for the man holding her and the feeling that she was getting everything she ever wanted…just a little faster than she'd planned.

"We both know that I can get you to say yes, Lena."

His hand skimmed down over her body. Need blasted through her, hot and hard.

"That's playing dirty."

"Maybe." His mouth sucked at the racing pulse at the base of her throat. "But I'll take what I can get."

She was on fire. And happy. And for the life of her, she couldn't come up with a reason not to say yes. She'd been ready to tie her life to a man who was completely wrong for her just two weeks ago. Then, she'd had jitters that she ignored. Now, the only thing jangling inside was an insistent little voice that said if they didn't find a bed soon the entire village was going to be shocked.

"Bring it on," she said, laughing with happiness when he spun her around.

They *were* perfect for each other. They had a history and a friendship that was the solid base for so much more.

She'd gone to the island hoping to find a few days of peace. To figure out how to put the pieces of her life back together. Instead, she'd found the love of her life…a man who'd been standing in front of her the whole time. She'd scoffed about the legend of Île du Coeur, but maybe there was more to it than she thought.

And when they were old and gray, they'd show their grandchildren the pictures from the island where they found their hearts' desire.

Epilogue

Marcy watched as Lena and Colt boarded the ferry back to St. Lucia. They'd only stayed for a few days to celebrate their honeymoon—something about finishing a project in Peru. But they'd promised to return often, and despite all the trouble they'd caused her, Marcy was looking forward to having them back. She liked those two. And she liked the fact that they'd both woken up and realized they were meant to be.

"Don't tell me you have a romantic side after all. It'll ruin my opinion of you."

Marcy's back stiffened at the sound of Simon's voice behind her. For once, she wished her boss had stayed locked inside his office where she'd left him.

"I have no such thing. Romance is a big hoax, lust wrapped up in a pretty package so that everyone feels better about their animalistic tendencies."

Simon walked up beside her, folding his arms over his chest and staring out after the ferry as it pulled into the bright blue water.

"You know, if you'd take that stick out of your ass,

Marcy, you might actually find that life is usually enjoyable. Oh, and that sex isn't half bad."

"You know nothing about my sex life, Simon, so stop pretending that you do."

He shrugged, his careless attitude pissing her off even more than his little digs. Part of her wanted him to care, wanted him to wonder who and what she was. But that was just asking for trouble.

And she had enough of that where Simon was concerned.

"The photography team will be here at the end of the week. I've cleared the new concept with *Worldwide Travel*. Everyone seems excited and I'm hopeful it might actually work out better."

"That's good, considering you're the one who screwed it up in the first place."

Marcy ground her teeth to keep from saying something that would get her fired. *I need this job, I need this job,* she chanted silently.

Simon hadn't even cared about the first photo shoot. And, honestly, she'd eat her own shoe if he cared about this one. He just loved the fact that he could throw the hiccup in her face.

Without waiting for her response—*coward*—Simon turned around and strode off. He was halfway up the walk when she remembered that she'd needed to talk to him about the shoot. She hated how he could make her forget things. It drove her insane.

"Simon," she called.

He turned to look at her, and she could tell by the faraway, distracted expression in his blue eyes that he'd already gone somewhere else. She wondered where it was, this place that could so easily engross him. Normally it bugged the hell out of her, especially when she wanted his attention. But today it worked in her favor, since he wasn't going to like what she needed to ask.

"The production crew would like to shoot in your office. It's the highest floor in the main building and the backdrop of the water and sky should work perfectly for the concept we're using."

She watched as he shook his head, trying to focus on what she was saying. That might not be good.

Before he could come around, she added, "I just wanted to remind you that you'd agreed to let them shoot there." Waving her hands, she sighed in relief as Simon turned on his heel and walked away.

She might regret that later—as in when the crew showed up at his office door—but she'd worry about it then.

She'd gotten awfully good at putting off until tomorrow what she didn't have to worry about today.

Her sigh of relief was a bit premature—at the head of the path Simon paused and turned slowly back toward her, pinning her with his eyes. Gone was the preoccupied expression, replaced by a sharp glint that had unwanted heat suffusing her body.

Marcy yanked her gaze away, swallowing. She did not want Simon Reeves.

Hell, she didn't even like the man....

* * * * *

RANCHER TO THE RESCUE

BY
JENNIFER FAYE

In another life, **Jennifer Faye** was a statistician. She still has a love for numbers, formulas and spreadsheets, but when she was presented with the opportunity to follow her lifelong passion and spend her days writing and pursuing her dream of becoming a Mills & Boon author, she couldn't pass it up. These days, when she's not writing, Jennifer enjoys reading, fine needlework, quilting, tweeting and cheering on the Pittsburgh Penguins. She lives in Pennsylvania with her amazingly patient husband, two remarkably talented daughters and their two very spoiled fur babies otherwise known as cats—but *shh…* don't tell them they're not human!

Jennifer loves to hear from readers—you can contact her via her website: www.JenniferFaye.com

This is Jennifer Faye's fabulous first book for Mills & Boon!

To my real-life hero, Eric,
who is the most positive, encouraging person
I've ever known. Thanks for cheering me on
to reach for the stars. You're my rock.

And to Bliss and Ashley.
You both amaze and impress me every day.
Thank you for filling my life with so much sunshine.

I'd also like to send a big thanks to my wonderful
editor, Carly Byrne, for believing in my abilities and
showing me the way to make my first book a reality.

CHAPTER ONE

WHY DO PEOPLE insist on pledging themselves to each other? Love was fleeting at best—if it existed at all.

Cash Sullivan crossed his arms as he lounged back against the front fender of his silver pickup. He pulled his tan Stetson low, blocking out the brilliant New Mexico sun. From the no-parking zone he glanced at the adobe-style church, where all of the guests were gathered, but he refused to budge.

His grandmother had insisted he bring her, but there was no way he'd sit by and listen to a bunch of empty promises. Besides, he'd met the groom a few times over the years and found the guy to be nothing more than a bunch of hot air. Cash would rather spend his time wrestling the most contrary steer than have to make small talk with that blowhard.

He loosened his bolo tie and unbuttoned the collar of his white button-up shirt. Gram had insisted he dress up to escort her in and out of the church—even if he wasn't planning to stay.

What he wouldn't give to be back at the ranch in his old, comfy jeans, instead of these new black ones that were as stiff as a fence rail. Heck, even mucking out stalls sounded like a luxury compared to standing here with nothing to do.

A woman in a white flowing dress caught his attention.

She was rushing along the side of the church. Abruptly she stopped and bent over some shrubs. What in the world was the bride doing? Looking for something?

This was certainly the most entertainment he'd had in the past half hour. He shook his head and smiled at the strange behavior. When she started running down the walk toward his vehicle, he tipped his hat upward to get a better view.

A mass of unruly red curls was piled atop her head while yards of white material fluttered behind her like the tail of a kite. Her face was heart-shaped, with lush lips. Not bad. Not bad at all.

Her breasts threatened to spill out of the dress, which hugged her waist and flared out over her full hips. She was no skinny-minny, but the curves looked good on her. Real good.

He let out a low whistle. She sure was a looker. How in the world had boring Harold bagged her?

He couldn't tear his gaze from her as she stopped right next to his pickup and tried to open the tan SUV in the neighboring parking spot. Unable to gain access, she smacked her hand on the window. Obviously this lady had a case of cold feet—as in *ice cold*—and hadn't planned an escape route. At least she'd come to her senses before making the worst decision of her life.

The bride spun around. Her fearful gaze met his. Her pale face made her intense green eyes stand out bright with fear. Alarm tightened his chest. Was there more going on here than a change of mind?

She glanced over the hood of his truck. He followed her line of vision, spotting a group of photographers rounding the corner of the church. In the next second she'd opened his passenger door and vaulted inside.

What in the world was she doing? Planning to steal

his truck? He swung open the driver's side door and climbed in.

"What are you doing in here?"

The fluffy material of her veil hit him in the face as she turned in the seat and slammed the door shut. "Drive. Fast."

He smashed down the material from her veil, not caring if he wrinkled it. He'd never laid eyes on this woman before today, and he wasn't about to drive her anywhere until he got some answers. "Why?"

"I don't have time to explain. Unless you want to be front and center in tomorrow's paper, you'll drive."

His gaze swung around to the photographers. They hadn't noticed her yet, but that didn't ease his discomfort. "You didn't kill anyone, did you?"

"Of course not." She sighed. "Do you honestly think I'd be in this getup if I was going to murder someone?"

"I'm not into any Bonnie and Clyde scenario."

"That's good to know. Now that we have that straightened out, can you put the pedal to the metal and get us out of here before they find me?"

He grabbed the bride's arm and yanked her down out of sight, just before the group of reporters turned their curious gazes to his pickup. Luckily his truck sat high up off the ground, so no one could see much unless they were standing right next to it.

"What are you doing?" she protested, struggling.

"Those reporters don't know you're in here, and I don't want to be named in your tabloid drama. Stay down and don't get up until I tell you to."

His jaw tensed as he stuffed the white fluff beneath the dash. He was caught up in this mess whether he wanted to be or not.

Her struggles ceased. He fired up the truck and threw

it in Reverse. Mustering some restraint, he eased down on the accelerator. Damn. He didn't want to be the driver for this bride's getaway, but what choice did he have?

He knew all about reporters—they were like a pack of starving wolves, just waiting for a juicy story. For their purposes he'd be "the other man." Scandals always made good sales—it didn't matter if you were an innocent by-stander or not. In the court of public opinion, when your face hit the front page you were crucified. He should know.

Cash pulled his cowboy hat low, hoping no one would recognize him. He didn't want to draw the attention of the reporters who were searching behind rocks, shrubs and cars. There would be no quick getaway. Slow and steady.

When the bride once again attempted to sit up, he placed his hand on the back of her head.

"Hey, you!" a young reporter, standing a few yards away, shouted through the open window.

Cash's chest tightened as he pulled to a stop. "Yeah?"

"Did you see which way the bride ran?"

"She ran around back. Think there was a car waiting for her."

The reporter waved and took off. Cash eased off the brake and rolled toward the exit. He hadn't had a rush of adrenaline like this since his last showdown with a deter-mined steer.

"What'd you say that for? You're making things worse," the bride protested, starting to sit up.

He pressed the side of her face back down. "Stay down or I'll dump you in this parking lot and let those hungry reporters have you."

"You wouldn't."

"Try me." He was in no mood to play around with some woman who didn't know what she wanted.

Now he needed to get rid of this bundle of frills so his life could return to its peaceful routine.

Before he could ask where she wanted to be dropped off she started to wiggle, bumping the steering wheel.

"Watch it." He steadied the wheel with both hands. "What are you doing down there?"

"Trying to get comfortable, but I think it's impossible. Are we away from the church yet?"

"Just approaching the parking lot exit, but don't get any ideas of sitting up until we're out of town. I'm not about to have people tracking me down and bothering me with a bunch of questions I can't answer."

"Thanks for being so sympathetic," she muttered.

He slowed down at the exit, checking for traffic before merging. "Hey, I didn't ask you to hijack my truck."

"I didn't have any other choice."

"Get cold feet?"

"No…yes. It's complicated." She squirmed some more. "I don't feel so good. Can I sit up yet?"

"No."

The rush of air through the open windows picked up the spicy, citrusy scent of the colorful bouquet she was still clutching. A part of him felt bad for her. He'd heard about how women got excited about their wedding day and, though he personally couldn't relate, he knew what it was to have a special moment ruined, like getting penalized after a winning rodeo ride.

He checked the rearview mirror. No one had followed him out of the parking lot. He let out a deep breath. So far, so good.

He tightened his fingers around the steering wheel, resisting the urge to run a soothing hand over her back. "Where am I taking you?"

"I...I don't know. I can't go back to my apartment. They'll be sure to find me."

"You're on the run?" He should have figured this was more than just a case of cold feet. "And what was up with the reporters?"

"My boss thought the wedding would be a good source of free publicity for my television show."

"You certainly will get publicity. *Runaway Bride Disappears Without a Trace.*"

She groaned. Her hand pressed against his leg. The heat of her touch radiated through the denim. A lot of time had passed since a woman had touched him—back before his accident.

He cleared his throat. "I suppose at this point we should introduce ourselves. I'm Cash Sullivan."

He waited, wondering if there would be a moment of recognition. After all, he hadn't retired from the rodeo circuit all that long ago.

"Meghan Finnegan." When he didn't say anything, she continued, "I'm the Jiffy Cook on TV, and the reason those men are armed with cameras is to see this hometown girl marry a millionaire."

Nothing in her voice or mannerisms gave the slightest hint that she'd recognized his name. Cash assured himself it was for the best. His name wasn't always associated with the prestige of his rodeo wins—sometimes it was connected with things he'd rather forget. Still, he couldn't ignore the deflating prick of disappointment.

"I don't watch television," he said, gruffer than intended. "Okay, we're out of Lomas and this road doesn't have much traffic."

When she didn't say anything, he glanced over. Her complexion had gone ghostly pale, making her pink glossy lips stand out. "You feeling okay?"

"No." Her hand pressed to her stomach. "Pull over. Now."

He threw on his right-turn signal and pulled to a stop in a barren stretch of desert. Meg barreled out of the vehicle, leaving the door ajar. She rushed over to a large rock and hunched over. So this was what she'd been doing when she ran out of the church. Must be a huge case of nerves.

He grabbed some napkins from his glove compartment and a bottle of unopened water. It was tepid, but it'd be better than nothing. He exited the truck and followed her. He wasn't good with women—especially not ones who were upset and sick.

"Um…I can hold this for you." He reached for the lengthy veil.

He didn't know if he should try talking to her to calm her down or attempt to rub her back. He didn't want to make things worse. Unsure what to do, he stood there quietly until her stomach settled. Then he handed over the meager supplies.

"You okay now?" he asked, just before his cell phone buzzed.

His grandmother. How could he have forgotten about her? This bride had a way of messing with his mind to the point of forgetting his priorities.

He flipped open his phone, but before he could utter a word Gram said, "Where are you? Everyone's leaving."

"I went for a little ride. I'll be there in a few minutes."

"Hurry. You won't believe what happened. I'll tell you when you get here."

He hated the thought of going back and facing those reporters. Hopefully there'd be too much confusion with the missing bride and the exiting guests that they wouldn't remember he'd been the only one around when Meg had disappeared.

He cast a concerned look at his pale stowaway. "We have to go back."

Fear flashed in her eyes and she started shaking her head. "No. I can't. I won't."

"Why? Because you changed your mind about the wedding? I'm sure people will understand."

She shook her head. "No, they won't."

He didn't have time to make her see reason. "I have to go back to the church. My grandmother is waiting. I can't abandon her."

Meg's brow creased as she worried her bottom lip. "Then I'll wait here."

"What?" She couldn't be thinking clearly. "I can't leave you here. You're not well."

"I won't go back there. I can't face all of those people... especially my mother. And when the press spots us together they'll have a field day."

"You can hide on the floor again."

She shook her head. "We were lucky to get away with that once. With all of the guests leaving, the chances of me staying hidden are slim to none."

She had a good point, but it still didn't sit right with him. "Leaving you here in the middle of nowhere, in this heat, isn't a good idea."

"This isn't the middle of nowhere. I'm within walking distance of town. I'll be fine. Just go. Your grandmother is waiting. There's just one thing."

"What's that?"

"Leave me your cell phone."

He supposed it was the best solution, but he didn't like it. Not one bit. But the chance of discovery was too great. Not seeing any other alternative, he pulled the phone from his belt and handed it over.

"You're sure about this?" he asked, hoping she'd change her mind.

She nodded.

"Then scoot around to the other side of that rock. No one will see you there—unless that veil thing starts flapping in the wind like a big flag."

"It won't." She wound the lengthy material around her arm. A look of concern filled her eyes. "You will come back, won't you?"

He didn't want to. He didn't want anything to do with this mess. All he wanted was to go home and get on with his life. But he couldn't leave her sick and stranded.

"I'll be back as fast as I can."

Meghan Finnegan watched as the tailgate of the cowboy's pickup faded into the distance. The events of the day rushed up and stampeded her, knocking the air from her lungs. How could Harold have waited until she'd walked up the aisle to tell her he'd suddenly changed his mind?

He didn't want her.

And he wanted her to get rid of their unborn baby—a baby they'd agreed to keep secret until after the ceremony. Meghan wrapped her arms around her midsection. She loved her baby and she'd do whatever was necessary to care for it.

She sagged against the rock before her knees gave out. Sure, she knew Harold hadn't wanted children—he'd made that clear from the start. And with her rising television career she'd accepted that children wouldn't fit into her hectic lifestyle. But this was different—it had been an accident. When she'd told Harold about the pregnancy a few weeks ago he'd been stunned at first but then he'd seemed to accept it. What in the world had changed his mind?

The sound of an approaching vehicle—perhaps depart-

ing wedding guests—sent her scurrying behind the out-
crop of large rocks. She wasn't ready to face the inquiring
questions, the pitying stares or the speculative guesses. At
twenty-eight, she'd prided herself on having her life all
planned out. Now she was pregnant and she didn't have a
clue what her next move should be.

She sank down on a small rock and yanked out scads
of hairpins in order to release the veil. At last free of the
yards of tulle, she ran her fingers through her hair, letting
it flow over her shoulders.

She glanced down at the black phone in her lap. She
should probably call her family, so they didn't worry, but
there was no way she was going to deal with her mother,
who would demand answers. After all, her mother had
been instrumental in planning this whole affair—from
setting up her initial date with the boy-next-door who'd
grown up to make a fortune in the computer software business to making the wedding plans. In fact the preparations
were what had finally pulled her mother out of her depression after cancer had robbed them of Meghan's father less
than a year ago.

Not that all of the blame could be laid at her mother's
feet. Meghan had been willing to go along with the plans—
anxious to put her father's mind at ease about her future
before he passed on. And, eager at last to gain her mother's hard-won approval, she'd convinced herself Harold
was the man for her.

Then, as the "big day" approached the doubts had
started to settle in. At first she'd thought they were just
the usual bridal jitters. But Harold had started to change—
to be less charming and thoughtful. It had been as though
she was really seeing him for the first time. But her options had vanished as soon as the pregnancy strip displayed
two little pink lines.

Meghan's hand moved to her barely-there baby bump. "It's okay, little one. Mommy will fix things. I just need some time to think."

First she had to call her family. She carefully considered whom to contact. Her middle sister Ella? Or her little sis Katie? At the moment they weren't all that close. Since their father's death the family had splintered. She'd hoped the wedding would bring them all together again, but nothing she'd tried had worked.

Never having been very close with her youngest sister, she dialed Ella's number. The cell phone rang for a long time. Meghan had blocked Cash's number and now she worried that her sister might think it was a prank call or, worse, a telemarketer and not answer. Maybe that was for the best. She could leave a message and have no questions to field.

"Hello?" chimed Ella's hesitant voice.

"Ella, it's me. Meghan."

"Meghan—"

"Shh…don't let anyone know you're talking to me. I'm not ready to deal with Mother."

"Wait a sec." The buzz of people talking in the background grew faint, followed by the thud of a door closing. "Okay. I'm alone. What happened? Why'd you run off? Where—?"

"Slow down."

Her first instinct was to tell Ella she was stranded on the side of the road. In the past they'd shared all sorts of girly secrets—right up until Ella's engagement had ended abruptly seven months ago. Her sister hadn't been the same since then. Now, it wouldn't be right to burden her sister with her problems—not when Ella still had her own to figure out.

Meghan heard herself saying, "Don't worry. I'm fine. I'm with a friend."

"But why did you run out on the wedding? I thought you wanted to marry Harold? He acted so broken up and shocked when you took off."

"What?" Her mouth gaped as her fingers clenched the phone tighter to her ear.

"Harold barely held it together when he told the family that he didn't have a clue why you ran out on him."

"He knew…"

That low-down, sniveling, two-faced creep. Her blood boiled in her veins. How could he turn the tables on her when he was the one who'd done the jilting?

He was worried about his image. It always came back to what would look best for him and his company. Why should he take any of the blame for the ruined wedding when she wasn't there to defend herself?

"Meghan, what did he know? Are you still there?"

"He lied," she said, trying to remain calm so she didn't say something she'd regret later. But she couldn't let her sister believe Harold's lies. "He knew exactly why I left."

"It's okay," Ella said as sympathy oozed in her voice. "I understand you got cold feet. Remember I was there not that long ago—"

"I didn't get cold feet. There are things you don't know."

"Then tell me."

"I can't yet. This is different from when you called off your engagement. And it seems to me you've been spending all of your time hiding in your bakery."

"This isn't about me." Ella sighed. "Harold hinted that the stress of planning such a large wedding might have driven you over the edge."

"But that's not what happened." Why hadn't she seen this side of Harold a long time ago? Had it been there all along? She'd thought he was honorable and with time he would accept the baby.

"It doesn't matter. Just come home. The whole family is worried. Mother is beside herself. She says she'll never be able to step outside again because she's too embarrassed."

"And what do you expect me to do?" she asked, tired of being the oldest and the one expected to deal with their mother. "Nothing I say will make her less embarrassed."

In fact it'd only make it that much worse when her strait-laced mother, a pillar of the community, found out her unwed daughter was pregnant by the boy-next-door—the same guy who'd dumped her and their baby at the altar.

"But, Meghan, you have to—"

"No, I don't. Not this time. You and Katie are going to have to deal with her. I need some space to figure things out. Until I do, I won't be of any help to anyone."

Ella huffed. "So when are you coming home?"

She wanted to go to her apartment and hide away, but she wouldn't have any peace there. And there was no way she was going to her mother's house.

"I don't know. I have two weeks planned for the honeymoon so don't expect to see me before then. I'm sorry, Ella. I've got to go."

There was nothing left to say—or more like nothing she was willing to say at this point. She knew Ella was worried and frustrated, but her sister was smart and had a good head on her shoulders. She'd figure out how to manage their mother.

As Meghan disconnected the call her concern over her family was replaced by nagging doubts about the cowboy returning for her. She glanced down at the new-looking phone with a photo of a horse on the display. Surely he wouldn't toss aside his phone with his photos and numbers inside?

He'd be back…

But then again she'd put her faith in Harold and look where that had gotten her. Pregnant and alone. Her hand moved to spread across her abdomen. She'd barely come to terms with the fact there was a baby growing inside her, relying on her. And she'd already made such a blunder of things.

CHAPTER TWO

CASH ARRIVED AT the church in time to witness the groom taking his moment in the spotlight, blaming everything on Meg in order to gain the public's sympathy.

The nerve of the man amazed Cash. Meg was distraught to the point of being physically ill, and here was Harold posing for pictures. His bride might have walked out on him, but Harold sure didn't look like the injured party. A niggling feeling told him there was more to this story than the bride getting cold feet.

Ten minutes passed before he pried Gram away from consoling the groom's family and ushered her to his pickup. At last they hit the road. Gram insisted on regaling him with the tale of how the bride ran out of the church without explanation and all the wild speculations. Cash let her talk. All too soon she would learn the facts for herself.

When he reached the two-lane highway he had only one mission—to tramp the accelerator and get back to the sickly bride. By now she must think he'd forgotten her.

Nothing could be further from the truth.

"Cash, slow down," Gram protested. "I don't know what you're in such an all-fired-up rush for. There's nothing at the Tumbling Weed that can't wait."

"It's not the ranch I'm worried about."

He could feel his grandmother's pointed gaze. "You aren't in some kind of trouble again, are you?"

He sighed, hating how his past clung to him tighter than wet denim. "Not like you're thinking."

He glanced down at the speedometer, finding he was well beyond the limit. He eased his boot up on the accelerator. As his speed decreased his anxiety rose. It was bad enough having to leave Meg alone, but when she didn't feel well it had to be awful for her.

At last he flipped on his turn signal and pulled off the road.

"What are we stopping for? Is there something wrong with the truck? I told you we should have gassed up before leaving town."

"The truck's fine."

"Then why are we stopping in the middle of nowhere? Cash, have you lost your mind?"

"Wait here." He jumped out of the truck and rushed over to the rock.

Meg wasn't there. His chest clenched. What had happened to her? He hadn't seen any sign of her walking back to town. Had someone picked her up? The thought made him uneasy.

"Meg!" He turned in a circle. "Meg, where are you?" At last he spotted her, on the other side of the road. She gathered up her dirty dress and rushed across the road. "What in the world were you doing?"

"I thought if any passing vehicles had taken notice of you dropping a bride off on the side of the road, it might be wiser if I moved to another location."

It seemed as though her nerves had settled and left her making reasonable decisions. "Good thinking. Sorry it took me a bit to get back here. Picking up my grandmother took me longer than I anticipated—"

"Cash, who are you talking to?" Gram hollered from inside the truck.

"Don't worry," he said, "that's my grandmother. Your number-one fan."

"Really? She watches my show?"

"Don't sound so surprised. From what Gram says, you've gained quite a loyal following."

"I suppose I have. That's why the network's considering taking the show national."

So she was a rising television star. Maybe Harold hadn't been up for sharing the spotlight? Cash liked the idea of Meg being more successful and popular than a man who played up the part of an injured party to gain public sympathy.

"Cash, do you hear me?" Gram yelled, her voice growing irritated.

"We'd better not keep her waiting," he said. "If she gets it in her mind to climb out of that truck without assistance I'm afraid she'll get hurt."

Meg walked beside him. "Your truck could use a step-ladder to get into."

"When I bought it my intent was to haul a horse trailer, not to have beautiful women using it as a taxi service."

He noticed how splotches of pink bloomed in her cheeks. He found he enjoyed making her blush. Obviously Harold, the stuffed shirt, hadn't bothered to lather her with compliments. No wonder she'd left him.

"Before I forget, here's your phone." She placed it in his outstretched hand. "I hope you don't mind but I called my family."

"No problem." He knew if she were his sister or daughter he'd be worried. Turning his attention to his grandmother, he said, "Meg, this is my grandmother—Martha Sullivan. Gram, this is—"

"The Jiffy Cook," Gram interjected. Her thin lips pursed together. Behind her wire-rimmed glasses her gaze darted between him and Meg. "You stole the bride. Cash, how *could* you?"

His own grandmother believed *he* was the reason the bride had run away from the church. The fact it had even crossed her mind hurt. He'd have thought Gram of all people would think better of him and not believe all those scandalous stories in the press.

Before he could refute the accusation Meg spoke up. "Your grandson has been a total gentleman. When he saw me run out of the church with the press on my trail he helped me get away without any incidents. I'm sorry if it inconvenienced you, Mrs. Sullivan."

Gram waved away her concern. "It's you I'm concerned about. Has this thing with my grandson been going on for long?"

Any color in Meg's cheeks leached away, leaving her pasty white beneath the light splattering of freckles across the bridge of her nose. "I…ah…we aren't—"

"Gram, we aren't together. In fact until she ran out of the church I'd never seen Meg before. She needed a lift and I was there. End of story. No one else knows where she is."

"My goodness, what happened? Why did you run away?" Gram pressed a bony hand to her lips, halting the stream of questions. Seconds later, she lowered her hand to her lap. "Sorry, dear. I didn't mean to be so dang nosy. Climb in here and we can give you a ride back to town."

Seeing alarm in Meg's eyes, Cash spoke up, "We can't do that, Gram."

"Well, for heaven's sake, why not? She obviously needs to get out of that filthy gown. And we sure aren't going to leave her here on the side of the road."

"I can't go home," Meg spoke up. "Not yet."

"But what about Harold?" Gram asked. "Shouldn't you let him know where you are? He looked so worried."

Meg's face grew ashen as she pressed her hand to her stomach. She turned to Cash, her eyes wide with anguish. She pushed past him and ran off.

"Meg—wait." He dogged her footsteps to a rock in the distance.

When she bent at her waist he grabbed at the white material of her dress, pulling it back for her. He'd hoped the nausea had passed, but one mention of the wedding and she was sick again.

Was she overtaken by regret about leaving old what's-his-name at the altar? Had her conscience kicked in and it was so distressing that it made her ill?

He considered telling her what he'd witnessed when he'd gone back for Gram, but what purpose would it serve? Obviously the thought of the wrecked wedding was enough to make her sick. Knowing the man she must still love had turned on her wasn't likely to help.

When she straightened, her eyes were red and her face was still ashen. She swayed and he put a steadying arm around her waist. He had no doubt the hot sun was only making things worse.

"I'm fine," she protested in a weak voice. "There's nothing left in my stomach. Just dry heaves."

He didn't release his hold on her until he had her situated in the pickup next to his grandmother. "Gram, can you turn up the air-conditioning and aim the vents on her?"

Without a word Gram adjusted the dials while he helped Meg latch her seatbelt. Once she was secure, he shut the door and rushed over to the driver's side.

He shifted into Drive, but kept his foot on the brake. "Where can we take you, Meg?"

When she didn't answer, he glanced over to find her

head propped against the window. She stared off into the distance, looking as if she'd lost her best friend and didn't know where to turn. In that instant he was transported back in time almost twenty years ago, a little boy who needed a helping hand. If it hadn't been for Gram…

"We'll take you back to the Tumbling Weed," he said, surprising even himself with the decision.

"Where?" Meg's weary voice floated over to him, reassuring him that he'd made the right decision.

"It's Cash's ranch," Gram chimed in. "The perfect place for you to catch your breath."

"I don't know." She worried her bottom lip. "You don't even know me. I wouldn't want to be an imposition."

"With there just being Cash and me living there, we could use the company. Isn't that right, Cash?"

"You live there too?" Meg looked directly at his grandmother.

Gram nodded. "So, what do you say?"

Cash wasn't as thrilled about their guest as his grandmother. Meg might be beautiful, and she might have charmed his grandmother, but she was trouble. The press wasn't going to let up until they found her. He could already envision the headlines: *Runaway Bride Stolen by Thieving Cowboy.* His gut twisted into a painful knot.

"You're invited as long as you keep your location a secret," he said, his voice unbending. "I can't afford to have the press swooping in."

"Oh, no," Meg said, pulling herself upright with some effort. "I'd never bring them to your place. I don't want to see any of them."

Honesty dripped from her words, and a quick glance in her direction showed him her somber expression. But what if she started to feel better and decided she needed to fix her reputation? Or, worse, made a public appeal to what's-his-name to win him back?

Then again, she wouldn't be there that long. In fact it was still early in the day. Not quite lunchtime. If she rested, perhaps she'd be up to going home this evening.

Certain she'd soon be on her way, he said, "Good. Now that we understand each other, let's get moving."

The cold air from the vents of Cash's new-smelling pickup breathed a sense of renewed energy into Meghan. She was exhausted and dirty, but thankfully her stomach had settled. She gazed out the window as they headed southeast. She'd never ventured in this direction, but she enjoyed the vastness of the barren land, where it felt as if she could lose herself and her problems.

Instinctively she moved her hand to her stomach. There wasn't time for kicking back and losing herself. This wasn't a vacation or a spa weekend. This was a chance to get her head screwed on straight, to figure out how to repair the damage to her life and prepare to be a single mother.

The thought of her impending motherhood filled her with anxiety. What she didn't know about being a good parent could fill up an entire library. The only thing she *did* know was that she didn't want to be like her own mother—emotionally distant and habitually withholding her approval. Instead, Meghan planned to lavish her baby with love.

But what if she failed to express her love? What if she fell back on the way she'd been raised?

"Here we are," Cash announced, breaking into her troubled thoughts.

The truck had stopped in front of a little whitewashed house with a covered porch and two matching rocking chairs. The place was cute, but awfully small. Certainly not big enough for her to keep out of everyone's way.

Cash cut the engine and rounded the front of the truck. He swung open the door she'd only moments ago been leaning against. She released her seat restraint as Cash held out his hands to help her down. As the length of her dress hampered her movements she accepted his offer. His long, lean fingers wrapped around her waist. Holding her securely, he lowered her to the ground in one steady movement.

She tilted her chin upward and for the first time noticed his towering height. Even with her heels on he stood a good six inches taller than her own five-foot-six stature. His smoky gray eyes held her captive with their intensity.

She swallowed. "Thank you."

"You're welcome." His lips lifted in a small smile, sending her tummy aflutter.

Before she could think of anything to say he turned to his grandmother and helped her out of the vehicle. Martha rushed up the walk, appearing not to need any assistance getting around. Meghan could only hope to be so spry when she got on in years.

Martha, as though remembering them, stopped on the porch. "See you at five o'clock for dinner."

She'd turned for the door when Cash said, "Wait, Gram. You're forgetting Meg."

"Not at all. She's invited too." She reached for the doorknob.

"But, Gram, aren't you going to invite her in?"

Martha turned and gave him a puzzled look. "Sure, she's welcome. But I thought she'd want to get cleaned up and changed into something fresh."

"Wouldn't she need to go inside?"

Martha's brows rose. "Um…Cash…you're going to have to take her to the big house."

"But I thought—"

"Remember after you built the house we converted your old room into my sewing room? She could sleep on the couch, but I think she'd be much more comfortable in one of your guestrooms."

This wasn't what Meghan had imagined. She'd thought they'd all be staying in one house together. The thought of staying alone with Cash sent up warning signals.

"I don't want to be a burden on either of you. If you could let me use your phone, I can call and get a ride."

Cash shot her a puzzled look. "I thought you didn't have any other place to hide from the press?"

"I don't." She licked her dry lips. Softly she added, "I'll just have to tell them…"

"What? What will you tell them?"

Panic paralyzed the muscles in her chest. "I don't know."

"Why *did* you run out on your wedding?" His unblinking gaze held hers, searching for answers.

"I…ah…"

"Why *did* you abandon the groom at the altar? Do you want him back?"

She glared at Cash. "I'm not ready to talk about it. Why are you being so mean?"

"Because that is just a small taste of what's waiting for you. In fact, this is probably mild compared to the questions they'll lob at you."

"What would a cowboy know about the press?" she sputtered, not wanting to admit he was right.

"Trust Cash," Martha piped up. "He knows what he's talking about—"

"Gram, drop it. Meg obviously doesn't want to hear our thoughts."

Meghan turned her gaze to Cash, waiting for him to finish his grandmother's cryptic comment. She'd already had her fiancé dupe her into believing he was going to marry her—that he cared about her. But if he had he wouldn't have uttered those words at the altar. Everything she'd thought about their relationship was a lie. And she wouldn't stand for one more man lying to her.

"What aren't you saying?" she demanded. "What do you know about the press?"

His jaw tensed and a muscle twitched in his cheek. His hands came to rest on his sides as his weight shifted from one foot to the other.

"I'll let you two talk," Martha said. "I've got some things to do."

The front door to the little house swished open, followed by a soft thud as it closed. All the while Meghan's gaze never left Cash. What in the world had made her think coming here was a good idea?

"I'm waiting." The August sun beat down on her in the layers of tulle and satin, leaving it clinging to her skin. Perspiration trickled down her spine. She longed to rub away the irritating sensation, but instead she stood her ground. She wouldn't budge until this stubborn cowboy told her what his cryptic comments meant.

Cash sighed. "I overheard your fiancé talking to the press and it sounded like you'll have a lot of explaining to do."

He'd turned the conversation around on her without bothering to explain his grandmother's comment. But Meghan didn't have time to point this out. She was reeling from the knowledge that Harold had not only gone to her family and blamed her for the wrecked wedding, but he'd also gone to the press with his pack of lies too. The revelation hit her like a sucker punch.

"Why would he do that?" she muttered. Her public persona was her livelihood. Was he trying to wreck her career?

"Maybe if you talked to him you could straighten things out."

She shook her head. At last she was seeing past Harold's smooth talk and fancy airs to the self-centered man beneath the designer suits. "He doesn't want to hear what I have to say. Not after what happened."

Cash's gaze was filled with questions, but she wasn't up for answering them. Right about now she would gladly give her diamond ring just to have a shower and a glass of ice-cold water.

"Could we get out of the sun?" she asked.

Cash's brows rose, as though he'd realized he'd forgotten his manners. "Sure. My house isn't far down the lane."

Alone with this cowboy. It didn't sound like a good idea. In fact, it sounded like a really bad idea. She eyed him up. He looked reasonable. And his grandmother certainly seemed to think the sun revolved around him. So why was she hesitating? It wasn't as if she was moving in. She would figure out a plan and be out of his way in no time.

"You're safe," he said, as though reading her thoughts. "If you're that worried about being alone with me, you heard my grandmother—you can sleep on her couch. Although, between you and me, it's a bit on the lumpy side."

His teasing eased the tenseness in her stomach. He'd been a gentleman so far. There was no reason to think he'd be a threat.

As she stood there, contemplating how to climb up into the passenger seat again, Cash said, "Let me give you a hand."

She knew without having any money or her own trans-

portation she was beholden to him, but that didn't mean
she had to give up every bit of self-reliance.

"Thanks, but I've got it." She took her time, hiking up
her dress in one hand while bracing the other hand on the
truck frame. With all of her might she heaved herself up
and into the seat without incident. While he rounded the
vehicle she latched her seatbelt.

"The lane," as he'd referred to the two dirt ruts, contained a series of rocks and potholes, and Meghan was
jostled and tossed about like a rag doll.

"Did you ever consider paving this?" She clutched the
door handle and tried to remain in her seat.

A deep chuckle filled the air. The sound was warm and
thick, like a layer of hot fudge oozing down over a scoop
of ice cream—both of which she could easily enjoy on a
regular basis. Ice cream had always been something she
could take or leave, but suddenly the thought of diving
into a sundae plagued her, as did pulling back the layers
of this mysterious cowboy.

In the next instance she reminded herself that she didn't
have the time nor the energy to figure him out—not that
she had any clue about men. She'd thought she'd understood Harold. The idea of being a parent must have scared
him—especially since he'd never planned on having kids.
It scared her too. They could have talked about it. Supported each other. But for him to cut and run at the last
minute, leaving her all alone to deal with this… That was
unforgivable.

She'd been so wrong about him.

And that was the real reason she found herself at this
out-of-the-way ranch. If she'd been so wrong about Harold
she didn't trust herself to make any more big decisions.

She glanced over at Cash. Had she been wrong to
trust him?

She smothered a groan. This was ridiculous. She was overthinking everything now. She wondered if this cowboy had ever questioned his every decision. She studied the set of his strong jaw and the firm line of his lips—everything about him said he was sure of himself.

He turned and their gazes connected. His slate-gray eyes were like walls, holding in all his secrets. What kind of secrets could this rugged cowboy have?

CHAPTER THREE

CASH PULLED TO a stop in front of his two-story country home and none too soon. Meg was giving him some strange looks—not the kind he experienced from the good-time girls in the local cowboy bar. These looks were deeper, as though she had questions but didn't know how to phrase them. Whatever she wanted to know about him, he was pretty certain he didn't want to discuss it.

This ranch had become his refuge from the craziness of the rodeo circuit, and now he couldn't imagine living anywhere else. Here at the Tumbling Weed he could be himself and unwind. Though the house had been built a few years ago, he'd never brought home any female friends. He didn't want any misunderstandings. He made it known that he was a no-strings-attached cowboy. Period.

"Thanks for everything," Meg said, breaking into his thoughts. "If you hadn't helped me I don't know what I'd have done."

"I'm certain you would have made do. You don't seem like the type of person who goes long without a plan." When she didn't say anything, he glanced over. She'd bitten down on her lower lip. "Hey, I didn't mean anything by the comment. You're welcome here until you feel better."

"I don't want to get in the way."

"Have you looked at this house?" He pointed through

the windshield. "I guess I got a little carried away when I had the plans drawn up. Tried to talk Gram into moving in but she flat-out refused. She said all of her memories were in her little house and she had no intention of leaving it until the good Lord called her home."

"Your grandmother sounds like a down-to-earth lady."

"She is. And the best cook around."

He immediately noticed Meg's lips purse. He'd momentarily forgotten *she* was some kind of cook. He'd bet his prize mare that Meg's scripted cooking couldn't come close to his grandmother's down-home dishes, but he let the subject drop.

Meg reached for the door handle. "Before I leave I'd love to hear about some of her recipes."

He'd met women before who only had one thing on their minds—what they could freely gain from somebody else. He didn't like the thought of the Jiffy Cook using his grandmother's recipes to further her career. If he had his way that would never happen. And the sooner he got her settled, the sooner she'd be rested and on her way.

"Shall we go inside? I'll see if I can find something for you to change into."

"That would be wonderful. Every girl dreams about their wedding dress, but they never realize how awkward it can be to move in."

"I couldn't even imagine."

He rushed around the truck, but by the time he got there Meg had already jumped out. Seemed she'd gotten the hang of rustling up her dress to get around. The woman certainly had an independent streak. What had convinced her to chain herself to Harold?

Love. That mythical, elusive thing women wanted so desperately to believe in. He refused to buy into hearts and Valentines. There was no such thing as undying love—at least not the romantic kind. His parents' marriage should have been proof enough for him, but he'd given it a shot and learned a brutal lesson he'd never forget.

He led Meg up the steps to the large wraparound porch. This was his favorite spot in the whole house. Weather permitting, this was where he had his mid-morning coffee, and in the evening he liked to kick back to check out the stars.

"This is really nice," she said, as though agreeing with his thoughts.

"Nothing better than unwinding and looking out over the pasture."

"You're lucky to have so much space, and this view is awesome. How big is the ranch?"

"A little more than sixteen hundred acres. Plenty of room to go trail riding."

"It's like having your own little country."

He chuckled. She'd obviously spent too much time in the city. "It's not quite that big. But it's my little piece of heaven." He moved to the door and opened it. "Ready to get out of that dress?"

Color infused her cheeks and she glanced away. He tightened his jaw, smothering his amusement over her misinterpretation of his words.

Meg kept her head down and examined the dirt-stained skirt. "Shame that all it's good for now is the garbage."

"Why would you want to keep a dress from a wedding you ran away from?"

A flicker of surprise showed in her eyes and then it was gone. "If you would show me where to go, I'll get out of your way."

"The bedrooms are upstairs."

She stepped toward the living room and peered inside. "This is so spacious. And the woodwork is beautiful."

Her compliment warmed his chest, and whatever he'd been meaning to say floated clean out of his head. This was the first time he'd shown any woman other than Gram around the house he'd helped design and build. He noticed how Meg's appreciative gaze took in the hardwood floors, the built-in bookcases and the big bay window with the windowseat.

Why in the world did her words mean so much to him? It wasn't as if they were involved and he was out to impress her. She was merely a stranger passing through his life.

"I'll show you upstairs," he said, anxious for a little distance. "I'm sure I'll have something you can change into. Might not fit, but it'll be better than all of that fluff."

"I'm sorry to put you to such bother. If you are ever in Albuquerque you should look me up. The least I can do is take you to dinner." She followed him to the staircase. "Didn't you say your grandmother is a fan of the Jiffy Cook?"

He stopped on the bottom step and turned. What was she up to? He hesitated to answer, but the twinkle in Meg's eyes drew him in. "She watches the show religiously. That's why she was thrilled to get an invite to the wedding."

"So why didn't you attend? You could have gone as her escort."

His gaze moved to the floor. "I don't do weddings."

"Is that from personal experience?"

His hands clenched. What was it with this woman, making him think about things he'd rather leave buried in the dark shadows of his mind? Refusing to reveal too much, he said, "Marriage is for dreamers and suckers. Eventually people figure out there's no happily-ever-after, but by then it's usually too late."

"You can't be serious! I've never heard such a cynical

view on marriage. And especially from someone who has never even tried it."

"Don't always have to try something to know it's a sham."

He didn't want to go any further with this conversation. He didn't want to think about the kids of those unhappy marriages that had no voice—no choice.

He turned his back and started up the stairs. Not hearing her behind him, he stopped to glance over his shoulder. She remained in the foyer and shot him a pitying look that pierced his chest.

"That's the saddest thing I've ever heard anyone say."

He knew better than to discuss romance and marriage with a woman. He'd thought a runaway bride would have a different perspective on the whole arrangement, but apparently today hadn't been enough to snuff out her foolish childhood fairytales.

"There's no such thing as Cinderella or happily-ever-after." He turned and climbed the rest of the stairs, certain she would follow him with that silly dejected look on her face as if he'd just told her there was no tooth fairy or Easter bunny.

Her heels clicked up the hardwood steps. There was a distinct stamp to her footsteps, as though she resented him pointing out the obvious to her. True, she had had a hard day, but what was he supposed to do? Lie to her? He didn't believe in romance. Plain and simple.

"Let's get you settled," he said, coming to a stop in the hallway. "Then we'll see about grabbing some chow…if you're up to it?"

"Actually, I'm feeling better now. And something to eat does sound good."

He opened the door and stepped back to let her pass.

"Is this your room?" she asked. "I don't want to put you out."

"No. Mine's at the other end of the hallway. This happens to be the only other bedroom I've gotten around to furnishing."

"You decorated this?" Her eyes opened wide as she began inspecting the green walls with the white crown molding.

"It isn't anything great, but I figured if I was going to have a shot at talking Gram into moving in here she might be persuaded by a cheerful room."

"It's definitely cheerful. You did a great job. And I just love the sleigh bed. It's so big you could get lost in it."

He nearly offered to come find her, but he caught himself in time. Apparently Meg's thoughts had roamed in the same direction as color flared in her cheeks and she refused to meet his gaze.

He smiled and propped his shoulder against the doorjamb. "This room has its own bathroom, so feel free to get cleaned up. I'll go find you something to change into. I'll be back."

"Thanks. Seems like I've been saying that a lot. But I mean it. I don't know what I'd have done if you hadn't been at the church."

One minute she was strong and standing her ground and the next she was sweet and vulnerable. She left his head spinning.

"I'll get those clothes."

He slipped into the hallway and strode to his bedroom. What in the world was he supposed to give her to wear? There really wasn't that much to her. She was quite a few inches shorter than him. And he recalled spying high heels when she lifted her dress.

Then there was her waist. She wasn't skinny, but still

none of his pants would even come close to fitting. Not even if they were cinched up with a belt. No, he'd have to think of something else.

Cash rummaged through his closet but found nothing suitable. Then he started sorting through his chest of drawers. He made sure to dig to the bottom, hoping to find something he'd forgotten about. He couldn't believe he was doing all of this for a woman who was obviously still in love with what's-his-face. Cash's hands clenched tight around the T-shirt he'd been holding.

So, if she still loved this guy, why had she run out of the church? He was tired of contemplating that question—he resolved to try again and ask her straight up what had happened. Get it out in the open. Once he understood he'd... he'd give her advice—you know, from a guy's perspective.

With a plan in mind, he grabbed a pair of drawstring shorts and a T-shirt. He knew she'd swim in them but it was the best he could do.

He returned to the guestroom and found the door shut. He rapped his knuckles against the wood. "Meg?" He waited a few seconds. Nothing. "Meg? It's me."

He didn't hear anything. Guessing she'd opted for a shower, he decided to leave the clothes on the bed before heading down to the kitchen to scrounge up some food.

With a twist of the doorknob he swung the door open and stepped inside. His gaze landed on Meg sprawled over the bed and he came to an abrupt halt. What in the world?

She was lying on her stomach in nothing more than white thigh-high stockings, a garter belt and lacy bikini panties that barely covered her creamy backside...

He swallowed hard and blinked. The sexy vision was still there. He shouldn't be here, but his feet refused to cooperate.

A soft sigh escaped her lips, snapping him from the

trance. He dropped the clothes on the cedar chest at the end of the bed and hightailed it out of the room. The image of her draped over the bed would forever be tattooed on his memory.

CHAPTER FOUR

MEGHAN SHOT UPRIGHT in bed. Something had startled her out of sleep. Her heart pounded in her chest. She shoved the flyaway strands back from her face and looked around. Where was she? Her gaze skimmed over the unfamiliar surroundings.

A knock sounded at the door. "Meg, it's dinnertime. Gram's expecting us."

The male voice was familiar. Cash. Flashes of the day's events came rushing back to her.

The wedding that would never be.

The narrow escape from the press.

Being sick on the side of the road.

And, lastly, her ride home with Cash and his grand-mother.

Thanks to him she was safe. Her breath settled as the beating of her heart eased to a steady rhythm.

An insistent pounding on the door ensued. "Meg? Are you okay? If you don't answer me I'm coming in."

She glanced down at her scant bra and white lace pant-ies. "I'm fine."

"You sure?"

"I fell asleep." She leaned over and grabbed the quilt she'd turned down earlier. With it snug over her shoulders, she was prepared in case Cash charged into the room.

"It's getting late." His deep voice rumbled through the door. "We should get moving."

Her bedraggled wedding dress lay in a heap on the floor. She never wanted to put that dress back on, but she couldn't go around wrapped in this quilt either, no matter how pretty she found the mosaic of pastel colors.

She worried at her bottom lip. Her gaze slipped to the window, where the sinking sun's rays glimmered. "But I don't have anything to wear."

"I left a few things on the cedar chest."

Relief eased the tension in her body. "Thanks. Give me five minutes to get changed."

She waited for his retreating footsteps before scrambling out from beneath the quilt. She couldn't believe she'd fallen asleep for—what? The whole afternoon? For the past couple of weeks if she hadn't been sick, she'd been tired. She wondered if it was the stress of the wedding or the baby. She pressed her hand protectively to her abdomen.

She rushed into the bathroom to wash up. When she'd finished, she stared in the mirror at her fresh-faced reflection. She had a rule about never going in public without her make-up—but that was before her life ran straight off the rails. The time had come to rethink some of those rules.

Back in the bedroom, she found the clothes where Cash had said he'd left them. Her face warmed as it dawned on her that he would have had to enter the bedroom—while she was sprawled across the bed in the lingerie she'd planned to wear on her wedding night.

The thought of the sexy giant checking her out sent a tingle of excitement zinging through her chest. A part of her wondered what he had been thinking when he realized she'd stripped down to her skivvies before sleep claimed her. Yet in the very next second a blaze of embarrassment rushed up from her chest and singed the roots of her hair—he'd seen her practically naked. Could this day get any worse?

She gave herself a mental shake and gathered the borrowed clothes. His earthy scent clung to the shirt. Her mind conjured up thoughts of the tall, muscular cowboy. If circumstances were different—if her plans were different—she wouldn't mind moving in for an up close and personal whiff of the man.

As quickly as the notion occurred to her she dismissed it. She didn't have room in her messed-up life to entertain thoughts about men. Right now she should be concentrating on more important matters, like trying to figure out her future. She had to make careful plans for the little baby growing inside her.

Not wanting to keep Cash waiting longer than necessary, she slipped on the clothes. Though the shorts and T-shirt were about five sizes too big for her, they were at least clean, and much cooler than the tattered dress she'd attempted to shove in the wastebasket.

In the bathroom, she gave her appearance a quick once-over, knowing there was no way she could make herself look good—presentable would have to do. She rushed to the top of the stairs and glanced down to where Cash was pacing in the foyer. His handsome face was creased as though he were deep in thought—probably about how soon she'd be gone from his life.

Her empty stomach rumbled. After only some juice and toast early that morning, her body was running on empty. She started down the steps.

Cash stopped and turned but didn't speak. She paused on the bottom step as his intense perusal of her outfit made her stomach flutter. Was he remembering what he'd seen upstairs when she'd been sleeping? For a moment she wondered if he'd liked the view.

She forced a tentative smile. "Ready to eat?"

He didn't return her friendly gesture. In fact, his face lacked any visible emotion. "I've been ready."

"Do you always eat at your grandmother's?"

He shifted his weight. "With it just being me here, and Gram all alone, I like to keep tabs on her. Sharing meals allows me to make sure she's okay without it seeming like I'm checking up on her. Speaking of which, we'd best get a move on."

Meghan glanced down and wiggled her freshly mani-cured, pink-painted toes. "I don't have any shoes."

He sighed. "Wait here. I think I have something that'll work."

She couldn't imagine what he'd have that would fit her size seven feet. A glance at his impressive cowboy boots confirmed her feet would be lost in anything he wore.

When Cash returned from the kitchen he was toting a couple of large bags. He stopped in front of her and dropped them at her feet. "Take a look in those."

Confused, she peeked inside, finding both bags full of clothes of varying colors. "I don't understand. Where did these come from?"

"This afternoon Gram needed some stuff in town. So while you were napping I drove her. We picked up some essentials. Whatever doesn't fit can be returned or ex-changed."

Her mouth gaped. She wasn't used to such generos-ity. Harold had always been a stickler for keeping their expenses separate. At first she'd found it strange, but she didn't mind paying her own way. In fact she'd soon learned she liked being self-reliant and the freedom that came with it.

"But I can't accept these," she protested.

Cash frowned. "Why not?"

"I don't have any money to pay you back…at least not on me."

"It's okay. I can afford it."

She shook her head. "I didn't mean that. It's just you hardly know me and you've already opened your home up to me. I can't have you buying me clothes too."

His brow arched. "Are you sure that's the only reason? After all, they aren't designer fashions."

"I'm not a snob. Just because I'm on television doesn't mean I'm uppity—"

"Fine." He held up his palms to stop her litany. "Consider this a loan. You can pay me back when you get home."

The idea appealed to her. She really didn't have too many options. "It's a deal."

She bent down and dug through the bag until her fingers wrapped around a pair of bubblegum-colored flip-flops. A little big for her, but it didn't matter. They fit well enough and they'd be cool in this heat. Double win.

Outside, he held open the truck door for her. She really wanted to walk and enjoy the fresh air and scenery but, recalling they were running late, she didn't mention it. Suddenly her plans to flee this ranch as soon as possible didn't seem quite so urgent. This little bit of heaven was like a soothing balm on her frazzled nerves. In fact Cash was making her feel right at home.

The bumps on the way to his grandmother's house didn't bother her so much this time, and thankfully it didn't kick up her nausea. She was feeling better after that nap. Amazing how sleep could make a new person out of you.

Cash pulled to a stop and turned to her. "Before you go inside, I know you're a fancy cook and all, but my grandmother is a simple woman with simple tastes. She's proud of her abilities. Don't make her feel bad if her food isn't up to your TV standards."

It hurt that he'd immediately assumed she'd be snooty about dinner. She might be on TV, but she loved home-cooking the same as the next guy.

Heck, if Cash knew she was pregnant and the father had dumped her on her keester, he probably wouldn't worry so much. However, she had no intention of telling him her little secret. He'd already witnessed her at her lowest point—she wasn't about to confirm that her entire life was completely out of control.

"I'd never say or do anything to upset your grand-mother. I'm very grateful for her kindness."

"You swear?"

She blinked. He didn't trust her? "I promise."

He eyed her, as if to discern if she were on the level. Apparently she passed his test because he climbed out of the truck and she met him on the sidewalk.

The fact he didn't trust her without even giving her a chance bothered her. Why did he seem so wary of her? Because she was on television? What did he have against TV personalities? Or was it something else?

She most likely wouldn't be here long enough to fig-ure it out. After she'd had something to eat she'd think up her next move. Yet it made her cringe to think of facing her mother and telling her that she was pregnant and the father didn't want her or the baby.

Cash trailed Meg into his grandmother's house. Even the sweet sashay of her rounded backside wasn't enough to loosen the unease in his chest. In fact it made the discom-fort worse.

His mind filled with visions of her bare limbs sprawled across the bed while her assets were barely covered with the sheerest material. It'd taken every bit of willpower to quietly back out of the room and shut the door. No woman had a right to look that tantalizing without even trying.

He couldn't believe he was letting her get to him. He thought he'd become immune to feminine charms. Take them or leave them had been his motto. And the way this little redhead could distract him with her shapely curves and heart-stopping smile were sure signs he should leave her alone.

"Remember what we talked about," he said.

"I'm not a child. You don't have to keep reminding me—like I'd *ever* be so rude."

"Good."

He followed her up the steps to the porch. He wanted to believe Meg, but he'd been lied to by his straight-faced ex-girlfriend. In his experience, when women wanted something badly enough they could be sneaky and deceptive. Now he preferred to err on the side of caution.

After all, Gram had been preparing for this meal ever since they'd returned from town. It'd only take one wrong look or word from the Jiffy Cook, his grandmother's favorite television celebrity, and Gram would be crushed.

Cash rapped his knuckles on the door of the modest four-room house before opening it and stepping inside. "Gram, we're here. And, boy, does something smell good."

His grandmother came rushing out of the kitchen wearing a stained apron, wiping her hands on a towel. "Good. I threw together a new dish. I hope you both like it."

"I'm starved," Meg said.

"Okay, you two go wash up. Cash can show you to the bathroom."

He nodded, then led the way. In silence, they lathered up. Even standing next to her, doing the most mundane thing, he couldn't relax. Every time he glanced her way he started mentally undressing her until she had nothing on but that sheer white underwear. His throat tightened and he struggled to swallow.

What was wrong with him? He barely even knew her, and he had absolutely no intention of starting up anything. His focus needed to be on rebuilding this ranch, not day-dreaming about a brief fling with the tempting redhead next to him.

Back in the kitchen, Gram said, "I'll warn you—dinner's nothing special."

Cash held back a chuckle at his grandmother's attempt to downplay this meal. He wished she'd made one of her tried-and-true dishes instead of taking a chance on something new to impress their guest. But no matter what it tasted like he would smile and shovel it in.

"What did you make?" Meg asked.

"I tried something a little different. I was hoping for your opinion."

"My opinion?" Meg pressed a hand to her chest and the light glittered off the rock on her ring finger. The wedding dress might be gone, but the impressive engagement ring remained. Obviously she wasn't quite through with what's-his-name.

"You're the expert."

Remembering his manners, he pulled out a chair for Meg. Having absolutely nothing to add to this conversation, he quietly took his usual seat.

"I'm no expert." Sincerity rang out in Meg's voice. "I just cook and I hope other people will like the same things as me."

"I'll let you in on a little secret," Gram said, leaning her head toward Meg. "I watch your show every day and I jot down the recipes I think Cash will like."

Meg leaned toward Gram and lowered her voice. "And does he like them?"

Cash wasn't so sure he liked these two women putting their heads together to discuss him. "You two *do* remember that I'm in the room, right?"

"Of course we do." Gram sent him a playful look. "Yes, he likes them."

So now he understood why he'd been eating some strange dishes for the past year—Gram had been imitating Meg. Interesting. But he still preferred Gram's traditional recipes, such as homemade vegetable barley soup and her hearty beef stew.

"Dinner isn't quite ready," Gram said. "The shopping today put me a little behind. I have some fresh bread in the oven, and I have to add the tortellini to the soup."

"Anything I can help with?" Cash offered, as he did at each meal.

Usually she waved him off, but today she said, "Yes, you could get us some drinks."

"Drinks?" Their standard fare normally consisted of some tap water. On really hot, miserable days they added ice for something special.

"Yes. I picked up some soda and juice at the store." Gram turned to Meg. "I'm sure you're probably used to something fancy with your meals, like champagne or wine, but I'm afraid we're rather plain around here. If you want something we don't have I'll have Cash pick it up for you the next time he's in town."

"That won't be necessary. You've already been too generous with the clothes. Thank you for being so thoughtful."

"I didn't know what you would wear, and Cash wasn't much help."

"I haven't had a chance to go through them." Pink tinged her cheeks. "I slept longer this afternoon than I'd planned…well, I hadn't planned to go to sleep at all."

"I'm sure you were worn out after such a terrible day. You poor child."

"You can help yourself to drinks," Cash said, trying to offset his grandmother's mollycoddling.

"Oh, no, she can't. She's our guest. You can serve her."

Cash swallowed down his irritation. The last thing in the world he'd wanted to do was upset his grandmother.

Gram and Meg discussed the Jiffy Cook's show while he kept himself busy. He opened the cabinet and sorted through a stack of deep bowls, trying to find ones that weren't chipped on the edges. He'd never noticed their worn condition before today. A sense of guilt settled over him like a dense fog. He'd been too focused on the rodeo circuit and hadn't paid enough attention to the small things at home. He made a mental note to get his grandmother some new dishes.

When Gram turned her back to check on the bread in the oven Meg held out her hands for the bowls. Cash handed them over. No need to stand on ceremony. It wasn't as if she was an invited guest or anything. He had no idea why Gram was treating the woman like some sort of royalty—even if her burnt-orange curls, the splattering of freckles across the bridge of her nose and the intense green eyes *were* fit for a princess.

He gathered the various items they'd need for dinner and laid them on the edge of the table. When he turned around he found Meg had set everything out accordingly. Maybe she wasn't as spoiled as he'd imagined.

Again the light caught the diamond on her hand and it sparkled, serving as a reminder of how much she liked nice things—expensive things. And, more importantly, that she was a woman who didn't take off her engagement ring after calling off the wedding—a woman with lingering feelings for her intended groom.

Cash's jaw tightened. Best not get used to having her around. After dinner he'd drive her wherever she needed to go.

Gram stirred the pot and set aside the spoon. "These are a couple of recipes that I pulled from one of my new cookbooks. Don't know how they'll turn out. If nothing else, the bread is tried and true. Cash can attest to how good it is."

"You bet. Gram makes the best fresh-baked bread in the entire county. With a dab of fresh-churned butter it practically melts in your mouth."

"You don't have to sell me on it." A smile lit up Meg's eyes. "I had a whiff of it when she opened the oven. I can't wait to eat."

"Well, if you're hungry we can start with the salad." Gram hustled over to the fridge and removed three bowls with baby greens, halved grape tomatoes and rings of red onion. "This is the first time I've made blue cheese and bacon dressing from scratch."

"Sounds good to me," Meg said. "But you know you didn't have to make anything special. Your usual recipes would have been fine."

"But those dishes aren't good enough for a professional chef."

"I'm not a chef. Just a cook—like you. And I'm sure your salad will be delicious."

Gram turned back to the fridge and pulled out a plastic-wrapped measuring cup. She moved it to the table before retrieving the whisk from the counter. In an instant she had the dressing unwrapped and was stirring the creamy mixture. Cash's mouth began to water. Okay, so maybe Gram didn't have to go to all this trouble, but he had to admit some of her experiments turned out real well, and this dinner was slated to get star ratings.

Cash passed the first bowl to Meg. He noticed how

the smile slid from her face. And her eyes were huge as she stared at the salad. He wanted to tell her to drown it in black pepper—anything so she would eat it. With his grandmother by his side, he was limited to an imploring stare.

For some reason he hadn't thought a chef—or, as she called herself, a *cook*—would be opposed to blue cheese. Was it his grandmother's recipe? Had Gram made some big cooking blunder?

"Eat up, everyone." Gram smiled and sat across the table from him. "There's more if anyone wants seconds."

He immediately filled his fork and shoveled it in his mouth. The dressing was bold, just the way he liked it. But *his* impression wasn't the one that counted tonight. He cast Meg a worried glance. He couldn't let this meal fall apart. He moved his foot under the table and poked Meg's leg.

"Ouch!" Gram said. "Cash, what are you doing? Sit still."

"Sorry," he mumbled. "This is really good."

"Thank you." Gram's face lit up.

It was Meg's turn to chime in, but she didn't. Her fork hovered over the bowl. *Eat a bite,* he willed her. *Just take a bite and praise my grandmother.*

"Excuse me." Meg's chair scraped over the wood floor and like a shot she was out of the room.

Cash inwardly groaned as he watched her run away. He turned back to find disappointment glinting in his grandmother's eyes. It didn't matter what he said now, the meal was ruined. Meg had gone and broken her word to him.

His fingers tightened around the fork. He should have listened to the little voice in his head that said not to trust a spoiled celebrity—one who hadn't even seen fit to stick around for her own wedding.

CHAPTER FIVE

A SPLASH OF cold water soothed Meghan's flushed cheeks but did nothing to ease her embarrassment. She was utterly mortified about her mad dash from the dinner table. One minute she'd felt fine, but after the stern warning from Cash to enjoy the dinner and his constant stares her stomach had twisted into a gigantic knot. The whiff of blue cheese had been her final undoing.

"Thank you for being so understanding," Meghan said, accepting a towel from Cash's grandmother.

"I've been there, child. I remember it as if it were yesterday. I was sick as a dog when I was carrying Cash's father."

"But I'm not—"

Martha silenced her with a knowing look. "Honey, there's no point trying to close the gate when the horse is obviously out of the corral."

There was no sense carrying on the charade. Meghan sank down on the edge of the large clawfoot tub. "I wanted to keep the news to myself for now. It's the main reason I'm here. The thought of being a single mother scares me, and I need a plan before I go home."

Martha patted her hand. "I won't say a word to anyone. And you can stay here as long as you need."

"But Cash—"

"Don't worry about him. He's gruff on the outside but he's a softy on the inside."

"I don't know… He already thinks I'm spoiled and self-centered. I can't tell him about the baby and have him thinking I'm irresponsible too."

"Give my grandson another chance. He can be extremely generous and thoughtful."

To those he loves, Meghan silently added. She admired the way he looked after his grandmother. Everyone should have someone in their life who cared that much.

Where she was concerned he wasn't so generous. She was an outsider. Although she had to admit he had willingly opened his home to her, and for that she was grateful.

Feeling better, Meghan agreed to try a little of the soup. Martha looked pleased with the idea and rushed off to dish some up for her.

Meghan moved to the mirror and inspected her blotchy complexion. She looked awful and she didn't feel much better. No one had ever warned her being pregnant would feel like having a bad case of the flu. She groaned. Or was it a case of overwrought nerves? The pressure and warning looks from Cash had made her entire body tense.

She shrugged and turned away. Either way, she'd gone back on her word to him and ruined the dinner. How in the world would she make it up to him?

She eased out of the bathroom and found him pacing in the living room. "I'm really sorry about that."

His brows drew together and he gave her a once-over. "You feeling better?"

She nodded, but didn't elaborate.

"Good. But you should have told me you still didn't feel well. I wouldn't have dragged you to dinner. I would have explained it to my grandmother."

Meghan eyed him. Was this the cowboy's way of apologizing for those death stares at the dinner table? The tension in her stomach eased. Something told her apologies, even awkward ones, didn't come easily to him.

"Apology accepted. But I was feeling fine and then it just hit me at once. I told Martha I would try a little broth and bread. Have you finished eating?"

"No."

"Sorry for disturbing everyone's dinner. If you want, we can try again."

On her way back to the kitchen her gaze roamed over the house, admiring all the old pieces of oak furnishing. Everything was in its place, but a layer of dust was growing thick. Definitely not the perfect home appearance her mother had instilled in Meghan. Her mother had insisted that the perfect house led to the perfect life and the perfect future. This motto had been drilled into her as a child. If only life was that easy.

She worried about how she'd scar her own child. How in the world would she instill confidence in them? Especially when she struggled daily with the confidence to follow her own dreams?

"You sure you're okay?" Cash asked just outside the kitchen.

"Yes, I'm fine."

She really should level with him about her pregnancy, but she couldn't bring herself to broach the subject. She didn't want him to look down at her—a single woman, dumped at the altar by her baby's daddy as if he was tossing out a carton of sour milk.

Definitely not up for defending herself, she stuck with her decision to keep her condition to herself. Besides, it was none of his business. Soon she'd be gone and their paths most likely would never cross again.

With Cash acting friendly, Meghan relaxed and savored

every drop of the delicious broth. She even finished every morsel of the thick slice of buttered bread. "That was delicious. I'd love to have more, but I don't think I should push my luck."

"Still not feeling a hundred percent?" Cash asked, concern reflected in his eyes.

The fact he genuinely seemed worried about her came as a surprise. "Not exactly. Would you believe I'm ready to go back to sleep again?"

He didn't say a word. Instead he kept his head lowered, as though it took all his concentration to slather butter on a slice of bread.

Martha reached out and patted her hand. "Cash can run you back to the house so you can rest."

His head immediately lifted. Deep frown lines bracketed his eyes and lips.

"I don't want to overstay my welcome," Meghan said. She wasn't sure what alternatives she had, but she'd come up with something. "If you could just give me a lift to the closest town."

Was that a flicker of relief that she saw reflected in his eyes? She'd thought they'd made peace with each other, but perhaps she'd been mistaken.

As though oblivious to the undercurrent of tension, his grandmother continued. "Nonsense. You barely made it through dinner. You're in no condition to go home and face those reporters. Cash knows all about how merciless they can be. Isn't that right, Cash?"

His blank stare shifted between his grandmother and herself. He merely nodded before dunking his bread in the remaining soup in his bowl.

Meghan couldn't stay where she wasn't wanted. If Cash wouldn't set his grandmother straight she'd have to do it herself. "But I can't…"

Martha's steady gaze caught hers. The woman quietly shook her head and silenced her protest. Maybe the woman had a point. Stress definitely exacerbated the unease in her stomach. But if Cash didn't want her, where would she spend the night? She'd already eyed up Martha's small couch with its uneven cushions. Her back hurt just from looking at it.

"So how long can you stay?" Martha asked.

"I do have two weeks of vacation time planned. It was supposed to be for my honeymoon."

"Well, there you have it. Plenty of time to rest up. We'll make your stay here as pleasant as possible." Martha got to her feet. "Cash can drive you back to his place."

Cash looked none too happy with his grandmother's meddling. "I will as soon as the kitchen is straightened up."

This wasn't right. She didn't want them going out of their way for her. "I'll stay on one condition."

His brow arched. "And what would that be?"

"I refuse to be waited on. I want to do my share—starting with cleaning the dinner dishes."

He shrugged. "Fine by me. I don't have time to wait on you with a ranch to run."

She nodded, understanding that he had his hands full. "I think your grandmother should go in the living room and put up her feet after she's slaved away all afternoon making this fantastic meal."

The older woman's gaze moved back and forth between her and her grandson. Meghan braced herself for an argument. She might be down and out right now, but that didn't mean she was utterly pathetic and in need of being waited on hand and foot.

"Thank you." Martha started for the doorway. "There's a classic movie on tonight and I don't want to miss it."

The woman slipped off her sunflower-covered apron and hustled out of the room without a backward glance.

Cash's gray eyes filled with concern. "Do you think she's okay?"

"I don't really know her, but she seems okay to me. Why do you ask?"

"It's not like her to leave the work to others. She's normally a very stubborn woman who won't rest until the house is in order."

During the meal, Meghan had noticed the kitchen needed some sprucing up, and the windows needed to be wiped down inside and out. Maybe his grandmother needed some help around the place. A plan formed in her mind as to how she could carry her weight while at the Tumbling Weed and keep from dwelling too much on her problems.

"Maybe she figured there was enough help in the kitchen and she wasn't needed. I wouldn't worry. Just be glad she's taking a moment to rest. She deserves it."

"She certainly does. I've tried to get her to slow down for years now, but instead I think she does more. Heck, a lot of days she invites the ranch hands to the house for lunch. And then she fights with me when I insist on helping with the clean-up. And when any of the neighbors need a helping hand she's the first to volunteer, whether it's to cook for another family or to care for a sick person."

"Your grandmother is amazing. I wish I still had my grandmothers, but one died before I was born and the other passed on when I was in grade school."

"Gram is definitely a force to be reckoned with. Maybe you can help keep an eye on her while you're here? Make sure there's nothing wrong? As you can tell, I'm not good at reading women. I had no idea that you were still sick."

He glanced down, avoiding her stare. "I thought you didn't like my grandmother's cooking."

She glanced over her shoulder to make sure they were alone and then lowered her voice so as not to be overheard. "Actually, I was going to suggest that I could earn my keep by being housekeeper and helping with the cooking. I'm thinking it's been a while since your grandmother's house has been washed top to bottom, so I could clean here. It would give me something to do all day."

"I don't know."

She pursed her lips together and counted to ten. "I'm not some spoiled actress. I'm a local television cook. Period. I still do everything for myself."

He stepped closer. "Then I'd say you have yourself a job. Do as much as Gram will let you."

With him standing right in front of her, she was forced to crane her neck to meet his gaze. When he wasn't scowling at her he really was quite handsome, with those slate-gray eyes, a prominent nose, stubble layering his tanned cheeks and a squared jaw.

And then there was his mouth. She found herself staring at his lips, wondering what his kisses would be like. Short and sweet? Or long and spicy? When his mouth bowed into a smile she lifted her gaze and realized she'd been busted. She grew uncomfortably warm, but she didn't let on.

This was a way to earn her keep and extend her time here, allowing her a chance to think. She liked the idea. This way she wouldn't feel indebted to the sexy cowboy who made her feel a little off-center when he stood so close to her—like he was doing now.

The next morning Meghan awoke to a knock. Had she slept in again? Her eyes fluttered open and she sat up in bed to find herself surrounded by darkness.

It was still the middle of the night. What in the world was going on?

"Cash, is that you?"

"Who else were you expecting?"

"No one." She yawned and stretched, enjoying the comfort of the big bed. "It must be the middle of the night."

"It won't be dark for long. You planning to sleep the day away?"

"The day? The sun hasn't even climbed out of bed."

"It'll be up before you know it. That's why a rancher has to get an early jump on the day."

Meghan groaned. "Fine. I'll be downstairs in a half hour."

"Ten minutes, tops."

"Ten?" she screeched before scrambling out of bed. The coldness from the bare wood floor seeped up her legs and shocked her sluggish body to life.

She didn't care what he said. She was getting a shower. Otherwise there was no way she'd make it through the day. She rushed into a hot steamy shower before sorting out a pair of blue jeans and a T-shirt, both of which were a little big. She supposed in her current condition that was a good thing. She pressed her hand to her almost non-existent baby bump. Shortly after she returned home she'd most likely be getting herself a whole new wardrobe—*maternity clothes, here I come.*

The assortment of supplies in the bag was quite extensive. Meghan located a hairbrush and ponytail holders. She made quick use of them, pulling her unruly curls back. Without worrying about her lack of make-up, she ran downstairs.

Cash reached for the doorknob. "It's about time."

"I hurried," she protested, still feeling a bit damp from

her shower. "Especially considering it's the middle of the night."

He chuckled, warming her insides. "Hardly. Gram probably already has breakfast started."

"Well, then, lead the way. We don't want to keep her waiting." And she had a job to do—a means to earn her keep.

"Are you feeling better this morning?"

"Much better. The sleep really helped."

He studied her. "Your stomach is okay?"

She nodded, touched by his concern. "In fact I'm ravenous. Now, quit with the overprotective act and get moving."

He grinned at her. "Yes, ma'am."

Her empty stomach did a somersault. How could his smile do such crazy things to her insides? She refused to dwell on its meaning as she rushed to the pickup. The short ride to Martha's house was quiet. Without caffeine, Meghan lacked the energy to make idle chitchat, even though Cash's mood appeared to have improved.

When he pulled to a stop in front of the steps leading to his grandmother's house Meghan glanced over to him. "Aren't you coming inside?"

"Later. Right now I have the animals to tend to."

"But don't you need something in your stomach?"

"I had a mug of stiff black coffee while I waited for you." He patted his stomach and rubbed. "It's the fuel this cowboy runs on."

Meghan scrunched up her nose. "I never learned how to drink that stuff straight up. I always add milk and sugar."

"Gram should have everything you need to make yourself a cup. I'll see you soon. Remember our deal."

"I won't forget. Your grandmother is my first priority." She didn't want to think about her other priorities—

not at this unseemly hour. "Maybe later I can help you in the barn."

"And break those pretty nails? I don't think so."

She held out her hands and for the first time noticed she was still wearing Harold's ring. She wanted to rip it from her finger and toss it out the window, but instead she balled up her hands and stuffed them back in her lap. Disposing of the ring now would only evoke a bunch of questions from Cash—questions she didn't want to answer.

"My nails aren't long. They can't be. Remember I'm a cook?"

"Long or short, you weren't born and bred to this kind of work. A pampered star like yourself will be much better off in the kitchen with my grandmother."

"I'm not pampered."

She pursed her lips together. She didn't like being told what she could and couldn't do. Harold had told her she needed to be a television personality because she was too pretty to hide in some kitchen. Looking back now, she wondered if he hadn't pushed her into taking the television spot, if she'd have chosen that career path for herself. Her love had always been for the creative side of cooking, and it rubbed her the wrong way to have recipes provided for her merely to demonstrate.

"I'll bet I can keep up with you in the barn," she said. Her pricked ego refused to back down.

He raised his cowboy hat. "You think so, huh?"

"I do."

Humor reflected in his eyes. "Maybe we'll put you to the test, but right now you're needed in the kitchen."

"I know. I haven't forgotten our deal. But that doesn't mean it's the only thing I can do."

She hopped out of the truck and sent the door swinging shut. With her hands clenched, she marched up the walk.

Just because she hadn't been fortunate enough to be born into such a beautiful ranch with dozens of horses, it didn't mean she couldn't learn her way around the place.

The time had come to prove to herself that she could stand on her own two feet. With a baby on the way, she needed to know she could handle whatever challenges life threw at her.

If earning her keep meant cleaning up after this cowboy and his horses, she'd do it. After all, it couldn't be that hard—could it?

CHAPTER SIX

CASH SAT ASTRIDE Emperor, a feisty black stallion, as the mid-morning sun beat down on his back. He brought the stallion to a stop in the center of the small arena. He'd spent a good part of the morning working with this horse in preparation for its new owner.

The stallion lowered his head, yanking on the reins. Cash urged the horse forward, which in turn raised Emperor's head, allowing him to retain his hold on the reins. Cash's injured shoulder started to throb, but he refused to quit. This horse was smart and beautiful. He just needed to remember who was the boss.

They started circling the arena again. The horse's hooves thudded against the dry earth, kicking up puffs of dirt that trailed them around the small arena. With the horse at last following directions, Cash's thoughts strayed back to the redhead with the curvy figure. It wasn't the first time she'd stumbled into his thoughts. In fact she was on his mind more than he wanted to admit.

"Nice horse. Can I ride him?"

The lyrical chime of a female voice roused him from his thoughts. Cash slowed Emperor to a stop and turned. He immediately noticed Meg's pink and white cowboy hat—the one he'd picked out for her. She looked so cute—too cute for his own comfort.

She wouldn't be classified as skinny, which suited him just fine. When he pulled a woman into his arms he liked to feel more than skin and bones. But she wasn't overweight either. She was someplace between the two—someplace he'd call perfect.

His pulse climbed. All he could envision was wrapping his arms around her and seeing if her lips were as soft as they appeared.

Meghan rested her hands on the fence rail. "After that challenge you threw down this morning about how I couldn't be a cowgirl because I wasn't born on a ranch, I came to prove you wrong."

He couldn't help but chuckle at the fierce determination reflected in her green eyes. This woman was certainly a little spitfire. And at the same time he found her to be a breath of fresh air.

"You wouldn't want to ride Emperor. He can be a handful. If you're serious, I'll find you a gentler mount." He turned Emperor loose in the pasture and joined her by the fence. "But what about our arrangement? Shouldn't you be helping my grandmother?"

"I did. After we cleaned up the breakfast dishes I ran the vacuum, even though Martha complained the entire time about how she could do it all herself. And then I dusted—before your grandmother shooed me out of the house, insisting her morning cooking shows were coming on and she didn't want to be disturbed. I'll go back and do more later."

"My grandmother does like her routines."

Meg climbed up and perched on the white rail fence. Her left hand brushed his arm as she got settled. He noticed something was different about her, but he couldn't quite figure it out—then it dawned on him. She'd taken off the flashy diamond. The urge to question her about the missing ring hovered at the back of his throat but he swallowed down his curiosity—it shouldn't matter to him.

"The horse you were riding is a beauty. You're lucky to own him."

"He isn't mine."

Her brows lifted. "He isn't?"

"No. I train horses and sell them. So technically he's mine, but only until the buyer shows up later this week to collect him."

"That must be tough. Spending so much time with the horses and then having to part with them."

He shrugged. "It's a way of life I've grown up around. You have to keep your emotions at bay when it comes to business. Now, don't get me wrong. I have my own horses and there's no way I'd part with *them*. They're family."

"I've heard about men and their horses." She eyed him speculatively.

"Yep, we're thick as thieves."

"Are you up for that ride now?" she asked.

Her jean-clad thigh had settled within an inch of his arm. It'd be so easy to turn around and nestle up between her thighs. He'd pull her close and then he'd steal a kiss from this woman whose image in lacy lingerie still taunted his thoughts.

What in the world was he thinking? He bowed his head and gave it a shake, clearing the ridiculous thoughts. It was then that he noticed her old cowboy boots. His grandmother must have lent them to her. He considered explaining how he needed to keep on working, but he liked her company—even if it were purely platonic—and he didn't want her to leave quite yet.

"I'll give you a quick tour of the ranch."

She leveled him a direct stare and then a smile tugged at those sweet lips. "I already like what I've seen."

His heart rammed into his windpipe. Meg's eyes filled with merriment as her smile broadened. Was she flirting with him? Impossible. She was only being friendly. After all, she was still hung up on what's-his-name. And that was for the best.

Cash cleared his throat, anxious to change the conversation to a safer subject. "We'll start here. This is the arena where I do a lot of work with the horses. And over there—" he pointed to an area behind the barn "—is a smaller corral where we break in the young ones."

"Can I watch you sometime?"

"Sure." He longed to show her some of his skills. He cleared his throat. "And this way leads to the barn."

Out of habit, he worked his sore shoulder in a circular motion. The persistent dull ache was still there—it was always there, sometimes better and sometimes worse. Right now it was a bit better.

"When did you hurt your shoulder?" Meg asked as she rushed to catch up with him.

He didn't like talking about that time in his life. When he'd been discharged from the hospital he'd made tracks, putting miles between him and the press. All he'd wanted to do was forget the whole scene and the events that had led up to his accident. And it wasn't something he wanted to delve into with this television personality. Sure, she was just a cook, and highly unlikely to be able to use any of the information he gave her, but she was closely linked to people who would love a chance to revisit the scandal. After all, it wasn't as if it was ancient history. It'd only happened a little more than three months ago.

He carefully chose his words. "It happened at my last rodeo in Austin."

"You're a rodeo cowboy?" A note of awe rang out in her voice.

"Not anymore. I walked away from it a few months back."

"Did your decision have something to do with your shoulder?"

He shrugged. "Maybe a little."

"What happened?"

"I made good time out of the gate, but the steer I drew stumbled during the takedown and we hit the ground together. Hard. I landed on my shoulder at exactly the wrong angle."

"Ouch." Meg winced. "Shouldn't you be resting and letting it heal?"

"I did rest after the surgery."

"Surgery? What did they have to do?"

"Pop a pin in to hold everything together. Not a big deal." He knew guys with far worse injuries, but it was best not to mention that to Meg. "I did my stint in rehab and now I'm back on horseback."

"I can't imagine loving something so much that you would take such risks."

"Don't you love being in front of the cameras, cooking up something new for your fans?"

Seconds passed, as though she were trying to make up her mind. "The fans are great. It's the rest of it that gets old. Watching what I eat because the camera puts fifteen pounds on me is pure drudgery. And it's frustrating being told what will and what won't be in each segment instead of having a voice in the show's content."

"I thought the stars were in charge?"

She shook her head. "Maybe if you're Paula Deen or Rachael Ray, but not for some no-name on a local network."

So she wasn't as big a star as his grandmother had built her up to be? Interesting. He wondered what else he had got wrong about her.

"If you were no longer a television personality, what would you do with your life?"

She paused and stared at him. Their gazes locked and his heart thump-thumped in his chest. His eyes dipped to her lips. What would it be like to kiss her? Maybe if he swooped in for a little smooch then he'd realize his imagination had blown her appeal way out of proportion.

"I...I don't know." Pink tinged her cheeks.

Could she read his mind? Was she having the same heady thoughts? Would it be so wrong to steal a kiss?

She glanced away. "Right now I'm rethinking everything. With my marriage being off, my life is about to take a very different direction, and I have to start planning what I'm going to do next."

The reminder of her almost-wedding washed away his errant desire to kiss her. She'd already run out on the guy she'd promised to marry—she was the kind of woman who'd let a man down without a second thought. And he didn't need someone like that in his life.

In no time at all Meghan was sitting astride Cinnamon, a gentle mare. Cash led her on a brief tour of the Tumbling Weed. She couldn't help but admire all the beautiful horses in the meadow, but it was the cowboy at her side that gave her the greatest pause. With his squared chin held high and his broad shoulders pulled back, he gave off a definite air of confidence. She couldn't help but admire the way he moved, as if he were one with the horse.

"Tell me a little about yourself," Cash said.

"You don't want to hear about me. You'd be bored senseless."

"Consider it part of you getting the job. After all, there'd normally be some sort of interview where I'd get to know at least the broad strokes of your life."

He had a point. If *she* had a stranger working and living with her, she'd want some background information too. But opening up about herself and her family didn't come easily to her.

Her mother had taught her to hide their family flaws and shortcomings from the light of day. And never, ever to let the man in your life know of them—not if you wanted to plan a future with him. Meghan had foolishly followed that advice with Harold and held so much of herself back. As a result they'd had a very superficial relationship.

She never wanted that to happen again. If a man was to love her, he had to see her just as she was—blemishes and all.

But that didn't make revealing her imperfections any less scary. Thankfully she could take her first plunge into honesty with a man she had no intention of getting romantically entangled with.

"Let's see—you already know I'm a professional cook. I grew up in Lomas, New Mexico. I have two younger sisters. And my parents were married almost thirty years before my father died of cancer this past winter."

"Are you close to your family?"

The easy answer teetered on the tip of her tongue, but she bit it back. The point was to learn to open up about herself. "The family splintered apart after my father died. Since I'm the oldest, I know it falls to me to keep everyone together. But too much happened too fast and I...I failed."

Seconds passed before Cash said, "I don't know about your particular situation, but in my experience I've learned some families are better off apart."

Sadness smothered her as the truth of his words descended over her. She didn't want that to be true of her family. But, more than that, she wondered what he'd lived through to come to such a dismal conclusion.

She wanted to ask. She wanted to offer him some hope. But she couldn't let herself get drawn into his problems when she had so many of her own.

Instead, she changed the subject. "How many horses do you have?"

"Fifty-one. I aim to have close to a hundred when all is said and done."

"That's a lot."

"Sure is. But with thousands of cowboys roaming through the West, and the right sort of advertising, I'm thinking soon I'll have more business than I can handle."

"Do you have a business plan?" She was curious to know if a cowboy could also have a mind for business.

"I do. Why do you ask?"

"Just curious. So, do you advertise?" She almost blurted out that she'd never heard of the Tumbling Weed before yesterday, but she caught herself in time.

"I have a website, and I've taken out ads in various publications, but the best form of advertising by far is word of mouth."

So he knew his stuff. She was impressed. She had a feeling that some day soon everyone in the Southwest would know of the Tumbling Weed.

"But don't you get lonely out here by yourself?"

A muscle in his cheek twitched. "Not at all. There are ranch hands to talk to and there's always Gram."

"But what about…?" Meghan bit down on her bottom lip, holding back her intrusive question.

"You surely aren't going to ask me about my social life, are you?"

Heat blazed in her cheeks. "Sorry. None of my business. An occupational hazard."

His dark brows rose, disappearing beneath the brim of his Stetson. "Do you interview people on your show?"

"Sometimes. It's always fun to have local celebrities on as guests. I really shouldn't have pried into your private life. I was just trying to get to know you."

"If it makes you feel better, I don't have a girlfriend or anyone special. I'm not into serious relationships."

His answer put her at ease. However, the fact that his status mattered to her at all was worrisome. He was her temporary boss—nothing more. As a single expectant mother, she didn't have any right to notice a man—even if he *was* a drop-dead sexy cowboy.

Tuesday's late-morning sunshine rained down on Meghan, warming her skin and raising her spirits. She had come to anticipate her daily walks to Martha's house. It provided her with a chance to stretch her legs and inhale the sweet fresh air. At this moment her problems didn't seem insurmountable. She could...no, she *would* conquer them.

Upon reaching Martha's place, she knocked on the door. From the beginning, Martha had insisted she not stand on formalities and let herself in, so Meghan eased open the door and stepped inside, finding the house surprisingly quiet.

"Hello? Martha? I'm here to help with lunch," she said loudly, in case her dear friend hadn't heard the knock. "I also have a question for you—"

The words died on her lips when she stepped into the kitchen and found it vacant. A closer inspection revealed lunch hadn't been started, which was quite unlike Martha, who always stayed a step ahead of everyone. Meghan's stomached tightened into a hard lump.

Please don't let anything have happened to her.

A search of the remainder of the house turned up nothing. Where in the world had she gone? Martha hadn't mentioned anything at breakfast. This just didn't make sense.

On her way out the door Meghan noticed a folded piece of paper propped up on the kitchen table. Her name had been scrawled across the front. She grasped the page and started to read.

Meg,

Sorry to leave in such a rush. Amy Santiago just gave birth to triplets and is having complications. She has no family in town, so I'm going to stay with them until their relatives arrive in a few days. Cash will make sure you have everything you need.

See you soon.
Martha

Meghan refolded the paper and slid it in her pocket. She couldn't help but wonder if this would change things with Cash. Would he want her to stay on? Or would this be the perfect excuse for him to send her packing?

CHAPTER SEVEN

"WHAT DO YOU mean, Gram's gone?"

Cash's spine straightened as every muscle in his body tensed. Why would Gram disappear without talking to him? Had it been an emergency? His chest tightened.

"You didn't know?" Meg asked, surprise written all over her delicate features.

"Of course not." He swung out of the saddle of a brown and white paint. In three long strides he reached the white rail fence where Meg waited. "Would I be asking you if I did?"

"It's just that I would have thought she'd tell you...would have asked you for a ride."

"Quit rambling and tell me where my grandmother went."

Meg yanked a piece of paper from her back pocket and held it out to him. He snatched it from her, eager to get to the bottom of this not-so-fun mystery.

His gaze eagerly scanned the page. Relief settled over him as he blew out a sigh of relief.

"Don't worry me like that again." He handed the paper back to Meg. "Gram is fiercely independent. And sometimes she gets herself into trouble."

"If you don't mind me asking, what sort of things does she do?"

"You wouldn't believe it." He shoved up his Stetson and ran a hand over his forehead. "One time I actually found her on the roof."

"The roof?" Meg's eyes rounded. "Why in the world was she up there?"

"She said it was the only way she could get the upstairs windows cleaned. There was a smudge, and she couldn't reach it from the inside. With her, I never know what's going to happen next."

A smile lifted Meg's lips, which stirred a warm sensation in him. He shoved aside the reaction, refusing to acknowledge that she held any sort of power over him.

"What did you do about your grandmother while you were away on the rodeo circuit?"

"I worried. A lot. I tried to call home every day, and I had Hal, my foreman, check in a couple of times a day."

"I can't even imagine how tough that must have been for you." She paused and her gaze lowered. "I suppose with your grandmother away you'll want me to pack my things?"

The thought hadn't crossed his mind until she'd mentioned it. Her leaving would certainly make his life a lot easier. He'd no longer have to worry about the press tracking her down. And he could relax, no longer tormented by his urge to see if she tasted as sweet as she looked.

He cleared his throat. "If you give me a chance to clean up, I can give you a lift wherever you want to go."

Her gaze didn't meet his as she shook her head. "I don't want to be a bother."

"You aren't. I'm the one who offered. Where do you want to go? Home?"

She caught her lower lip between her teeth. When she lifted her head, he saw uncertainty reflected in her green eyes. She didn't have any clue what her next move would be. Sympathy welled up in him.

No. This wasn't his problem. She'd be fine.

Or would she be?

He couldn't just kick her to the curb. If his grandmother had dismissed *him* as not her problem he'd have ended up as a street urchin at best... At worst— No, he didn't want to go there. He'd slammed the door on his past a long time ago.

Against his better judgment he heard himself say, "On second thought, if you aren't in a hurry to go I could use your help."

Surprise quickly followed by suspicion filtered across her face. "I don't need charity."

She still had her pride. Good for her.

"What I have in mind is purely business. With you here acting as housekeeper and cook I've been able to get more work done than ever before. Besides, my grandmother won't be gone long."

The stress lines eased on her face. "Are you sure?"

Absolutely not. It was crazy to invite this sexy redhead to stay here...alone...with him. But what choice did he have?

"I'm sure," he lied.

A hesitant smile spread across her face, plumping up her pale cheeks. "Since it's just the two of us, maybe we could christen your new kitchen?"

"Fine by me."

She climbed down from where she'd been perched on the fence. "Any special request for dinner?"

"Meat and potatoes are my favorite, but the fridge and pantry are almost bare. So whatever you come up with will do. I'll pick up a few things in town later today."

"I noticed there isn't any wine. Sometimes I like to cook with it. Would you mind picking up some red and white?"

Cash clenched his jaw. He knew it wasn't her fault. She didn't know about his past, and that was for the best. If only she'd let the subject drop.

"You *do* like wine, don't you?" Her gaze probed him. "If you tell me your preference—"

"I don't drink," he said sharply.

She jumped. Regret consumed him for letting his bottled-up emotions escape. But he couldn't explain himself. He couldn't dredge up the memories he'd found so hard to push to the far recesses of his mind.

"Uh…no problem. I can cook without it."

He lowered his head and rubbed the back of his neck. "I didn't mean to startle you."

"You didn't."

She was lying, and they both knew it, but he didn't call her on it. He just wanted to pretend the incident hadn't happened.

Meg had turned to walk away when he called out, "If you'd make up a store list it'll be easier for both of us."

She glanced over her shoulder. "I'll do it first thing."

"Good."

"I'll have to remember to add a pie for dessert." She turned fully around. "You *do* like pie, don't you?"

His previous tension rolled away. "I thought the Jiffy Cook would whip one up from scratch."

"Not this girl. I can cook almost anything, but when it comes to baking I'm a disaster. Trust me, you wouldn't want to try one of my pies. Last time I tried the crust was burnt on the edges and raw in the center."

"Hard to believe someone as talented as you can't throw together a pie."

Color infused her cheeks. "My younger sister, Ella, got all the baking genes. In fact she runs her own bakery."

"If she bakes half as good as you cook, her pies must be the best in the land."

Meg's beaming smile caught his attention. His gaze latched onto her lips—her very kissable lips. His stomach dipped like it had when he was a kid riding a rollercoaster.

Damn. What had he gotten himself into by agreeing to let her stay?

A slight tremor shook Meghan's hands.

Why in the world was she letting herself get so worked up about this meal? So maybe she'd experimented a bit? That wasn't anything new. She'd been putting her twist on recipes since she was a kid.

But this was her first attempt to cook for Cash without his grandmother taking charge of the meal. Tonight's menu was spicier than anything they'd had since she'd arrived. She could barely sit still as she waited for his opinion.

"What do you think?" she asked as the forkful of flat enchilada slipped past his lips.

His eyes twinkled but he didn't answer. She watched as he slowly chewed. When his Adam's apple rose and fell as he swallowed she couldn't stand the suspense.

"Well—tell me. Did you like it?"

He rested the fork on the side of his plate, steepled his fingers together and narrowed his eyes on her. Her nails dug into her palms as she awaited his verdict. Patience had never been one of her strong suits.

Unable to stand it anymore, she blurted out, "Enough with the looks. Tell me the good, the bad or the ugly. I can take it."

She couldn't. Not really. His opinion meant more to

her than a judge's at a national cooking competition. Her breath was suspended while she waited.

"So you want my real opinion, right?" he asked, poker-faced. "The unvarnished truth?"

She pulled back her shoulders and nodded.

"The enchiladas were…surprising. I wasn't expecting a fried egg inside. And the sauce was tangy, but not hot enough to drown out the Monterey Jack or the onion." He broke into a smile. "Where did you find the recipe? I'll have to try it sometime."

The pent-up air whooshed from her lungs. "Honest? I mean you aren't saying this just to be nice?"

"Me? Nice? Never."

She started to laugh. "Would you quit joking around?"

"You still didn't say where you got the recipe."

She sat up a little straighter. "That's because I didn't have a recipe. I made it up."

He grabbed her fork and held it out to her. "Then I suggest you try your own dish."

He had a good point. She'd been so wrapped up in his reaction that she'd forgotten to have a bite. How could she let this man's opinion matter so much to her? When had he become so important?

By dwelling on this current of awareness sizzling between them she was only giving it more power over her. And the last thing she or her baby needed was another complication—even if this complication came with the most delightful lips that evoked spine-tingling sensations.

She stared down at her untouched food.

Concentrate on the food—not the cowboy.

Even as a portion of the casserole rested on her plate it held its shape. Of course, she'd let it cool for about ten minutes before serving. Presentation was half the battle. No one wanted to slave away in the kitchen and have their masterpiece turn out to be a sloppy, oozing mess on the plate. And you never wanted one dish to flow into the other. That would be enough to ruin the whole meal.

So aroma and presentation passed. Now for texture and taste. A dish that turned to mush was never appetizing, nor would it be fulfilling. There had to be solidity. Kind of like Cash, who was firm and solid on the outside, but inside, on those rare insightful moments, his soft center showed.

Oh, boy, now she was comparing the man to her culinary creation. Yikes, was she in trouble?

She lifted the fork to her lips. The dish was good, but it was those riveting eyes across the table that held her captive. If only she could create a dish that made a person think they'd floated up to the heavens with each mouthful—like Cash could make her feel whenever his gaze held hers—then she'd be the most famous cook in the world.

"Something wrong with the food?" His brows creased together.

"Um…no." Heat crept into her cheeks. Thank goodness one of his talents wasn't reading minds.

"You should be writing your own recipes."

His statement triggered a memory. "You know, it's funny that you mention it. There was this book editor once who wanted to know if I'd be interested in writing a cookbook."

"What did you tell her?"

Meghan shrugged. "That I'd think about it."

"If this is any indication of your other recipes I'd say you'd be a big hit." He helped himself to another heaping forkful of enchilada.

She couldn't hold back a grin. She did have a lot of fun creating unique food combinations. She couldn't imagine it'd be too hard to come up with enough recipes to fill a book. In fact it might be fun, now that Harold wasn't around discouraging her.

"You know, I received an email from the editor not too long ago."

"Why don't you talk to her and see what she has to offer?"

Cash was so different from Harold. Where Cash encouraged her to follow her dreams, Harold had insisted writing a cookbook would be a waste of time. She'd been so intent on pleasing him—on earning his love—that she'd gone along with his decision. She'd been willing to sacrifice her dreams to fulfill her mother's wish for her to become the perfect wife. The memory sickened her.

"I'll get back to her," Meghan said with conviction.

For a while they ate quietly. Meghan tried to focus her thoughts on anything but the sexy cowboy sitting across the table from her. Giving in to this crush would not be good. Soon she would be leaving the Tumbling Weed, and she needed to keep her focus on her baby and her options for the future.

"So what happened?" Cash asked, drawing her back to the here and now. "What made you run away from your own wedding?"

Wow! That had come out of nowhere. Her fork clanked onto her plate. She sat back and met his intense gaze. She'd suspected he'd ask sooner or later, but this evening she'd wanted it to be all about the food—the one thing she could do well. Not about her failings as a woman.

"We...we wanted different things."

His gaze continued to probe her. "You guys didn't talk about the future and what each of you wanted?"

She stared down at her still full plate. "We did. But things changed."

"And Harold wasn't up to handling change?"

What was up with all of these questions? Why the sudden curiosity? She pulled her shoulders back and lifted her chin. The determined look in his eyes said he wasn't going to let the subject rest until she'd answered him—but it didn't have to be the whole truth.

"A couple of weeks before the wedding I told him about some changes to our future and...and he seemed to accept it. It wasn't until the day of the wedding that he called everything off."

"I don't understand. If he called off the wedding why were you both at the church? Why did you walk down the aisle?" Before she could say a word, Cash's eyes widened. "Wait. You mean he waited to dump you until you were standing at the altar in front of your family and friends?"

She nodded, unable to find the courage to add that Harold had not only rejected her, but their unborn baby too. The memory of the whole awful event made her stomach churn.

"The jerk! How could he do that to you? You must have been horrified. No wonder you ran. You must hate him."

"No," she said adamantly. When Cash sent her a startled look, she added, "I can't hate him. It...it wasn't all his fault."

She'd been the one to forget her birth control pills. She'd strayed from their perfectly planned-out life. Maybe the problem was that they'd planned everything out *too* well—leaving no room for the unexpected.

"How can you stand up for him after what he did to you?"

She couldn't spout hateful things about the father of her baby—no matter how hard it was to smother the urge. "I don't want to talk about him."

"You mean you're still hung up on this guy?"

She didn't answer as she picked up her dinner plate and

headed to the kitchen. Maybe she should have told Cash about the baby. Guilt gnawed at her over this lie of omission. But she couldn't see how revealing her pregnancy would change things for the better.

The last thing she wanted was for Cash to look at her as if she was an utter fool. She valued his opinion and needed him to respect her. If only she could keep her secret for a little longer he'd never have to know.

CHAPTER EIGHT

MEG'S STOMACH FLUTTERED with nerves. What had gotten into her yesterday when she'd promised Cash that she'd contact the book editor?

What if the woman had already found someone else? Or, worse, what if the editor had completely forgotten about the offer *and* her? This wasn't a good idea.

But she had promised, and she always tried to do her best to keep her word. So she sat down at Cash's computer and started it up.

Without her cell phone she felt totally disconnected from the world—cocooned in the safety of the sprawling Tumbling Weed Ranch. The thought of having to face the reality of her life and the aftermath of the wedding disaster made her heart palpitate and her palms grow moist.

Staring at the blank screen, she realized she was being melodramatic. It wasn't as if anyone was going to know she was online and confront her.

Slowly her fingertips poked at the keyboard. As was her ritual, she visited the discussion thread on the Jiffy Cook's television show website.

Any other day she'd log on to find out how people had responded to her previous broadcast. Today was different. Today her morbid curiosity demanded to know how her fans were reacting to her wedding debacle.

What would happen to her television career if her followers bailed on her? The thought of being jobless and pregnant had her worrying her lower lip. That wouldn't happen. It couldn't. Her show was doing well.

Meghan scrolled down to find over nine hundred comments. *Wow!* That was a record. Apparently people had a lot of emotions concerning her runaway bride act. Now the question remained: did the majority side with her or the groom?

She clicked on the comments and waited for them to load on the screen.

Jiffy Cook Discussion—Comment #1
Hey, Jiffy Girl, hang in there. You did what you had to do. Now stick to your guns. We're behind you.
SexyLegs911

The message brought a smile to her lips. SexyLegs911 had been Ella's screen name for years. It was a private joke since her sister had inherited their mother's short legs. And with Ella being a baker she wasn't skinny. A point their mother stressed regularly. But that didn't keep the young guys from turning their heads when Ella strolled by. It just went to show that some men liked curves on their women—no matter what their mother said.

Meghan continued skimming over the comments until she spotted a heart-stopping link: *Fickle Cook Bails on Groom for Hotter Dish.*

The backs of her eyes stung. Part of her just wanted to shut down the computer and run away, but a more powerful urge had her clicking on the link. In seconds, a picture popped up on the screen. It was from a distance, but it showed her as she'd run out the church doors.

Meghan's face flamed with heat and she blinked repeatedly as she read the malicious article. They accused her of running out on Harold for a hottie from her stage crew.

It was libelous! Outlandish! Horrible!

But it also had thousands of hits. Her shoulders slumped. By now even her own mother must think she was a two-timer with no conscience.

An internet search of her name brought up another trashy article. It included a picture of someone claiming to be her, and with the picture being slightly out of focus observers just might believe it really was. Her look-alike was on some beach, making out with a tanned, muscular guy that she'd never laid eyes on before in her life. And this headline was even more outrageous: *Jiffy Cook Dishes up New Dessert on Solo Honeymoon.*

What in the world was her family thinking after reading that scandalous trash? Her once stellar reputation was beyond tarnished—singed beyond repair. What was she to do now?

Cash was in the middle of exercising Emperor when he spotted Meg walking down the lane. He was about to turn away, but there was a rigidness in her posture—an unnatural intensity in her movements—that didn't sit right with him.

Something was wrong—*way* wrong.

"Hey, Hal!" he called out to his ranch foreman. "Can you finish up with Emperor? I need to take care of something."

Hal cast a glance in Meg's direction. "And if you don't hurry, at the pace she's moving, you'll need the pickup to catch up to her."

Cash didn't waste time responding. He swung out of the saddle and ran, vaulting over the fence. All the while he searched his memory to recall if he'd done something wrong. He couldn't think of anything. In fact she'd seemed to be in a good mood at lunch, having created a delicious frittata recipe.

"Racing off to any place in particular?" he asked, taking long strides to keep pace with her short, quick steps.

"Like you'd care," she said in a shaky voice.

Cash grabbed her arm, bringing her to a stop. "Whoa, now. What has you so riled up? And, by the way, I do care. Now, out with it."

She glanced up at him with red-rimmed eyes. The pitiful look tugged at him, filling him with a strong urge to pull her to his chest and hold her. But her crossed arms and jutted-out chin told him the effort would be wasted.

"I'm waiting," he said. "And we aren't moving until I know what's going on."

A moment of strained silence passed. "You'll think it's stupid."

"I doubt that."

"Why?"

"Because you don't strike me as the type to get this upset over something trivial."

Surprise closely followed by relief was reflected in her bloodshot eyes. "I went online to contact the book editor and…"

"She turned you down that fast?"

Meg shook her head. "There were these articles online…about me. They were…awful. Full of lies."

Her shoulders drooped as she swiped at her eyes. He inwardly groaned at his own stupidity. If he hadn't urged her to contact the editor she wouldn't have run across the bad press.

He had to make this better for her. Throwing caution to the wind, he reached out and wrapped his hands around her waist. Surprisingly, she came to him without a fight. Her cheek pressed to his chest.

His heart hammered as he ran a hand over her silky hair. She felt so right there. So good.

"I'm sorry," he murmured.

She yanked out of his hold. "Why should you be sorry? You didn't write those malicious lies."

He lifted his hat and raked his fingers through his hair. "No, but I've been on the receiving end of the tabloid press. I know how bad it can hurt."

She eyed him. "Is that why you hide away here—all alone?"

"I'm not hiding." Or was he? It didn't matter. This wasn't about him. "Don't try and turn the tables on me."

"Just seems, with you being a good-looking guy and all, you wouldn't have a hard time finding someone to settle down with."

His heart thumped into his ribs. She thought he was good-looking?

Now wasn't the time to explore what that might mean. Right now she was upset and trying her hardest to change the subject. But he couldn't let the press stop her from having the brilliant future she so deserved.

"Meg, this isn't about me and my decisions. You have to ignore the lies. Because the more you say about the matter, the more headlines you'll make for them. And you don't want them to make a bigger deal of this, do you?"

A fire lit in her eyes. "Of course not."

"Good. Anyone who knows you will know it's nothing but a pack of lies. Give it a little time and they'll move on to the next story."

The stress lines eased on her face, which in turn eased the tightness in his chest. He wanted to go online and call those people out on their lies—he wanted to tell the whole world that Meg was the kindest person he'd ever met. She'd no more intentionally hurt someone than he would return to the grueling life of the rodeo circuit.

He fought back the urge. He couldn't make this any worse for her. All he could do was be there for her when she needed a friend.

Not liking the thought of her returning to a career where the press took potshots at her, he asked, "Did you contact the book editor?"

Meg shook her head, letting the sunshine glisten off the golden highlights in her red hair. "I was going to, but then I saw those awful articles—"

"Don't dwell on them. They aren't worth it. Pretend they don't exist and go ahead with your plan to email the editor."

"But if my reputation is already smeared in the press, what's the point?"

He *hated* that some lowlife had made Meg doubt herself. "Trust me, those articles aren't such a big deal."

Her gaze narrowed. "Really? Or are you trying to make me feel better?"

"I'm serious." And he was. He doubted anyone would give those headlines any credence. "Now, promise me you'll contact the editor."

A wave of expressions washed across her pale face. Seconds later her shoulders drew back, her chin tilted up and her gaze met his. "I'll do it."

Late the next afternoon, Cash stared down at the large check made out to the Tumbling Weed and couldn't help but smile. Emperor's new owner had just picked up the black stallion. The sale couldn't have come at a better time. The ranch could certainly use a few more profitable sales like this one.

He couldn't wait to share the good news with Meg. His

strides were long and fast as he made his way to the house. Inside, he found some pans on the stove, but no sign of his beautiful cook.

"Hey, Meg?" Nearly bursting with pride over his biggest sale to date, he searched downstairs for her.

"I'm in the family room."

In his stockinged feet, he moved quietly over the hardwood floors. Meg turned as he entered the room. Her smile was bright like the summer sun. It filled him with a warmth that started on the inside and worked its way out. He tamped down the unfamiliar response. He couldn't let himself get carried away.

"You never told me you were a world champion steer wrestler." A note of awe carried in her voice as she held up a trophy. "I'm not sure this room is big enough to display all of your accomplishments. Shame on you for hiding all of these awards in a box in the corner."

His chest puffed up a little. "You really like them?"

"I think they're amazing—*you're* amazing. And very brave."

Brave? No one had ever used that word to describe him. He could tell her some horror stories from his days on the rodeo circuit, but he didn't want to ruin this moment. He felt a connection to her—something so strong he wasn't sure he'd ever experienced it before.

"I was lucky," he said. "I retired before anything too serious happened to me."

"I'm glad." She picked up another trophy. "Any particular place you want these?"

"Wherever you think is best works for me."

She immediately turned and began positioning the two awards on the mantel. "What did you come rushing in here to tell me?"

Oh, that's right. He'd gotten so caught up in Meg and

her compliments that he'd forgotten his big news. "The buyer just picked up Emperor. I've made my first big sale. And the man promised to be back for more."

"That's wonderful! Congratulations. I've got some good news too."

"Are you going to make me guess?"

She grinned like a little kid with a big secret. "I followed your advice and found the email from that book editor. I reread it. She sounded very excited about the project. I can only hope she's still interested. I emailed her and now I'm waiting to hear back."

Cash basked in Meg's happy glow. He'd never seen anyone look so excited and hopeful. With all of his being he willed this to work out for her.

"The editor's going to jump on this opportunity."

"We need to celebrate," she said. "And I just happen to have your favorite meal started in the kitchen. I'd better go check on it."

She remembered his favorite meal? He paused and looked at her. He couldn't deny it. He was impressed. She was a diligent worker—in fact his house had never been so clean, with a fresh lemony scent lingering in the air—she'd befriended his grandmother in record time, and she was thoughtful.

He liked this—he liked *her*. There was so much more to Meg than he'd originally thought possible for a television celebrity. She wasn't at all concerned about herself, but she cared for others.

He trailed behind her into the kitchen. His gaze latched onto her finely rounded backside as she sashayed across the room. His blood warmed at the sight, bringing his body to full attention.

His gaze slid down over her shorts to her bare legs. He stifled a murmur of approval. Still, he couldn't stop his mind from imagining what it would be like to run his hands over her creamy smooth skin.

She turned to him and heat flamed from beneath his shirt collar, singeing his face. His mouth grew dry and he struggled to swallow.

He should turn away, but he couldn't. He liked staring at her too much. Every day he swore she grew more beautiful. She was like a blooming flower. Even the dark circles under her eyes had faded since she'd been here. He'd also taken note of her increased appetite. For the second time the blue skies and fresh air of the Tumbling Weed had worked its magic and healed a broken person—he'd been the first, when he'd returned here a few months back.

Meg rushed around the kitchen. "Do you see the hot mitts?"

He spotted them on the counter and moved into action. "Let me get the food from the oven."

"I've got it." She snagged the mitts from his hand, moved to the oven and removed the aluminum foil from a casserole dish. "Not yet. The roast needs a few more minutes."

"Sure smells good," he said, making small talk since his grandmother wasn't around to fill in the silent gaps.

"Thanks." She adjusted the oven and reset the timer. "I hope you like it."

"If it tastes half as good as I think it will, you don't have a thing to worry about."

She grabbed a serving spoon from the ceramic canister on the counter and turned to him. Her smile sparked a desire in him that raced through his body like wildfire, obliterating his best intentions.

The tip of her pink tongue swiped over her full bottom lip. "I experimented with it. You might be taking your life in your hands by trying it."

"Where's the fun if you don't take a risk now and then?" His gaze never wavered from her mouth. "Have I thanked you properly for all you've done?"

"No, you haven't." Her eyes grew round and sparkled with devilry. "What did you have in mind?"

He stepped up to her and wrapped his hands around her waist. Any lingering common sense went up in smoke. With a slight tug, she swayed against him. Her hands splayed across his chest. Could she feel the pounding of his heart? Was hers pounding just as hard?

Her voluptuous curves pressed against him and all he could think about was kissing her…holding her…having her. His gaze met hers. The want…the need…it was written in her smoldering eyes. Was this the way she'd stared at Harold?

Cash froze. His chest tightened. The thought hit him like a bucket of icy water. The last thing he wanted to think about was old what's-his-name. And he certainly didn't want to think about him or anyone else kissing Meg.

The brush of her fingertip along his jaw reheated his blood. Dismissing the unwanted thoughts, he gazed back at Meg. Before he could make his move she stood up on her tiptoes and leaned into him. Was this truly happening? Was she going to kiss him? Or had he let his daydreams run amok?

Her breath tickled his neck and her citrusy scent wrapped around him. This was certainly no dream. And if by chance it was he didn't want it to end. Meg fit perfectly in his arms, like she'd been made for him.

With her pressed flush against him he was helpless to hide his most primal response to her. Her mouth hovered within an inch of his, but she stopped. Had she changed her mind?

When she didn't pull away he dipped his head. His lips

brushed tentatively across hers. He longed for a deeper, more intense sampling, but he couldn't rush her. This moment had to be right for both of them. He'd never wanted someone so much.

A slight whimper met his ears. He hoped it'd come from her, but at this point he couldn't be sure. He took the fact she was still in his arms as an invitation. Their lips pressed together once again and there was no doubt in her kiss. She wanted him too. His hold on her waist tightened until no air existed between their bodies.

She tasted sweet like sun-warmed tea. He didn't want to stop drinking in her sugary goodness. Their kiss grew in intensity. His fingers worked their way beneath her top. Her skin was heated and satiny smooth. He wanted to explore every inch of her. Here. Now.

He'd never met anyone like Meg—a woman who could drive him to distraction with a mere look or the hypnotic sway of her luscious curves. Yet in the next moment she could make him want to pull his hair out with her fierce determinedness.

Now, as her hips ground into his, he wanted nothing more than to shed the thin layer of clothing separating them and make love to her right there in the kitchen. What would she say? Dared he try?

His fingers slid up her sides until his fingertips brushed over her lacy bra. He'd slipped his hands around to her back, anxious to find the hook, when an intrusive beeping sound halted his delicious plan.

"The food!" Meg pushed him away and rushed over to the oven. "I can't let it burn."

If anything was burning it was him. His body was on fire for her and his chance of being put out of his misery had slipped right through his fingers.

He strode across the room, stopping by the window—

as far as he could get from Meg without walking out on her. His clenched hands pressed down on the windowsill. His gaze zeroed in on the acres of green pasture. But it was the memory of Meg's ravaged lips and the unbridled passion in her eyes that held his attention. He raked his fingers through his hair. What was he doing? He hadn't been thinking. He'd merely acted on impulse.

As he cooled off he realized that for the first time in his life he'd let his desires overrule his common sense. Meg had teased him with those short-shorts and tempting lips, and he'd forgotten that she was a runaway bride, hiding out here while she pieced her life back together. The mere thought of how he'd lost control shook him to the core.

Thankfully they'd been literally saved by the bell. Otherwise she still might be in his arms, and things most certainly would have moved beyond first base. He expelled a long, frustrated sigh. He'd really screwed up. How in the world were they supposed to forget that soul-searing kiss and act like housemates now?

CHAPTER NINE

MEGHAN FLOPPED ABOUT her bed most of the night. She couldn't wipe that stirring kiss from her memory, but it was Cash's reaction—or rather his lack of a reaction—since then that ate at her. Life had merely returned to the status quo.

She rose long before the sun and hustled through her morning routine. With her energy back and her stomach settled, Meghan couldn't stand the thought of spending another day cooped up in the house. Besides, Cash made her job easy since he had a habit of picking up after himself. She appreciated the fact he didn't take advantage of her being the housekeeper. He was such a gentleman.

He'd certainly make some woman a fine husband—if only they could lasso him. A frown pulled at her lips. The thought of another woman in his arms left her quite unsettled.

Still, with his stirring kisses it was only a matter of time before someone took him permanently off the market. She'd certainly never experienced such passion in a kiss before. Not even close. So what was different? What was it about Cash that made her insides do gymnastics? Or was it simply that the grass was greener on the other side of the fence?

She tried to recall her first dates with Harold. They

were hazy and hard to remember. Not a stellar commentary on the man she'd almost married and the father of her unborn baby.

The harder she thought about it, the more certain she was that Harold had never once excited her with just a look. He'd never watched her with such rapt interest. They had simply started as good friends with parallel goals. Somewhere along the way they'd gotten caught in a dream of being the perfect power couple.

But, even though Cash's kiss had touched her in a way no other kiss ever had, she had to put it out of her mind. With no firm plans in place to return to her life, she needed to make sure things were all right between her and the sexy cowboy.

The allure of the stables and the horses called to her. Heck, she could work a shovel and wheelbarrow with the best of them. She'd used to help her mother every spring by turning the soil in the vegetable garden—a garden which had expanded each year. How different could it be cleaning up after horses? What she didn't know, she'd learn.

Dressed in blue jeans and the borrowed boots, she trudged to the barn, ready for work. She glanced around the corral but didn't spot Cash. The doors were open on the stables, as they had been since she'd arrived here. Shadows danced in the building as a gentle breeze carried with it the combination of horses, hay and wood. The rustic scents reminded her of a certain cowboy and a smile pulled at her lips.

Cash stepped out of a stall leading a golden-brown mare. He stopped in his tracks. "Did you need something?"

"Point out what needs to be done out here and I'll get started."

"You mean you want to shovel horse manure?" When

she nodded, he lifted his tan cowboy hat and scratched his forehead. "Don't you have enough to do inside?"

She crossed her arms and didn't budge. "I need a change of pace."

"Wait here," he said. "I'm taking Brown Sugar outside."

"No problem. Growing up, I spent a lot of time at my best friend's ranch. I loved it and wished I'd grown up on one." She shrugged. "Anyway, I still remember a thing or two."

Cash walked away, leaving her alone except for the few other horses still lingering in their stalls. The place was peaceful. She understood why Cash loved this ranch. Perhaps if the cookbook deal worked out and she made some extra money she could buy a small plot of land for herself and the baby. The thought filled her with hope.

Meghan strolled down the wide aisle, peering into the empty stalls. At the far end she made her way over to one of the occupied stalls. An engraved wooden plaque on the door read "Nutmeg." The mare stuck her head out the opening and Meg ran her hand down over the sleek neck.

"Hey, girl. Ready to stretch your legs?"

The horse, as though understanding her, lifted her chin.

"Have you made a new friend?"

The sound of Cash's voice caused Meghan to jump.

She whirled around to face him. "You startled me."

He held up both hands in defense. "Sorry. But you've got to pay more attention to your surroundings if you intend to spend time around the horses."

"Where would you like me to start?"

He eyed her up. "You're really serious about this?"

She nodded.

"Do you think you're up to walking Nutmeg out to the corral?"

"Definitely. We were just becoming friends."

When he stepped closer to help with the horse the quivering in her stomach kicked up a notch. No man had a right to be so good-looking. If he smiled more often he'd have every available female in New Mexico swooning at his feet. And she'd be the first in line.

Meghan got to work. She wasn't here to drool over him. She wanted to earn her keep and prove to him that they could still get along.

Cash watched as she led the mare outside. Meg's curly ponytail swished from side to side. He couldn't turn away. He drank in the vision of her like a thirsty man lost in the desert. There were no two ways about it: he was crazy to agree to work with this beautiful redhead who could heat his blood with the gentle sway of her hips.

He should have turned her away, but when her green eyes had pleaded with him he'd folded faster than a house of cards in a windstorm. He sighed. No point in beating himself up over his weakness when it came to Meg. Besides, maybe it'd do her some good, having a chance to live out her childhood dream of living on a ranch. He wondered how real life would compare. Probably not very well.

When he'd first arrived at the Tumbling Weed he'd believed all his problems were in the past. Not even close. As a child, he hadn't had the capacity to realize his father had most likely got his mean streak from Cash's grandfather.

Cash had started for the tackroom when the sound of an approaching vehicle had him changing directions. He couldn't think who it would be—perhaps a potential buyer? His steps came a little faster. Slowly but surely the reputation of Tumbling Weed had been getting out into the horse community, drawing in new customers.

He stepped out of the stable and a flash went off in his face. He blinked, regaining his vision only to find a stranger with a camera in his hand. A growl rose in the back of Cash's throat. He didn't need anyone to tell him that this smug-looking trespasser was a reporter.

"Aren't you Cash Sullivan, the two-time world steer-wrestling champion?" The man, who appeared to be about his own age, approached him with his hand extended.

Cash's shoulders grew rigid. His neck muscles tightened. He'd bet the whole ranch this reporter wasn't here to do an article on his horse-breeding business. He crossed his arms and the man's hand lowered. "What do you want?"

"A man who gets straight to the point. Good. Let's get down to business—"

"You can start by explaining why you're on my ranch."

The man's brows rose. "So you're admitting you're Cash Sullivan? The man who started a life of crime at an early age? What was it?" He snapped his fingers. "Got it. You held up a liquor store with your old man."

The muscles in Cash's clenched jaw throbbed. This reporter had certainly done his homework and he wasn't afraid to turn up the heat. Cash refused to defend himself. No matter what he said it'd be twisted and used against him in the papers.

When silence ensued, the reporter added, "And weren't you a suspect in the rodeo robbery earlier this year?"

Cash lowered his arms with his hands fisted. Every bit of willpower went into holding back his desire to take a swing at this jerk. A little voice in the back of his mind reminded him that an assault charge certainly wouldn't help his already colorful background.

With all his buttons pushed, Cash spoke up. "Funny how you forgot to add the part where I was never charged with either crime. If you guys don't have a good story you conjure one up. Now, get off my property."

The man didn't budge. "Not until you tell me if you've stolen another man's bride."

Cash glared at the man. Did this fool have a clue how close he was to being physically removed from the Tumbling Weed?

"How do you know her? Have you two been lovers all along?"

Cash flexed his fists and stepped forward. "For your own safety, leave. Now."

The man's eyes widened but he didn't retreat. "So my question struck a chord? Where are you hiding the runaway bride?"

The man peered around. Cash wanted to glance over his shoulder to make sure Meg hadn't followed him out of the barn, but he couldn't afford to give anything away. There was no way he'd let this man get anywhere near her.

"I don't know what you're talking about. There's no woman around here."

"You don't remember being at that church at the time of the bride's mysterious escape?"

Cash's gaze narrowed in on the man. This was the reporter who'd asked him if he'd seen which way Meg had gone. How much did he know?

"Why bother me? Shouldn't you be checking out her home? Or speaking with her family?"

What had led this man to his doorstep? Were there more reporters behind him? A sickening sensation churned in his gut.

The reporter rubbed his stubbled jaw. "The thing is she hasn't been home and her family doesn't have a clue where she is. Seems you're the last person to see her. I'm thinking she tossed over the groom for her lover. I'll just have a look around and ask her myself."

Cash's open hand thumped against the guy's chest,

sending him stumbling back toward his car. "You're tres-passing. If you take one more step on my ranch you'll be facing the sheriff."

The man narrowed his gaze on him, as though trying to figure out if he was serious. Cash put on his best poker face, meeting the man's intense stare dead-on. At last all those late nights of card playing out on the rodeo circuit had paid off.

"What if my publisher was willing to make this worth your while?"

"I don't have anything to tell you. You're sniffing 'round the wrong cowboy and the wrong ranch. You've been warned."

The man yanked a card out of his pocket. "If you change your mind, call me. Don't take too long. If the rumors and public interest die so does my offer."

When Cash didn't make a move to accept the card, the man reached out and boldly stuffed it in Cash's shirt pocket. Finally the man turned and climbed back in his car. Cash didn't move until the vehicle had disappeared from sight.

He pulled the card out and ripped it up. This wasn't over. As sure as he was standing there on this red earth the rumors would begin to swell. His past would be dug up—again.

No matter what he did, he'd never escape his past. In the end he would only end up damaging Meg's reputation even more. If he'd ever needed a reminder of why he was better off alone this was it.

He'd never be a good boyfriend, much less husband material.

This fact stabbed at his chest deeply and repeatedly.

Cash turned and headed for the barn. At least Meg had

had the presence of mind to stay hidden while the reporter had been snooping around.

"Meg, you can come out now."

He detected a whimper. His eyes took a moment to adjust to the dim lighting after being in the bright sunshine.

"Help me…" Meg's voice wavered.

He scanned the area and saw her lying on her side. His heart galloped faster than his finest quarter horse. He rushed to her side and crouched down.

"Did you break something?" Her watery eyes stared up at him. He wished she'd say something—anything. "Meg, you've got to tell me what's wrong."

"I was running to hide from the reporter and…and I slipped." Her bottom lip quivered.

He reached out and tucked a loose strand of hair behind her ear before letting his hand slide down to caress her soft cheek. "Do you think you can get up?"

"I…I think so. But what if I hurt the baby?"

The baby? A shaft of fear sliced into him. He snatched his hand back from her. She sure didn't look pregnant.

"How…how far along are you?"

"Not very. But I can't lose it." A silent tear splashed onto her pale cheek.

"I'll call an ambulance." He reached for his cell phone.

"No—wait."

"You're in pain. You should go get checked out right away."

"Help me up." She held out a hand to him.

"You sure that's a good idea?"

"Never mind." Exasperation threaded through her weak voice. "I'll do it on my own."

Figuring he couldn't make things any worse than having her struggle to get up on her own, he moved swiftly and slipped his hands under her arms. She was a solid girl, but he easily helped her to her feet. His hands lingered around her as he studied her face for signs of distress.

"Any pain?" If she said yes he didn't care how much she protested. He was throwing her in his truck and rushing her to the emergency room.

She shook her head.

"You're sure?"

She nodded.

He wished she'd talk more. It wasn't like her to be so quiet. "Let's get you inside."

Guilt and concern swamped his mind, making his head throb. This whole accident was his fault. He should have kept a closer eye on her. He'd never forgive himself if something happened to her or her baby.

A baby. Meg was pregnant. The fragmented thoughts pelted him, leaving him stunned. What was he supposed to do now?

Once the shock wore off Meghan breathed easier. Thank goodness there was no pain or cramping. Before she could take a step toward the ranch house Cash swung her up in his arms.

"What are you doing? Put me down."

He ignored her protests as he started for the house at a brisk pace. Her hands automatically wrapped around his neck. A solid column of muscle lay beneath her fingertips. A whiff of soap mingled with a spicy scent teased her nose.

She wanted to relax and rest her head against his shoulder, but she couldn't let herself get caught up in the moment. Cash had so many walls erected around his heart that she doubted a wrecking ball could break through. With all her own problems she didn't need to toy around with the idea of getting involved with someone who was emotionally off-limits.

He carried her into the family room and approached the leather couch. Meghan glanced down. A manure smudge trailed up her leg. "Don't put me down here. I'm filthy."

"It'll clean up."

"Cash, no."

Ignoring her protest, he deposited her with the utmost care onto the couch. The man could be so infuriating, but she wasn't up for an argument. Once she'd rested for a bit, assured herself everything was all right with the baby, she'd grab the leather cleaner and spiff everything up. After all, it was her job.

"Can I get you anything?" he asked, breaking into her thoughts.

"No, thanks. I'm okay now."

He sat down on the large wooden coffee table and leaned forward, resting his elbows on his knees. "No aches or pains? The baby—?"

"Is fine." When Cash made no move to leave, she added, "You don't need to sit there the rest of the day, staring at me."

He leaned back and rubbed the stubble lining his jaw. "You have to tell me the honest truth. Do you need a doctor?"

She reached out and patted his leg, noticing the firm muscles beneath his denim. "Other than needing another shower, I feel fine. If things change you'll be the first I tell."

"Promise?"

Her hand moved protectively to her abdomen. "I've got a little one to protect now. I'll do whatever it takes to give him or her the best life."

"Does that include sticking by the father even if he doesn't deserve your loyalty?"

CHAPTER TEN

MEGHAN STUDIED CASH'S face, wondering what had given him the idea she was in any way standing by Harold. After the thoughtless, hurtful manner in which he'd dumped her, nothing could be further from the truth.

"Why in the world would you think I feel loyalty toward Harold?"

Cash's dark brow arched. "I don't know. How about because you wanted to save your wedding dress? You wore your engagement ring until you started doing housework, and you refuse to say a bad word about him."

Oh, she had a whole host of not-so-nice things to say about Harold, but she refused to give in to the temptation—it'd be too easy. And she didn't want her child exposed to an atmosphere where animosity was the *status quo*.

However, Cash had opened his home to her, and he hadn't needed to. And once he'd gotten to know her he'd been kind and generous. It was time she trusted him. He deserved to know the unvarnished truth.

She inhaled a steadying breath and launched into the events leading up to her mad dash out of the church, including how Harold had rejected not only her but also their baby.

Cash's eyes opened wide with surprise. "He doesn't want his own baby?"

She shook her head.

Cash's expression hardened and his eyes narrowed. "How can he write off his own kid as if it was a house-plant he didn't want? Doesn't he realize how lucky he is? I'd give anything to have my baby…"

The impact of his words took a few seconds to sink in. Dumbfounded, she stared at him. Lingering pain was reflected in his darkened eyes.

At last finding her voice, she asked, "You're a father?"

His head lowered. "I never got the chance to be. My ex didn't want to be tied down."

Meghan squeezed his hand. His fingers closed around hers and held on tight.

"I'm so sorry," she said. "But maybe someday—"

"No. It's better this way." He released his hold on her and took a step back. "Are you sure you want to be a mother?"

Meghan nodded vigorously. "Besides, even if I had done what Harold wanted he still wouldn't have married me. It just wasn't meant to be."

"So there's no chance of a reconciliation?" Cash's direct gaze searched her face.

"Absolutely none." Instead of pain and regret, all she felt was relief.

"I guess this is the part where I'm supposed to say I'm sorry it didn't work out, but it sounds like you were lucky to find out the truth before you married him."

Meghan sighed. "My mother wouldn't agree with you. She had this perfect wedding planned. In fact, she expected me to be the perfect wife to the perfect husband and live out the perfect life."

"That's a tall order, considering nothing and no one is perfect."

"Try explaining that to my mother. She likes to run

with the 'in' crowd and pretend our family is better than we are. No matter how hard I've tried I've never earned her approval. But when I started dating Harold she became a little less critical of me and she smiled a little more."

"I'm guessing she isn't happy about the wedding being called off."

Sadness over not being able to turn to her own mother during this trying time settled over her. "Once again I've disappointed her. And she doesn't even know that I'm about to become a single parent."

"Doesn't sound like your mother is going to be much help with the baby. What will you do?"

"For the time being I'm going to keep my pregnancy under wraps and go back to my job as the Jiffy Cook."

"I thought you didn't like the job? Why not try something else?"

"I can't. I'm pregnant. I no longer have the freedom to pick and choose what I do for a living. I have to do what is best for my child."

Cash's brow arched. "And you think being the Jiffy Cook is the best option?"

"It provides a comfortable income and excellent health benefits."

"But if you aren't happy—"

"I don't have a choice."

"What about Harold? He's still the baby's father."

The thought of her child growing up without a father deeply troubled her. Both of her parents had played significant roles in her life. Her mother had given her the gift of cooking, for which she'd be forever grateful, and her father had taught her to keep putting one foot in front of the other, day after day, no matter the challenges that lay ahead. How in the world would she ever be enough for her child?

"For the baby's sake I'll make peace with Harold. We'll work out visitation. Or, if he really wants nothing to do with the baby, I'll have him sign over his rights."

Cash nodded in understanding. "Sounds like you've been doing a lot of thinking since you've been here. You know there's still the press to deal with? Seems they're more fascinated with you than I first thought."

The memory of why she'd slipped and fallen came rushing back to her. "What did you tell the reporter when he was here?"

"Nothing." Stress lines marred his face. "The reporter was the same man I spoke to at the church when we were leaving. I don't think he knows anything definite, but I can't promise he won't be back."

She noted how his lips pressed together in a firm line. In his gray eyes she spied unease.

"What else is bothering you?"

The silence engulfed them. She wouldn't back down. She had to know what was eating at him.

Cash got to his feet and paced. He raked his fingers through his hair, scattering the short strands into an unruly mess. He stopped in front of her, resting his hands on his waist.

His intense gaze caught and held hers. "Fine. You want to know what keeps going through my mind?" She nodded and he continued. "You didn't tell me you were pregnant."

He was right. She'd been lying by omission. And none of the excuses she'd been feeding herself now seemed acceptable. She'd never thought about it from his perspective. "I…I'm sorry. The timing just never seemed right. I shouldn't have let it stop me. I should have worked up the courage to be honest with you—"

All of a sudden there was a movement in her abdomen. Her hands moved to her midsection.

Cash rushed to her side and dropped to his knees. "Is it the baby? Are you in pain?"

She smiled and shook her head. It was the first time she'd ever felt anything like it.

"Meg, talk to me or I'm calling an ambulance."

Pulling herself together, she said, "I swear I'm not in pain."

"Then what is it?"

She grabbed his hand and pressed it to her tiny baby bump. "There it is again."

He pressed both strong hands to her stomach. His brows drew together as though he were in deep concentration. "I don't feel anything. Was the baby kicking?"

"When I found out I was pregnant I started to read a baby book. At nine weeks the baby's too small to kick, but there was a definite fluttering sensation."

"Sounds like you have a feisty one in there." His expression grew serious. "Promise me you'll be more cautious from now on? That little one is counting on you."

She blinked back a sudden rush of tears and nodded. She wasn't a crier. It must be the crazy pregnancy hormones that had her all choked up.

When Cash moved away a coldness settled in where his hands had been pressed against her. She didn't want him to go. Not yet. But she didn't have a reason for him to stay.

"Don't move from that couch until I return." He bent over and snatched his cowboy hat from the coffee table. As he stood, his gaze met hers. "I won't be gone long. I have to speak with Hal and let him know if he needs me I'll be right here, taking care of you."

His orders struck her the wrong way. "No."

"Meg, don't be ridiculous. You need to rest. And I'll be here to make sure that you do just that."

The idea of listening to him sounded so good—so

tempting. But the fact she wanted to let him take charge frightened her. She couldn't need him—want him. The last time she'd leaned on a man he'd taken over her life. This time she needed to make her way on her own.

She swallowed hard. "I can take care of myself."

"Quit being stubborn."

"Just leave me alone," she said, struggling to keep her warring emotions in check. "I don't need you. I don't need anyone. I can take care of myself and my baby."

Cash expelled an exasperated sigh but didn't say another word.

His retreating footsteps echoed through the room. Once the front door snicked shut a hot tear splashed onto her cheek. She dashed it away with the back of her hand, but it was quickly followed by another one. These darn pregnancy hormones had her acting all out of sorts.

She refused to accept that her emotional breakdown had anything to do with her wishing Cash was her baby's daddy, not Harold. Because if she accepted that then she'd have to accept she had feelings for him. And she didn't have any room in her life for a man.

Cash stomped out to the barn, tossed his hat on the bench in the tackroom and raked his hair with his fingers. His thoughts kept circling over the conversation he'd had with Meg. He was trying to figure out where it'd run off the tracks. One minute he was offering to help her and the next she was yelling at him.

No matter how long he lived, he'd never understand women. They'd be mankind's last unsolved mystery. He kicked at a clump of dirt, sending it skidding out into the aisle.

What was he supposed to do now? The thought of Meg packing her bags and leaving played on his mind. Worry inched up his spine. He hoped she wouldn't do anything so foolish.

He was thankful for one thing—Gram wasn't here to witness how he'd screwed things up. If Meg left early because of him...because he'd overstepped the mark...his grandmother wouldn't forgive him—he wouldn't forgive himself.

His cell phone buzzed. He didn't feel like talking to anyone, but with a ranch to run he didn't have the luxury of ignoring potentially important calls. "Tumbling Weed Ranch."

"Cash, is that you?" Gram shouted into the phone as though she were having a hard time hearing him.

"Yep, it's me. Ready to come home?" Talk about lousy timing. What he didn't need at this moment was a lecture about how he'd blown things with Meg.

"I'm not ready to leave yet. Amy's mother had problems catching a flight, but she's supposed to be here by next week. I agreed to stay until then. How are things there?"

Talk about a loaded question. He couldn't tell Gram about Meg—not over the phone. Besides, Gram already had her hands full caring for a new mother and her babies. She didn't need to hear about *his* problems.

"Cash?" Gram called out. "Cash, are you still there?"

"I'm here. Things are going well. Not only has Meg finished cleaning your house, but she almost has mine spiffed up too."

"You aren't working that poor girl too hard, are you? She needs to take care of herself and get plenty of rest."

Gram *knew* Meg was pregnant. The knowledge stole his breath. Why had he only just learned about it? A slow burn started in his gut. He'd been the last to know when his mother and father had run out of money. And the last to know when his dad had planned to hold up a liquor store.

Then, earlier this year, he'd been the last to know when his girlfriend, who'd worked in the office at the rodeo, had been in cahoots with a parolee. Behind his back they'd ripped off the rodeo proceeds and framed him for the job. She'd claimed he owed her. Instead of giving her his prize money, to fritter away at the local saloon, he'd always sent it home to Gram for the upkeep of the ranch. Thank goodness he'd had an alibi.

And now this. Meg had confided in his grandmother about her condition but she hadn't seen fit to share it with him, even though he'd opened his home up to her. His hand tightened on the phone.

"When did she tell you?" he asked.

"Tell me about what?" Gram asked a little too innocently.

"Don't pretend you don't know she's pregnant. You've known all along."

A slight pause ensued. "It wasn't my place to tell you."

"What else have I been kept in the dark about?"

"Nothing. And why does it bother you so much? It's not like you're the father."

Gram paused, giving him time to think. He might not be the biological father but he already had a sense of responsibility to this baby and its mother. His jaw tightened. He knew it'd lead to nothing but trouble.

"Cash, you're not planning to get involved with Meghan, are you?"

"What?" He would have thought his grandmother would be thrilled with the idea of him settling down with Meg, not warning him against it. "Of course not."

"Good. I know you've had a rough life, and trusting people doesn't come easily to you. That girl has been through enough already, and with a baby on the way she doesn't need another heartbreak. She needs someone steady. Someone she can rely on."

His grandmother's warning shook him. He wanted to disagree with her. But she was right. This wasn't his baby.

"Don't worry," he said. "Nothing's going to happen. Soon she'll be gone."

"I didn't say to run the poor girl off. She has a lot to deal with before she returns home. I have to go. One of the babies is crying. Tell Meghan I've come across some unique recipes while I've been here. We can try them out when I get home."

Without a chance for him to utter a goodbye the line went dead. Gram was expecting Meg to be here when she returned. If Gram found her gone she'd blame *him*. He'd already caused his grandmother enough heartache for one lifetime. He didn't want to be responsible for Meg leaving without Gram having an opportunity to say good-bye.

Around the corner she spotted a wash. She would be protected from the wind.

Around the corner she spotted the wagon. She rushed to close the distance. Near the wagon sat the horses, but the woman was nowhere to be seen. Meghan's heart leapt to her throat...

CHAPTER ELEVEN

THE WARM GLOW of the afternoon sun filled Cash's bedroom. Meghan swiped a dust rag over a silver picture frame with a snapshot of a little boy cuddled in a woman's arms. She pulled the picture closer and studied the child's face. The familiar gray eyes combined with the crop of dark hair resembled Cash. She smiled back at the picture of the grinning little boy. Was the beautiful woman gazing so lovingly at the child his mother? Meghan wondered what had happened to her. And where was Cash's father?

So many unanswered questions. She shoved away her curiosity. None of this was any of her business. She ran the rag over the frame one last time before placing it back on the dresser.

His bedroom was the last room to be cleaned. She gave the place a final inspection, closed the windows and dropped the blinds. Sadness welled up in her as she pulled the door shut behind her. With both houses clean she needed to make plans to leave—especially after her total meltdown the day before.

Even so, she'd come to love this house and ranch so much in such a short amount of time. She'd been able to relax here and be herself. If only she could get her life back on track—back to normal. Whatever *that* was. Then she'd be just as comfortable back in Albuquerque as she was here. Wouldn't she?

After putting away the cleaning supplies and grabbing a quick shower she realized it was five o'clock and she still hadn't started dinner. With exhaustion settling in, she decided to go with an easy meal. Spaghetti marinara with a tossed salad.

While the sauce simmered, Meghan took a moment to check if there'd been a response from the book editor. This time she made a point of avoiding any blogs or articles about herself. Her empty stomach quivered in anticipation as her fingers clicked over the keyboard.

She opened her email account, finding a bunch of new messages. The third one down caught her attention. It was from Lillian Henry, the editor. Meg's heart skipped a beat before her nerves kicked up a notch. Was Lillian still interested? Or had the bad press swayed her decision? Questions and doubts whirled through Meghan's mind as her finger hovered over the open button.

Taking a deep breath, she clicked on Lillian's name and the email flashed up on the screen.

To: JiffyCook@myemail.com
From: Lillian.Henry@emailservice.com
RE: Cookbook
Hello, Meghan. I was surprised to get your email, considering everything that's been happening in your life. I'm happy to hear you're interested. Let me know when you're available to discuss a theme for the book series. I'm looking forward to some sample recipes. Lillian

Meghan jumped to her feet and did a happy dance around the kitchen island, laughing and squealing in delight. *A series. Wow!* Things were looking up for her at last. She couldn't stop smiling.

She'd need to rethink how to fit in enough time to work up additional recipes and figure out themes for these books. There was so much to plan—but then again, planning things was her forte. Now, with a baby to care for, a demanding television show and books to write, she'd definitely need a new strategy to make time for everything.

She started for the door to tell Cash, but as her hand touched the doorknob she paused. Since she'd told him to leave her alone, he'd done just that. Other than a couple of inquiries about her well-being and the baby's, no words had passed between them.

Meghan's excitement ebbed away.

With no one to talk to, Meghan returned to the computer. She scrolled down through the list of unrecognizable names until she came across one from her producer at the TV studio.

To: JiffyCook@myemail.com
From: Darlene.Jansen@myemail.com
RE: Urgent!
Meghan, where are you? What happened? We need to talk right away. Call me. Darlene Jansen

Guilt washed over Meghan. She'd been MIA longer than was appropriate, but her time at the Tumbling Weed had been so nice—so stress-free. Now it was all about to end.

She grabbed the phone and dialed her producer. On the second ring she picked up.

"Where have you been?" Darlene asked, cutting straight to the chase. "Do you know what has been going on around here? The suits upstairs were real unhappy when the television special about your wedding fell through. All the buildup and the money we spent on advertisements to pique viewer interest and we ended up having to air a rerun. Ratings plummeted."

A baseball-sized lump swelled at the back of Meghan's throat. She swallowed hard and it thudded into her stomach. Television was a ratings game. Up until this point her ratings had been impressive—so impressive they'd been working on moving the Jiffy Cook to a larger audience.

"I'm sorry, Darlene." Now wasn't the time to remind her producer that she had been opposed to promoting the wedding week after week. They'd covered everything from floral arrangements to choosing the right wedding dress. It'd just been too much.

"Couldn't you have gone through with the ceremony?" Darlene asked. "If you really didn't want to be married, you could have had it annulled later."

Meghan's mouth gaped. Was she *serious?* Sure, she might have been planning to marry Harold out of obligation to their child, but that was different than saying "I do" to impress the public while planning an annulment the next morning.

Trying to smooth the waters, Meghan said, "Listen, I'll be back in town tomorrow. How about we get together for lunch and discuss how you want to handle things for the next show?"

Ignoring the lunch invitation, Darlene plowed on. "Why did you walk out on the ceremony when you knew it was being taped to air on the next show?"

With her job on the line, Meghan decided it was time she came clean and let the broken pieces of her life fall as they may. Surely Darlene would sympathize with her after she'd heard the details.

"I'd just found out I'm…I'm pregnant."

A swift intake of air filled the phone line, followed by an ominous silence. Not at all the reaction Meghan had been expecting. Darlene had always been friendly and supportive before. She obviously didn't know her as well as she'd thought.

Too late to turn back, so Meghan ventured forth. "Harold waited until we were at the altar to tell me he didn't want…the baby." She exhaled an uneven breath. "He didn't want me. I…I couldn't think about anything but getting away from him…from the church."

A tense silence ensued. Unsure what else she could say in her own defense, Meghan quietly waited.

"This won't help us," Darlene said in a firm tone. "After you ran out on your wedding, the execs got the impression you're fickle. They're not going to pick up the show on a national basis."

"But they don't know the circumstances. The wedding was personal, not business."

"None of that matters to them. They believe you're spoiled and selfish. That you'll balk at the first rough spot."

Meghan's body tensed. "Who gave them that impression?"

"Doesn't matter."

She didn't need confirmation. Her gut said it had been Harold. He could be a wonderful ally, but if he thought someone had crossed him he wouldn't rest until he'd leveled his enemy. Apparently he truly believed she'd intentionally gotten pregnant and he'd done her out of her job. How could he be so vindictive?

She paced back and forth, needing to keep her rising temper in check while she approached this conversation from a different direction. "But I've been working toward this point in my career since I took my first waitress job when I was sixteen. I've always worked in the food industry."

"Your work history is a long list of pitstops before you moved on to the next rung on the ladder. It doesn't display any stability."

Meghan's hand spread over her abdomen. "There has to be a way to renew my show in its former spot. Surely they'll understand. I can bring the numbers back up."

"Your old time slot has been filled. You knew it was going to be a gamble when we put the show out there to be picked up on a larger platform."

Meghan's mouth gaped and she sucked in a horrified gasp. She remembered the meetings about moving the Jiffy Cook from her half-hour spot for a small audience around Albuquerque to an hour-long broadcast for a national audience. She'd met with Darlene and the executives. And then she'd discussed it with Harold. Everyone had been in agreement that with the rising ratings the sky was the limit. Now the sky was raining down all over Meghan, and there wasn't an umbrella big enough to protect her.

"You've been great to work with," Darlene said in weary voice, "and I thought you had a bright future ahead of you. But the suits want what they were promised—a career-oriented woman. Now, with the ratings at an all-time low, I have to tell the execs that your priorities will soon be split between your career and being a single mom."

Meghan blinked away the sting at the back of her eyes. "I can manage a career and a family."

"They don't care. All they care about is the bottom line. That's why I've been trying to reach you. Word came down on Monday to shut down the show."

A sob caught in the back of her throat as her eyes burned with unshed tears. This couldn't be happening. Her life kept spinning out of control and she didn't know how to stop it.

* * *

Cash strode up to the house late that evening. He'd put off talking to Meg as long as possible. But a sandwich and chips just didn't go far when you were spending the afternoon breaking in a horse. And not even the most stubborn stallion could erase his thoughts of Meg. In fact at one point he'd lost his hold when the horse had bucked and nearly landed on his injured shoulder. Another slip like that and he'd be back in the hospital—a place he hoped never to see again.

A part of him knew he'd let himself begin to care about Meg more than he should, but this silent treatment was a bit of overkill. Maybe he should apologize…but for what?

His temples began to throb. He didn't know what he'd done wrong. Could he have overreacted when he found out about the baby? That had to be it. He'd apologize and they'd make peace.

He hoped.

Cash quietly let himself into the mudroom at the back of the house. His motions were slow after his rugged workout. His shoulder ached from the repeated abuse. He rubbed the tender area with his other hand.

He pulled off his dirty boots and set them aside. In his stockinged feet, his footsteps were silent as he crossed to the entrance to the kitchen. He spotted Meg with her back to him. The soft glow of the stove light illuminated her curves. His immediate reaction was to go to her and wrap his arms around her before nuzzling her neck. But he held himself to the spot on the hardwood floor. He didn't need to muddy the waters by sending her mixed signals.

Cash took a closer look and noticed the way her head was bent and her shoulders slumped. Had she been lying when she'd told him she was okay after the fall? Was something wrong with the baby? Or maybe this was just one of those pregnancy hormone fluctuations?

A sniffle caught his full attention. His chest tightened. If there was something wrong with her or the baby and he'd left her alone all day he'd never forgive himself.

He strode over to her. "Are you okay?"

Her spine straightened, but she kept her back to him. "I'm fine. Your dinner is ready."

He placed his hand on her shoulder. "I'm not interested in the food. It's you I'm concerned about. Turn around and talk to me."

She didn't budge. "Go wash up."

Alarm sliced through him. *Please don't let anything be wrong with the baby.*

The child might not have his DNA but he felt a connection to it. He knew what it was like to be rejected by your biological father. No child should ever go through that pain.

The fact the baby was part of Meg had him conjuring up an image of a little girl. Cute as a button with red curls and green eyes just like her mother. But soon Meg was leaving, and he'd never get the chance to know the baby.

"Meg, you aren't listening to me. I don't want dinner. I want you to face me and tell me what's wrong."

"Nothing. Just leave it alone." The pitch of her voice was too high.

"I'm not moving until you start giving me some answers."

Not about to continue talking to her back, he tightened his hand on her shoulder as he pivoted her around to face him. Her eyes were bloodshot and her cheeks tearstained. He didn't take time to consider his next action. He merely reached out and pulled her into his embrace.

Her lush curves pressed against his hard length. He was surprised when she willingly leaned into him. Her arms draped around his midsection while her head drooped against his chest. She fit so perfectly against him—as though she'd been made for him.

Her emotions bubbled over and he let her cry it out of her system. He pressed his lips to her hair and breathed in her intoxicating scent. His hand moved to the length of red curls trailing down her back. For so long he'd ached to run his fingers through the silky mass and at last he caved in to his desire. Nothing should feel so soft or smell so good. He took a deep breath, inhaling the faint floral scent. It teased his senses, making him want more of this woman.

His body grew tense as he resisted the urge to turn this intimate moment into something much more—a chance to caress her body and chase away those unsettling tears. He knew it was wrong—she was pregnant, and a local celebrity, totally out of this broken-down cowboy's league. But that didn't douse his longing to protect and comfort her. Nor did it diminish the mounting need to love away her worries.

When her tears stopped, he mustered up all his self-restraint and moved so that he was holding her at arm's length—a much safer distance. What she needed now was a friend, not a lover. If only his libido would listen to his mind.

"Meg, if it's not the baby, what has you so upset? Let me help you."

She shook her head. "You can't."

CHAPTER TWELVE

CASH REFUSED TO give up. Meg needed him, and he intended to find a way to make things better for her. "If this is about me overreacting about the baby, I'm sorry."

She pulled back to look up at him. "It doesn't have anything to do with that."

Her eyes shimmered with unshed tears and her face was blotchy. Her pouty lips beckoned to him. If only a kiss could make her worries disappear he'd be more than willing to ride to her rescue. He gave himself a mental jerk. A kiss would only complicate matters.

"Will dinner be okay for a little bit?" he asked, wanting to get her off her feet.

She nodded. "I turned the burners off."

"Come with me." He led her to the family room, where they sat side by side on the couch. "Now, tell me what has you so worked up."

When a fresh tear splashed onto her cheek, his body tensed. Not sure what to do, he grabbed a handful of tissues from the end table and stuffed them in her hand. His gaze strayed from her to the door. He stifled the urge to make a beeline back to the stables. Out there, he knew what to do. In here, he didn't have the foggiest idea if he should hold her again or sit by patiently until she stopped sniffling and started talking.

"Did someone die?" he asked, needing to know the severity of the situation.

She hiccuped and shook her head. "It's nothing like that. I think the pregnancy hormones have me overreacting."

He let out a pent-up breath and squeezed her hand. "It's okay. You just worried me."

Long seconds passed as Meg dashed away tears with a tissue and blew her red nose. "I heard back from the book editor."

Oh, no, had the editor changed her mind? The woman had to be crazy, because Meg made the most delicious dishes. He should know—his waistline was increasing from the second and third helpings he had regularly at each dinner.

"What did she say?" he asked, already searching for words of support.

"She wants to get together and discuss the idea of writing a series of cookbooks."

Confused, he said, "Sounds like good news to me."

"You think so?"

"Of course I do. Otherwise I wouldn't have encouraged you to contact her."

"That's one of the things I like about you—your straightforward answers."

One of the things she liked about him implied there were more. A warm sensation filled his chest and made his heart pound. He wanted to know what other things she liked, but resisted the urge to ask.

He was having trouble figuring out her problem, but he didn't want to say too much and get the waterworks flowing again. He was certain if he waited she'd tell him more. Women liked to talk about what bothered them—wasn't that what his grandmother had told him?

Meg balled up the tissue in her hand. "While I was checking my email I came across one from my television producer." The color drained from her cheeks. "She needed to talk to me so I called her. She…she told me the deal to move my show to a bigger platform had fallen through."

Ah—now he understood. "I'm sorry." His sympathy did nothing to ease the pain etched on her face. He should say something else—something to calm her worries and give her hope. "Maybe if your show keeps doing well they'll make the change next year?"

She shook her head. "You don't understand…there's no show. *The Jiffy Cook* has been cancelled. I was worried this might happen if we went ahead with plans to move to a larger platform, but Darlene assured me with the ratings the show was generating it'd be a sure thing. And I believed her. I thought she was my friend. I thought wrong. I've been so wrong about so many people in my life."

Cash sat back on the couch, resisting the urge to pull her back in his arms and kiss her until she forgot her problems. He didn't want to end up being another person who let her down. And leading her on when they had nowhere to go would certainly qualify.

"What am I going to do?" She threw herself back against the couch and hugged her arms over her chest. "I need those health benefits."

Secretly, he thought this was for the best. Meg could find a better job—a more stable one. A job that would make her happy.

He glanced over at her. The light had gone out in her eyes. It knocked him for a loop. Meg was a gutsy woman. Someone he'd come to admire for her spunk and determination. Until now, he'd never seen her utterly give up—not even after the father of her baby dumped her at the altar.

This reaction had to be some sort of shock. She'd snap out of it. He just might have to give her a nudge.

"Don't let this defeat you," he said with conviction. "You can make new plans. Let me help you."

Her chin lifted. "I have to do this on my own."

"But why? I've got friends and they've got friends. Surely someone needs a fabulous chef?"

She shook her head. "I let myself rely on Harold and look where that got me. This time I have to do it my way."

Was she comparing *him* to Harold? The thought stung. He was nothing like that self-righteous, pompous jerk. He wanted to call her out on her comment, but the wounded look in her eyes subdued his indignation. This was about Meg, not his wounded ego.

"There's still the plan to work with the book editor," Cash offered.

Meg's green eyes opened wide and at last a little light twinkled in them. "That's true. And she didn't seem to be fazed by the wedding falling through. She said she's looking forward to receiving sample recipes."

"Sounds promising."

"I just can't believe she wants to do a whole series. How in the world will I come up with so many new dishes?"

As quickly as the light in her eyes flicked on, it dimmed again. Meg leaned back on the couch. Her emotions were bouncing up and down more than a bucking bronco. He raked his fingers through his hair. Pregnancy hormones should be outlawed. He didn't know what reaction to expect from her.

"How about we grab some food?" he asked, anxious for a distraction. "I always think more clearly on a full stomach."

"I *am* hungry." Meg rose to her feet. Her shoulders

drooped, as though every problem in the world was weighing on them. "I'll set the table."

He grabbed her hand. Her fingers were cold—most likely from nerves. His thumb stroked her smooth skin as he guided her down next to him. Just a mere touch quickened his pulse. He pulled his hand away.

"You've done more than enough today. You stay here and put up your feet." He picked up the remote for the large screen television and held it out to her. "Find us a good show to watch."

He was at the doorway when Meg called out, "Cash, thank you."

"No problem. After all, you cooked it."

"Not for dinner. For listening to me and not judging me for losing my job." She got to her feet and moved until she stood directly in front of him. Her emerald eyes held a sadness which tugged at his heart. "I feel safe here with you—like I could tell you anything and you'd understand."

Her words touched a spot deep inside him. He swallowed hard, feeling a thump-thump in his chest. It was a place he'd thought had all but died, but Meg had shown him that his heart might be damaged but it could still feel the intensity of her words. Maybe somewhere, somehow, with Meg around, there was a spark of hope for him.

"We'll get through this together." He pulled her into his arms and held her close, drawing on her strength to bolster his own. "I won't let you down."

"I know you won't."

Her faith in him made him want to move the sun and the stars for her. But what was he doing, making promises to a pregnant woman? Especially promises he didn't know if he could keep—if he *should* keep.

* * *

Meghan's bare feet were propped up on the coffee table, exactly where Cash had placed her after the comforting hug. How had she gotten so lucky to have someone so caring in her life?

She flipped through the various television stations. She wasn't used to a man waiting on her. Her father had been old-fashioned and had expected to find dinner on the table. Then there had been Harold, and he'd liked to be waited on as though he were royalty. At first she hadn't minded. She'd thought he'd eventually do the same for her. But he had never returned the gesture. And she'd begun to wonder if all men expected to be catered to.

Cash had renewed her belief that there were still gentlemen in this world. She hoped when the right lady came along and landed him she would realize what a wonderful man she'd married. The thought of another woman sitting here, waiting to share a cozy meal with him, brought a frown to Meghan's face. She was being silly. It wasn't like she had any claim on him. They were friends. Period.

"Here you go." Cash held a big plate of spaghetti in one hand and the salad in the other. "I'll be right back with your drink."

When he handed over the food their fingers touched. Awareness pulsed up her arm and settled into a warm spot in her chest. As he returned to the kitchen she found herself turning to appreciate his finer assets. How had this man managed to stay single all these years?

The fact he didn't mind treating her like a princess only added to his irresistibility. In that moment she knew the man she married would have to have this quality. Thoughtfulness went a long way in her book. But, sadly, this sexy cowboy no more fit into her city life than she could be a world-famous cook on an out-of-the-way ranch.

At last they settled side by side on the couch with their feet up. Meghan worked the remote, scanning the television stations. When they stumbled over a crime series she paused and turned a pleading look to Cash. "Do you like this?"

"It's fine by me."

She grinned. "I love this show. But you have to guess the killer."

"I do?"

She nodded, excited to have someone to share her favorite television show with at last. "It's no fun otherwise."

He glanced over at her with an arched brow. "And what if—?"

"Shh…it's on. We'll miss the clues."

He chuckled as he settled back against the couch. She couldn't remember the last time she'd been home to catch an episode. It seemed as though the past year of her life had been one long string of dinners out on the town or mandatory appearances at various events.

An hour later the empty dishes were piled at the end of the coffee table because neither wanted to risk missing any of the show. Each threw out guesses about the villain's identity, and at the end Cash got it right.

"Since you guessed the killer, I'll clean up," Meghan said, getting to her feet.

"I don't think so." He picked up the stack of dishes and started for the kitchen. "You cooked. I'll take care of the rest."

This man was offering to clean up? Had she died and gone to heaven? Even if all he did was rinse them off and stack them in the dishwasher she'd be tickled pink.

She followed him. "Are you serious?"

"Would you quit acting so shocked?" He sat his load on the counter and turned to her. "It isn't that big a deal."

"If you're sure." He nodded and she added, "I should give my sister a call."

He momentarily frowned. "Is this sister the one you called right after the wedding?"

"Yes. Ella is a couple of years younger than me. We used to be really close."

"Maybe with the baby on its way it'll draw you two back together."

She smiled at Cash's encouraging words. He reminded her of her father and his peacemaking tendencies. "I hope so. I'm pretty sure my mother will want nothing to do with me or the baby after the way I screwed up the wedding."

Disappointment and frustration welled up in her as she faced the fact that she'd come so close to receiving her mother's approval at last, only to have it snatched away. She promised herself never to be so hard on her own child.

"I take it your sister won't be so judgmental?" he asked.

"I don't think so. You should meet her sometime. I think you'd like her." She regretted the words as soon as she spoke them.

He smiled and the dimple in his cheek showed. "I'd like that."

His comment implied they had a future, but she knew that wouldn't be the case. Once she left the Tumbling Weed she'd never be back. She'd mail him a check for all the clothes and then this part of her life would be done—over—a memory.

Sorrow settled in her chest. So many doors were being closed to her. She needed to start throwing open some windows until she found a way out of this mess.

CHAPTER THIRTEEN

CASH YAWNED AS he strolled to the kitchen early the next morning and flicked on the ceiling light. He wanted to help Meg, but she'd told him point-blank not to. It just wasn't in his nature to stand by and not lend a hand. What would it take to get that stubborn redhead to see reason?

He moved to the cabinet where he usually kept the coffee grounds but found none. Funny…he'd just picked some up at the store. They must be around somewhere. A quick search revealed they were on the bottom shelf of the fridge. He smiled. Little changes had been made all over the house but he didn't mind a bit. It was nice to share the place with someone.

"Morning." A long yawn followed Meg's greeting. "I slept in."

He turned, ready to shoo her back to bed, but when his gaze landed on her cute pink cotton top and sleeper shorts, all rational thoughts fled his mind. His gaze lingered on her skimpy outfit, which revealed her smooth, bare legs. His blood stirred. With each heartbeat his temperature shot up another degree.

Realizing he was staring, he jerked his line of vision upward. Another yawn overtook her and she stretched. The tiny T-shirt rode up, giving him a glimpse of her creamy midriff. He shifted uncomfortably, fighting the urge to go to her.

"Sorry I'm still in my PJs. When I saw the time I rushed down here. I didn't want you to skip breakfast."

"You should go back to bed." He forced himself to turn away from the tempting view. He breathed in a deep, calming breath before he proceeded to add grounds to the coffeemaker. "I've got everything under control."

With the machine armed with coffee and water, he switched it on. Having regained his composure, he turned to find her heading for the refrigerator.

"Stop," he said. "You aren't cooking this morning."

She paused. The overhead light made her squint as she turned to him, but it was the return of the dark shadows beneath her eyes that concerned him.

"Of course I am."

"Did you get any sleep last night?"

She shrugged. "After I talked to my sister I had trouble falling asleep."

And he knew exactly what had kept her awake—the loss of her job. His hands clenched and his jaw tightened. He could help alleviate some of her worries if she'd just let him.

Unable to keep his mouth shut, he said, "I'll make some calls today and see if I can track down some leads for you."

Her shoulders squared and her hands balled and rested on her hips. "We talked about this, I don't need charity. If I'm going to be a mom I've got to learn to do things on my own."

"But it's just a little help—"

"No. Thank you."

He'd certainly give her credit for fierce determination to gain her independence. And, as much as he wanted to argue with her, the pursing of her lush lips and the slant of her eyes told him he needed to find another tactic.

All this stress couldn't be good for her or the baby. If she wouldn't let him help her find a job, he could at least help distract her from her problems for a little bit.

"You know, you've been working too hard around here," he said. "When we made our agreement I never meant for you to clean the house top to bottom."

"But I wanted to do it. You didn't have to open your house up to me but you did. And I'm extremely grateful."

"And I'm glad I was there to help. But I don't want you to overdo it. Especially with the baby and all…"

Pink tinged her cheeks. "I am a little tired."

"Then go crawl back in bed."

"But what about breakfast—?"

"I can grab something to eat. I'm not helpless." Not giving her time to protest, he added, "If you do as I ask I've got an offer for you. How would you feel about packing us a picnic lunch?"

"A picnic?" Her face lit up.

"I'll saddle up a couple of horses and we'll take off about eleven. What do you say?"

"I say it's a date." Another yawn had her covering her mouth. "It's been years since I was on a picnic. I can't wait."

She sauntered out of the kitchen. His gaze followed the pendulum movement of her hips until she turned the corner. He expelled a sigh of regret.

Soon she'd be gone and, boy, was he going to miss everything about her. No one but his grandmother had ever gone out of their way for him. His house not only sparkled, but bit by bit she'd made it into a home. Somehow he would find a way to pay her back.

* * *

Meghan sat atop Cinnamon, trying not to frown. In between preparing food for the picnic she'd searched the online job notices. She hadn't found any openings for a chef, but she refused to let it defeat her.

She'd taken the time to update her résumé and sent it out to a number of restaurants in Albuquerque. It was only after she'd hit "send" that the nerves had settled in. What if none of them called her? What would she do next?

She'd deal with that later.

Right now, with the sun's rays warming her back and the handsomest cowboy on her left, she made a concerted effort to shove her problems to the back of her mind. It wasn't every day such a sexy guy asked her out on a picnic.

With a gentle breeze at their backs, they quietly rode along with no particular destination in mind. Out here it was just them, their horses and an abundance of nature. Meghan inhaled deeply, enjoying the fresh air laced with the scent of grass and wildflowers.

Cash was easy to be around. He talked when he had something to say, but never just to hear himself talk. And he listened to her—really listened. He made her feel special. She only wished she could make him feel the same way.

He worked so hard, from dawn until late in the evening, never once complaining, but instead insisting on helping her with the dinner dishes. That was why she'd worked extra hard on this picnic lunch. He deserved a special treat.

After riding for an hour or so they came upon a winding creek. Off to the side was a lush green pasture, just perfect for a secluded picnic—a romantic rendezvous. Was it possible Cash had more in mind for today's outing than just food? She cast him a sideways glance. He wasn't acting any different than normal.

"Can we stop here?" she asked.

Her overactive imagination conjured up an image of her spreading out a blanket and sinking down into Cash's arms. His gaze would catch hers, stealing her breath away. And before she knew it his lips would be pressed to hers. The daydream sparked heat in her cheeks.

The level of her desire for him struck her. She'd never hungered for a man in her life. She worried at her bottom lip. She was carrying one man's baby and craving the touch of another. Did this make her some sort of hussy?

"Why are you frowning?" His voice cut into her troubled thoughts. "Did you change your mind about stopping?"

"No, this is fine. In fact it's beautiful. You're so lucky to own this little bit of heaven on earth."

"Really? Because you looked like something was bothering you."

"Nothing." She forced a smile. "Although I'm getting hungry. How about you?"

"Definitely. The aroma of fried chicken has been pure torture."

She was being silly and worrying for no reason. But when he helped her out of her saddle she noticed how his hands lingered a little longer than necessary. His gaze caught hers and his Adam's apple bobbed.

In the next breath he pulled away. "I'll grab the food."

In no time Cash set the supplies down at her feet. They included a container of homemade potato salad, macaroni and cheese and some deviled eggs. "If you don't need anything else, I'm going to take the horses down to the creek."

"Go ahead. I'll be fine here. Lunch will be ready when you get back."

"I won't be gone long." His gaze paused on her lips,

causing her insides to flutter. "Promise you won't start without me?"

She swallowed and tried to maintain an easy demeanor. "Now, would I do something like that?"

He strolled over to the horses. Wise or foolish, she couldn't ignore the magnetic attraction pulling at them. Cash felt it too. She was certain of it.

And it wasn't just now that he'd felt it. This morning in the kitchen she'd caught his hungry glances. And there had been other times when he'd eyed her up, all the while thinking she hadn't noticed.

She licked her dry lips. She'd most definitely noticed.

No more than ten minutes later Cash had tended to the horses and was heading back to join Meg. The aroma of fried chicken floating along in the gentle breeze was tempting, but not as tempting as having a taste of Meg's sweet kisses. This picnic was his best idea so far. And Meg looked more delicious than the cherry pie she'd packed for dessert.

When he entered the clearing she flashed him a smile. His chest puffed up. No one had ever looked at him quite that way before.

She got to her feet and moved to meet him partway. Her beauty mesmerized him, from the pink tingeing her cheeks to the spark of mischief in her emerald eyes.

"Thanks for bringing me here," she said, stopping in front of him. "I didn't think it was possible, but I'm feeling much better."

"That's great. I thought a change of scenery might help."

Her palms rested on his chest. Could she feel how her mere touch made his heart beat out of control? He hoped not. The last thing either of them needed was to let this physical attraction get out of hand.

"It's not the scenery," she said, her voice growing soft with a sexy lilt. "It's you."

Before he could make sense of what was happening she leaned closer. He couldn't let this happen—no matter how much he wanted it. He turned his head and her lips pressed against his cheek.

Meg jumped back. Her face flamed red. His gut knotted with unease. He knew that he was responsible for her embarrassment and was unsure where this would leave them.

"I thought you…um…don't you like me?" she stammered.

He lowered his head, realizing he'd been too obvious with his interest in her. "You're wonderful. It's not you, it's me."

"Seriously? You're going to throw that tired old cliché at me?" She stepped forward and raised her chin so they were making direct eye contact. "You like me. You're just afraid to admit it."

"Drop it." He tried to walk away but she grabbed his arm.

"Admit it. Admit that you can't forget about that kiss we shared back at the house. Admit that you want to do it again."

She was right. He did like her. And he thought about that stirring kiss far too often for his own sanity. Heck, he'd offer up his prize stallion to taste her lips once more—but he couldn't—they couldn't.

"Meg, stop it! This—you and me—it can't happen."

He pulled away from her touch. He had to convince her that he wasn't good enough for her. She could do so much better.

He strode over to the picnic area.

A blue-and-white quilt was spread over the ground with the food in the center. He stopped next to the blanket, unable to tear his gaze from the familiar hand-sewn material. His throat tightened and the air became trapped in his lungs.

"Why can't we happen?" Meg persisted.

He knelt down on the edge of the quilt. His outstretched fingers traced over the interlocking blocks of material. This was a physical reminder of why he had to stop this romance with Meg before it got started.

"You don't know me," he said.

Her intense stare drilled into him. "Then tell me. I'm listening."

He didn't want to have this talk—not with her—not with anyone. But he'd already said too much, and now he might as well fill her in. Maybe then she'd understand why they could never share more than a few kisses—no matter how much he longed for more.

"This quilt is older than me. My great-grandmother made it for my mother. It kept me warm in the winter, but most of all it kept me safe from the war between my parents. When I was hidden beneath it I pretended no one could see me."

He paused, wondering how many people described their parents' relationship as a war. He sure hoped not many. No child should ever live through what he'd endured. No one should ever feel the need to become invisible to stay safe.

Meg opened her mouth, obviously to offer some unwanted sympathy, but when he turned a hard gaze to her she pressed her lips back together and knelt down beside him. He'd never get it all out if she showered him with compassion. He needed to say this once and for all. Revealing his past was necessary. It'd set both of them free from this magnetic attraction.

His muscles tensed and his stomach churned as he reached into the far recesses of his mind, pulling forth the memories he'd tried for years to forget. "My mother wasn't a bad person. But she was young when she became pregnant. She wasn't ready for a husband and a child. And my father…well, he was a piece of work."

"Your mother must have been a brave woman. I'm scared to death about bringing a child into this world."

"You don't need to be afraid. You'll make a wonderful mother."

Her eyes lit up with hope. "You really think so?"

He nodded. He envisioned Meg with a baby in her arms—a baby with red hair and green eyes just like her. Sadness welled up in his chest when he realized he'd never witness mother and child together. Once she left the Tumbling Weed there'd be no looking back for either of them—it had to be that way.

"Tell me some more about your mother," she said, with genuine interest in her voice.

"She was the most beautiful woman I'd ever seen. I remember her singing me to sleep. She sang like an angel."

Meg's hand moved to her stomach. "I hope my son or daughter will have such wonderful memories of me."

Cash shook his head. "It wasn't all good. She tried to be a good mother, but she couldn't stand up to my father. He blamed her for his washed-up rodeo career. Heck, he blamed her for everything that went wrong. I'll never understand why she didn't just leave him. When the money ran out she sold our possessions—anything that would buy us food for just one more day."

"I can't imagine not knowing where your next meal was going to come from," Meg said softly. "So this is why you treat the people in your life like the horses you sell. By holding them at arm's length they can't hurt you."

"You don't understand." His hands clenched. "There's

more to it. Some people shouldn't be allowed to reproduce, and my father was one of them."

Cash threw his hat down on the blanket and stabbed his fingers through his hair. Memories bombarded him. He chanced a glance at Meg. Her features had softened and her eyes were warm with…was that *love?*

His heart skipped a beat. No, it couldn't be. It had to be compassion. If it was love, they were in far more trouble than he'd ever imagined. He had no choice now but to get the rest of his past out in the open.

"When there was nothing left for my mother to sell or barter, my father's answer wasn't to get a job. Not him. Instead he loaded the family up in the car and we headed into town. We pulled up to a liquor store and he made me get out…"

Cash drew in an unsteady breath, refusing to meet Meg's unwavering stare. What was she thinking? It didn't matter. Nothing she'd imagined could come close to the horror of his dreadful tale.

"I didn't want to go. I was a frightened nine-year-old who wanted to stay in the car with my mother. My father grabbed me by my collar and yanked me out of the backseat." Cash rubbed his hand over the back of his neck, still able to recall the burn where his shirt had been pulled taut across his skin. "He dragged me to the liquor store door, pulled it open and pushed me inside. I knew by the fierce look on his face that it was going to be bad. I had no idea how bad. I was shaking when he shoved a handgun at me."

Meg expelled a horrified gasp. "What on earth was he *thinking?*"

"Probably about how to get his next drink." Cash spat out the bitter words. "When I didn't take it, he forced it into my hands. I think he said if anyone tried to come in the door I was to shoot them. I'm not real sure. I'd started crying by then."

Meg reached out to him, but he jerked back before her fingers touched his.

He gave her a hard stare, which stopped her hand in midair. "You wanted to know why I'm damaged goods, so I'm telling you."

"I don't care what you say. You're a good person."

He ignored her protest while he dredged up the courage to finish telling her this nightmare. "I stood in the liquor store, crying and shaking. The gun dangled from my fingertips. My father yelled at the salesclerk and the next thing I heard was a gunshot. I ran out of the store and kept running until my mother pulled me into the car."

Meg placed a hand on his jean-clad thigh and this time he didn't move it. He needed her strength to get through the next part—the part that had haunted his dreams for years.

"I can't imagine how scared you must have been." Meg's soft voice was like balm on his raw scars.

"My father had left the car running, so when he ran out of the store and jumped in he punched the gas pedal. He ranted about what a wimp I was and I believed him. If I had been stronger I would have stayed by his side. I climbed into the backseat to get away from him. I knew all too well what the back of his hand felt like. In no time there were sirens behind us but my parents continued to fight. I hunched down on the floor to keep out of his reach. He started chugging stolen whiskey. That stuff always made him meaner. When he couldn't grab me, he smacked my mother. The car jerked and my mother screamed. The next thing I knew the car was wrapped around a tree and both of my parents were dead."

"That's the saddest story I've ever heard." Pity echoed

in her voice, making him feel worse. "Nobody should ever have to put up with a bully like him."

"It wasn't until I was a teenager, after being around my grandfather, that I realized the apple hadn't fallen far from the tree. Both of them were tough men to get along with under the best of circumstances, but put some liquor in front of them and they became mean."

"So that explains it," Meg said.

"Explains what?"

"The reason there's no liquor in your house or Martha's. And why you reacted so negatively to my suggestion of picking up some wine in town."

"When he had the money Dad always started his evenings with a cheap bottle of wine at dinner. From there he'd move to the stronger stuff."

"I'm sorry. I should have figured there was a reason both houses are completely dry. I just wasn't thinking."

This time it was Cash who reached out and squeezed her hand. "There was no way for you to know. But now that you do you have to understand, with a father like mine, why I'm better off keeping to myself."

CHAPTER FOURTEEN

WATER SPLASHED ONTO the back of Meghan's hand. Had it begun to rain? She glanced up at the clear blue sky. There wasn't a cloud in sight. Then she lifted a hand to her cheek, finding it damp.

She didn't know when during that sad story she'd begun to cry, but it didn't matter. All that mattered now was Cash.

She sat there in the meadow, wanting nothing more than to ease his pain. She stared across at him, noticing how the color had drained from his complexion.

What did you say to someone who'd lived through such an abusive childhood? *I'm sorry* seemed too generic—too empty. She wanted him to know how much she cared about what had happened to him. Still, words of comfort remained elusive.

She got to her knees and leaned forward. Unwilling to let the firm set of his jaw or his mask of indifference deter her, she wrapped her arms around him. With a squeeze, she wished she could absorb his pain.

"Cash, you can't beat yourself up for something that happened when you were a kid. You were a victim...not an accomplice."

He unwound her arms from his neck. "You don't understand. The bad stuff—it's in my genes."

"I don't believe it. You're nothing like your father or

grandfather. But if you let the past rule your future it won't matter. You'll miss out on all of the good bits—"

"I've got to check on the horses." Cash jumped to his feet.

"Wait. Don't go." Her heart ached for him. She once more held out her hand, hoping this time he'd grab on. He had to know he wasn't alone. "I'm here for you."

Inner turmoil filtered across his tanned face. He glanced at her hand. She willed him to take it. Instead he turned and, like a wooden soldier, marched away without so much as a backward glance.

She lowered her hand to her lap. This trip down memory lane hadn't brought them closer together. In fact she'd wager their talk had only succeeded in confirming Cash's belief that he should remain a lone cowboy. The thought left a sad void inside her.

His story was so much worse than she could have ever imagined. The fact he'd lived through such horrific events and still turned out to be a caring, generous soul amazed her. But it explained why he distanced himself from everyone in his life. He was afraid of being hurt again.

Her heart clenched. She knew all too well what *that* felt like.

Giant chocolate chip cookies.

That was Meghan's answer to Cash's stony indifference. Since he'd revealed that intimate part of his life yesterday he'd locked her out. Other than a nod here or a glib answer there, they hadn't really interacted.

At dinnertime the back door clattered shut a few minutes before six. Meghan tossed a clean kitchen towel over the large platter of still warm cookies. Then she placed a homemade Mexican pizza smothered in Monterey Jack and cheddar in the oven.

With the timer set, she dusted off her hands and turned. "Dinner's just about ready."

His gaze didn't meet hers. "There's no rush."

"I made something special for dessert." She held her breath, hoping it'd pique his interest.

"That's nice." He headed out of the room, most likely on his way to get cleaned up.

The air rushed out of her lungs. Not a smile, not a glimmer of interest in his eyes or even some basic curiosity. So much for getting to a man's heart through his stomach. Obviously the person who'd made up the saying had never encountered anyone as stubborn as Cash.

She pressed her fingers to her lips, holding back a litany of frustration. She'd had it with him. If only she hadn't made such a fool of herself back at the picnic by throwing herself at him they'd still be friends. Life would still be peaceful.

With the salad made, she had twenty minutes to herself. Time to see if her résumé had hooked any interested employers. It was high time she got out of Cash's way—permanently.

She rushed to the computer. Her fingers flew over the keyboard. Though the thought of never seeing Cash again bothered her, she refused to dwell on it. Maybe by the end of the week she'd have an interview lined up—no, make that two or three.

Out of habit, she started to type the address for the Jiffy Cook website. She stopped herself just before hitting "enter." That was her past. Her future was waiting for her in her inbox.

With the correct address entered, her fingers drummed on the oak desktop. At last the screen popped up. She had a number of new emails. She held her breath in anticipation as she opened the first one:

To: JiffyCook@myemail.com
From: admin@TheTurquoiseCantina.com
RE: Employment
Thank you so much for considering the Turquoise Can-
tina in your employment pursuit. However, at this time we
don't have any openings. We wish you the best with your
continued endeavors.

Disappointment slammed into Meghan. She hadn't realized until that moment how much she'd been counting
on an eager reception to her inquiries.

She swallowed hard. There were still other responses.
She opened each of them. One after the other. All were
polite. But each held the same message: thanks, but no
thanks.

Meghan's eyes stung as she stared at the monitor.

"Ready?"

The sound of Cash's voice jarred her from her thoughts.
After a couple of rapid blinks she shut down the computer.
She'd figure out what to do tomorrow. It'd always seemed
to work for Scarlett O'Hara.

"I'll get your dinner," she muttered through clenched
teeth. With her shoulders rigid, she strutted past him to
retrieve a plate from the cabinet.

"Aren't you eating too?"

She could feel his curious stare drilling into the back
of her head, but a girl could only take so much rejection
without it getting to her. Cash hadn't just rejected her kiss,
he'd then proceeded to treat her like she had the plague.
She slammed the plate on the table.

"Would you talk to me?" Cash's voice rumbled with
agitation. "Tell me what's bothering you."

With only seconds to go on the timer, Meghan turned

off the oven and pulled the pizza out. She placed it on the stovetop and threw down the hot mitts.

Her patience stretched to the limit, she swung around to face him. "That's rich, coming from you. You've done nothing but give me the cold shoulder since I mistakenly tried to kiss you."

Cash crossed his arms, his face creased into a deep frown. "I thought I explained why starting anything between us would be a mistake. I should never have suggested the picnic. I'm sorry. Now, will you join me for dinner?"

"I'm not hungry."

He stepped closer. His voice lowered. "Listen, I know I've been a bear lately—"

"A bear with a thorn in his paw."

His lips pressed into a firm line. "I guess I deserve that. But if I promise to be on my best behavior will you eat dinner with me? After all, you have the baby to think of."

She shook her head. "I've got more than that on my mind."

"Such as?"

Her gaze met his. Genuine concern was reflected in his eyes. At last Cash was being his usual caring self. She breathed easier, knowing that the grouchy version of him was gone. Still, she wasn't so sure she was up for sharing her latest failure.

"Meg, I'm not going anywhere until you spit it out."

His unbending tone let her know that he was serious.

"Fine. If you must know I just got a slew of responses to my job search. Seems no one needs an out-of-work Jiffy Cook."

Cash stepped forward. His hands rose as if to embrace her. She glared at him. She didn't want his pity. Not now. She needed to hold it together. His arms lowered.

"Maybe I gave up on my television show too soon. I should ask—no, *beg*—for my job back."

"Don't do that. You already told me it didn't make you happy."

She clenched her fists. His calm, reasonable tone grated on her last nerve as panic twisted her stomach in knots. "But I don't have much savings. And with the baby coming I need a steady paycheck."

Cash pulled out a kitchen chair and helped her into it. He knelt down in front of her. "You tried—what? A half-dozen restaurants?" When she nodded, he continued, "There are dozens more you haven't contacted. Keep going. Keep trying. You'll find the right position in no time."

He was right. Her search had only just begun. Her stomach began to settle. "I know you're right. But with the baby on the way it's just so scary not to have a reliable job."

"Quit worrying. You and that little one will be just fine. My offer still stands. Any time you want some help—"

She shook her head. "I'm fine now. I can do this. But thank you."

He got to his feet. "Stay there. I'll get you a plate. And no protests. That little one you're carrying is hungry."

Cash amazed her with his ability to be so supportive. No one in her life had ever rallied behind her like he had. The others had barged in and told her what to do.

But not Cash. He was willing to step aside and let her find her own way. How would she ever repay him?

Cash chugged down his third mug of coffee and trudged off to the barn. Another yawn plagued him. After his talk with Meg the previous evening he'd been troubled by his conscience.

He'd spent a sleepless night, staring into the darkness,

wrestling with what he should do: honor his word to Meg and let her find a job on her own? Or make a few phone calls on her behalf?

After witnessing the toll her unemployment was taking on her, he couldn't imagine that the ensuing stress was any good for the baby. And the knowledge that she was considering begging for her television job back tipped his decision.

He'd made a lot of contacts while working the rodeo circuit. After all, he was a world champion twice over. He'd had influential sponsors. He'd never asked for any special favors in the past so he had a few chips to cash in.

He was hesitant, though, to reconnect with that part of his life. He had always thought that when he'd decided to walk away after that last scandal selling horses to cowboys would be the extent of his involvement with the rodeo crew.

However, there was more here to consider than his own comfort. Meg and her baby deserved a good life, and if he could do anything to make that happen he had to at least try.

He grabbed for his phone. The echo of Meg's determined voice filled his mind. Surely she'd forgive him? After all, he was only offering her a helping hand.

He dialed the phone number scrawled on an old slip of paper. "Hey, Tex. It's Cash. I was hoping you could help me out with something…"

Meghan sat down at Cash's computer with her bottom lip clenched firmly between her teeth. A couple of days had elapsed since she'd received that handful of passes on her résumé, but after Cash's pep talk she'd contacted more potential employers. Now it was time to see if anyone was willing to give her a chance.

She sent up a short, hopeful prayer and opened her

email. The first few were more of the same—"thanks, but no thanks" notes. The fourth email was from someone whose name and address she didn't recognize.

To: JiffyCook@myemail.com
From: Tex.Northridge1@emailRus.com
RE: Inquiry
Ms. Finnegan, it has come to my attention that you're looking for a position in the restaurant industry. I'm currently in the process of establishing the Golden Mesa Restaurant, a 5-star culinary delight in Albuquerque. If you were to forward me your résumé and a list of references, I'd like to consider you for our kitchen staff.

At last her luck was turning around. She couldn't quit grinning. She squealed with delight.

Cash ran into the room. "What's wrong? Is it the baby?"

"Nothing's wrong. Nothing at all."

She jumped to her feet. In a wave of happy adrenaline she rushed over, threw her arms around his neck and hugged him. At first he didn't move, but then his arms snaked around her blossoming waistline to give her a squeeze. It'd only take the turn of her head for them to be lip to lip.

He was so tempting.

So desirable.

So...

No. She couldn't set herself up to be rebuffed once again. If he wanted her, he'd have to make the first move.

She pulled back. Pretending not to be affected by their closeness, she explained to him about the email she had just received. "I don't know how the owner got my name, though."

Cash's throat bobbed. "Hey, you're a celebrity. I'm sure

the word is out that your talent is available to the right restaurant."

"You really think people in the know are talking about me?"

"Of course I do. Did you email back?"

"No. I was so excited I forgot. But with it being Friday I probably won't hear back until Monday."

In that moment she realized her two weeks at the Tumbling Weed were almost over. She'd been hoping that by the time she had to face her family and friends she'd once again be gainfully employed.

"Don't worry," Cash said, as though reading her troubled thoughts. "We'll get through the weekend together. Maybe there will be some more murder mysteries on television for us to guess the culprit."

She smiled. Her chest was filled with a grateful warmth over the way he'd so smoothly made it possible for her to stay on a little longer without putting her in the difficult position of having to ask.

It'd all work out. She wasn't worried. She had a good feeling about this job—a real good feeling.

With a thump, she settled back into the desk chair. It was time to put her best foot forward. She began to type an eager response.

CHAPTER FIFTEEN

HE'D CHICKENED OUT.

After witnessing Meg's excitement over the job inquiry Cash hadn't been able to bring himself to snuff out her glow by confessing that he might have opened the door for her with Tex. Besides, all he'd done was make a few phone calls and throw out her name. It would be Meg's talent that landed her that job. And he had no doubt she'd get it.

In all honesty, it hadn't been easy to convince Tex to consider Meg. News of her canceled television show and the ensuing bad press hadn't died down yet. In an effort to counter the negativity Cash had mentioned in confidence Meg's upcoming cookbook deal, assuring Tex that the public would love it. In addition, Cash had thrown out the idea of having a large press presence and a sizeable crowd for the ribbon cutting. Tex had liked the thought of creating some media buzz about the grand opening. Now Cash was in over his head. But he couldn't back out.

Tex had held up his end of the deal by taking Meg into consideration for executive chef. Now Cash had to come through with his part of the deal. And he wasn't looking forward to it.

But the thought of Meg and the baby with a secure future would make it tolerable. He'd do almost anything for them.

He'd done some research on the internet and now he had a plan of action. Only it'd take more manpower than he could muster single-handedly in such a short space of time. Remembering Meg's sister's phone number was still on his cell phone, he strode outside for privacy and placed a call. He could only hope her sister was as trusting of strangers as Meg.

A warm voice answered.

"Is this Ella? Meg's sister?" he asked, hoping he wasn't about to make a fool of himself.

"Possibly. And who would this be?"

She was cautious. Good for her.

"This is Cash Sullivan. I think your sister might have mentioned me."

"Is Meghan all right?" Ella asked in a rushed, anxious voice.

"Yes, she is. I didn't mean to alarm you. There's a problem, but it has nothing to do with her health."

"Did one of those reporters track her down? I told her eventually they'd find her. They're worse than bloodhounds."

His gaze moved to the empty country lane. "So far she's avoided them. The reason I'm calling is because I need your help if we're going to get your sister a new—a *better* job as the celebrity chef of a new five-star restaurant."

"I still can't believe they canceled her show." A note of anger rumbled through the phone. "You know, I saw Harold talking to some TV executives at the church. I'm certain he's somehow mixed up in this. I never did understand what Meghan saw in him."

That made two of them. But Cash didn't want to get started listing all Harold's faults or they might be there all evening. They had more pressing matters to discuss.

"Your sister is returning home soon, but it's going to be

tough for her to face her friends and family with no husband and no job." He didn't elaborate on her need for this job because he wasn't going to spill the beans about the baby. Meg had a right to her privacy, as his grandmother had pointed out. "I have a plan, but we'll need to act fast."

"*We?* As in you and me?" Her tone sounded doubtful.

"Yes." His neck and shoulders tightened as he thought of the way this must sound to her.

"But I don't even know you."

"True. But what devious motive could I have by helping Meg get a job?"

A slight pause ensued. "Are you in love with her?"

What? Talk about a crazy idea—this ranked at the top of the list. It was a physical attraction between them—pure and simple.

"Of course not. Your sister has been a big help to me and my grandmother. All I want is a chance to pay her back."

"I'm listening."

"There's one condition, though. Would you be willing to keep this from Meg until we work out all the details?" He almost mentioned how the stress wouldn't be good for the baby. Instead he settled for, "After the wedding she was so upset she ended up physically sick. I don't want to get her worked up again, especially since she doesn't quite have the job yet."

"Aren't you rushing things, then?"

"I have faith in your sister's abilities."

"Are you sure there isn't something else going on between you two?"

Her suspicion made him uneasy. Memories of the steamy kiss they'd shared stirred his body. Did that constitute something going on? No. He'd certainly made it to a lot more bases in the past without any strings attached. This was no different.

"I'm certain. She's a friend. Nothing more," he lied.

"If you say so."

She didn't sound as though she'd bought his line. Her warm voice was a lot like Meg's and, just like her sister, she wasn't easily swayed.

He brushed off Ella's suspicions. They had more important matters to address, and soon Meg would come looking for him for dinner. "The thing is, this will take more coordination and planning than I have time to do on my own. Will you help?"

"Depends on what you have in mind. Start talking."

Her interest in hearing him out eased his tension. With some help, his plan had a real chance. He prayed it would all work out the way he envisioned. Then Meg and the little one would have a stable, happy life—something *he* could never offer them.

Talk about a joyous homecoming.

Meg pulled up to the ranch house at Tumbling Weed after returning from her job interview on Tuesday morning with Tex Northridge. She smiled as she recalled how well the meeting had gone. She'd left him with a sample menu and he'd assured her that he'd be in contact "real soon."

She climbed out of the truck to find Cash standing on the porch as though he'd been there for a while, waiting for her. The thought filled her with warmth and her smile broadened.

"I'd ask how the interview went, but by the look on your face I'd say you have the job."

"Not quite. But I have a good feeling about it."

"I never doubted you could pull it off."

She climbed the steps and stopped next to him. "That's one thing I love about you." When surprise was reflected in Cash's gray eyes she realized her poor word choice hadn't gone unnoticed. Not wanting to make an even bigger deal of it, she continued, "You're always so encouraging and optimistic…about my life. I just wish you'd take some of your own advice. Forget your past and make a future for yourself."

He looked at her thoughtfully. "You still think that's possible after everything I've told you?"

"I honestly do. The trick is you have to believe it too."

Cash shuffled his feet. "We best get moving or we'll be late for lunch. And you know how Gram likes to eat on time."

"She's home?" Meghan grinned.

Cash nodded and led her back to the pickup.

She couldn't wait to see her dear friend. It felt like she'd been gone for a month or more. What was she going to do when she returned to Albuquerque? The thought of never seeing Martha—or Cash—deflated her good mood.

Lunch was filled with nonstop talk about Meghan's interview and Amy Santiago's babies. Cash remained unusually quiet and ducked back out the door before he even swallowed his last bite of sandwich.

After the dishes were washed and the kitchen put to rights Martha shooed her out. "Go and work on some new recipes for that cookbook."

"Are you sure? I could stay and help you unpack, or do laundry."

"Nonsense. You have more important things to do. And it's great you're putting my grandson's new kitchen to use."

"I can work on the recipes another time," Meghan insisted, preferring to stay here and talk.

"Go," Martha said, chasing her through the door. "I'll be over for dinner at six. Yell if you need any help."

My, how things were changing. Dinner at Cash's house and *she* was in charge of the meal. As Meghan strolled up the lane she realized those meals were numbered. She'd already stayed beyond what they'd originally agreed to. Once she heard back from Mr. Northridge, which was supposed to be by the end of this week, she'd be gone.

Sure, she could keep finding excuses to stay longer, and Cash was too much of a gentleman to boot her out. But it wasn't fair to him, and it was high time she stood firmly on her own two feet. If this job didn't pan out she'd find another.

She might have lost her television career, but her life wasn't over. In fact it was just beginning.

But somewhere along the way she'd started picturing Cash as part of that new beginning. Not a good thing to do with a man who'd shut himself off from love. If only she could get through to him...

Once she stepped into the kitchen she concentrated on creating fabulous new recipes. She whipped up sauces and marinades. She discarded the ones she'd classify as merely "good." She was looking for something with a "wow" factor. She knew Cash liked her cooking, but tonight she planned to knock his boots off.

All too soon the back door banged shut. Her gaze shifted to the wall clock above the sink. Half past five. When had it gotten so late? Martha would arrive soon and she wasn't ready.

Meghan dropped a hot mitt to the counter and ran a hand over her hair. After slaving over the stove all afternoon she must look a sight, but it was too late to go spruce herself up.

Cash strode into the kitchen. "Something sure smells good."

"Thanks. Umm...I didn't have a chance to clean up. I was working on recipes for the cookbook."

"Does this mean we're going to dine on another of your soon-to-be famous recipes?"

"Are you offering to be my guinea pig again?"

His dimple showed when he smiled. "If it's as good as your other creations, count me in."

"You know I won't be around much longer to tempt your palate?"

The light in his eyes dimmed. She'd thought he'd be relieved to know he'd soon have the place back to himself. Was it possible he wasn't anxious for her to go?

Before she could figure out how to ask him such a delicate question he excused himself to go wash up for dinner.

He was so sweet and kind. It was a shame he had no intention of letting some lucky woman into his life. Next to her father, he was the most dependable man she'd ever known.

Meghan had finished setting the dining room table when Cash strolled back into the kitchen, looking fresh and dangerously sexy with his damp hair. His Western shirt was unbuttoned, giving her a glimpse of the light smattering of dark hair on his chest. Heat rushed to her cheeks and she glanced away, trying to focus on cleaning up the kitchen island.

He approached her and she inhaled a whiff of his spicy cologne. It was darn near intoxicating, and she nearly dropped the mixing bowl she'd intended to place in the sink. He reached out to take the bowl from her and their fingers connected.

The heat of his touch zinged up her arm and settled in her chest. She turned her head to him. His very kissable lips hovered only a few inches from hers. Would it be so wrong to take one more sizzling memory with her when she left?

She tried to tell herself this wasn't right—for either of

them—but the pounding of her heart and the yearning in her core drove her beyond the bounds of caution.

The breath caught in her throat and the blood pounded in her veins. She was totally caught up in an overwhelming need to have him kiss her—here—now. For just this moment she wanted to forget their circumstances and lose herself in his arms.

His hungry gaze met and held hers. He wanted her too. She'd never experienced such desire. Her stomach quivered with excitement. But she held herself back. She'd promised herself the next time *he'd* be the one to make the first move. She couldn't risk being shunned again—no matter how much she wanted him.

As though reading her thoughts, he lowered his head. Thankfully she didn't have to test her resolution. As light as a breeze, his lips brushed hers.

He pulled back ever so slightly. A frustrated groan clogged her throat. He couldn't stop yet. She needed more. Something hot and steamy to fill the long lonely nights ahead of her.

"Kiss me again," she murmured over the pounding of her heart. "Kiss me like there's no tomorrow."

His breath was rushed as it brushed her cheek. "You're sure?"

"Stop talking and press your lips to mine."

In the driver's seat, she reveled in the exhilaration of telling Cash what she desired. His eyes flared with passion before he obliged her by running his lips tentatively over hers. A moan swelled inside her and vibrated in her throat.

When he pulled back and sent her a questioning gaze, she said, "Again."

His mouth pressed to hers with urgency this time. As their kiss deepened excitement sparked and exploded inside her like a Roman candle. He sought out her tongue with his. He tasted fresh and minty. Her arms trailed around his neck and she sidled up against him. She wanted more of him—so much more.

In the background, she heard a bowl hit the countertop with a thud before his hands slid around her waist. His fingertips slipped beneath the hem of her top to stroke her tender flesh. She lifted her legs and wrapped them about his waist, never moving her mouth from his. His kisses were sweeter than honey and she was on a sugar high. She'd never get enough of him. *Ever.*

Just then it sounded like someone had cleared their throat, but Cash didn't miss a beat as he rained down sweet kisses on her. Obviously she'd been hearing things. She let herself once again be swept away in the moment.

"Excuse me?" The sound of Martha's voice startled Meghan, ending the kiss. "I hate to intrude, but I think something is burning."

Meghan lowered her feet to the floor as a blaze of heat flamed up her neck and set her cheeks on fire. She felt like a naughty teenager, having just been busted making out with the hottest guy in school.

"You need to do something with the stove." Martha pointed over Meghan's shoulder. "Dinner is going to be ruined."

"Dinner!" Meghan shrieked, coming out of her desire-induced trance.

She rushed to the stove, glad to have a reason not to face Martha. She had no excuse for losing her mind and begging Cash to kiss her. Between the steam from her sauce and the heat from her utter mortification she thought she was going to melt.

"Gram…we…um…didn't know it was so late," Cash stuttered.

"Obviously. Good thing I showed up before this place went up in smoke."

Martha's voice held a note of amusement, which only added to Meghan's discomfort.

Though the bottom layer of the Dijon sauce was burnt, she was able to ladle off enough for the three of them. Thankfully Martha didn't make a fuss about the scene she'd walked in on. In fact she seemed rather pleased with the idea—mistaken though it was—that they were a couple.

Someone needed to set Martha straight, but with Meghan's lips still tingling and her heart doing double-time she couldn't lie to the woman. There was no way she'd be able to convince anyone that the kiss had meant nothing to her. In fact it'd shaken her to her core.

Instead of saying goodbye, it had been more like hello.

Please ring.

Meghan lifted the phone Friday morning and checked for a dial tone. Satisfied it still worked since she'd checked it a half hour ago, she hung up. What was the problem? Why hadn't she heard about the job yet?

Maybe it was bad news and they were dragging their feet about making an uncomfortable call. Her stomach plummeted. Or it could be good news and they were notifying all of the other candidates first. Her spirits rose a little.

She sighed. Staring at the phone wouldn't make it ring. She needed to get busy if she was going to maintain her sanity. After all, there was a pile of dirty laundry with her name on it.

She'd just started up the stairs when the chime of the phone filled the air. Like a sprinter, she set off for the kitchen.

She paused, gathered herself, and blew out a deep breath.

"Hello?" She hoped her voice didn't sound as shaky as she felt.

"Good morning, Ms. Finnegan. This is Tex Northridge…"

In her frenzied mind his words merged into an excited blur. However, she caught the most important part—she'd got the job!

Her heart thump-thumped with excitement. She grinned until her cheeks grew tired. She couldn't wait to tell Cash the news.

In the end, the position had come down to her and one other. It was her sample menu with its unique flair which she'd thought to include with her résumé that had tipped the balance in her favor. *She* would be the executive chef.

Still in a daze, she hung up the phone. At last she had what she'd wanted since she'd arrived at the Tumbling Weed—a new beginning for herself and the baby. She should be bubbling over with joy, but as her gaze moved around the room which had come to feel like home to her the smile slid from her face.

It was more than the house—it was Cash. Now that she had a job the time had come for her to leave…leave *him*. The thought tugged at her heart.

She shoved aside her tangle of feelings for the cowboy and forced her thoughts back to her new job. Her mouth gaped open when she realized in her excitement that she'd forgotten to ask how soon Mr. Northridge would need a full menu to approve. She immediately called back.

"I thought Cash would have told you," Mr. Northridge said. "We have the ribbon cutting coming up in a few weeks. We need to have everything in place by then."

Cash was involved in her getting this job? Her heart

rammed into her throat, choking her. *How? Why?* Questions bombarded her. She choked down her rising emotions. There had to be a mistake.

"Cash knows?"

"Well, sure. We go back a long way, to when he was a rodeo champ. So when he called me about you I was eager to help."

Stunned to the point of numbness, she asked, "This was his idea?"

"You're lucky to have a man who'll go out of his way for you. He's really outdone himself arranging press coverage. They're all anxious to find out what the Jiffy Cook is up to. It was a brilliant idea to reveal your upcoming cookbook deal at the restaurant opening."

She blinked repeatedly, holding back a wave of disappointment. Feeling as though someone had ripped out her heart, she hung up the phone.

Meghan sank down in a kitchen chair and rested her face in her hands. Cash was behind this whole job offer. He had gone behind her back and done exactly what she'd asked him not to do.

Her chest ached and her head throbbed. How could he have done this? She'd trusted him.

He was no better than her ex. He'd manipulated her into doing what he thought was right for her—or was it what worked for *him?*

CHAPTER SIXTEEN

THE CLOSER CASH got to the house, the faster he moved. He was a man on a mission and his plan was beginning to fall into place. The night before, when he'd taken Gram home, he'd explained about his involvement in getting Meg the interview. No arm twisting had been necessary to convince his grandmother to call her friends and invite everyone to attend the upcoming ribbon-cutting ceremony. The only part she'd balked at was keeping his involvement a secret from Meg, but upon revealing how Meg had refused his offer of help Gram had relented.

With it being almost lunchtime, he slipped off his boots and stepped into the kitchen, expecting to find Meg hard at work on a new recipe. The room was empty and the counters were spotless. He supposed it was possible she'd never returned from Gram's house after breakfast. He wouldn't know as he'd been busy in the tackroom, making phone calls and fighting with the internet to push ahead with advertising the big event.

"Meg?" No response. "Meg, are you here? It's time to head over to Gram's for lunch."

His mood had lifted ever since that kiss—the kiss Meg had insisted upon—the one that had spiraled so wonderfully out of control. If Gram hadn't intervened dinner wouldn't have been the only thing overheated.

The memory made his mouth go dry. The last thing he should do was stir up the embers, but he'd loved how he hadn't been the only one getting into the moment. Meg had been demanding and it had only heated his blood all the more.

"What are you smiling about?"

Meg's serious tone wiped the grin from his face.

"Nothing. Are you ready for lunch?"

"It can wait." She crossed her arms and her brows knit together in a frown. "We need to talk."

Oh, no. What had happened? His body grew tense.

"Why don't we eat first?" Somehow food seemed to calm people. "Gram will be waiting."

"I phoned Martha a while ago and explained that we'd be late." Meg didn't wait for him to say a word before she turned on her heels and headed for the family room.

His body tensed as he followed her rapid footsteps. What was bothering her? He couldn't think of anything he'd done wrong, but that didn't mean he hadn't missed something.

He followed her as far as the doorway, where he propped himself against the doorjamb. She paced in front of the stone fireplace, her forehead creased as though she were in deep thought.

His gut churned with dread. "Whatever it is, just spit it out."

She stopped and stared at him. "I got that executive chef position…but I'm sure that's no surprise to *you,* since Mr. Northridge said you went out of your way to make it happen."

Cash rubbed at the tightness in his chest. So much for keeping his involvement off the radar. And now that Meg knew she sure didn't look grateful. He'd guessed that one wrong.

"You aren't going to deny it?" When he shook his head, she continued, "How could you do it?"

Justification teetered on the tip of his tongue, but he knew it would be a waste of breath. He'd been busted. And it didn't matter that he'd had the best of intentions—he'd broken his word to her.

"I asked you to leave my employment issue alone, but you couldn't trust me to handle it. I was *so* wrong about you. You're just like my ex. Both of you think you know what's best for me. And you don't!"

Her comparison between him and Harold was like a sucker punch to the gut. "That's not true. I'm not like that jerk. It isn't like I dumped you at the altar. I only tried to help."

Meg pulled her shoulders back and jutted out her chin. "How? By helping me out the door?"

"That's not true."

"Why?" Her lips pursed together. "Are you saying you want me to stay?"

He couldn't give Meg the answer she wanted—the words inside his heart. It was impossible. He was crazy even to contemplate the idea.

The Sullivan men repeatedly hurt those around them. He thought of the physical and mental anguish he'd witnessed between his parents. And then how he'd come to the Tumbling Weed, where his grandfather had verbally abused him. The men in his family lacked the ability to be gentle and caring. But Meg had showed him that he wasn't like them. He was different. So what was holding him back?

Clarity struck with the force of a sharp blow to his chest. All this time he'd had it backward. It wasn't that he feared hurting her, but rather he feared that by letting her in she'd let him down—like most everyone else.

"Cash, say something." She wrung her hands. "Are you saying we have something beyond an employer/employee relationship?"

He wanted to say yes. He wanted to trust her and believe what she was saying. But once bitten, twice shy…

He swallowed hard. "Weren't you listening the other day in the meadow? I'm not good for you—for anyone."

"You're hiding away from life here on this ranch!" she shouted. "Any man who takes such loving care of his grandmother and takes in a total stranger is a good man."

Meg continued to cling to the idea that he could fit into her life like a dog clutching a bone. Cash's neck tensed. He had to get her to forget about this foolish notion.

"Meg, listen to me. I'm not the man for you. My past isn't dead and gone. It still haunts me. It will ruin your future."

"No, it won't. It's old news. The only one keeping it alive is you."

He wished she was right, but the reporter who'd visited the ranch proved his point. Now he had no choice but to reveal his latest embarrassing scandal.

Cash sucked in a deep breath and straightened his shoulders, feeling the heavy weight of his past pushing down on him. He slowly blew out a breath, all the while figuring out where to start.

"Remember how I told you I left the rodeo after I busted my shoulder?" When she nodded, he continued, "That wasn't the only reason I pulled out. My ex-girlfriend framed me for a robbery in Austin. Being a child armed robber sticks to a person worse than flypaper. The rodeo circuit is a small world and people have long memories. Even that reporter who showed up here knew all about my past. He accused me of moving from robbing liquor stores and rodeos to stealing the bride from her own wedding."

Sympathy was reflected in Meg's luminous green eyes as she stepped closer. Her tone softened but still held a note of conviction. "You've got to stand up and prove to everyone—most of all to yourself—that there's more to you than those nasty tabloid stories. You're a strong, hardworking cowboy who cares deeply about his family."

Cash had never thought anyone would fight for him—certainly no one as special as Meg. In the time they'd spent together she'd snuck past his defenses and niggled her way into his heart, filling it up—making him whole.

But she didn't belong here at the Tumbling Weed. Her future was in the spotlight. Soon she'd realize that and then she'd be miserable here.

The thought of what he had to do next turned his stomach. He met Meg's determined gaze head-on. She refused to back down.

You can do this. It's the best thing for her.

"I need you to listen to me," he said. "You've read too much into what we've shared."

She shook her head. "I *know* you felt that strong connection too."

He had, but that was beside the point. Right now it was about getting her to see sense.

"It was a physical thing," he forced out. "Nothing more."

He stood rigid, resisting the urge to turn away and miss the pain that was about to filter through her emerald eyes. It would serve as his punishment for letting himself get too close to someone—a lesson he would never forget.

You can do this. You're almost there.

Soon Meg would be set free to have the wonderful life she deserved.

He swallowed. "I knew things were getting out of control between us. That's why I contacted Tex. It's…it's time you got on with your life—"

"Stop." She held out a shaky hand. "I don't want to hear any more."

Her eyes shimmered with unshed tears. She pressed a hand to her mouth and fled the room.

He felt lower than pond scum. What had he done?

He followed, but she'd already made it to the second floor. The resounding bang of her bedroom door shattered the eerie silence.

"I'm so sorry. I only wanted what was best for you and the baby."

The too-late words floated up the empty staircase and dissipated. He felt more alone in that moment than he had ever felt in his life.

Meghan sat by the bedroom window as tears fell one after the other. Stupid hormones had her crying over every little thing. It wasn't like Cash had told her anything she didn't already know. Of *course* there was nothing between them.

Memories of the moments she'd spent in his arms flooded her mind. The kisses they'd shared—had they all been a fleeting fancy for him? How could that be?

They'd been so much more for her. Why, oh, why had she read so much into his soft touches and passionate embraces?

Every time she replayed how he'd admitted he'd found the job for her so she'd leave, the aching hole in her chest widened. She blamed her out-of-control emotions on her pregnancy. In the future she'd work harder at keeping them under wraps.

When she saw Cash jump into his pickup to head over to Martha's for lunch she knew her time at the Tumbling Weed was up. She needed to head home and face the music—or, in her case, face her mother and any lingering reporters.

CHAPTER SEVENTEEN

ONE LONELY, MISERABLE week stretched into two…then three.

All alone, Cash stood in his kitchen, holding a mug full of coffee. His thoughts strolled back to the day Meg had left him, leaving only a brief note thanking him for his hospitality. Instead of asking him for a ride into town she'd called upon his ranch foreman, Hal, whom she'd befriended during her stay. Cash hated how she'd slipped away without so much as a "good to know you," but he couldn't blame her after his not-so-gentle letdown.

Without her around, the house was so quiet it was deafening. There was nowhere to go, and nothing he did let him escape his thoughts. He couldn't hide behind the excuse that by turning her away he'd done the right thing. The glaring truth was he'd let her go because he was afraid of taking a chance on love.

He gazed out the kitchen window as the late evening sun glowed liked a fireball, painting the distant horizon with splashes of pink and purple. Still he frowned.

A sip of the now-cold brew caused him to grimace and dump the remainder down the drain. Food no longer appealed to him. It was just one more reminder of Meg. Not even Gram's down-home cooking stirred his appetite. Everything tasted like sawdust.

Everywhere he looked he saw Meg's image. Next to the stove, serving up eggs and bacon. In the laundry room, folding his clothes. In the family room, watching television. Even the stables didn't provide him with an escape. Her memory lurked in every inch of the Tumbling Weed.

While doing some overdue soul-searching he'd realized he had accomplished something his father never had—he owned his own home. And he couldn't imagine ever demeaning anyone the way his grandfather had done.

Could Meg be right?

Had he avoided the Sullivan curse?

Cash sighed. What good did the knowledge do him now? He'd already turned Meg away, and each day he regretted that decision even more.

He'd tried to move on with his life, but it was so hard when he was working night and day to make her new career a huge splash in all the news outlets. It was his parting gift to her and the sweet baby she was carrying. Sadness engulfed him as he thought of all he would miss.

The telephone buzzed, drawing him from his list of regrets. He grabbed the phone, but before he could utter a greeting he heard, "Cash, what exactly did you do to my sister?"

The female voice was familiar, but it definitely didn't belong to Meg. "Ella? Is that you?"

"Of course it's me. How many women do you have calling you about their sister?"

The implication of her initial accusation sank in. "What's wrong with Meg? Is it the—?"

He stopped himself before blurting out about the baby. He recalled how Meg had planned to keep the pregnancy to herself for a while. The last thing he wanted to do was further complicate her life.

"The baby is fine," Ella said, as though reading his

thoughts. "She had a doctor's appointment earlier this week and she got a clean bill of health."

"What's wrong with Meg?"

"She doesn't laugh," Ella said in an accusatory tone. "She doesn't smile. She wasn't this way until she stayed at your ranch. What happened? Did you break her heart?"

Was it possible Meg missed him as much as he missed her? Was there still hope for them?

Nonsense. She'd hate him by now.

"Meg will be fine." It was what he'd told himself every day since she'd left the Tumbling Weed. "She's probably just nervous about the new job. Wait until she sees everything that's planned for the ribbon-cutting ceremony."

"That's another thing. Do you know how hard it's been to keep her away from the internet? I think we should let her in on all of the details."

"Is everything in place?"

"Yes."

He supposed there was no longer a reason to keep Meg in the dark. "Go ahead and tell her how her publisher has agreed to go public at the ceremony with news of her three-book deal. It'll cheer her up."

"I hope so. Nothing else has." Ella sighed. "I could show her the outpourings of caring viewers on the new blog we set up for the Jiffy Cook cookbook series. The response has been huge. I can't believe we pulled this off."

"You did most of it," he said, not wanting to share the spotlight. He preferred to remain the man behind the curtain.

"You know that's not true. You've worked round the clock, drumming up support and lining up press coverage. It's amazing what you've been able to accomplish in such a short amount of time. When Meghan finds out how you went above and beyond for her she'll be indebted to you."

"No."

"What do you mean, *no?*"

"I don't want her to know I'm still involved. She'll think I'm trying to control her life."

"No, she won't. She'll be grateful."

"Trust me. I know your sister, and the less said about my involvement the better."

"You're acting just as strange as Meghan. I'm thinking there was a lot more cooking at your ranch than those recipes for the cookbook."

"The past is the past. Leave it be. After tomorrow afternoon Meg won't have time to think about her stay at the Tumbling Weed. She'll have a classy kitchen to run and a baby to plan for."

"You're going to be at the ceremony, aren't you?"

He shouldn't go. For his sake as well as Meg's. But the thought of seeing her just one more time—even from a distance—was too tempting to pass up.

"I promised my grandmother I'd drive her."

Meghan rushed into the bedroom of her Albuquerque apartment, clutching the now signed custody papers. She'd just come from a meeting with Harold. He hadn't changed his mind about the baby—he didn't want to be involved in any part of its life, and had willingly signed away his rights.

She couldn't believe she'd come so close to marrying a man so different from herself. And then there was Cash, who'd missed out on a chance to be a father—something he wanted. She was certain he'd make a fine parent if he would give himself the chance.

"About time you got here," Ella said, entering the bedroom. "You'll have to hurry or you'll be late for the ceremony."

Meghan stuffed her copy of the custody papers in her purse before going to touch up her barely there make-up. Her hand trembled, smearing brown eyeliner.

With the custody issue settled she should be focused on her career, but all she could think about was Cash. Every time her phone rang she hoped it would be him. But not once in the past few weeks had he attempted to contact her.

Was it possible he'd dismissed everything they'd shared so easily? The thought whipped up a torrent of frustration. Did he *have* to be so stoic and resolute about his lonely life?

Her wounded pride was willing to wallow in his rejection, but her heart wasn't ready to lie down and accept defeat. His spine-tingling kisses had contained more than raw hunger. They'd been gentle and loving. And she recalled how he'd opened up to her about his past. He'd let her in and revealed his vulnerable side. He wouldn't have done that with just anyone. He cared about her, and somehow she had to get him to admit it.

"I'm so nervous I can't hold my hand steady enough to put on my make-up." Meghan tossed the eyeliner pencil on the counter. "At this rate I'm going to look like a clown."

Ella walked over, handed her a tissue, and propelled her toward the bathroom. "Wash off your face and we'll start over. We don't want the Golden Mesa's executive chef looking anything but phenomenal in front of the press."

"I can't believe you pulled all this together. I couldn't have asked for a better sister."

"Hey, what about me?" chimed in her little sis Katie.

Meghan peeked her head around the doorway. "Correction. I couldn't have asked for *two* better sisters. You guys rock."

She added a few drops of water to the tissue and some facial cleanser. Even though she'd made a mess of her life her sisters were right there, rallying behind her. Thank goodness. At last her siblings had set aside their problems and banded together. Why in the world had she thought she had to go through all this alone? She should count her blessings, but a part of her wished Cash could be there for her too.

Her mother, on the other hand, had been mortified when she'd learned the reason for Meghan's disappearing act. Meghan scrubbed at the messed-up make-up with more force than necessary. Her mother hadn't been quiet about her disapproval over the way Meghan had handled the situation with the wedding. In fact she'd flat out refused to attend today's ribbon cutting.

What surprised Meghan the most was her ability to accept her mother's decision to stay away. She might love her mother, but it didn't mean they were good for each other. They'd always had a strained relationship. There was no reason to think it would change now...or ever.

"If you scrub your face much longer there won't be anything left," Ella called out. "And we've got to go soon."

Meghan glanced in the mirror at her blotchy complexion, noticing the dark shadows under her eyes. Her sister had her work cut out for her if she was going to make her look more human again instead of like something the cat dragged in.

"What's up with you? You sure don't look thrilled about finding such a great job," Katie said.

Ella elbowed their younger sister, frowning at her to be quiet.

Meghan pulled her shoulders back and tried not to frown. "Sorry, guys. I just have a lot on my mind."

"I thought landing the top position at a five-star restaurant would be a dream come true." Katie flounced down on the bed next to her and crossed her legs. "I'd love it if someone would give *me* a kitchen to run. Can you imagine all of the chocolate desserts I could create?"

Meghan found herself smiling at her little sister's different take on life. "We could swap places today."

Both sisters froze. Their smiles faded and they turned startled glances in her direction.

"Would you guys quit staring at me like my face has broken out in an ugly rash?" Meghan pressed her fingers to her cheeks, relieved to find no hot bumps.

Ella turned to grab some foundation from the dresser. "It's just that we've never heard you talk like this before. Your career has always been so important to you."

"Yeah," Katie chimed in. "You don't seem the least bit excited about today."

Meghan mentally admonished herself. Her sisters had chipped in with her boss to make this grand opening a huge event, and she was being nothing but a downer. "I think it must be these hormones. They have me moody most of the time."

Ella dabbed make-up on her cheeks. "I'd be willing to bet it isn't hormones. In fact I'd wager my bakery that your problem has something to do with a cowboy named Cash Sullivan."

"I agree," Katie piped up as she started to brush Meghan's hair.

The breath stilled in her lungs. How had they found out? She'd made sure to say very little about him since she'd come home. "What do you two know about him?"

Ella flashed her a guilty look. "I promised not to tell you, but…"

CHAPTER EIGHTEEN

"STEP ON IT, Cash," Gram insisted.

He chanced a startled glance at his grandmother. "Aren't you the one who usually tells me to slow down?"

"This is different. It's an emergency."

Since when had a ribbon-cutting ceremony qualified as an emergency? But he wasn't about to argue. He pressed harder on the accelerator. It felt like an eternity had passed since Meg had left. Enough time for him to realize that she'd not only invaded every part of his life but most especially his heart.

He'd finally had to accept that life was a series of choices. And now he had to face the most important choice of his life. Stay secluded on the Tumbling Weed and miss out on the good things life has to offer, or go after the woman he'd come to love—the woman who'd given him the desire and courage to admit he wanted to be a family man.

He chose to have Meghan in his life.

One question still remained: would she still want him?

His chest tightened with nervous tension as he braked for yet another red light. They were only seconds away from the Golden Mesa Restaurant.

Until now he'd been so anxious to set things straight with Meg that he hadn't taken time to contemplate the

scene he'd have to face. The parking lot would be swarm-
ing with press. He'd made sure of it.

With each passing second the churning in his gut grew
more intense. When the light changed, he tramped on the
gas pedal. He'd wanted Meg to get as much coverage as
possible to undo the damage her canceled television show
and runaway bride episode had done to her reputation.
While he'd been talking to the reporters over the phone
about the ceremony he'd been able to cover up his own
identity. But once he stepped anywhere near Meg the camera flashes would start, followed by probing questions.

His hands grew moist against the steering wheel. But
he had to do this—there was no backing out now. Meg
had finally opened his eyes and he accepted that he could
never have anything worthwhile unless he was willing to
accept the inherent risks.

He didn't want to end up a lousy husband, like his father and grandfather. All he could do was promise Meg
to do his best not to fall into bad habits. With her at his
side, he believed he could be a husband and father worthy
of his family's love.

Parked cars lined both sides of the street. Couples, families, young and old all filed down the sidewalk headed toward the restaurant. The turnout was phenomenal.

"There!" Gram shouted. "Someone's pulling out. Grab
that parking spot."

"But it's a hike to the restaurant. I'll drop you off and
then park."

Gram smacked his arm. "I'm not a helpless old lady.
And we don't have time for you to play the thoughtful gentleman. You have to find Meghan and set things straight."

His grandmother was right. He was running out of
time to find Meg before she took the stage. He glanced at
his watch. Seven minutes until the ceremony began. The

twisted knot inside him ratcheted tighter, squeezing the air from his lungs.

They parked and Cash rushed to help his grandmother out of the vehicle. Gram still got around quite well for her age, but as they started down the walk her modest pace held him back. He checked the time again. It would all work out. He forced a deep breath into his lungs.

"What are you doing?" Gram grumbled.

"Walking with you. What else would I be doing?"

"How about hurrying to the woman you love? Unless you've changed your mind about marrying her?"

He shook his head. He had doubts about being here, around all this press, but he didn't have any doubts about proposing.

"Then go," Gram said. "Don't let her get away. Tell her how you feel."

"Are you sure you'll be all right walking on your own?" he asked, not wanting to leave her alone in this crowd.

"I promise I won't get lost."

"Thanks, Gram." He kissed her cheek.

He sprinted up the walk, weaving his way through the throng of people. He couldn't miss this chance to prove to Meg that he'd changed—that at last he was ready to take a chance. A chance on *them*.

The number of supporters in the Golden Mesa parking lot was impressive. Ella had been right about advertising free giveaways—who didn't like something for nothing? They were also providing finger food, balloons and a Mariachi band. It was a very festive gathering, with lots of smiles.

The attendance surpassed Cash's wildest estimations. In fact there were so many people he had trouble threading his way to the stage. Tex Northridge stood in the spotlight, holding the microphone as he extolled the virtues of the newly opening Golden Mesa. Cash didn't have time to stop and listen.

He moved faster, bumping into people in his haste, yelling an apology over his shoulder. His gaze scanned left and right. Where in the world *was* she?

"Cash?" a female voice called out.

He stopped and turned, finding a woman waving her arms over her head. She looked familiar, but he couldn't put a name to the face. He considered ignoring her, but she might know Meg's whereabouts. He sidled over to the stranger and gave her a puzzled look. When she smiled, she bore a striking resemblance to Meg.

"Are you Ella?"

She eyed him and then smiled. "Good guess."

"Do you know where Meg is?"

She eyed him again. "What do you want with her?"

He deserved her suspicion. He just didn't have time to answer all her impending questions. "Let's just say I came to my senses. Now, where's your sister?"

"Well, it's about time you admitted it. She's over there."

He followed the line of her finger and spotted Meg just as she stepped onto the stage. The only way to convince her that he was willing to do whatever was necessary to make this relationship work was to step up on that stage with her. He had to show her that he was stronger than those tabloid stories—that at last he was willing to step forward and take chances.

The closer he got to the stage, the more his gut churned. His gaze swept over the sea of unfamiliar faces and the army of cameras. His chest tightened to the point where he could barely suck in a breath. Maybe he should wait here in the shadows until Meg had given her speech.

Yet if he fell back into his old routine and shied away from the public…if he didn't make the choice to step outside of his comfort zone…how would he prove that he'd changed? If he couldn't make the right choice now, what made him think he'd have the courage, the strength, to do right by Meg and her baby?

Meghan stood in front of the microphone. "Thank you all for coming here today." She swallowed, easing the tickle in the back of her throat. "I'm so honored to have been offered the awesome position to head up the kitchen at the Golden Mesa, as well as to be offered a cookbook deal. Dreams really do come true!"

A round of applause filled the air.

Meghan's insides quivered with nerves. As she stood there she was more certain than ever of what she had to do. She was about to tell everyone how much she appreciated their support, but she couldn't accept the Golden Mesa position.

When Ella had spilled the beans about Cash being the mastermind behind this amazing ceremony it had confirmed that he still had feelings for her.

In the past couple of months she'd learned that life didn't always have to follow a plan—sometimes the best things in life came when you least expected them. Her mind filled with Cash's image. She knew exactly what she wanted—Cash. But first he'd have to admit he loved her. And the only way to find out was to go back to the one place she'd been happiest.

Frustration knotted up her stomach when she realized that for all of her best intentions—her attempts to put herself out there and chase after her dreams—she'd failed to do the most important thing of all.

She'd never spoken the actual words "I love you" to Cash.

Tex Northridge took control of the microphone. "Wait

until you see the carefully planned menu we have to tempt your tastebuds!"

Meghan caught sight of Cash stepping onto the stage. What was he doing here?

"Ladies and gentlemen," continued Mr. Northridge, "in order to share this culinary experience with many of you, we have a number of gift cards to give away to some lucky winners."

Another round of applause and whistles filled the air, but all Meghan heard was the pounding of her heart. Her gaze remained glued to the rugged cowboy stepping into the spotlight. The fact he was willing to push past his fear of standing in front of a swarm of reporters to get to her made her love him all the more.

She wanted to run to him and shield him from the cameras, but her rubbery legs refused to move. A hush fell over the crowd. Even Mr. Northridge paused as Cash crossed the stage. He dropped to his knee and took her left hand in his. Camera flashes flared in the background, lighting up the sky like the Fourth of July.

"What are you doing?" she whispered.

He smiled up at her, causing her stomach to flutter and rob her of air. "I came here to stake my claim on the woman I love."

The fluttering in her chest increased and she grew giddy. Had she heard him correctly? She stared into his unwavering gaze. He was perfectly serious. "But you didn't have to come here. In front of everyone."

"Yes, I did. You taught me that I can't run or hide from my past. I no longer need to lurk in the shadows, always worrying about someone digging up ancient history."

"Oh, Cash." She swiped at her moist cheeks. "You're a great man, inside and out. Anyone who can't see that is blind."

His grip on her hand tightened. "Miss Meghan Finnegan, I love you."

This was her chance to put herself out there in front of everyone and reach for her dream—her happiness. "I love you too."

His confident gaze held hers. "Would you agree to be my bride?"

Her free hand pressed on her abdomen. The public didn't know she was in the family way, and she didn't want to announce it here, but she hoped Cash would know what she meant.

"Are you sure? I come with a lot of baggage."

"I wouldn't have you any other way. I love you and all of your baggage."

She pulled on his hand until he got to his feet, and then she held up her index finger for him to wait. She turned back to Tex Northridge and retrieved the microphone.

"Wow! I can't believe this day. I think I must be—no, I *know* I am the luckiest woman in the world. Thank you, everyone, for sharing this special moment with me." Tears of joy slipped down her cheeks.

Her new boss's brow arched. "Are you sure you want to pin your future on this cowboy?"

She couldn't think of anything she wanted more. She grinned. "I'm absolutely positive."

"Then let me be the first to congratulate you both." Mr. Northridge's tanned face lifted into a smile as he leaned toward Meghan. Loudly he said teasingly, "I hope Cash knows what a wonderful woman he's getting."

Cash stepped up and placed an arm around her waist. "I'm the luckiest man in the world."

Her unwavering gaze held his.

The crowd broke out into applause, shouting, "Kiss her!"

Cash swept her into his arms. "I've wasted enough time. What would you say to a brief engagement?"

He pulled her close for a deep, soul-searing kiss that gave way to a round of hootin' and hollerin' from the on-lookers.

"I'd say when do we leave on the honeymoon?"

* * * * *

Give a 12 month subscription to a friend today!

Call Customer Services
0844 844 1358*

or visit
millsandboon.co.uk/subscriptions